THE TANGLED LOCK

ALSO BY BILL ROGERS

BILL ROGERS

THE TANGLED LOCK

THOMAS & MERCER

Text copyright © 2017 by Bill Rogers
All rights reserved.

Published by Thomas & Mercer, Seattle

www.apub.com

Amazon, the Amazon logo, and Thomas & Mercer are trademarks of Amazon.com, Inc., or its affiliates.

ISBN-13: 9781542049986
ISBN-10: 1542049989

Cover design by @blacksheep-uk.com

Printed in the United States of America

This book is dedicated to the memory of those who died as a result of the events of the 22nd of May 2017 in Manchester.

It is also dedicated to those who worked tirelessly and selflessly in the immediate aftermath to support the injured, bereaved, and traumatised, and those professionals and others who will continue to support them in the years to come.

Finally, it is dedicated to the indomitable spirit of the citizens of Manchester, Greater Manchester, and the North West of England, who have yet again shown the capacity to treat triumph and disaster as the same. Who through their small acts of kindness, their prayers, and their comradeship have brought comfort to the grieving, and demonstrated so eloquently that acts of terror are ultimately self-defeating.

In the words of the Mancunian poet Tony Walsh

'Forever Manchester . . . Choose love.'

She is the fairies' midwife, and she comes
In shape no bigger than an agate-stone . . .
That plaits the manes of horses in the night,
And bakes the elflocks in foul sluttish hairs,
Which once untangled, much misfortune bodes.

Romeo and Juliet, William Shakespeare, circa 1595

Chapter 1

Sunday, 30th April

'It's quiet tonight.'

Tricia stuffed her trainers into her bag.

'Is there something we don't know?'

Mandy followed the other woman's gaze. There was a solitary girl on the corner of Fairfield Street. Trackie bottoms and a hoodie, mobile phone glued to her ear. Magda turned up whatever the weather. Her pimp made sure of that.

A car, its headlights dimmed, crawled past, and accelerated away.

'Checking the goods,' Tricia observed. 'He'll be back.'

Two minutes later the same car appeared and turned into the railway arches. They watched as Magda stepped forward, more in hope than expectation, then gave him the finger as he drove past.

The car slowed as it approached them.

'Good luck,' said Mandy, stepping back a pace.

They had a pact to take it in turns, unless the punter insisted on choosing one of them rather than the other. It was what best friends did.

Tricia placed her hand on the car roof, leaning forward as the driver lowered the window. The transaction was clearly acceptable because

Tricia made her way to the passenger door, opened it, and looked across at her friend.

'You take care,' she said. 'See you in a bit.'

'You too,' Mandy replied, her eyes focused on the driver. The punter smiled at her briefly before averting his gaze. He was fiftyish, clean-shaven, respectable-looking. But you never could tell. That was why they took precautions, in more ways than one. As the car set off, she made a mental note of the make, and number plate. Just in case. Hopefully it would never happen. Hopefully. She watched the rear lights recede until the car turned a corner, and disappeared.

Twenty minutes later Tricia had still not returned. Several cars had crawled by, but none had stopped. Magda had moved on to try her luck closer to Piccadilly station. A car approached. A BMW saloon packed with young men, the high-octane beat of the stereo reverberating around the arches. The car slowed to a halt. The windows rolled down.

Mandy's pulse began to race. She felt in her bag for the reassuring presence of the spray, and the rape alarm.

She need not have worried. Like dozens before them, they only wanted to hurl insults and abuse. To inform her of all the things they would love to do to her. A final flurry of obscene gestures, three blasts of the horn, and off they sped with a screech of tyres, and the smell of burning rubber. The remnants of the bass beat echoed through the tunnel. Silence returned.

Standing in the cold and dark, Mandy found herself falling prey to a sense of foreboding. She gave herself a hug for reassurance. Shortly the drizzle would abate. She would try her luck on Fairfield Street. There she would have the security provided by street lights. She shivered, zipped up her parka, and started walking.

From the shadows of the alley beside the Star & Garter public house, he watched as the woman turned left, and walked slowly and provocatively towards Ardwick, her soft, silky, shoulder-length hair swaying in time with her hips. Just like his mother's.

His heart lurched. A predator observing its prey. He sensed instinctively that this was the one. He patted the zipped pockets of his jacket, and then, both for remembrance and protection, he stroked the locket hanging from the chain around his neck. Finally, he made sure that he was not himself the focus of unwanted attention, and set off after her.

Chapter 2

MONDAY, 1ST MAY

Jo relaxed while Rico worked his magic.

He had persuaded her to try a new style. A short crop cut with loads of texture, with the promise that it would broaden her face and give her a slightly mischievous expression. Jo liked the sound of that. Her existing style had become increasingly severe. She needed a little frivolity in her life.

'Have you finished, Trenton?' Rico asked.

The apprentice held up his broom, and the bag full of hair.

'Yes, Mr Romano.'

'Good. Now you can go and tell those students to tidy the magazines and wash up the cups and saucers in the kitchen. As soon as you've done that, you can come back here, and watch me finish this cut and blow. And before you go, turn up the volume on the television for Miss Stuart.'

'Yes, Mr Romano.'

'He's a good boy,' Rico confided. 'I have hopes for him.'

Jo barely registered what he was saying. Her attention had been grabbed by a news headline about the discovery of a woman's body. Rico's arm kept blocking her vision, but she could hear the commentary.

'*Greater Manchester Police have issued a statement confirming the body is that of a woman in her mid-twenties and that they believe there are suspicious circumstances surrounding her death. When asked if they have reason to suspect that it may be linked to the discovery of the bodies of several other women in the region that are part of an ongoing murder investigation, their spokesman declined to answer.*'

Jo's pulse quickened. It had been over three months since Operation Juniper resulted in the capture of the region's most prolific serial rapist. She had spent that time preparing pretrial evidence while she kicked her heels, waiting for the Independent Police Complaints Commission to decide if the discharge of her weapon, and the consequent wounding of the suspect, had been lawful and proportionate. Last week their decision exonerating her had come through. Now she was desperate for another challenge.

Rico stood back to admire his handiwork.

'*Perfetto*, even if I say so myself,' he declared. '*Veramente bellissima!*'

Jo was delighted with her new look but anxious to pay as quickly as possible and get to her office on The Quays.

As she turned to say goodbye, the door swung inwards and she collided with a young man who had entered carrying a stack of cardboard boxes, three of which fell to the floor.

'I'm so sorry,' she said, staring down at a mass of curly black hair as the young man bent to pick the boxes up. 'I wasn't looking.'

'Don't worry, Joanna, you go,' said Rico. 'No harm done.'

Chapter 3

Jo held her security pass against the entry pad, and glanced at her watch. Ten minutes past nine was not bad, she reflected, given that she had been to the gym, and had her hair done. She heard the click, and pushed the door open.

Max Nailor, her fellow senior investigator, and Ram Shah, the serious crime analyst, were in relaxed conversation by the coffee machine.

'What time do you call this?' Max asked.

She slipped her jacket off, and hung it over her chair.

'Where's Andy?'

'He called to say he's stuck in traffic in Trafford after dropping his kids off at school,' said Ram. 'And Dorsey's setting up a video link next door. Harry wants a word. Do you want a coffee to take through with you?'

'No, thanks. Just had one.'

She went to join them.

'I was just asking Ram how his mother's attempt to find him a bride is going,' said Max.

'You're incorrigible,' Jo replied. 'Don't listen to him, Ram.'

'Don't know what that means,' Max retorted. 'I'm only a simple police officer, remember.'

'It means, among other things, persistently unruly and unmanageable,' she said.

He grinned. 'That's what my governor at the Met threatened to put on my annual performance review.'

'Have you seen the news?' she asked. 'About the body they've found?'

They nodded in unison.

'I didn't catch the location,' she said.

'A wooded track just off Pin Mill Brow,' Ram told her. 'Do you know it? You're the local.'

'It runs alongside the River Medlock, into woodland.'

'GMP aren't saying much,' said Max. 'But the press are hinting that she was a prostitute.'

Jo nodded. 'It makes sense. That close to the city's largest red-light district.'

'How many are there?' said Ram.

'Three within a mile of the city centre.'

'Ready to go!' Dorsey Zephaniah, the unit administrator, stood at the far end of the office holding open the door into the conference room. As the three of them walked towards her, Andy Swift burst into the room.

'It's hell out there,' he said, tugging off his helmet. 'That's the last time I do the school run.'

'You did the school run on your bike?' said Ram. 'Where did you put the girls? In the saddlebags?'

'I dropped them off in the car,' the psychologist replied. 'Drove it home, and came in on my MZ Charly. He's a jam buster.'

'You'd better get in here now,' Max told him. 'The Boss is on the video link.'

'I love what you've done with your hair, Ma'am,' said Dorsey. 'Very sassy.'

'Thank you for noticing,' Jo replied.

'I'd have mentioned it too,' Max muttered, 'but I was worried that might be considered politically incorrect.'

'For future reference,' she said, 'anything above the neck is fine. As long as it's complimentary.'

They followed Dorsey into the conference room, and took their seats, facing the screen.

Harry Stone looked tired, and drawn. And it wasn't just the quality of the video link. Jo was surprised how much he seemed to have aged in the nine months since the team had been created.

'I assume you've all seen BBC's North West England news?' His tone was sombre. 'The body discovered close to Piccadilly station?'

There was a general murmur of agreement.

'Good,' Harry continued. 'Because GMP have made an official request for our assistance. Not merely with this investigation, but with two others which they believe to have been committed by the same perpetrator.'

'The two working girls found murdered in the borough of Wigan?' Max asked.

'Precisely. It will soon become official. It looks as though they have a serial killer on their hands. Or should I say, on *our* hands. The Chief Constable specifically asked for the assistance of the National Crime Agency, and specifically of the Behavioural Sciences Unit.'

'When you say *assistance*, Boss,' said Jo, 'what exactly are they looking for?'

Harry leaned back, as though distancing himself a little before replying. 'Detective Chief Inspector Gordon Holmes will head up the Force Major Incident Team Syndicate as senior investigating officer. I have agreed that the Behavioural Sciences Unit will provide intelligence, analytical and technical advice, and you, SI Stuart, will undertake specific investigative activities agreed with the senior investigating officer.'

Jo heard a sharp intake of breath beside her. 'What about me, Boss?' asked Max. He looked and sounded both disappointed, and surprised.

'This is no reflection on you, Max,' said Harry. 'Firstly, the SIO specifically asked for Jo because the two of them go back a long way.'

Max began to protest, but Harry's meaty hand filled the screen.

'Hang on,' he said. 'I know what you're about to say, and I'll save you from having to say it. Just hear me out. GMP wants to keep our involvement low-key at this stage. You can hardly blame them given the way in which the media focused all their attention on us last time, and the time before. There was barely a mention of Greater Manchester Police. That made for some awkward discussions at regional liaison meetings, and a fair amount of bridge building.'

Jo knew that he was referring to her. The fact that she had been the one to confront both predators, and had twice narrowly avoided being killed had led to sensational headlines that exaggerated and distorted the role of the NCA while minimising that of GMP. The last thing anyone wanted was to undermine the relationship between the NCA and regional police forces while it was still being shaped.

'However,' Harry continued, 'I informed the Chief Constable that the deployment of the BSU was my responsibility, and that on this occasion I felt it was important that both of my senior investigators be involved. My understanding, Max, is that you're still tied up at court with the Lancashire rape case – Operation Gannet.'

'I've been back and forth to Crown Court,' Max told him. 'But the case for the defence concludes this afternoon, and then it will just be a matter of the judge's summation, and waiting for the verdict of the jury.'

Harry allowed himself a thin smile. 'In that case you can catch up with this new investigation as soon as the verdict is in. I want you all to follow the same protocols as the last major investigation. Is that understood?'

'Yes, Boss,' they chorused.

'Good,' he said. 'In which case, SI Stuart, I suggest that you get over to the crime scene as quickly as possible, and take Mr Swift with you.'

For Max's sake, Jo did her best to hide her excitement, but she couldn't get out of there fast enough.

'Come on, Andy,' she whispered as she grabbed her jacket and shoulder bag. 'You can forget about your beloved scooter. I'm driving.'

Chapter 4

'Bloody ghouls!'

Cars and vans crawled bumper to bumper up Pin Mill Brow as drivers rubbernecked. Two Traffic policemen stood at the junction with the Mancunian Way, frantically waving them on. Jo activated the blue flashing lights behind her grille and the whoop of the siren as she tried to force her way between a van, and a new Mini Cooper.

'Look at this idiot!'

She gesticulated at the woman in the Mini, who, oblivious to the siren, had stopped dead, and was filming the scene on her smartphone.

'Why do they do this?'

'The American psychologist Carney Landis conducted experiments back in the '20s,' Andy told her. 'He concluded that there are many reasons why we have this compulsive need to observe the macabre. Part of it is down to the resultant flood of chemicals into our brain that make us more alert and curious.'

'I've got another theory,' she said. 'It's called *Thank God it's you, and not me.*'

'That too,' said Andy. They watched impotently as the woman calmly placed her phone on the passenger seat before driving slowly forward, all the while deliberately avoiding eye contact.

Jo drove through the gap and on to a narrow tarmacked lane. She stopped at a metal gate strung with blue-and-white crime scene tape.

'I could understand if there was something to see,' Jo muttered, releasing her seat belt, and lowering her window.

Behind them two police vans, two unmarked cars, and a mortuary van were parked on the pavement at the entrance to the lane. Ahead, a white plastic partition had been placed across the path that led down to the woods. She handed their IDs to the crime scene loggist, who recorded them on her clipboard, and handed them back.

'You'll have to back up, and pull over to the left I'm afraid, Ma'am,' the officer told her. 'And you'll need to suit up and boot up before you proceed any further. If you don't have your own, I have a supply here.'

Beyond the gate they followed one of two sets of metal plates that marked the common approach paths. Rounding the incident screen, they came to an abrupt halt. Less than five yards ahead, two men, their backs towards them, stared down at a woman on her knees beside a body partly hidden from view. Jo coughed discreetly. They turned.

'Jo, glad you could make it,' said the older of the pair with a grim smile. 'You too, Mr Swift.'

'Thank you for inviting us, Gordon,' Jo replied with a wry smile. 'And congratulations on your promotion. Not before time. Did I miss the party?'

Gordon grimaced. 'Haven't had time for one. This came through straight after I heard.'

Jo turned to the younger, taller man. 'Good to see you too, Nick.'

'Likewise.'

'This is Andy Swift, our resident crime behaviour analyst,' Jo said. 'DCI Holmes, you've met, Andy. And this is Detective Sergeant Nick Carter. We go back a long way.'

'Come and join us,' said Gordon. 'Dr Tompkins was just finishing up.'

The body lay at the side of the track at the foot of a grassy bank beneath overhanging trees, whose buds had newly burst. It was a woman in her late twenties. She lay on her back, her arms by her sides. Long auburn hair formed a halo around her head, which was tilted back-wards. Her eyes stared blankly skywards. Her mouth was open. Her lips were drawn back, exposing a full set of unnaturally bright white teeth. There was something other than the normal rictus of a violent death about her face, but Jo was damned if she could place it. The victim wore a brown fur-lined parka that had been unzipped. Beneath it was a white silk blouse, and a burgundy miniskirt that exposed long, bare, tanned legs, slightly parted. A red stiletto hung from the left foot. The other shoe lay several yards away beside a yellow plastic crime scene marker.

Carol Tompkins, the forensic medical examiner, sat back on her heels and tucked an errant lock of silver hair beneath her hood. 'I'm done,' she said. 'I suggest you erect a tent to preserve the scene until Professor Flatman gets here.'

'Before you go,' said Gordon, 'could I trouble you to give SI Stuart and her colleague here a headline summary?'

Tompkins sighed, stood up, and turned to face them. 'I arrived at 8.27am. At 8.28am I confirmed that the victim was deceased. According to the senior crime scene investigator, the ambient temperature at that time was 7.3 degrees Celsius. Because of the likelihood that there had been sexual activity before death I took a reading from the external auditory meatus to establish the internal body temperature. This was 27 degrees Celsius. Allowing for a lower ambient temperature of around 2 degrees during the night, I estimated the time of death as somewhere between midnight and 2am this morning. This is consistent with the degree of rigor mortis. The body was warm and stiff, suggesting that death had occurred between three and eight hours prior to my arrival. The state of dress was as you see it. As to the cause of death, there were traces of blood in the nostrils and the ears.'

She turned and bent over the body, gently moving the collar of the parka to expose the neck.

'These marks around the neck are consistent with the use of a ligature.'

Gordon stepped back so that their NCA colleagues could move closer. There was a faint ring of bluish-purple discolouration around the neck approximately two centimetres wide.

'She was strangled?' asked Andy.

The FME smiled wearily. 'SI Stuart knows better than to jump to conclusions,' she said. 'There was a foreign object placed around the victim's neck that constricted sufficiently to cause bruising. Whether or not that amounted to deliberate strangulation, and whether or not it was the cause of death, will have to wait on the post-mortem results. The cause may have been asphyxia, vagal inhibition, venous congestion, or cerebral anoxia as a result of strangling or something else entirely.'

She sat back on her haunches, and looked up at them. 'If you look closely, you'll see that there is a foreign substance in the mouth. If I were to hazard a guess, I'd say it looks like hair. The quantity is such that it may have obstructed her airways enough to cause suffocation.'

'Could it be the victim's own hair?' Jo asked.

The FME stood up. 'It's impossible to determine without removing it for comparison. My initial impression was that it is not. But don't quote me on that or anything else I've shared with you. As ever, my advice is to wait for the post-mortem. Now, if you'll excuse me, I have to get back and file my report.'

Someone else's hair? Jo reflected. What the hell was that all about?

Chapter 5

'The victim's name is Mandy Madden,' said Gordon. 'She's a known sex worker. Never convicted but frequently moved on, in accordance with current practice. Her body was discovered by a security officer on his way back home to the estate. This was found right here, close to the body.' He held up a sealed evidence bag containing a large brown small-grain leather designer tote bag.

'Not the real thing of course, but all of her possessions are inside. A pair of trainers, two hundred and sixty-eight pounds sterling in a side compartment, purse, mobile phone, two pairs of women's panties, two packs of condoms, a self-defence spray, and a rape alarm.'

'Much good that did her,' Nick Carter remarked.

'She has a decent enough watch on her left wrist. There is no evidence to suggest that the motive was robbery. And although it'll be a miracle, given her occupation, if the post-mortem doesn't find some evidence of recent sexual activity, there is nothing to suggest that she was raped or otherwise seriously sexually assaulted at the scene.'

'So, you are assuming that this was where she was killed rather than the deposition site?' said Andy.

Gordon raised his eyebrows. 'Not *assuming*, Mr Swift. We have good reason to believe that this was where she died. There are no drag marks. Then there is the presence and position of the bag and the shoes.

Furthermore, Dr Tompkins found that the only area of lividity visible without removing the clothing completely was on the back of the legs, thighs, and buttocks. Nothing around the ankles or on the sides or upper surface of the legs, where you might expect to find it had she been carried here or been lying in any other position post-mortem.'

Jo remained silent and expressionless. She was well aware that, like herself, Andy had comprehensive knowledge of such matters, and had only been trying to elicit the detail. To his credit, he had kept that to himself. 'Thank you for explaining,' he said without a trace of sarcasm.

Two suited and booted men approached. Jo recognised the taller as Jack Benson, a Major Incident Team senior crime scene investigator.

'SI Stuart,' he said. 'It's good to see you again. Please tell me you're joining the investigation.'

'Just assisting the DCI,' she said tactfully.

'Brilliant!' Benson beamed at Jo and Andy, but the smile fell from his face the moment he looked at Gordon.

'Is this a social visit?' asked Gordon. 'Or was there something you wanted to tell me?'

Jo had no idea if Gordon was miffed because Jack was so pleased to see her, or because the CSI's manner was inappropriate this close to the body.

'Neither, Boss,' the CSI replied. 'I merely wanted to ask if it was okay to erect the tent now. Only, the wind is picking up, and if it starts blowing leaves and other debris around it's going to play havoc with our attempts to lift any meaningful trace evidence from the body.'

'Go ahead,' Gordon told him. 'But for God's sake don't do anything that's going to piss off Sir James Flatman, or there'll be hell to pay.'

'Thank you,' said Benson. He turned, gave the thumbs up to a group of his technicians standing by the gate, and waved them forward.

'Do you mind if I have a look around?' Andy asked. 'I'll stick to the common approach path.'

Gordon shrugged. 'Feel free.' He turned to Jo. 'I need to wait for Flatman to arrive, but then I suppose I'll have to go to the victim's house, and break the news. I wondered if you'd come with me.' He shrugged apologetically. 'She lives alone, except for her son.'

'He's on his own in the house?'

Gordon shook his head. 'There's an Eastern European nanny looks after the kid along with another kid belonging to Tricia Garbett, one of the other working girls. Garbett reported her friend missing about an hour or so before the body was discovered.'

Jo knew from experience how awkward Gordon was with other people's children. It didn't help that he looked like a cross between a rugby player and a nightclub bouncer.

'No problem,' she said. 'I'll be with Andy when you've finished.'

Andy stood to one side of the plastic screen across the path. He had his tablet in his hand, and was making notes.

'What do you see?' she asked.

'What do *you* see, Jo?' he said without looking up.

Jo recalled how her mentor, DCI Caton, had first introduced her to what he called visualisation and playback. A mental walk through the scene that, when vocalised, was as easy to recall as video footage and even more meaningful. She turned west to face the road.

Several more vehicles crowded the entrance. A van bristling with antennas and a satellite dish, a radio car, and an estate car. A female uniformed officer was holding back a bunch of cameramen, sound technicians, and reporters.

'For a start,' she said, 'I can see that the circus is in town.'

She closed her eyes. When she opened them again, she began the playback, turning slowly through 360 degrees as she did so.

'I see large grey windowless retail units on the far side of a busy dual carriageway. There is a central reservation with two sets of traffic lights. Immediately ahead of me is the tarmacked entrance to the path on which I am standing. There are street lights on either side of the entrance. There is a blue-and-green footpath signpost, and a larger black-and-white sign on one of the street light stanchions. Looking down the tarmac, away from the road, I see a green metal gate, beyond which the path broadens out into a sandy track approximately five yards wide that after twenty yards follows the River Medlock south in a curve that takes it out of sight among trees on either side. To my left, a low sandstone wall borders the river as far as the gate, beyond which a low iron fence continues the task of separating path and river. On the far bank of the river is a wood consisting of a variety of deciduous trees, including wild fruit trees full of blossom. To my right, a grassy bank beside the path rises steeply. Mature silver birch trees populate the bank. Beneath the trees, on both sides of the river, bushes have created dense undergrowth. The body of a deceased female is lying on its back at the side of the path. The head and shoulders are on the grassy bank, beneath overhanging branches. There is a faint musty smell from the river, and a metallic taste of diesel fumes in the mouth. The grass is damp from dew.'

She paused, and turned full circle.

'It feels as though there is a choice to be made standing here halfway between the hum of the city, and the promise of tranquility just around the corner, beside the river, and among the trees. In the dead of night, from the victim's perspective, that choice must have been between the relative safety of the streets, and the dark menace of the woods. It is self-evident why the perpetrator chose the latter.'

Andy looked up from his tablet. 'I'm very impressed,' he said.

'I was taught by the best,' Jo replied. 'You have to immerse yourself in a crime scene. Especially when it's where a murder has taken place or a body has been deposited.'

'Because it raises so many questions?' he said.

'And possibilities.'

'Such as?'

'Apart from the obvious ones, such as camera footage from the ring road and the Mancunian Way, and drivers who may have witnessed either the unsub or the victim making their way here? Take the vegetation. There will be millions of potential transfers from here to the unsub's clothing. Leaves, twigs, seeds, plant hairs, pollen, algal cells from the river.'

Andy nodded. 'And the questions?'

Jo began to count them off on her fingers. 'Why was the body left where it is when there was an opportunity to drop it in the river or hide it in the undergrowth? Why was this place chosen, in plain sight of the road? He – if it is a he – was taking a hell of a chance.'

'Not so much a chance, more a risk,' said Andy. 'GMP suspect that this is the unsub's third killing. He is supremely confident. What better display of his omnipotence than to do it in plain sight? That would be wholly consistent behaviour for a psychopathic unsub.'

'Why do you guys use the term *unsub*?'

They turned to find Jack Benson behind them. Alongside him was the shorter male detective who had been with Benson earlier.

'Good question,' said Andy. 'Because "unidentified subject" is more appropriate than "suspect". We don't yet have any suspects, but we do have good reason to believe that the same person has committed at least three identical killings. That person is the unidentified subject of our investigation.'

'Why not "person of interest"?'

'Because that term,' said Jo, 'is often applied to people who have been identified in some way or other but have yet to come forward or to be arrested.'

'Or is it just because you're wannabe FBI?' asked Benson's companion.

It sounded light-hearted, but Jo could tell there was an element of rancour. From the outset, she had been surprised that most of the animosity towards the NCA came from the junior ranks.

'Watch it, DC Henshall,' said Gordon, coming up behind him, 'or you'll be back in uniform before you know it. Go up to the road, and wait for Professor Flatman to arrive. Make sure he isn't hassled by any of the press, or the media.' He waited until the detective was out of earshot and turned to Jo. 'Thinks he's a joker. But he's not in DC Hulme's league.' He rubbed his chin with the heel of his latexed hand. 'I'm going to have to wait for the pathologist. Apparently Flatman is stuck in traffic on the M6. I told him Dr Tompkins has done a great job, we've documented the scene, got all the photos and video footage, but he said he's not prepared to do the post-mortem unless he's seen the body in situ. It's all about *context* apparently.' He shook his head dolefully. 'That's Home Office pathologists for you.'

Jo wasn't the least bit surprised. She also knew what Gordon was leading up to. She decided to save him the trouble of asking. 'If you like, I'll do the home visit for you,' she said. 'I assume you have a specialist search team on standby.'

Gordon's face lit up. A weight lifted from his shoulders. 'They're on their way. And I've asked for a family liaison officer.'

'I'll drop Andy off at The Quays,' she said. 'Tell them to wait till I get there.'

Jo and Andy walked back towards the road and shouldered their way, tight-lipped, through the crush of reporters beyond the crime scene tape. As Jo opened her car door, a woman appeared beside her. She was petite with ash blonde hair, and striking blue eyes.

'I believe I may be able to help you,' she said, pressing a business card into her hand. 'Call me.'

Jo glanced at the details. Agata Kowalski. Investigative News UK. Reporter. There was a press accreditation logo in one corner. When she looked up again, the woman had melted into the media scrum. Jo pushed the card inside her jacket pocket, and ducked inside the Audi. As she waited for Andy to fasten his seat belt, she gripped the steering wheel, and took a deep breath. Performing a home visit with the family of the deceased was a task she always dreaded.

Chapter 6

One patrol car, and two unmarked cars were parked outside a row of tired maisonettes. Jo deadlocked her Audi, walked over to the lead vehicle, and showed her ID.

'Who's in charge?' she asked.

The front seat passenger leaned across. 'That would be me. DS Muller. What are we dealing with, Ma'am?'

'I'll be able to tell you when I've been inside. Bottom line is this is the victim's home. Not a primary crime scene. You'll be looking for anything that might lead us to suspect that she was targeted as opposed to a random victim. Also the names of friends or associates. In particular, anything that suggests she may have had a pimp. And anything to suggest that she may have had a drug habit.'

Muller nodded his understanding. 'Do you want me to come in with you?'

She shook her head. 'There are two young children, one of whom has just lost his mother. Give me a few minutes. You can brief the team and remind them they need to be sensitive to the situation. I'll give you a shout when I'm ready for you.'

Jo pushed open the wooden gate, and walked down the concrete path. Women stood watching her from the doorsteps of three neighbouring houses. A curtain twitched in a downstairs kitchen window. As she raised her hand to ring the bell, the door swung open.

A young woman stood there, her face grief-stricken. One hand on the door, the other scrunching her tee shirt between her breasts. There were dark rings beneath her eyes and dried tear stains on her cheeks. Jo guessed she was in her early twenties. She looked like a frightened teenager.

Jo held her ID up, and began to introduce herself, but the young woman had already turned and was leading the way down the narrow hall.

In the tiny lounge, another woman in her early thirties was sitting on a couch with her arm around two infants, a boy and a girl, their heads buried in her chest. She looked up as Jo entered the room. The younger woman stood nervously by the fireplace.

'My name is Joanne Stuart,' Jo said. 'I am a senior investigator with the National Crime Agency. You must be Tricia.'

The woman nodded. The little girl turned her head to sneak a look at the newcomer. Tricia Garbett hugged the girl closer, and pointed to the only other chair in the room. She waited for Jo to sit down.

'It's about Mandy, isn't it?' she said. 'You've found her.'

'Is this your daughter?' Jo asked.

'Michaela. And this is Sean.' Tricia gave the children a squeeze. Both looked to be about three years old.

'I think it would be best,' Jo said, 'if . . .' She looked up at the young woman by the fireplace.

'Kat,' said Tricia.

'Would it be possible for Kat to take them somewhere else down here while we have a chat?'

Tricia gently released her grip on the children.

'Come on, Michaela – and you, Sean. Kat is going to take you into the kitchen for a little treat.'

As the young woman stepped forward, the little girl squirmed off the couch, and grasped an outstretched hand. The boy tried to burrow deeper into Tricia.

'Come on now, Sean,' she said, gradually prising him free. 'Show the nice lady what a brave boy you are.'

Reluctantly, the boy allowed the nanny to take his hand and lift him from the couch. He immediately clasped his other arm around her leg.

'One biscuit each, and a juice tube,' Tricia called after her.

When Tricia turned back to face Jo, the full extent of her own grief became apparent. Despite the artificial tan, her face was ashen. Her eyes were smudged with blue mascara. Tears had left track marks down heavily made-up cheeks. She groped down by the side of the couch and retrieved a near-empty box of tissues. Taking one, she blew her nose and dropped the tissue on the floor, where the box had been. She raised her head and looked at Jo.

'It's her, isn't it?' Tricia said, nodding at the blank television screen in the corner.

'You saw something on the news?' Jo guessed.

Tricia nodded. 'That body found by the River Medlock. It's Mandy, isn't it?' She clasped her hands tightly together. Tears began to trickle down her cheeks.

'We don't know that for certain,' said Jo. 'That's why I'm here.'

Tricia wiped her cheeks with the heels of both hands. 'It is her. It's the only explanation. She wouldn't just go off without warning and leave Sean. There's not been so much as a phone call. I've tried texting and ringing since five this morning. It just goes to voicemail.' She shook her head. 'We always met up at the end of the night and walked back here together. It wasn't just for company. It was so we'd know the other one was alright.' She started crying again. 'That's how I knew.'

Jo waited while Tricia took another tissue, dabbed her cheeks, and blew her nose again. When she seemed to have composed herself, Jo leaned forward.

23

'I'm very sorry about your friend,' Jo said. 'You do understand that I'm going to have to ask you some questions so that we can find out what happened.'

Tricia nodded. 'Of course.'

'What did you do when Mandy failed to turn up?'

'After half an hour and no replies on her phone, I started looking for her. It was hopeless. None of the other girls had seen her since about 1am. So I came back here. When she still wasn't home by 7am, I rang 999.'

'What did they say?'

'What do you think they said?' Tricia's tone was scornful. 'They wanted to know why I'd rung the emergency line. I told them because I was worried she was at serious risk of harm, if something hadn't already happened to her.' She scowled. 'I could almost hear them laughing on the other end of the line. A street worker has been missing for a few hours? She isn't answering her phone? Maybe she's got a client who's taken her back to his. They told me to ring the local station.'

'Did you?'

She nodded.

'They said they'd send someone round to get a description. I'm still waiting.'

Jo knew from experience that the response would have been much the same if the missing person had not been a sex worker. It wouldn't help to say so.

'That description,' she said. 'Can you tell me what Mandy was wearing when she went out last night?'

Tricia took a deep breath and exhaled slowly. 'A brown parka with a fur-lined hood. A white silk blouse. A red leather skirt. Red stiletto shoes. She'll have had a pair of Nike trainers in her bag.'

She looked up at the ceiling. Jo followed her gaze. There was nothing to see.

'We bought identical pairs at the Trafford Centre last month.' She lowered her head and stared straight at Jo.

'And there was a large brown leather bag.'

Her stare was desperate and relentless. She began to sob.

'I am truly sorry,' said Jo.

She had lost count of the number of times she had said those words to families and friends of victims torn from them by the senseless actions of others. Yet still she found it hard to repeat the words without feeling some of their pain. She hoped it would always be so. That more than anything was what spurred her on and gave her the strength and determination to bring to justice those responsible for upending their lives.

Chapter 7

Jo left Tricia Garbett checking on Katalina, the nanny, and the children while she briefed the search team and set them to work upstairs. She also called Gordon and asked him to chase up the family liaison officer. Jo had a feeling that some very difficult decisions might have to be made.

'So, Tricia,' she said on her return to the front room, 'how long had you and Mandy known each other?'

'Forever. She was my best friend. We were like sisters.' Tricia dabbed her eyes with a tissue. 'We grew up together on the same street on the Cardroom Estate. Where that posh New Islington development is now.'

Jo remembered the development from her early days on the Force. The slums had been cleared in the 1960s to create a brand-new council estate, bordered by the Rochdale and Ashton canals. Devoid of any through roads, with many inward-facing properties and a lack of boundaries between the gardens and open spaces, the estate had proved impossible to police. Inexorably it had become a sink estate. As aspirational families moved out, the council moved problem families in. Alcoholism, drug use, and antisocial behaviour took root. It was out of bounds to taxis and pizza deliveries. If this was where the two friends had grown up, it was hardly surprising they had gravitated towards sex work.

'Did you both move out at the same time?'

'More or less. Mandy's mum and dad moved to Openshaw in 2004. Mine clung on for another year to get the maximum compensation when the whole place was demolished. Three years later we both moved in here together.'

'So you live here too?'

Tricia shook her head. 'I live with Michaela's father in Miles Platting. It's only ten minutes away.'

Jo was confused.

'He works nights,' Tricia explained. 'As a hotel night porter. That's why I drop Sean off for her. I go halves with Mandy . . .' She paused to take a breath. '*Went* halves with Mandy, to pay Kat.'

Jo wondered if Tricia's partner was aware she was a prostitute. Tricia saved her the trouble. 'And before you ask – because everybody does – yes, he knows I'm a sex worker. And no, he isn't my pimp. We have separate bank accounts. He doesn't touch a penny of my money. I've promised him that as soon as we've saved enough for a small mortgage, I'm going to pack it in. He's fine with that.'

Jo doubted he would be now, after what had happened to Mandy Madden. She also wondered if either Tricia or her partner were aware that buying a house with money she had earned this way would be interpreted as his benefiting from the proceeds of prostitution and leave him open to prosecution.

'Did Mandy have a partner or a boyfriend?' she asked.

'No.'

'What about Sean's father?'

Tricia shrugged. 'Long gone. They'd been going together for six months. As soon as he found out she was pregnant, he legged it. Before he did, he told her there was no way it was his. That as far as he was concerned it could belong to any one of a hundred blokes she'd slept with, and she wasn't going to pin it on him. What's more, she could kiss goodbye to child support payments. That was never going to happen. The bastard!'

'Do you know where he is?'

'Liverpool, the last we heard.'

Jo made a note to get the father's details, though she thought it highly unlikely he could be involved after all this time. 'Did Mandy have a pimp?' she asked.

Tricia looked offended. 'No way. Never. Neither of us did. The foreign girls do. Most of them were either trafficked or brought here under false pretences, had their passports and other papers taken off them, and given no choice but to work in a brothel or on the street. You go down that route you lose all your independence. You do all the work, he takes most of your money. For what? A promise of security? Don't make me laugh.'

Her voice trailed off as she tried to convince herself that they had made the right decision. That having a pimp would have made no difference to what had happened last night.

'Did Mandy have a drug habit?'

'No! Neither of us ever have. Not even legal highs. We saw what that did to people on the Cardroom. What it did to her brother, Ronnie.'

She began to cry again. Jo waited patiently. DS Muller tapped on the door and stepped gingerly into the room. Jo ushered him back out into the hall, where she joined him, pulling the door closed behind her.

'We've finished upstairs, Ma'am,' Muller said. 'Is it alright if we have a look in the kitchen?'

'Did you find anything?'

'Bugger all.' He looked disappointed. 'Not so much as a spliff. Her iPad's not even password-protected. It's full of kids' stuff, literally. Games and videos mainly. She hardly uses her email account, and she doesn't even have a Facebook page. We found two hundred and fifty pounds in cash in a box in the wardrobe. Hardly sinister.'

He was right. For someone who was paid a considerable amount each night in cash, it was chicken feed.

'What about names?'

'There were only a couple of dozen in her contacts file. There's also a card index by the landline phone. That's mainly takeaways and tradesmen.'

'What about bank accounts?'

'Looks like she banked online. Without the username and password you'll have to speak to the bank.'

'Look at this, Sarge.'

They both turned to look up at the officer leaning over the banisters. He was waving a large purple dildo.

'Put it back where you found it, and then go and wait for me in the van,' Muller snapped. He turned to Jo. 'I'm sorry about that, Ma'am. He's a new member of the team. He's close to becoming an *ex*-member.'

'I'm not finished in there,' she said. 'And I've yet to speak with the nanny. Do you mind taking what you've got out to your car and asking the team to sit pretty until I'm ready? Ten minutes should do it.'

Muller smiled grimly. 'No problem, Ma'am. It'll give me a chance to explain to that plonker the meaning of the word *sensitive*. Before I kick him somewhere where that is.'

When Jo went back inside, Tricia was crouching in the doorway to the kitchen, talking to her daughter. She gave her a hug, kissed her on the cheek, gently closed the door, and came back into the room.

'Will this take much longer?' she asked. 'Only . . .'

'I understand,' said Jo. 'I've only a few more questions. You mentioned that Mandy had a brother, Ronnie.'

'A year younger than her. Life was difficult at home. Her dad is a control freak. Ronnie rebelled. He got in with a gang of youths and started taking drugs. Two days before his sixteenth birthday he overdosed on some really bad stuff and died. Mandy and me, we vowed we'd never ever do drugs.'

She grimaced.

'Alcohol didn't count. There was a time a couple of years ago where we drank so much so often that we were both heading for rock bottom. It was Mandy who saw the light. If it hadn't been for her, I'd be homeless and Michaela would be in care.'

The thought brought more tears to Tricia's eyes. She bent down, picked up the box of tissues, dabbed her eyes, and blew her nose. Jo waited for her to sit down.

'Tricia,' Jo said, 'I need you to think carefully about these next two questions.' She paused until she had eye contact. 'Last night from the time that you left here until you arrived back, did you see or hear anyone or anything out of the ordinary? Anything unusual?'

Tricia bowed her head and closed her eyes. She hugged herself and began to rock slowly backwards and forwards. When she opened her eyes, she looked despondent. 'No, I don't remember anything strange happening, or anyone behaving differently from how they usually do.'

'Which is?'

'Shifty, furtive, abusive, patronising, sexist, desperate. Take your pick.'

'Did you see any of the punters Mandy went with?'

She shook her head.

'No. I was the first to pull a client. When I got back to our pitch, she was gone. I had another five clients before I started looking for her.'

'So you never saw her in between clients that night?'

'No.'

'Was that usually the case?'

She thought about it.

'It varied. I suppose about once a week we might not see each other until it was time to go home.'

That explained why Mandy was not missed until shortly before dawn.

'The place where Mandy was found,' Jo said. 'Off Pin Mill Brow. Do you know it?'

Tricia nodded. 'Limekiln Lane. It runs beside the Medlock all the way up to Holt Town. We used to play in those woods as kids. As teenagers too.'

'Can you think of any reason why Mandy might have been there?'

Tricia raised her eyebrows. 'Why do you think?'

'I'd rather you told me, Tricia.'

'Because a client took her there in his car.'

'Was it somewhere she might have suggested to a client?'

A shake of the head. 'That's unlikely. I wouldn't. Nor do any of the other girls as far as I know.'

'Why not?'

'It means driving on to the ring road and then turning off near the lights. It spooks the clients if we take them somewhere that close to a main road. And it's too exposed. You can only drive as far as the gates, which means the car can be seen from the road. And there's always a chance of someone using it as a shortcut to the Viaduct Street estate. And at night your lot sometimes park there to watch for speeding motorists and drink-drivers jumping the lights.'

'So it would definitely be a client's choice, not hers.'

'That was what I thought when I saw it on the news.'

There was a long silence while Jo considered the implications. If a punter had taken Tricia there, it suggested he was either unaware of the risks he was taking or oblivious to them. Tricia interrupted her thoughts.

'What's going to happen to little Sean?' she asked.

'I'm sorry,' said Jo, 'that's not for me to say. Someone from social services is on their way. They'll have to decide. They'll want to talk to Mandy's next of kin.'

'Her parents?' Tricia sounded incredulous. 'You can't force him to live with that miserable drunken bastard. He all but killed Ronnie, and he was the reason Mandy left home. It's the last thing she'd want.'

'You'd better tell . . .' Jo began.

'I'll keep him!' Tricia declared. 'I'll adopt him. Sean and Michaela are like brother and sister. I'll keep Kat on full-time.' She was excited at the prospect. Desperate to convince Jo. 'I can persuade my partner. We're getting married. We'll be a stable family. That's what Mandy would want.'

'Talk to the social worker when she gets here,' said Jo. 'They will want to consider all of the options.'

She knew from experience that Tricia's proposal had about as much chance of being accepted as her winning the lottery. Probably less.

'Do you have an address for Mandy's parents?' she asked.

'Of course.'

'Could you write it down for me? And then would you ask Kat to join me please? I'll need to speak with her too. I won't keep her long. I promise.'

Chapter 8

'What is your full name, Kat?'

The nanny was sitting on the sofa, head down, wringing her hands nervously. Her face was hidden by wavy shoulder-length black hair, which had fallen forward. When she spoke, it came out in a whisper.

'My name is Katalina Szabó. I come from Hungary.' It sounded like a response she was used to giving. To officials and complete strangers.

'There is nothing to be afraid of,' said Jo.

She wondered if the young woman knew that this wasn't strictly true. Katalina raised her head and pushed her hair back from her face. Despite the grief, fear, and lack of sleep, she was still attractive. High cheekbones and oval hazel eyes were set in a teardrop face. Jo realised she had overestimated her age.

'How old are you, Katalina?'

'Twenty.'

'How old were you when you started working in this house?'

'Seventeen.'

That seemed very young to be caring for two infants on her own when their mothers were out all night. Alarm bells were ringing. Had she been trafficked?

The young woman seemed to read Jo's expression. 'I have five sisters and two brothers,' she said. 'I was eldest. My mother worked at night also, in factory. I was carer. I also studied one year at college in Budapest. How do you say? Childcare?'

'Who did you come to England with?'

'With my uncle. He works here in Manchester. You wish to speak with him?'

'Not at the moment, Katalina.'

'You wish to see my passport? My papers?'

Katalina was becoming anxious again. Jo needed to reassure her before she became distressed once more.

'Not now. Later maybe. But as I said, you have nothing to worry about. I just need to ask you a few questions about Ms Madden. Then you can get back to the children. Do you understand?'

'Yes.'

Katalina's eyes were beginning to well up. She reached down, took a tissue from the box on the floor beside her, and dabbed them.

'You must have got to know Mandy really well,' said Jo.

Katalina nodded.

'Did she seem at all worried lately?'

'Worried?'

'Nervous, preoccupied, jumpy? Unusually anxious about anything?'

Katalina crumpled up the tissue but clung on to it. Then she shook her head slowly. 'No.'

'Did she have a boyfriend at all?'

Katalina's eyes widened. She hesitated. 'A boyfriend?'

'Someone she was seeing regularly?'

'No.'

'What about Sean's father?'

She shook her head.

'I never see him. She never talk about him.'

Jo was running out of questions.

'Have you seen anyone hanging around outside the house?'

'Hanging around?'

'Watching the house. From a car perhaps.'

'No. Never.'

There was a polite knock on the door. It was DS Muller. 'Excuse me, Ma'am,' he said. 'The FLO is here.'

'I'll be right there,' Jo said.

She turned back to Katalina. 'One last question. Do you know what kind of work Ms Madden and Ms Garbett have been engaged in?'

Panic flitted across Katalina's face. She shook her head. 'They work nights somewhere in the city. Is all I know.'

It was the right answer, if not a truthful one. Katalina was right to be afraid. She must also know that Jo had not been entirely truthful herself. Under UK law, whilst Katalina's employers could not be prosecuted for selling their services, she herself could, for living off the earnings of prostitution. Fortunately it was not Jo's decision. She smiled at the other woman, and was rewarded with a nervous lopsided grin.

'Thank you, Kat,' she said. 'You've been very helpful.'

'I can go back to children now?'

'Yes, you can go back. And I suggest you give your uncle a call and let him know what has happened.'

The young woman stood up.

'What will happen to Sean? Can he stay with us? I look after him.'

'I don't know,' Jo replied. 'That will be for social services and the courts to decide.'

Her second half-truth of the morning. There was no way Sean would be allowed to stay here, however happy and settled he might appear. Even if in the long run it might prove the best solution. Jo could tell from the way Katalina's shoulders drooped as she left the room that the nanny knew it too. There were four people in this house whose lives would never be the same following Mandy Madden's cruel murder.

Jo briefed the family liaison officer and the social worker, who arrived within minutes of each other, and checked with Muller to see if anything relevant to the murder had been found. It had not. Finally, she rang Gordon and told him she was going to visit the victim's parents at the address Tricia Garbett had given her.

'They'll need to make a positive identification,' he said.

'I know,' she told him. 'If they have a problem with that, Tricia Garbett is willing to do it. She's known her since they were babies, and they were best friends and co-workers.'

'Must have hit her hard then.'

'That's why I'd like to spare her the identification if I can. Better that she remembers Mandy as she was in life.'

Chapter 9

Jo pulled up outside the modest semi-detached house in Newton Heath, just off Briscoe Lane. Less than two miles from their daughter's maisonette and yet they had no contact, not even with their grandson. This was going to be interesting.

The door opened until it met the resistance of a chain. Through the narrow gap she could see a woman in her early sixties. She had a nervous, haunted look and a voice to match.

'Mrs Madden?'

Her eyes narrowed.

'Who's asking?'

'I am a special investigator with the National Crime Agency,' said Jo, holding up her ID. It had been so much easier when all she had to say was 'Police'.

Suspicion was replaced by confusion and even greater nervousness.

A male voice barked from the inner recesses of the house. 'Sandy! Whoever it is, tell 'em to bugger off.'

Jo placed her hand against the door and inserted her foot between it and the doorjamb. 'I need to talk with both you and your husband, Mrs Madden. Inside the house.'

Mandy's mother slipped the chain and stepped back inside the hall. Jo followed her down a bright clean hallway into an open-plan kitchen-diner and lounge. The first thing that struck her was that every-thing was spotless. The stainless-steel sink, the range cooker, the faux-marble worktops, and the tiled floor all gleamed. The beige carpet in the lounge was immaculate. A man lay with his back towards them, sprawled on the couch, watching *Homes Under the Hammer* on the television. His stockinged feet were up on the coffee table. An open can of cheap full-strength lager stood on the floor beside him.

'Who is it this time?' he snarled. 'Bloody double glazing again?'

'It's the police, Mr Madden,' Jo told him. 'The National Crime Agency to be precise.'

Mr Madden tried to turn his head to look at her, but his immense bulk made it impossible. He slid his legs off the coffee table, sending the beer can flying, placed his hand on the arm of the couch, and began to push himself up. His wife rushed to the sink.

'What the fuck!' he said.

Jo bent to pick up the can, and walked over to the fireplace, step-ping over the spreading pool of amber liquid. She put the can down on the mantelpiece, turned to face him, and held her ID out in front of her.

'Turn the television off, Mr Madden,' she said. 'I need you to hear this.'

His wife was already on her knees mopping the stain with a sponge and dabbing at it with kitchen roll.

'You too, Mrs Madden.'

Mr Madden scrabbled around the sofa with his hands until he located the remote and then switched off the TV.

'Mrs Madden,' said Jo.

'For fuck's sake, Sandy!' shouted the husband.

Jo flinched. Mrs Madden stopped scrubbing and sat back on her heels.

'I think you had better sit down, Mrs Madden,' Jo said.

'What's this all about?' said the husband. 'We've done nothing.'

His wife's face had paled, and her hands were trembling. Whether that was because she suspected why Jo was here or because of her husband's belligerence, it was impossible to tell.

'I am afraid that I have some bad news for you both,' Jo said. 'This morning the body of a woman was discovered close to the city centre. We have reason to believe it may be your daughter, Mandy.'

The husband's expression remained fixed. Jo could not tell from his rheumy eyes if he had registered what she'd said or was trying to compute it. The blood had drained completely from his wife's face. She began to fall forwards. Jo moved to catch her, but Mrs Madden was now rocking back and forth, softly wailing.

'Mr Madden,' Jo said. 'Did you hear what I said? We think—'

'I heard,' he said, cutting her off. 'It's her, isn't it? On the news. The body they found down by the Medlock. It's her.'

'We think it may be your—'

'What did I tell you?' Mr Madden yelled at his grieving wife. 'What did I fucking say? I told you this was how she'd end up. I told *her*, didn't I?' He turned back to address Jo. 'I told her. I said one of these days you're going to end up dead in some dark alley or dumped in the canal. That's where you're heading, mark my words. And it'll serve you right. And don't think you can come crawling back when it all goes tits up. You made your bed, you can bloody well lie on it.'

Jo couldn't tell if this was the kind of bluster she had witnessed from grieving relatives before – almost exclusively men, for whom anger was a way of expressing their grief – or simply a cold-hearted statement of fact that he had been proved right. Jo sensed it was the latter. She turned her attention to his wife.

'Mrs Madden,' she said, 'can I get you a drink? Some water? A cup of tea?'

'If you're putting the kettle on, I'll have a coffee,' said Mr Madden. 'You'll find it in the cupboard above the kettle.'

Jo was tempted to tell him where to stick his coffee, but she knew it would be like water off a duck's back. She ignored him, and placed her hand on his wife's shoulder.

'Mrs Madden?'

Sandra Madden took her hands away from a face wet with tears, and seized Jo's arm. 'Little Sean,' she said. 'Is he alright?'

'Yes, he's fine, Sandy. Tricia and the nanny are looking after him.'

The husband snorted. 'Tricia? She's another slag. She's the reason our girl left home. The one who led her up the garden path.'

'Mr Madden!' Jo said. 'Your wife is grieving. If you have an ounce of humanity in you, I suggest you keep your thoughts to yourself. Better still, why don't you go and make her a cup of tea? Assuming you know how.'

For a moment it looked as though he might object. Instead he muttered to himself. Then he used the coffee table and the arm of the couch to haul himself upright. He began to waddle towards the kitchen area and then paused to stare down at his wife.

'And you, woman, if you think her brat is coming to live here, you can think again. Over my dead body!'

Ten fruitless minutes later Sandy Madden followed Jo to the front door.

'I'll do it,' she whispered. 'The identification. I need to see her one last time. I need to tell her . . . I'm sorry.'

This close up, Jo realised that she was at least ten years younger than she had first assumed. Jo touched her lightly on the arm. There was a slight tremor beneath the flimsy blouse. This was, she realised, not a reaction to her daughter's death but an enduring condition. Her nerves were shot.

'Mrs Madden,' she said, 'what happened to Mandy had nothing to do with you.'

40

It did not matter that it was yet another half-truth; it was what this poor woman needed to hear right now.

'A car will come to pick you up,' Jo said. 'And I'll make sure someone from Victim Care is waiting for you at the morgue. And, Mrs Madden, I suggest you make an appointment with your doctor to help you through this.'

And beyond, Jo thought as she walked to the car. Both children dead. Her grandchild lost to her forever. The future bleak and hostile. It didn't bear thinking about.

Chapter 10

Jo pulled the car door to, and laid her head back on the seat rest. She was sure that if she'd stayed a moment longer she would have said or done something she'd regret. As for Sean moving there, it was out of the question. Social services would take one look at the relationship between husband and wife, and the father's drink habit, not to mention his attitude towards his dead daughter and her child, and that would be it. Sean would be taken into care. He'd be found a long-term foster home or, better still, adoptive parents, who could give him the life every child deserved. She hoped that the manner of his mother's death would never come back to haunt him. Her phone rang.

'Gordon,' she said. 'I was just about to phone you. I'm outside the parents' home.'

'Coming or going?'

'Leaving.'

'How did you get on?'

'Not good. The mother's in pieces. The father's a drunken bully. He reckons his daughter got what she deserved. He's even refused to come and identify her.'

'What about the wife?'

'She waited until we were out of earshot and then told me she wanted to do it. I said we'd send a car when the morgue is ready for her.

I assume you can arrange for someone from Victim Care to accompany her.'

'No problem. How did you get on at the victim's house?'

'Okay,' she said. 'Here are the headlines. The search team found nothing that might suggest there was anyone in her life with a grudge against her. Her best friend, who reported her missing, and the nanny confirmed that. We won't know for sure until Forensics have analysed the victim's laptop and mobile phone. Everything points towards your initial belief that this was an opportunist attack on a random victim by a serial killer.'

'How's the kid?' Gordon asked.

Jo was pleasantly surprised that this big bluff bear of a man should reveal his gentler side at a time like this. But then she had always known there was a soft heart beating beneath that tough exterior. Not least when she saw the tearful expression of guilt after she had been taken from under his nose by the Bluebell Hollow killer, and his relief that she survived the ordeal.

'Confused,' she said. 'He's only three. Too young to know what's going on, other than that his mum is late home and the other women in his life are very sad.'

'Poor little sod,' he said. 'Why is it always the innocent that suffer, Jo?'

She shook her head.

'God knows.'

'I doubt it,' said Gordon. 'Or he'd do something about it.'

Neither of them spoke while they processed the eternal question that haunted their professional lives, and explained why they did what they did.

'I'm off back to the incident room to make sure everything's set up right,' he said. 'We've started door-to-door interviews in the area, although what use that will be round there God only knows. It's like a graveyard at night. No pun intended. Factories and warehouses mainly. That's why it's a red-light district.'

'I do know, Gordon,' she said. 'I did do a spell with Vice.'

'Course you did,' he said. 'I've arranged for night patrols to stop and question motorists using Pin Mill Brow between 11pm tonight and 4am tomorrow morning just in case they happen to be regulars, and may have seen something. It'll play havoc with the street sex workers, but I doubt there'll be many around somehow. Any that are will also be interviewed.'

'You'll have people going through the CCTV footage?' she said.

'Number one priority,' he replied. 'I've got a team of three on it.' He sighed. 'There's not a lot more we can do till after the post-mortem. It's scheduled for 10am. Would you join me?'

'Of course.'

'Even though it's Flatman?'

She laughed. 'He seemed to lose interest when he realised I was gay. I wonder why.'

'I've scheduled a briefing as soon as we get back from the PM,' he said. 'I've been given Major Incident Room One at North Division HQ, Central Park.'

'Is it alright if I ask Andy and Ram to join us?'

'The more the merrier. I could do with all the help you can muster right now. What about Nailor?'

'Max is tied up in court. Our boss said he can pitch in as soon as he's free, if that's okay by you.'

'The way things are shaping up, the sooner the better,' said the GMP detective. 'The sooner the better.'

That's interesting, Jo reflected as she pulled away from the kerb. *I thought GMP was supposed to be antsy about the NCA muscling in on their territory.* Either that was all about Fourth Floor politics or Gordon was under real pressure to deliver results. Either way, this was what the BSU was all about. And she, for one, was ready.

Chapter 11

Jo silently cursed the M60 superhighway improvements as she hurried along the corridor of the Clinical Services Building. She had been further delayed commiserating briefly with Mrs Madden, who, having identified her daughter, was just leaving with the Victim Care officer. Jo had never been late for a post-mortem before. Now that she was, it had to be one performed by the redoubtable Professor Flatman. If she crept in quietly, and sat at the back of the viewing gallery, there was an outside chance he might not notice her.

The dissection and examination were over. The skullcap had been replaced and the face flap pulled forward. Benedict, the technician, was busy sewing up the chest cavity. Dr Hope, the assisting pathologist, was labelling samples on one of the gleaming stainless-steel shelves. Professor Flatman stood beside her, his back towards the gallery. Gordon and Nick sat four rows below Jo. They appeared not to have heard her enter. Professor Flatman turned around, and scanned the gallery.

'Well, well,' he said. 'Detective Inspector Stuart has graced us with her presence. What a pity you were late, DI Stuart. I was on excellent form today.'

Gordon and Nick turned to look up at her. Gordon nodded solemnly. Nick grinned. Jo knew it was a waste of time explaining or apologising. Flatman would only seize on that as another opportunity to demonstrate his wit. He moved closer to the observation window, hands on hips.

'And I suppose that you would like me to repeat everything just for you.'

Jo was determined not to let him faze her. She leaned into the microphone on the ledge in front of her.

'If you could see your way to giving me a summary of the salient details, Sir James, that would be most generous of you.'

The Home Office pathologist raised his eyebrows, and half turned towards Dr Hope, who was watching the verbal exchange with an amused smile.

'The salient points!' he said. 'Now what would those be, do you think, Dr Hope? It does rather suggest that our efforts here today may be reduced to a morsel or two. Rather like asking what the best bits of Laurence Olivier's rendition of *Hamlet* are.'

He turned back to Jo.

'However,' he said, 'for you, Detective Inspector, I am prepared to make an exception.'

'That is most considerate of you, Professor Flatman,' Jo said. She pointed to the three overhead video cameras recording the proceedings. 'And for the record, it is Senior Investigator now. I am currently with the National Crime Agency.'

Four rows below, Gordon Holmes had his head in his hands. Even from behind she could tell Nick Carter was smirking.

'La-di-da,' Flatman exclaimed. '*National* indeed. How we have risen, Miss Stuart. And how quickly. It seems like only yesterday that you first sat there, hanging on to DCI Caton's coat-tails, fresh-faced and bursting with youthful zeal.'

Jo smiled sweetly back at him. 'My zeal is undiminished, Professor,' she said. 'Which is why I'm bursting to hear your findings.'

He laughed, taking it with good grace, then folded his arms. He adopted a more serious tone. 'There were no obvious marks to indicate a struggle other than a pinprick of blood below the right ear. There was a folded lock of hair in the vestibule, extending into the oral cavity, one hundred and twenty-one millimetres long, knotted in two places. It was inserted post-mortem. It is not the victim's hair. The cause of death is manual restriction of the airways. She was strangled with what I suspect, from the marks on the skin and tiny traces in the grooves, to have been a twisted and knotted rope of hair. The pressure marks on one side of the neck suggest that the perpetrator is right-handed. The fact that the ligature appears to have moved vertically several times also suggests that the perpetrator may have repeatedly released, and reapplied the pressure. There is historical vaginal and anal scarring consistent with her profession. Internal bruising and absence of seminal fluids suggest that the victim had had protected sex at some time close to her death. There is no evidence of incipient disease. From the stomach contents, Dr Hope has adduced that the victim's final meal was probably chow mein. I concur.'

He unfolded his arms, and placed his hands back on his hips. 'DCI Holmes. Have I in your opinion missed any of the *salient* points?'

'No, Professor,' said Gordon. 'I believe that covers everything.'

Flatman beamed. 'Splendid. Do any of you have any questions?'

The two detectives shook their heads. Jo leaned forward. 'I have one,' she said.

The pathologist folded his arms again. 'Why am I not surprised?'

'When you examined the deceased's hair, did you find any evidence that a lock of hair had been removed?'

47

The pathologist frowned. 'I thought I had made it clear that the lock of hair in the deceased's mouth was a foreign body. It did not belong to her.'

'You did, Professor. I am curious as to whether a lock of hair may have been removed to create another ligature. Or to place on his next victim. Or as a trophy.'

Flatman nodded thoughtfully. He eased the latex gloves down over his wrists, and turned back to the dissection table. The technician stood back to give him room. Dr Hope brought him a stainless-steel comb, with which he proceeded to comb through the victim's hair, beginning on the crown. When he reached the back of the skull on the right side, he paused, bent closer, and then straightened up.

'A close-up on this please,' he ordered.

On the overhead screens they watched as the cameras zoomed in. It was obvious that a small rectangular section had been removed from the hair. Flatman held out his arm, and Dr Hope placed a ruler on his gloved palm. Dr Hope then held a sheet of white card beneath the fringe of hair while the pathologist measured the missing section.

'Fifty-two millimetres by seventeen millimetres,' he said. 'A clean cut.'

Benedict took a series of photographs with a digital camera.

Flatman handed back the ruler, and turned towards the gallery.

'Congratulations, *SI* Stuart,' he said. 'I can see why you made detective. It is not often that I miss something as significant as this. What I can tell you is that if this was the work of the killer, the section that has been removed could not possibly serve as a ligature. Nor is it of the dimensions of the knotted hair inserted in the victim's mouth.'

At least, Jo reflected, *we now know what he took as a trophy.*

Chapter 12

The incident room buzzed with energy and anticipation. This was the largest single syndicate Jo had seen in her time with GMP. Every chair and desktop was spoken for. She and her three colleagues were forced to stand. The jury in the trial Max had been involved in was still out, and so he had been able to join them. All eyes were on the television monitor.

A hush fell over the room as Helen Gates, the Assistant Chief Constable, responsible for Serious Crime, Counter Terrorism, and Public Protection, drew her microphone towards her. Beside her loitered Greg Dunsinane, the newly elected Mayor of Greater Manchester, and the female Head of the GMP Press Office.

'Got the heavy guns out,' someone observed from the back of the room.

'Shut it!' Gordon ordered.

'I can confirm,' Gates began, 'that the body of a young woman discovered close to the Mancunian Way yesterday morning has been identified as that of Mandy Madden, twenty-seven years old, a single parent, from Ancoats, in Manchester. Following a post-mortem carried out this morning, I can also confirm that we are investigating her death as a suspected murder. Relatives have been informed, and the investigation is ongoing. I will take questions, but I am sure that you realise that at this early stage there is a limit to the amount of information I can share with you.'

The screen showed a forest of hands in the packed press room.

'*How was she killed?*'

Helen Gates frowned.

'Don't tell them,' Gordon muttered. Earlier they had agreed to hold that information back, but the ACC was known for flying by the seat of her pants.

'She was strangled,' said Gates.

'Bugger!' said Gordon.

'*Had she been sexually assaulted?*'

'There was no evidence to suggest that she had been sexually assaulted,' Gates replied.

'*Or that she hadn't?*'

Jo recognised the voice.

'Ginley,' she said. 'The investigative reporter who caused us so much trouble during Operation Juniper.'

'Stirring it as usual,' said Max.

Helen Gates ignored the question. Unfortunately the implications were not lost on the rest of the assembled reporters.

'*Was the victim a prostitute?*' someone asked.

The Mayor looked alarmed. Gates, the Head of Crime, calmly placed her hand over her mic, and inclined her head towards the Force press officer. A whispered conversation ensued.

'She may as well tell them,' said Nick. 'They'll already know she was.'

Gates turned back to the mic.

'I can confirm that the victim was a known sex worker. However, I want to remind everyone that this in no way lessens the gravity of this despicable crime. Outside of her work Mandy had a life like everyone else here. She has parents and friends, who will mourn her, and a three-and-a-half-year-old child, who has lost his mother.'

'Nicely done,' said Jo.

Andy Swift shook his head.

'It won't make any difference. The right-wing papers will use it to push for draconian action against prostitution, and the gutter press will say she should have expected something like this to happen.'

'Are you linking this to the deaths of the two prostitutes in Wigan?' asked the crime reporter from the Manchester Evening News.

'Here we go,' said Gordon.

'There are sufficient features common to all three crime scenes to suggest that they may be connected.'

'What are these features, Assistant Chief Constable?' asked the woman from the Guardian.

Gates shook her head. 'I am not at liberty to disclose those details. To do so would compromise the investigation.'

All of the hands were waving now.

'*You're looking for a serial killer then?*'

'*Is this Ipswich all over again?*'

The press officer leaned forward.

'One question at a time! Through me please.' She pointed to someone in the front row. 'Mr Grice. BBC North West.'

'Are you looking for a serial killer?'

An expectant hush descended on the room.

Even though she must have anticipated the question, Helen Gates took her time, choosing her words carefully.

'At this stage of the investigation we are working on the assumption that all three murders were committed by the same person.'

The room erupted. The panel waited for the noise to subside.

'Ms Gates will take one more question?' said the press officer. 'John Delaney, ITN.'

'What reassurances can you give to the public, ACC Gates?'

The Mayor cupped his hand over his mouth and whispered urgently to the Head of Crime. Helen Gates frowned, and sat back, her hands folded over her chest. The Mayor leaned forward.

'I can assure you that GMP will be accorded every resource necessary to bring this killer to justice,' he said. 'The largest team of detectives ever deployed by the Force is already working on the case, and an elite team from the National Crime Agency is working alongside them. The Chief Constable has assured me that he is determined to bring this investigation to a speedy conclusion.'

'No pressure there then!' murmured Gordon.

As far as Jo was concerned, whatever external pressure might be brought to bear, none of it would compare with her own determination to catch the killer.

Helen Gates held up an imperious hand.

'I would now like to appeal directly to the public,' she said.

'In your dreams,' said someone in the MIR. 'Certainly doesn't appeal to me.'

Both Gordon and Nick turned to see if they could identify the culprit. Jo was sure it was the same detective constable she had met at the crime scene. What was his name? Hen something or other?

Gates had already begun her appeal. '. . . anyone who may believe they have any information, however small, that may assist us in this investigation, to contact us directly by dialling 111, or by speaking anonymously with Crimestoppers on 0800 555111, or going online at www.crimestoppers-uk.org. We are particularly interested in anyone who may have seen someone acting suspiciously in or around Fairfield Street, Crane Street, Raven Street, Helmet Street, and Pin Mill Brow, in Ardwick, between the hours of midnight on Sunday the 30th of April 2017, and 2am on Monday the 1st of May 2017. No one need feel anxious about coming forward. We are not interested in why you may have been in one of these locations, only in catching the person who murdered Mandy.'

'Tell that to the punters,' murmured the office comedian. 'You want to wake up, love, and smell the coffee.' This time he won a few sniggers.

But not from Gordon Holmes. 'DC Henshall!' he growled. 'What did I warn you?'

Morton Henshall. That was the man's name. The one who had questioned their use of the term 'unsub'. He was treading a fine line, Jo realised, even though on this occasion he was probably right. Most of the punters who had been there that night would be keeping their heads down in the mistaken belief that their dirty little secret would stay that way.

Chapter 13

'Welcome to Operation Firethorn!'

Gordon Holmes took his jacket off and draped it over his chair. 'I brought you in here because we'd never have been able to hear each other with all the phones going, the conversations, and the keyboards tapping away.'

Jo looked around. She was impressed. The small room had been turned into an office for himself, and a space for meetings. Through the magic of digital technology, facsimiles of the information on the whiteboards in the MIR appeared on the three of their own back at The Quays. A large chart on the left-hand wall headed *Investigative Strategy* documented actions taken and planned.

Gordon sat down. 'We've brought together the two small syndicates that were dealing with the investigations into what we now know were victims one and two, together with my own larger syndicate. At this rate we may need to requisition a sports hall.'

Jo had been involved in several cases where they had done just that. Gordon drew their attention to the first of the boards. 'Victim number one, Jade Scott. Twenty-three years of age. Single. Living with a male partner the same age. Both heroin addicts. A freelance prostitute, she started working the streets just two months before her death. Her body was discovered on a patch of waste ground off Cemetery Road, in

Ince-in-Makerfield, Wigan, at 3pm on Saturday, 25th of February this year, by a man out walking his dog.'

He gave them a moment or two to take in the images. A young pale face, bottle blonde, cropped hair, brown eyes that stared at the camera with an air of bemusement, and a half-hearted attempt at a smile. From the clarity of the eyes, and complexion, Jo guessed this was a photo selected by someone close to Jade, taken before the ravages of her addiction set in.

Beside the photo were others that had been taken at the scene. A crumpled body lay on its side on a pile of broken bricks colonised by grass and weeds. A long shot showed the position of the deposition site, eighteen yards from the road, accessed through a gap between blue railings.

There was a post-mortem photo of the victim's head and shoulders. A ring of bruises around the neck appeared to mirror those around the neck of Mandy Madden. In this photo, discounting the fact she was now a corpse, Jade Scott appeared to have aged a decade in just a few years.

Gordon pointed to the second set of photos on the neighbouring whiteboard. 'Victim number two. Kelly Carver. Twenty-one years of age. Single. Still living at home with her mother and two siblings. Also a drug user. She had a previous for possession of crack cocaine. She had a pimp, whom we have now established was also her supplier. Her body was found in woods at Aspull Common, Lowton St Mary's, again by a dog walker, at 7.12am on Saturday, 19th March this year.'

The first photograph, almost certainly the mugshot taken when she was charged with possession, showed a defiant, hard-faced young woman with long emerald-green hair. In the crime scene photo the hair was black, straggly, and plastered to her face as though soaked by rain. The now-familiar band of bruises encircled her neck.

'Victim number three, Mandy Madden. Twenty-seven years of age, a single mother. She was found on the morning of Monday, 1st of May, on Lime Bank Street by a sous-chef who lives on the Viaduct Street estate, as he cycled to work.'

On the third whiteboard Mandy Madden's face stared back at them. It was the photograph slipped into Jo's hand at the mortuary by Mandy's mother after she had identified her daughter. Taken on her twenty-first birthday, it showed an attractive young woman, happy in the moment, and full of hope. There was so much about that face – the eyes, the nose, the quirky smile – that resembled little Sean. Jo clenched her fists, the fingernails biting into the palms of her hands, choking back the tears, deepening her anger and resolve.

The door opened. Max stood hesitantly on the threshold.

'Come in, why don't you?' said Gordon. 'You haven't missed much.'

Max took a seat beside Jo.

'How did you get on?' she mouthed.

'Unanimous verdict,' he whispered back.

'Congratulations,' said Gordon. 'I can lip-read, so there's no need to whisper.'

He nodded to Nick, who proceeded to distribute manila folders across the table to the members of the Behavioural Sciences Unit.

Gordon flipped open his folder. 'This is what we have so far,' he said. 'The investigations relating to victims one and two – Jade Scott and Kelly Carver – have so far drawn a blank. From what I've seen, you can't fault the two syndicates involved. The searches of the crime scenes were exhaustive. Hundreds of statements were taken from door-to-door enquiries, from motorists, dog walkers, joggers, and cyclists who frequent the area around the deposition sites. Family, relatives, friends, and acquaintances have been interviewed. Known associates, including other sex workers, drug dealers, and pimps, have also been questioned. Over three thousand hours of CCTV from traffic and ANPR cameras, and domestic and business premises have been scrutinised. They have not unearthed a single lead. Conclusions?'

'Chummy is either very clever or very lucky,' said Nick.

'Or both,' said Max.

'Probably the latter,' Andy Swift observed. 'As you know, psychopaths are generally of above-average intelligence, and extreme high-risk takers.'

Gordon nodded. 'Unfortunately for Mandy Madden,' he said, 'but fortunately for us, a critical mass of evidence is beginning to form. If nothing else, we have been able to identify the features common to these three murders. As I understand it, this is where your expertise can assist us.'

'In as much,' said Jo, 'as those common factors represent a pattern of criminal behaviour that can tell us a great deal about the unidentified subject carrying out these murders, then yes, this is what the BSU is all about.'

She realised that all three of her colleagues were gazing at her. Here was she, the newest recruit to the team, acting as spokesperson. To her relief Andy nodded in agreement, Max winked, and Ram just grinned. Neither of the GMP detectives seemed to have noticed.

'So this is what we have,' said Gordon. 'All three victims are prostitutes. Specifically, street sex workers. Two of the three were drug users.'

Jo was not surprised. Research had shown that in the UK between forty per cent and ninety-five per cent of street prostitutes, depending on location, were crack cocaine or heroin addicts. And it was a vicious circle. Addiction often led to prostitution as a means of supporting the habit. So-called survival sex. And prostitutes were much more likely to become drug users or to escalate to injecting drugs, either as a coping mechanism or because of peer pressure.

'In all three cases the locations in which the bodies were left,' Gordon continued, 'which also appear to have been where they were killed, were areas of wasteland or woods close to roads and habitation. The modus operandi was the same in each case. The victims were strangled with a garrotte consisting of long twisted strands of human hair. Knotted locks of human hair were also found in the mouth and throat of each victim.'

He looked up, and nodded towards Jo. 'Following SI Stuart's intervention and the PM this morning, I have asked for the bodies of Jade Scott and Kelly Carver to be re-examined to determine if any hair had been cut from their heads in the same way in which it was from Mandy Madden.'

Gordon paused, sighed, and continued. 'His most recent killing offers us our best hope of nailing this bastard. The city never sleeps. Someone will have seen him, even if they don't know it yet. He had to get into, and out of, the killing zone. There are more cameras per square metre than I have eggs for breakfast. Somewhere there will be a picture. We just have to find it.'

Jo hoped he was right. Her experience, however, had taught her that sometimes the best place to hide was in plain sight. Where better, for example, than in the warren of streets around the railway station?

Gordon sat back, and rubbed his chin with the heel of his hand. 'Right,' he said. 'Your turn.'

Chapter 14

'One thing that occurs to me,' said Jo, 'is that all three crime scenes are close to bodies of water.' She pointed to each of the sets of photos in turn. 'Victim one by Pearson's Flash and Scotsman's Flash, victim two close to Pennington Flash, and victim three beside the River Medlock.'

'Your point being?' said Max.

'Might this be significant for our unsub? Or is it just that most wastelands, green spaces, and brownfield sites tend to be near water?'

She had no idea how it might be significant, and was hoping that nobody would press her to explain. Fortunately Max had moved on.

'I assume that you've noticed,' he said, 'that all three sites are very close to motorways or A roads, and that it's almost as though the unsub is travelling from east to west in what is very nearly a straight line between Wigan and Manchester.'

'Absolutely,' said Gordon. 'Our assumption is that he's been working his way along the East Lancs Road. Which is why I've asked for resources to increase patrols, and set up covert observations in the red-light districts to the east of the most recent attack, out as far as the boundary of the Force area with Derbyshire.'

That was some commitment, Jo realised, to try to cover the whole of East Manchester, Tameside, and Ashton-under-Lyne.

'Presumably you'll be giving specific warnings and advice to the working girls,' she said. 'After all, there is a real and present threat to life.'

Gordon nodded. 'Duty of care,' he said. 'DS Carter?'

Nick opened a plastic box on the table beside him. He removed a bundle of white cards secured with a rubber band, removed four cards, one for each of them, and slid them across the table. Jo picked up hers. It had the GMP logo at the top, a series of bullet points, and Helen Gates's name at the bottom. She read the bullet points.

A. You may be aware that three sex workers in this region have been murdered over the past three months. The person responsible has not yet been identified, and is still at large. I am therefore obliged to warn you that there is a real and credible threat to street sex workers such as yourself carrying out their profession within, or close to, what are often referred to as red-light districts.

B. There are things that you can do to minimise this threat:

- *Cease working on the streets.*
- *If you do continue to work, you should avoid unofficial red-light districts.*
- *A colleague should always accompany you, and on no account should you separate.*
- *Be especially aware of your surroundings, and of the people around you.*
- *Do not get into a vehicle alone, or allow yourself to be led to a place that does not have a potential escape route.*
- *Never travel to and from work alone. If you have to, then vary both your route and the time that you travel so that you are not a predictable target.*
- *Carry with you a police-approved personal attack alarm. If you do not possess one, your local community officers will be happy to provide one.*

- *You may also wish to carry a legally approved self-defence criminal identifier spray. When deployed, these sprays will mark the attacker's clothes and skin for up to 7 days. More importantly, they have been found to prevent attacks from escalating, and allow time for you to escape.*
- *Please note that the carrying of weapons for self-defence, and the use of pepper sprays, are illegal in the UK, and will result in prosecution. There is also a serious risk that your own weapon will be used against you.*

If you do see anything suspicious or believe that you have any information that may help us to identify and arrest the perpetrator, please let us know immediately, either by dialling 111 or by phoning or texting Crimestoppers on 0800 555 111.

Helen Gates,
Assistant Chief Constable,
Greater Manchester Police

This is a group Osman warning,' said Jo. 'That was brave of ACC Gates. I wonder how the right-wing press are going to react when they find out.'

'Not her problem,' Gordon replied. 'It was the Chief Constable who signed it off.'

'Only right and proper,' said Max. 'Though I doubt it'll change anything. Most of them – especially the addicts – won't take any notice, and the others will look elsewhere to ply their trade. That'll disperse the problem, and make it more difficult for you to police.'

'I don't disagree,' said Gordon. 'It's a no-win situation. We're damned if we do, and damned if we don't.'

'I've been running a series of filters on the list of known sex offenders on the HOLMES 2 system,' said Ram.

'Which filters?' Jo asked.

'Attacks on prostitutes between eighteen and thirty years of age; on any women where there was known to have been an attempt to employ manual strangulation or garrotting; any attacks where human hair was placed in any orifice; and any who have in any way cut their victim's hair. I then ran the same filters against all reported crimes – not just sex offenders – and all ages of victim.'

He opened the folder he had brought with him, and distributed one sheet of A4 paper.

'There were thirty-two matches to one or more of the filters. As you can see, there were only three that matched both category one and two. One of those is dead. The other two are still in prison. And before you ask, I did check. Neither involved the use of a garrotte. There were a further two who were convicted of sexual assault that involved use of a ligature – a scarf in one case, and a belt in the other, which was repeatedly used to briefly stop the victim from breathing before reviving them again. One is three years into a seven-year sentence; the other is seventy-six years old, and living in Pontypridd, in the Rhondda. Nevertheless I've requested a local police check on his whereabouts at the relevant time for our three murders. None of the above involved either the placement of human hair or the cutting of human hair in the commission of the offence. There were twenty-seven cases of the illegal removal of a female's head hair by cutting with scissors or a knife. Seven of those – two of which are female – were classified as actual bodily harm to a child occasioned by a relative or friend, in which the perpetrator either cut the child's hair themselves or took them to a hairdresser without the custodial parent's approval. Ten cases were for commercial gain, in which tresses were cut for sale.'

He looked up at the rest of the group. 'I know,' he said. 'Hard to believe. Apparently it's common in Eastern Europe and right across the Middle and Far East. Three were pranks under the influence of drink – a hen night, a stag do, and an office party. That left seven in which a definite sexual/fetish motivation was recorded. They are highlighted in bold at the end of the page. One is under fifteen, three are in their sixties. Of the other three, one lives in London, one in Belfast, and one in Somerset.'

'Thank you,' said Gordon.

Jo could tell from his tone and expression that Gordon was far from happy. None of these people looked promising, but all of them would have to be interviewed as part of the meticulous elimination process of a murder investigation. That was a lot of favours to call in from other forces, and precious GMP resources would be tied up for as long as it took.

Chapter 15

'That just leaves the crime behaviour analysis,' Gordon said. 'Please tell me you're going to make my day.'

'I am afraid not,' said Andy Swift.

'Better hang on tight then,' said Nick, grinning broadly.

'What?' asked Gordon.

'A frayed knot?'

Gordon shook his head, more in sorrow than irritation. 'The only reason DC Hulme gets away with crap jokes like that,' he said, 'is because we know he can't help it. This is a triple-murder investigation, Nick, not open mic night at The Comedy Store. Please carry on, Mr Swift.'

Andy Swift pushed his spectacles up the bridge of his nose with his index finger. 'The first thing to say is that in my opinion we are more likely to be dealing with a psychopath than a sociopath. My initial, and inevitably tentative, analysis is based on that assumption. I have a copy of my analysis for each of you, which I will distribute in a moment.'

Ever the lecturer, Jo reflected. At least this time he had chosen not to stand up.

'I have divided the analysis into three parts,' Andy continued. 'The first is a very quick reminder of the general characteristics of psychopaths. The second relates to those characteristics specific to the behaviours exhibited in these three murders, from which certain conjectures can be made. The third relates to those things about the unsub about which we can be certain.'

He opened the folder, and removed a typed sheet of paper.

'Recent research has confirmed a general perception that psychopaths are born, not made. Brain scans of known psychopaths in the criminal justice system have discovered a significant deficit in a linkage between two areas of the brain that regulate behaviour and aggression. It is believed that this deficit explains the following behaviours.'

He paused to pour some liquid from a flask into his beaker. He screwed the top back on, and took a drink before continuing.

'Psychopaths tend towards extreme egotism. The world revolves around them, and them alone. If they are extrovert, they will like the sound of their own voice, and often think of themselves as comedians. They will appear confident and boastful, but their arguments will be shallow and superficial. They are all inveterate liars, and they use their lies to manipulate others. They will say whatever they think it is that others want to hear in order to gain their confidence, respect, or support. They will often contradict themselves. They may exhibit unusual patterns of speech. They have no sense of guilt, remorse, or empathy. Despite their own lack of feeling and emotion, they read others well, just as predators do in the animal kingdom. They are impulsive. When threatened or insulted, they are prone to short explosive outbursts, which may include physical assault. They tend to be excitement junkies, driven by the anticipation of a thrill. As a child they may have a history of antisocial behaviour, and cruelty to animals. They do not share universal moral or ethical codes. They play by their own rules, which they will often make up as they go along. It is this, above all, combined with the absence of any sense of responsibility or conscience, which makes them so successful in life, and so dangerous. We all know psychopaths. Most of them are successful businessmen and women or political leaders.'

He looked up from his notes and scanned the room. 'Remind you of anyone?'

He waited until the comments died down. 'Thought so,' he said. 'Which brings us to part two. The unsub has chosen vulnerable females in their twenties as his victims, has used considerable force to kill them, and has taken a trophy most commonly associated with a sexual fetish. The absence of foreign bodily fluids or hairs with an identical DNA on the three victims means there is no evidence that the unknown subject had either consensual or non-consensual sex with any of his victims.'

'Might he be impotent?' Nick asked.

'Or have a sexual aversion to women?' Max suggested.

'Or used a condom, and shaved his body hair?' said Jo.

'All are possible,' the psychologist replied. 'I am inclined to think he is sexually immature. As to his age, he is probably in the twenty-to-forty age range. Towards the younger end if these are his first offences. Older if he has offended before, has managed to remain undetected, and only now decided to exhibit his handiwork publicly.'

Jo knew that was possible, however unlikely it seemed. As many as twenty in every thousand people in Greater Manchester went missing every year. The majority were female. Two per cent of them remained unaccounted for. The last time she checked, there were fifteen unidentified bodies or human remains in GMP morgues. They were the ones that had been found.

Andy was moving on. 'Given the manner in which he has left his victims, he is both egotistical and arrogant. The taking of hair as a trophy, and the placement of the knotted locks of hair in the victims' mouths indicate a sexual fetishist. The use of a garrotte and the absence of evidence of penetration or climax place him in the category of a power/control killer. Such killers are driven by a contradictory combination of egotism and feelings of inadequacy.'

He looked up from his notes, and peered over his spectacles. 'He is clearly comfortable in the loci of the "take", the "kill", and the "dump", and given the absence of defence wounds on the victims, we can assume that they feel comfortable in his presence. Taken together with the distance between the three crime scenes, I believe he has taken the time to research those areas and the movement of street workers within them, possibly to establish himself as a familiar presence within them.'

Jo raised a hand. 'Do you think this means he may be someone these women might expect to be approached by, such as a social worker, community volunteer, police community support officer, even a police officer? Or be comfortable masquerading as such?'

Andy nodded. 'Absolutely. He could be pretending to be what he is not. Although his behaviour is somewhat contradictory, overall I would say that he is an organised and non-social predator with an IQ in the normal to above-average range. Quite possibly educated to further or even higher education level. He would make a very convincing imitator.'

'I take it he'll be watching with interest to see what we're doing,' said Gordon.

Andy's sigh was the first sign that the interruptions were irritating him. 'He will be watching the investigation as it unfolds through the media reports. He may engage anonymously with social media, including our GMP and NCA Facebook and Twitter accounts. He might even return to the scene of his crimes either as an onlooker or in the professional guise that he may have created for himself.'

He removed his spectacles, and made a show of cleaning them with a microfibre cloth that he magicked from his back pocket. 'I would appreciate it,' he said, 'if you could wait until I have finished before asking any more questions. I am nearly there.'

He replaced his glasses, had a sip from his beaker, and picked up his notes. 'The murders all took place at the weekend – a Friday, a Saturday, and a Sunday. This strongly suggests that he is employed, possibly working nights. On the other hand, there may be something about weekends that facilitates his crimes. He is socially adequate, by which I mean that he is not the classic introverted loner we associate with a disorganised psychopath. It is possible that he may be married or have a long-term partner. In either case that person may not be aware of his fetish. Given what I said earlier about his being sexually immature, it is more likely that he has short-term unfulfilled relationships.'

Andy put his notes down, and held up his hand. 'There are only five things about the unsub that we know for certain.'

He counted them off on his fingers. 'He is murderous. He has a trichophilia fetish, in which he finds human hair both erotic and sexually arousing. He is playing with the police. He is escalating his attacks. Oh, yes, and he is right-handed. As I explained, everything else in this analysis was merely informed conjecture.'

Jo believed that a lot of that so-called informed conjecture could help in eliminating some potential suspects, and zeroing in on others. The tricky thing was that you had to have them down as suspects in the first place. Both the Yorkshire Ripper and the Suffolk serial killer were interviewed or spoken to by police on multiple occasions without raising suspicion. An analysis such as this one of Andy's might well have identified them both as prime suspects much earlier, and saved lives.

Nick Carter had his hand raised. 'One thing that occurs to me,' he said. 'Could he possibly be a copycat killer?'

'I take it you're referring to the Yorkshire Ripper and the Suffolk Strangler,' said Andy.

'Well, they did both kill prostitutes,' the detective sergeant replied. 'But I was really thinking about the Suffolk Strangler. He didn't have sex with his victims, and he strangled them. And it was exactly ten years ago.'

'Good point. And it is likely that the unsub will be aware of those murders. They may even have stimulated his imagination, and informed his planning. But the hair fetish is distinctively different.'

'Could that be an attempt to muddy the waters?' Jo asked. 'A distraction if you like? Or perhaps he wanted to add his own calling card or signature.'

'Both are possible,' Andy said. 'But in my view they are too elaborate for that. Copycats tend to do just that. Copy. I'm certain he is a genuine fetishist.' He looked around the table. 'Any more questions?'

There were none.

'Thank you, Mr Swift,' said Gordon. 'Now all we have to do is decide what all of this means in relation to Operation Firethorn's next actions.' He rolled a marker pen across the table towards Jo. 'As I remember, this is one of your fortes. Why don't we brainstorm, and you give it some semblance of order?'

Jo picked up the pen and made her way to the blank marker board. 'I hope you're not gender-stereotyping, DCI Holmes,' she said with a grin.

Gordon rolled his eyes.

'Perish the thought.'

'Good.' She flourished the pen. 'Because as far as I'm concerned, this is what gives me the power.'

Chapter 16

'Let's start with pointers for anyone examining the passive data from the CCTV or talking to street workers,' Jo said. 'Who should they be paying special attention to? The sort of people the victims might have expected to come across?'

There was a flurry of responses.

'Pimps.'

'Drug dealers!'

'Soup kitchen volunteers.'

'Regular punters.'

'Community workers.'

'Slow down,' she said.

Jo finished writing, and stepped away from the board. 'Those first three categories,' she said. 'I agree we can't exclude them, because they are potential suspects and witnesses in their own right, but given how far apart the crime scenes are, I think it unlikely that the same individuals in any of those categories would be popping up in all three red-light districts.'

'I agree,' said Andy Swift. 'But what about someone who may have been passing himself off as a community worker, health worker, or police officer, for example? Especially if they were pretending they were new to the area.'

Jo wrote that down. 'How about anyone they come across or hear mentioned by witnesses who has links to the hair and beauty industry?' she suggested.

'Absolutely,' Andy agreed.

Jo turned around. 'What's next?'

'I'll carry on work with GMP's HOLMES 2 officer to see if we can tweak the filters we're using,' said Ram. 'And I'll chase up a geolocation analysis to see what that tells us about where the unsub might be living.'

'I can offer to look at the witness statements,' said Andy, 'and see if I can spot anything worth following up.'

'Good,' said Gordon. 'Obviously my team are continuing the street and door-to-door interviews around the latest crime scene, analysing the direct calls from the public and via Crimestoppers, and hammering the CCTV footage. I'll also push for as much additional forensic analysis as I can get away with.' He paused and gave his chin a characteristically vigorous rub with the heel of his hand. 'I do have one difficult decision to make. Do we flood the local red-light districts with officers?'

'That would allay the fears of street sex workers and members of the public alike,' said Nick. 'And reduce the likelihood of another murder.'

'On the other hand,' said Jo, 'it's going to deter punters, and that will force the prostitutes out of the area. It might have the effect of moving them, and the unsub, into less well-policed and protected areas.'

'Furthermore,' said Andy, 'as I've already pointed out, the unsub is escalating. He will regard the flooding of red-light districts as a challenge, as part of the game. He will adapt, and adopt new tactics in new areas. This will make it harder to catch him.'

'Besides,' said Max, 'there is no single defined area for us to target. The first and third deposition sites were fourteen miles apart, suggesting the unsub is mobile. He could seek new hunting grounds beyond Greater Manchester.'

There was silence while everyone pondered the dilemma.

'It's my call,' said Gordon. 'Together with distributing to the street workers the advice cards that have already been prepared, I'm going to propose heightened covert surveillance. One pair of plain-clothes officers plus a surveillance van in every red-light district. And we'll retain existing levels of drive-by uniformed patrols.'

'Eleven divisions and sixteen red-light districts,' said Nick. 'That's thirty-two detectives and sixteen surveillance vans, Boss. We don't have anything approaching that number of vans.'

Less than the fingers on one hand if Jo remembered rightly. 'I'm sure the NCA can help out,' she said. 'I'll ask Mr Stone. He may even be able to put some pressure on neighbouring forces.'

'Thanks,' said Gordon. 'Every little helps.'

He stared at the list of actions Jo had recorded with an air of quiet desperation. She knew what he was thinking. Without a single suspect to go at, operations like this were dispiriting for everyone involved. Keeping them motivated and focused was part of his role. After that, it was all a lottery.

'What have we forgotten?' he said.

'I know it's obvious,' said Jo, 'but is it worth reminding everyone that all of the details of his modus operandi must remain completely confidential?'

'Don't worry,' said Gordon. 'I'll make it clear that divulging any of this will be grounds for dismissal on grounds of gross misconduct. Plus I'll rip their balls off!'

'Works for me,' said Nick.

Speak for yourself, thought Jo. *I just hope that horse hasn't bolted.*

'Jo and Max,' said Gordon, 'Nick is going to be busy working as my deputy, so if it's alright with you I'd like you both to carry out targeted interviews with any key witnesses, with known associates of the victims, and with any potential suspects that emerge. Are you up for that?'

They looked at each other, and smiled.

'It's what we do best,' said Max.

Gordon closed his file, and rubbed his chin.

'I'm glad someone's feeling confident,' he said.

Chapter 17

'This is ridiculous,' said Max.

In the absence of credible suspects, he and Jo had decided to go to the red-light district where Mandy Madden had begun her fateful evening. Perhaps one of the street workers would be willing to tell them something they had not shared with Gordon's officers.

'None of them are prepared to talk to me, and this lot aren't helping,' Max told her.

They were watching a video camera crew follow a pair of prostitutes in the vain hope of securing an interview. There seemed to be reporters on every corner. One had narrowly missed being mown down right in front of them by a prospective punter desperate to avoid being photographed.

'If nothing else,' said Jo, 'their presence is a bigger deterrent to the unsub than the odd marked car passing through.'

'It also means there are less girls and punters for us to stop and question,' he pointed out. 'And that surveillance van is wasting its time.'

'Do you think the unsub would be brazen enough to pose as a reporter?' Jo wondered, recalling how audacious the Falcon Tattooist had been.

The railway arches had turned into a wind tunnel. Max rubbed his hands together. 'I bloody well hope so,' he said. 'It might be our only way of getting him on our radar. Gordon has got a couple of officers checking their credentials as they enter or leave the area. Anyway, how did you get on?'

'At least one or two of them were willing to talk to me,' Jo said. 'Mainly the home-grown girls. I think the others are worried word might get back to their pimps or that I might be from Border Force.'

'What are they telling you?'

'Nothing we don't already know. None of them saw anything unusual. The punters were mostly regulars. None of them came up against one that was off the scale for creepiness or violence. Not that that says much. The last sighting of Mandy was her walking into Helmet Street at about ten minutes past one.'

'You know this patch,' said Max. 'Is that significant?'

'I'm not sure. It runs for about a quarter of a mile, with a right-angle bend in the middle. There are factories and warehouses on either side. Some trees and bushes, all behind railings. There are street lights, but they're further apart than on the main roads. Some of the girls take their punters down there. There's plenty of room to park up, and a quick getaway on to the ring road. It does emerge on to Pin Mill Brow sixty-five yards east of the spot where Mandy's body was found. And the timing's right.'

'Must be worth a look,' Max said.

Jo nodded. They had nothing else to do. 'Come on,' she said. 'I'll show you.'

The street was deserted. Moths danced in the lamplight. Bats swooped low above their heads. There was an intermittent hum of traffic on the ring road.

'What strikes me,' Max said, 'is we haven't passed a single CCTV camera trained on the pavements. They're all focused on the entrances and loading bays. And I'll be surprised if these lights are on all night.'

Jo was not paying attention. Fifty yards ahead of them a woman had just turned the corner, and was walking slowly towards them, looking from left to right at the buildings on either side of the street. There was something about her that tugged at Jo's memory banks.

'What is it?' said Max.

She held up her hand.

'Hang on.'

The woman stepped into a pool of light from one of the lamps.

'I knew it!' said Jo.

'What?'

'It's that reporter, Kowalski. Agata Kowalski. What the hell is she doing here?'

'Let's hope she hasn't decided on a career change,' said Max. 'Whatever, she's certainly got guts walking these streets alone.'

The reporter looked up, and began to hurry towards them. Her eyes shone bright in the street lights. She looked and sounded relieved to discover it was Jo.

'Officer Stuart,' she said. 'I was hoping I might bump into you.'

'Ms Kowalski,' said Jo. 'You don't give up, do you?'

'No,' she replied. 'It is not in my nature. And if it was, what kind of investigative reporter would that make me?'

'A live one,' said Max. 'You do know how dangerous it is walking around here at night alone?'

She stared at him defiantly. 'The working girls do it every night of the week, Mr . . . ?'

'Senior Investigator Nailor,' Jo told her. 'SI Nailor is my colleague.'

Kowalski acknowledged this with a nod. 'And if you're talking about the killer,' she continued, 'he's hardly likely to come back with all the police and media swamping the area, is he?'

'In which case,' said Jo, 'what were you hoping to discover here?'

Kowalski shrugged. 'The same thing as you. Mandy Madden was last seen entering this street. I thought that if I traced her probable route back from the spot where she was found I might find something significant.'

'Such as?' said Max.

'Something her killer may have discarded. A cigarette butt. A weapon. A piece of clothing.'

'And did you?'

Kowalski shook her head. 'Not yet.'

'What makes you think this was the last place the victim was known to have been?' asked Jo.

'One of the girls that I spoke with told me. Another of the girls said she also saw her.'

'How come they spoke to you?' asked Max. 'I couldn't get a word out of any of them.'

'Six months ago I interviewed many of these girls across the city. And in other cities across the UK. I've been working for a film company making a TV programme investigating the pros and cons of having legalised prostitution here, as they have in Canada, and elsewhere.'

She arched an eyebrow.

'As for them not being willing to speak to you, Officer Nailor, I am not at all surprised.'

Max bristled.

'And what's that supposed to mean?'

'Nothing personal. There is another reason. An important one. That was why I was hoping to see your colleague here. So that I could tell her.'

'Tell me what?' said Jo.

'Best you hear it from the girls themselves.' She smiled. 'Would you like me to see if I can persuade them to tell you?'

Chapter 18

It took ten minutes to track down three of the girls to whom Agata Kowalski had spoken earlier. They all agreed to talk, but only with Jo. Max had to retreat to the car, where they left him to nurse his wounded pride.

'It's difficult,' said Danielle, their spokeswoman, 'with you being police.'

'Why would that be difficult?' said Jo. 'You know that we're here to help. To protect you. To find the person that killed Mandy.'

'That's as maybe. But how do we know we can trust you?'

'I told you,' Kowalski interjected. 'Ms Stuart is different. You can absolutely trust her.'

Magda shuffled her feet.

'They always look after their own,' she said. 'Is the same in my country. Never trust police. They all corrupt.'

'Not in this country,' Kowalski assured her.

Jo's mind raced with possibilities. None of them good. 'What do you mean, look after their own?'

Two of the girls began to study their feet. The third looked away towards the railway arches.

'Come on, girls,' said the reporter. 'You promised. I told you, she is not one of them. She is with the National Crime Agency, not the local police. Not like *him*.'

Jo's fingernails bit into the palms of her hands. 'Agata is right,' she said. 'Whatever you tell me, I promise I will follow it up myself. Nothing will be swept under the carpet. Nobody who has broken the law will be protected. I give you my word.'

More shuffling of feet. Backs turned. A whispered discussion. Decision made, the women turned to face Jo, their faces full of apprehension.

'He's a policeman,' said Danielle.

Jo's heart skipped a beat. She suddenly felt the chill night air more keenly. 'Who is?'

'This man we agreed to tell you about.'

'Go on.'

'He says he will arrest us.'

'He *did* arrest me,' said Magda. 'Threw me in van. Took me to station. Said he would charge me. That I would go to prison. Then they would send me back home.'

Jo had a sinking feeling. 'And did he? Charge you?'

Magda looked at the ground, and shook her head.

'He didn't charge you?'

'No.'

'Why not?'

She had to lean closer to hear the reply.

'Because . . .'

Jo waited.

'Because . . . I did what he wanted.'

Danielle put her arm around her. The other girl, Vicky, took Magda's hand and squeezed.

'We all did,' said Danielle. 'It wasn't just Magda. All of the girls know the Viper. We all knew the score. He wasn't the first and he won't be the last.'

'Just to be sure that I understand,' said Jo, 'this man you call the Viper claims to be a police officer and he threatens to arrest you, and have you charged unless you avail him of your services.'

'Yes,' chorused Magda and Vicky.

'He didn't just *claim* to be a policeman,' said Danielle. 'He *is* a policeman.'

'How do you know?' said Jo.

'Because he used to pick us up in a police van.'

'And he wore the uniform,' added Vicky.

'Used to?'

'He doesn't wear the uniform any more,' Danielle told her. 'He wears ordinary clothes, like you.'

Jo's heart sank.

'He's a detective?'

'Not only that,' said Agata Kowalski, 'but I'm sorry to have to tell you that he is part of your team. The team investigating Mandy Madden's murder.'

Jo stared at Agata in disbelief. The reporter's expression conveyed her conviction. Jo knew too that she had a name. Sometimes you had to think the unthinkable.

The unsub had been hiding in plain sight.

Chapter 19

WEDNESDAY, 3RD MAY

'Henshall?'

Gordon Holmes slumped down on the corner of his desk. He looked shaken to the core. Jo had expected a torrent of profanity, but clearly the DCI was too busy processing the enormity of this news.

'That was the name she gave. Detective Constable Henshall.'

'How did she know, this reporter? Did the girls tell her?'

'No,' said Jo. 'He never showed them his ID. He just flashed it at them. Kowalski saw him with us at the Mandy Madden crime scene. He was only too keen to give her his name when asked.'

Gordon nodded. 'Probably thought she was from the Times.'

'You don't seem that surprised.'

'In the short time since he's been with us, DC Henshall has gained a reputation for borderline homophobic, racist, and misogynist comments. I've had to warn him on several occasions for sailing too close to the wind. He's also boastful, and an attention seeker.'

'That doesn't make him a sex pest, let alone a serial killer,' Nick pointed out.

'True,' said Jo. 'But we all know it goes on. There have been three cases of police officers being convicted of wilful abuse of a public office for sexual gain in England this year alone. Two with prostitutes, one with a vulnerable victim he was supposed to be helping. None of those men were serial killers.'

'It could still be him though,' said Nick. 'Either that or it's a highly inconvenient coincidence.'

Gordon turned on him. 'Highly inconvenient? Have I ever told you you're a master of understatement?'

'No, Boss.'

'Well, you are. It's a bloody disaster whatever way you look at it.'

Gordon was right. At best it was a terrible embarrassment for the force, and at worst it could mess up the entire investigation, resulting in a new team having to start from scratch.

Unless, of course, Henshall really was the unsub.

Jo wondered if that was possible. Even if he had carried out the two earlier murders in Wigan and Leigh, he was hardly going to carry one out on his own patch, where so many of the girls could identify him. But then who knew what went on in the mind of a psychopath? Apart from Andy.

Gordon rubbed his chin aggressively. 'They could be making it up.'

'That wasn't the impression I got,' said Jo. 'But you can decide for yourself. I managed, with Agata Kowalski's support, to persuade them to come in and make a formal statement. Her and Max are babysitting them downstairs.'

Gordon looked fit to burst. Jo pre-empted his objection. 'It was the only way I could get them to cooperate. Without her help we wouldn't know any of this. And to be fair, she could have gone public without warning us first.'

Gordon scowled. 'She's not sitting in on the interviews.'

'She doesn't expect to. I've already made that clear.'

He grabbed his jacket, and shrugged it on. 'Come on,' he said. 'Sooner we know the worst, the sooner we can sort it.'

'Gordon,' she said, 'they are all terrified about doing this. They're convinced that nobody will believe them. That you'll do anything to protect your own.'

'That's not going to happen,' he said. 'I'm disappointed in you, Jo. I thought you knew me better than that.'

'I do. But it's not down to you, is it? Granted, the Crown Prosecution Service will have the last say, but with something like this it'll go all the way to the Chief Constable before they get to see it. And he'll have to tell the Mayor. Once it goes political, anything can happen.'

'She's got a point, Boss,' said Nick. 'As soon as Madden's body was found, Henshall must have known there was a chance he'd be outed. He'll already be covering his tracks. It's going to be his word against a couple of prostitutes.'

'Hopefully more than a couple,' said Jo. 'But that will depend on how these interviews go.'

Gordon had one arm stuck in the sleeve of his jacket. He wriggled it free, and made eye contact.

'Whatever it is you're trying to say, just spit it out.'

She took a deep breath. 'I think you should let me take the lead on these interviews.'

'You don't want me in the room?'

She shook her head. 'On the contrary. I think it's important you are there. So they can see that the senior investigating officer from GMP is taking their allegations seriously.'

He cocked an eyebrow. 'But?'

'But I know that you'll want to prod and probe. To try and find any weakness in their stories.'

She held up a hand before he could interrupt.

'I would if I was you. If I still worked for GMP. It's only natural. You need to be sure before you take it any further. All I'm asking is that you let me do that. If you come across as accepting their story, sympathetic even, I'll be better placed to find any flaws in their stories. They already trust me . . . Besides . . .' She paused, preparing for the reaction her next words were bound to generate.

'Besides?' Gordon prompted.

She took a deep breath. 'Shouldn't Professional Standards be handling this?'

Nick stared at his boss, waiting for the inevitable eruption. To their surprise Gordon appeared to take it in his stride. He sat down slowly on the edge of a desk.

'I've already thought about that,' he said. 'The last thing we need is that lot trampling all over Firethorn. The first thing that'll happen is an internal struggle between the Investigation Branch and the Counter Corruption Unit about who gets to handle the complaint.'

He shook his head slowly. 'We can't have that. Not till we're sure there's something to investigate and that something has nothing to do with Mandy Madden or any of the other killings. Then they can take Henshall and do what they like with him just so long as they leave Firethorn alone.'

'They're bound to say you should have handed it over straight away,' Nick ventured nervously.

Gordon smiled. 'Depends on what you mean by *straight away*.' He turned to Jo. 'You didn't take a formal statement from any of them?'

'No,' she said. 'Given how serious it was, I thought you'd want it on the record here at the station.'

Jo could tell that he was about to say 'Good girl', something he'd done frequently in the early days of their professional relationship. But then he saw her expression, and clearly thought better of it. They exchanged knowing smiles, to Nick's obvious bemusement.

'Quite right,' Gordon said. 'Which means there is no complaint until we've given them the chance to make it official. In the meantime, we assess if it's got legs and, if so, what this means for Firethorn. If it's a sideshow, PSB can take it over, and leave us to get on with the big one.'

'And if it isn't?' said Nick.

Gordon slid off the desk, and brushed the knees of his trousers.

'Then we've got our unsub,' he said. 'Case closed.'

Chapter 20

'So you're saying that you believe them, DCI Holmes?' said Helen Gates. Her furrowed brow and anxious tone suggested she had been hoping otherwise.

'I'm afraid so, Ma'am,' he replied. 'As does SI Stuart.'

Jo nodded her agreement.

Mark Davis, the Deputy Chief Constable, whose roles included oversight of the Head of Professional Standards Branch, leaned forward. 'On what basis exactly?' he asked.

Gordon cleared his throat. 'We formally interviewed them both last night separately. All three of them described identical behaviours on the part of DC Henshall. The way in which he first approached them, the exact nature of the threats he made against them, even the nature of the sex acts he forced them to perform on him.'

'Acts they *alleged* he forced them to perform,' said Gates. 'For God sake, let's not rush to judgement.'

'Alleged,' Gordon acknowledged.

'They also described,' said Jo, 'a rug that he kept in the back of his van on which they were expected to perform these alleged acts. They claimed that when he started using an unmarked car he'd take the rug from the boot, and drape it over the rear seats. Presumably to minimise trace evidence.'

'How do we know they didn't cook all this up between them?' said Davis. 'It wouldn't be the first time a group of sex workers conspired to make false allegations against a serving officer.'

Gordon shook his head. 'All of their statements were similar enough to provide corroboration without being so alike as to suggest collusion.'

'There were small pieces of detail in each of their statements,' Jo added, 'that were both unique and credible enough to give the whole thing the ring of truth. That's not something they are likely to have thought of themselves.'

Gates sat back in her chair.

'Damn!' she said. 'What a mess.'

'There will have to be an immediate investigation, Helen,' said the Deputy Chief Constable. 'Especially in light of Operation Firethorn. If he's the killer and we don't act quickly, the press will crucify us. If he's not, the sooner we know and take him out of the equation, the better.'

He addressed the two detectives. 'Have either of you formed an opinion on how best to substantiate or disprove these allegations?'

Jo and Gordon looked at each other.

'You first,' said Gordon. 'You've had more time to think about it.'

'The rug is an obvious starting point,' she said. 'If we find it in his possession, that will back up their stories. Even better, it may hold vital trace evidence that will link him to them. The same with the vans he used, and his current car. The girls told us they still have the clothes they wore on the dates of the alleged incidents with DC Henshall. It would just be a matter of comparing any fibres from Henshall's vehicles to those clothes.'

She looked at Gordon. 'We have dates and times for at least five of the occasions when he is alleged to have solicited sex from them,' he said. 'It would be easy to check them against DC Henshall's work records to establish whether he had the opportunity to be in those places at those times, or alternatively if he has rock-solid alibis. I could also interview the officers he was scheduled to work with when he was in uniform to see if they were aware of anything at all suspicious about his movements.'

'You said *I*,' said the Deputy Chief Constable. 'Given the serious nature of these allegations, I hope you don't think for a moment that it's appropriate for you to be investigating one of your own officers. This is clearly a matter for the Professional Standards Branch Investigations Unit.'

Gates began to nod her agreement.

Gordon raised a tentative hand.

'Go on,' Gates said, her tone advising caution.

'Ordinarily I would agree,' Gordon said. 'But given that we don't know for certain that this isn't connected with Operation Firethorn, I believe that my team should be involved until that possibility has been eliminated.'

'He has a point, Mark,' Gates said.

The DCC frowned. 'It's far too risky. For a start this is serious enough for us to have to inform the IPCC.'

Gates looked askance at him. 'The Independent Police Complaints Commission?' she said. 'It'll take a week for them to agree the terms of reference, let alone who should lead the investigation. What about inviting the NCA to take on Firethorn until these allegations have been dealt with? After all, they are already involved.'

'We don't have the resources to do that,' said Jo hurriedly. 'Besides, our role is serious and organised crime.'

Mark Davis raised both eyebrows. 'You're saying a serial killer isn't serious and organised?' he said.

'Stop splitting hairs, Mark,' said Gates. 'You know very well what SI Stuart means.'

Jo was beginning to wonder if there was more than a professional relationship between these two. Why else the Christian names and the absence of the normal acknowledgement of rank?

'Can I make a suggestion?' Jo said. 'What if I liaise with your Professional Standards Branch to gather initial intelligence and evidence relating to DC Henshall? That would leave DCI Holmes free to concentrate on Firethorn. As soon as you have enough evidence to proceed one way or another, our focus would be back on Firethorn, and the PSB could handle the abuse-of-public-office investigation.'

She could feel Gordon staring at her, and studiously avoided his gaze. She had no idea what he was thinking. Gates and Davis looked at each other. There was a brief nodding of heads.

'That would work for me,' said the Deputy Chief Constable.

'What about you, DCI Holmes?' said Helen Gates.

Gordon shuffled uncomfortably in his seat. 'It would also work for me,' he said. 'As long as the rest of SI Stuart's team will still be supporting Firethorn.'

'Absolutely,' said Jo, secretly praying that Harry Stone would agree with that to which she had just committed herself.

'Splendid!' said the Deputy Chief. 'Let's agree first steps here and now. Number one, have the complainants been warned not to tell anyone else that they have talked to the police?'

'Yes,' said Jo. 'We impressed on them that to do so could undermine the investigation.'

'What about this reporter, Kowalski? Can you persuade her to keep quiet until we are in a position to move on Henshall?'

Jo nodded. 'I've already done that. But she will expect some exclusivity. At the very least she'll want to be free to set out her role in bringing the allegations to our attention.'

'We can't stop her doing that,' said Gates. 'But she can forget exclusivity. Whatever the outcome there'll be a very carefully worded press release that they all get at the same time.' She shrugged. 'I suppose you can promise her some privileged details after that.'

'Thirdly,' said the Deputy Chief, 'the PSB investigation unit will place Henshall under surveillance, and start digging into his professional and personal background. And finally, you, DCI Holmes, will find a pretext to give him a role that keeps him away from Firethorn. You'll also turn over to my team his work schedules and records for the period covered by the Firethorn killings.'

'What about the period before he joined my syndicate?' said Gordon. 'He's only been with us for a couple of months.'

'Leave that to us.'

Jo raised a hand. 'What about my role?' she asked.

'I suggest that you work that out with the PSB senior investigator,' Davis said. 'But since you already have a rapport with the complainants, why don't you get some samples of those clothes you mentioned, DNA swabs from each of them, and see if either they or any of the other sex workers can produce anything else that may help us to resolve this PDQ?'

———

'He's sidelined you already,' said Gordon as the two of them headed for the stairwell.

'We'll see,' said Jo.

'Smart move of yours,' he continued, 'handing it to him on a platter.'

She stopped, forcing him to do the same. 'That's not fair, Gordon,' she said. 'They were never going to let you handle the Henshall investigation. You know that. This way you get the best of both worlds. The resources of the PSB investigations branch to get it resolved quickly and cleanly, and me on the inside making sure that neither you nor Firethorn is compromised in any way.'

He smiled sheepishly. 'You're right,' he said. 'Of course you are. Can't deny me a bit of male vanity though, can you?'

They carried on down the stairs.

'One thing I don't understand,' Gordon said, speaking to the back of Jo's head, 'is that Henshall hasn't exactly been keeping a low profile since we started Operation Firethorn. Instead he's carried on playing the jackass. You'd think he'd either want off the case or keep his head down.'

'That's just a measure of his overweening self-confidence. He probably thought the girls would be too scared to say anything. That's why he tried it on in the first place. Because he saw them as vulnerable.'

She paused.

'Just like our unsub.'

Chapter 21

'What do you think?'

It was the second time of asking. Andy Swift appeared not to have heard. His head was bent over the notes he had been making for the past half an hour.

It was nine in the evening. Thirty-two long hours since the decision had been made to create parallel investigations for Firethorn, and the allegations against DC Henshall. DCI Harvey Ince, the Public Standards Branch Senior Investigator, together with Jo, Ram, and Andy, from the Behavioural Sciences Unit, had been at The Quays reviewing the data they had thus far.

'Andy?' said Jo, touching him lightly on the arm.

Andy jumped like a startled hare. 'What?' He stared at each of them in turn.

'DCI Ince was asking what you think. About Henshall.'

Andy nodded sagely, as though it suddenly made sense. 'It's not him,' he said.

'What's not him?' said Ince, visibly irritated by Swift's laconic response.

'He is not the unsub.'

'Are you sure?' asked Jo.

'But he is certainly capable of the offences of which he has been accused,' Swift replied, ignoring the question.

'Whoa,' said Ince. 'I don't recall asking you to look at Henshall as the Firethorn unsub. This meeting is about alleged abuse of office.'

Andy removed his glasses, and rubbed his eyes. It reminded Jo of just how tired she was. They had been working crazy hours ever since Mandy Madden's body had been found. The psychologist replaced his glasses, and turned to her. 'I'm confused,' he said. 'I understood that Max, Ram, and I were still focusing on Operation Firethorn.'

'You are,' she told him. 'But it makes sense to get your perspective on these allegations, and on what DCI Ince has discovered about DC Henshall.'

She turned to Ince. 'Harvey, this was always about eliminating Henshall from Firethorn as well as investigating the complaints. Why not hear Andy out?'

It had been clear from the outset that Ince was one of those officers who needed to be seen to be in charge. According to Gordon there had been sighs of relief all round in FMIT when he moved over to Professional Standards. She was beginning to understand why.

Ince shook his head but demurred. 'Go on then,' he said. 'So long as it doesn't take too long. I'm due back at Central Park in an hour and a half.'

Andy smiled. 'I can do brief,' he said, sitting back in his chair, and placing his hands behind his head. 'Let's see. Henshall is in the age range that we might expect either as the potential unsub or as the alleged perpetrator who coerced those three women into giving him sexual favours.'

Jo found herself smiling. *Sexual favours* was exactly the kind of coy phrase she would expect Andy to use.

'He is generally regarded as being overconfident,' Swift continued. 'And below average on the empathy continuum, as a result of which his application to become a detective was only narrowly approved. His initial training tests placed him in the centre of the average to above-average IQ range. His role places him in a position of power vis-à-vis the complainants. He lives alone, having been divorced . . .' Andy turned to Ram, eyebrows raised in a question.

'Two years ago,' said the intelligence analyst.

'Two years ago. The grounds cited were . . .'

'Irretrievable breakdown resulting from his unreasonable behaviour,' Ram supplied. 'I'm waiting for the transcript to discover the exact nature of this unreasonable behaviour.'

Jo made a mental note to go and see Henshall's former wife as soon as practicable, probably after he had been arrested, in case she might tell someone else, who might then alert him that he was under investigation.

'All of these factors,' said Swift, 'are wholly consistent in relation to both scenarios. Serial killer, and sexual predator.'

He raised one finger as a warning.

'However, there are elements of the known behaviour of our unsub that are not consistent with the known behaviour allegedly attributed to DC Henshall.'

'Such as?' said DCI Ince.

Swift frowned. 'I find it easier to order my thoughts in a form that is most likely to meet the brief required of me when I am neither prompted, nor interrupted.'

His tone was completely neutral. A simple statement of fact. It had the desired effect.

'Sorry,' said Ince. Jo sensed the apology was both rare and difficult for him to give.

'That's alright,' Andy said cheerfully. 'Now, where was I?'

Nobody dared to prompt him.

'Oh yes,' he said. 'The unsub. In addition to the known characteristics attributed to DC Henshall, we have the following. The unsub's modus operandi suggests trichophilia, an obsessive fetishism in which the person finds human hair sexually arousing and/or erotic. There is no evidence of actual sexual arousal or penetration on his part. He kills his victims using a garrotte constructed from twisted human hair. He leaves a signature in the form of knotted human hair in his victims' oral cavity. And he removes a lock of hair as a trophy of his subjugation and annihilation of his victims. None of that is consistent with DC Henshall's known behaviours, or his alleged attacks on the complainants. Ergo, Henshall and the unsub are not one and the same person.'

'It's not impossible though, is it?' said Ince sceptically. 'You can't be that certain. This is only an opinion surely.'

Swift sat up straight, removed his glasses, took that small blue microfibre cloth from his breast pocket, and began to polish the lenses.

'In my humble opinion,' he said, 'it's about as likely that the two are one and the same as it is that President Putin will retire and found a transgender religious order in Texas.'

Jo suppressed a smile.

'But Henshall *is* a credible suspect in relation to the allegations made against him,' said Ince.

'Absolutely,' Swift replied. 'I'd bet my MZ Charly on it.'

'Nice place you've got here,' said DCI Ince.

The meeting had broken up. The others were preparing to go home. Andy to his wife and children. Ram to his lonely apartment.

Jo followed his gaze to where the purple floodlit outlines of The Lowry Theatre and footbridge were perfectly mirrored in the still waters of the Huron Basin. Myriad white and gold lights from the buildings on the far side led the eye east past MediaCityUK to the red-and-white toast rack of the Manchester United stadium, and north to where the city was laid out like a fantasy model village. It was hard to accept that a serial killer had chosen to make this his playground. Easy to see why it was so hard to find him.

'Yes,' she said. 'It is. Not that I get much time to enjoy it.'

Ince glanced at his watch. 'I'd better get going. I have to brief the Deputy Chief about our plan to bring Henshall in early on Sunday morning. I take it you want to be there.'

'Are you kidding?' she said. 'I'm the one who started the ball rolling.'

Ince nodded, and fingered the collar of his donkey jacket. 'When this is put to bed,' he said tentatively, 'I don't suppose . . .'

'Go on,' she said.

'You'd fancy coming out for a drink with me. Or . . . a meal.'

Jo fought to keep a straight face. He had clearly not done his home-work, which was bad news for a detective. She, on the other hand, had. Ince had two children, and his marriage of twelve years was rumoured to be on the rocks. The last thing she wanted to do was humiliate him when they still had to work together.

'Ask me again nearer the time,' she said. 'Right now I'm too knack-ered to even contemplate it.'

'Fair enough,' he said.

The two of them headed for the door. 'By the way,' Ince said, 'who was that *Charlie* that Swift was talking about?'

She laughed. 'MZ Charly. It's his precious electric scooter. Believe me, if Andy is prepared to gamble that, you might want to think about betting your house, your car, and everything else you've got on it. Henshall may not be our unsub, but I'm afraid he's as guilty as hell.'

Chapter 22

Flora inhaled slowly, paused, then drew in a deep draught of clean air that pushed the smoke and vapour into the furthest recesses of her lungs. She rested her back against the wall, and waited.

Fifty seconds later cannabinoids leaped the blood–brain barrier. Her pulse quickened. She was now acutely aware of the traffic on Cheetham Hill Road, several streets away. The street lights seemed brighter, more intense. Time stood still.

The door of the Queens Arms burst open. She heard the sound of bubbling conversation from within, and raucous laughter. Two middle-aged men emerged, swaying unsteadily. The shorter of them stopped to zip up his black leather jacket. His companion spotted her, and nudged his friend, knocking him off balance, so that he fell back against a wooden picnic table.

'What the feck!' he cried, struggling to push himself upright.

'Would you look at this?' said the taller man. 'Are they getting younger, or are we getting older? Does your mother know you're out, sweetheart?'

'Leave her alone,' said Shorty. 'You don't know where she's been.'

'Oh but I do,' the other retorted. 'That's the thing. That's why I wouldn't be asking for more than a kiss.'

He stepped towards her. 'How about it, sweetheart? A little freebie for Uncle Jack?'

Flora took a final toke, and dropped the stub on the ground, grinding it beneath the toe of her shoe. She unclasped her handbag, slipped her hand inside, and began to walk diagonally away from them.

Never completely turn your back, Natalia had taught her. Make sure you can see them from the corner of your eye. If they start to follow, get your hand on your spray. If they keep coming, turn and point it at them. Feel for your rape alarm with the other. That usually stops them. If not, use both and then get the hell out of there. Don't stay in the area. Go home. There's nothing more dangerous than a wounded animal.

Flora's heart was pounding now, her anxiety magnified by the cannabis. Her hand tightened around the canister. His companion had hold of his arm and was pulling him back.

'Leave her, Jacky,' he mumbled. 'She's not worth it.'

The tall man hurled a stream of abuse at her, hawked from the back of his throat, and spat on the pavement with the finality of a full stop.

Part of her was sorry he hadn't kept coming. Flora would love an excuse to use her spray. Just once. How the hell would he have explained to his wife – the worst ones all had wives or partners – the dye on his face and clothes, which would take days to remove, and the foul sulphurous odour of garlic? Come to that, how would this one have explained the 130-plus-decibel screech of the alarm, which would surely have brought people, curious, from the pub. She had never used the canister except to warn them off. On those occasions when men had hurt her, it would have been impracticable, and potentially deadly dangerous, even to try. That was the dilemma they all faced. Knowing which ones to warn off. Sensing which ones might turn nasty before it was too late to do anything about it.

She clicked the clasp shut, thrust her hands into the pockets of her coat, and turned right to begin the Collingham Street circuit. Had Natalia been with her, she might have chanced the much more lucrative stretches between Red Bank and Cheetham Hill Road, but a pimp for some of the other girls had warned her off once tonight, and she wasn't going to risk it again.

It was miserable here, and dark. The security lights above one of the steel-shuttered factories lit a narrow path beside the storage units.

Where was Natalia now, Flora wondered? Why had she left without saying goodbye? After all they had been through together. The two of them leaving Dunakeszi with her cousin, and the promise of jobs in England. The cousin introducing them to that monster Arpad and then disappearing. Their passports and papers taken away. Locked in separate rooms. Raped. The two of them forced into a brothel near King's Cross. It was Natalia who hatched the plan. Hitched a lift for them with a Polish lorry driver. Persuaded the owner of the Hungarian food store to rent them a flat above the shop. And then she had suddenly disappeared. Her few belongings gone. Just that note left behind.

Got to move on. Sorry. Look after yourself. XXX. N.

It made no sense. But then nothing in Flora's world made sense any more. All she saw was a road stretching ahead leading nowhere. A road just like this one.

⌣

He cursed silently. It had taken forever for those two idiots to move on. Then, just as he was about to break cover, the door of the public house had opened again and two couples emerged. Finally the streets were empty. Now the girl was gone.

He left the shadows, crossed the road, and turned into the street he had seen her take. One small van had entered this street while he had been waiting. He could only hope that it was not a punter, or if it was, that she had turned him down. Otherwise he would have to try his luck in the crowded triangle, fraught with difficulty, between North Street and the A665. There were risks worth taking. Ones that set the pulse racing. But there were limits he had set himself. Even here in this carnal backwater, this fetid tributary. The same police patrol car had cruised by twice in the past two hours. Close enough for him to see the garrulous driver and his bored companion, one hand on the grab handle, the other cradling a Styrofoam beaker. Too close for comfort.

The moon emerged briefly in a gap between menacing clouds. He glimpsed a moving silhouette up ahead, and a flash of gold in the moonlight. Gold, the colour of her flaxen hair. His hand moved to the locket around his neck. He smiled, and hastened his steps.

The quarry was marked.

The hunt was on.

Chapter 23

Monday, 8th May

A pale glow, low on the horizon, heralded the dawn of a new day. The first of countless days this young woman would never experience. One that would bring grief knocking at the doors of her parents, family, and friends. Grief fuelled by guilt and rage, which would haunt some of them for the rest of their lives.

Jo had no idea if the sickness in the pit of her stomach was down to the shock of rising yet again in the early hours or anticipation of what lay ahead. Not that it mattered. All that counted was catching the sick bastard that was killing these women. Bringing a crumb of comfort to the bereaved in the form of justice, whatever that really meant. Above all, preventing him from doing it again, and again.

She tucked a wayward wisp of hair beneath her hood, wiped droplets of rain from her eyes with the back of a gloved hand, and trudged through the stream of water running from the crown of the road.

Up ahead, two telescopic LED lights shone 1,200 unforgiving lumens on to the scene below. Casting shadows. Illuminating the protective suits of the figures bent over the small skip. Five faceless hooded creatures straight from a horror movie. There was even a cameraman.

One of the figures moved. In the gap he left behind, a pathetically thin arm hung limp over the side of the skip. A ghostly slash of brilliant white beneath the stark lighting.

The skip was tiny. Four foot long perhaps by two and a half feet high. Twisted as though it had been dropped from a great height. A mass of red-brown rust, and random flakes of yellow paint. Jo stepped into the space that had been vacated, and swallowed to suppress the sudden rush of bile rising from her stomach.

The young woman lay on her right side. Knees tucked in. The right arm hidden from sight. Her head and shoulders lay propped up against the rear end of the skip. Sodden long blonde hair all but obscured her face. She wore what under normal circumstances would have been a stunning red dress, with a sexy square neckline, short sleeves, and a scoop back with an exposed zipper. A belt marked the start of a full-circle, fit-and-flare-style skirt that had risen up to expose alabaster legs and thighs.

The figure beside Jo turned to face her.

'Glad you could make it,' said Max. 'But I assumed you'd be calling on DC Henshall.'

There was no criticism implied.

'I wanted to see this first,' she said, 'so that we knew exactly what we were dealing with. DCI Ince has gone to check in with the surveillance teams. I said I'd join him shortly to bring him up to speed. Then we'll move in.'

The figure opposite her spoke. It was Nick Carter. 'Can't see it being him though. Not with two pairs of eyes on him all night.'

'It wouldn't be the first time someone gave a surveillance team the slip,' Jo said.

She sensed the reproach in his eyes, and instantly regretted her words.

'I'm sorry,' she said. 'I didn't mean . . .'

To hide his embarrassment, Nick stared down at his hands, gripping the sides of the skip. Gordon shrugged it away. Max stared at her quizzically. She said nothing. She didn't need to. All of her BSU colleagues knew the story of how the Cutacre killer had plucked her from under the noses of such a team. But not who else had been involved. Max would piece it together eventually.

'Is it the unsub?' Jo asked, breaking the silence.

'If it isn't,' said Nick, 'it's a copycat who knows every detail of the unsub's modus operandi.'

Dr Carol Tompkins lifted a handful of sopping-wet strands of hair away from the victim's neck, revealing the telltale circular bruising. With her other hand, she gently tilted the head towards them. Sweetheart lips the colour of the dress surrounded a gaping mouth, in which was visible a tangled mat of raven hair. It seemed to Jo a cruel humiliation. An evil, senseless desecration.

'A trophy?' Jo asked.

The police surgeon's hands let the hair go, and gathered up some more strands at the nape of the neck. The uniform length was interrupted by a three-inch-wide by five-inch-long gap where the hair had been excised.

'He's becoming more ambitious,' Max muttered. 'At this rate he'll be removing it all.'

'When did she die?' Jo asked.

'Between three and six hours ago,' said Tompkins.

'Between 11.30pm and 2.30am,' said Nick needlessly.

'Probably closer to midnight than two thirty,' said the doctor.

'Did she die here or was she moved?' Jo asked.

Carol Tompkins carefully unzipped the dress and pointed to the light purplish discolouration along the side of the body lying against the end of the skip. 'Based on this livor mortis, I would say here. Or very close to this spot.'

'That's where we found one of her shoes,' said Jack Benson from the opposite end of the skip.

Jo turned and stepped back to see where he was pointing. A yellow CSI marker was partly submerged in a pool of water close to the fence a yard or so from where Carol Tompkins was standing.

'The other one,' he said, 'was fifteen yards further away up against the fence. Where we also found the coat we believe she must have been wearing, and her handbag. We are working on the assumption that she was killed over there, lifted up, and carried to this skip, where he then dumped her.'

'I would suggest laid rather than dumped,' said Tompkins. 'I don't see any evidence that she was dropped, although we won't know for sure until after the post-mortem.'

Jo was staring at three large waste bins on wheels – one red, one blue, one beige – between here and the spot where the belongings had been found. Closer still was another, larger static bin, containing scrap metal. Above them towered a corrugated-iron fence, behind which the tip of a heap of scrap metal threatened to topple over on to the street.

'Why did he choose this skip,' Jo asked, 'rather than one of those bins?'

'Because he wanted to display her, not hide her?' Max suggested.

'So she'd be found sooner?' said Nick.

'Because it was easier to drop her in. Hardly any lifting required,' Benson proposed.

'Or all three,' said Jo. 'Who found the body?'

'Security van man,' said Gordon, pointing towards the other end of the street, where a white van with a roof-mounted amber beacon response light, and a pair of halogen floodlights was parked up with its sidelights on. 'Canine Protect Security Services. They do two sweeps a night of all of the industrial units round here. His dog found her stuff first and then this.'

Jo turned back, and stared at the body. 'If you have her bag, do we know who she is?'

'There was nothing in it to tell us that,' said Gordon. 'But local officers have been busy speaking to some of the other sex workers. We've got a street name for her. Clara. Eastern European. Only been on this patch for a couple of months. She used to have a friend with her until a week or so ago. Kept themselves to themselves. Rumour has it she lives over the top of a Hungarian food store on Bury New Road.'

'Nick and I were just about to make our way there,' said Max.

'I'd better leave too,' Jo said. 'I'll call DCI Ince, and tell him I'm on my way.'

By the time she reached her car, the rain had stopped. In the east, rays of the rising sun streaming through a squally shower had created a perfect rainbow. It seemed to Jo both incongruous and appropriate. *Which is it?* she wondered. *A sign of hope, a bridge between this world and the next? Or a beguiling promise, doomed to disappoint?*

Chapter 24

'What are the chances it was Henshall?'

Jo felt obliged to ask. Harvey Ince pointed to a modern semi-detached house forty yards down the road. It looked unloved compared to the houses on either side. The small garden was overgrown. Paint peeled from several of the window frames.

'He's been in there since 2pm yesterday afternoon. We've had eyes on him all that time, back and front.'

Jo frowned.

'Two pm? Why wasn't he at work?'

'Good question. It seems that shortly after the DCI informed him he was being loaned out to one of the Category B Cold Case teams for a couple of weeks, he complained of feeling unwell, and signed himself off work.'

'The transfer may have spooked him,' said Jo. 'Perhaps he suspects we're on to him.'

'Fortunately one of my teams was already in situ. The other one followed him home and then took up residence in the street whose houses back on to Henshall's.'

'He could still have left by the back door,' she said. 'Clambered over the fences of the adjoining gardens, then slipped out through a side gate while your officers were watching the front.'

Ince shook his head. 'He didn't.'

'How can you be so sure?'

'State-of-the-art surveillance. Both of our vehicles have cameras giving three-sixty-degree CCTV capture. One operative watches the target, another watches the screens. Plus we've got directional microphones trained on his house. They know what he's watching on the television, listening to on the radio, even when he goes to the loo. Trust me, he hasn't left the house.'

'You have to make sure though,' she said. 'Besides, if he does suspect he's under investigation he could be quietly destroying evidence. I would if it was me.'

'I'll remember you said that.'

It sounded like a joke, although with Professional Standards Branch you could never be sure. She remembered when it had been changed from Internal Affairs. Someone had pointed out that there were that many affairs between serving officers, including some of the most senior ones, that the name had become a running joke. Not just within the Force, but among the public too.

'You are going in though,' she said.

'Yes.'

'When?'

He reached into his inside breast pocket, removed a neatly folded A4 sheet and held it up.

'Right now.'

He pressed the button on the radio transmitter.

'Papa 2 report please.'

There was a brief pause.

'Nothing to report,' came the reply. 'All clear here.'

'Papa 3 report please.'

There was a brief pause.

'Target has just entered the lounge, and switched on the television.'

Jo stared at the house. The curtains were still drawn. There was no telltale flicker of light from either of the downstairs rooms.

'Papa 1 to all units,' said Ince, 'we are good to go. Charlie Sierra India, with me please. Romeo Sierra 4, Papa 2, and Papa 3, remain on station. Let's keep it low-profile, everybody. No need to wake the neighbours.'

Jo looked at her watch. It was 5.45am. Lights were on in some of the other houses. A car was backing out of a drive three houses down from Henshall's, the driver staring in their direction.

Ince had already unbuckled his seat belt and was opening the door. Together they walked towards the house. An unmarked car pulled up across the drive to Henshall's house. Two men and a woman climbed out. One of the men opened the boot and took out a large cardboard box, and a clipboard. The female officer removed a sleek aluminium case, and closed the boot. The five of them walked down the tarmacked drive and gathered at the front door.

Ince's finger hovered over the doorbell. There was muted laughter from behind the blackout curtains. He looked over his shoulder to check they were ready.

'This is a serving officer,' he said, 'assessed as minimum risk. We are not doing shock and awe. Understood?'

'Yes, Boss,' the search team chorused.

He pressed the bell. The response took them all by surprise.

'Ding dong! Ding dong!' yelled a familiar American cartoon voice. *'If that's my pizza, keep it hot till I get there.'*

'What a joker,' Ince observed sourly.

The greeting was repeating for a third time when the length of curtain closest to the front door was drawn back. Henshall peered out at them. He was unshaven, his hair dishevelled, and his face pale and drawn. There were dark rings beneath his eyes. He looked surprised. The curtain fell back. Thirty seconds later the door opened.

Henshall turned, and walked back down the hall without a word. He led them into the first room on the right. The search team closed the door behind them, and remained in the hall. Jo and DCI Ince followed Henshall into what proved to be a lounge.

Henshall sat down on a three-seat sofa. He was wearing a dressing gown that had seen better times over a pair of pyjama bottoms. His feet were on a coffee table. Beside them were a half-empty mug of tea, a box of flu powders, and a man-size box of tissues. There was a *Frasier* repeat on the television.

'This is what I call over the top,' he said, his gaze fixed on the television. 'Coming mob-handed to check if I'm pulling a sickie.'

It was a brave attempt, Jo thought, but for the quaver in his voice.

'Are you,' said Ince, 'pulling a sickie?'

Henshall looked up at him. 'Could be man flu, could be the real thing. I didn't want to take the risk of infecting the syndicate, did I?'

'Very noble of you,' said Jo. 'Nothing to do with your being loaned out then.'

Henshall attempted a smile. 'Far from it. I regard that as a promotion. Just me, a DI, and a load of old pensioners. Makes me his deputy, doesn't it?'

Ince decided to put an end to the charade. He picked up the TV remote, switched the television off, and dropped the remote on the sofa.

'Detective Constable Henshall,' he said, 'my name is Detective Chief Inspector Harvey Ince. I am with the Professional Standards Branch. SI Stuart you already know. I am here to arrest you in order that you may be questioned in relation to possible misconduct in a public office. You do not have to say anything. But it may harm your defence if you do not mention, when questioned, something which you later rely on in court. Anything you do say may be given in evidence. Do you understand?'

Despite Henshall's attempt to maintain a mask of total incomprehension, Jo spotted the tiny flicker of fear in his eyes.

'No, I don't,' he said.

'What don't you understand?'

'What I'm supposed to have done. I have the right to be told.'

That was true. And although they were under no obligation to tell him until he was formally interviewed, Jo could see no reason not to tell him. If he was guilty, he would know anyway. If he was innocent, it would make no difference. Ince arrived at the same conclusion.

'You will be questioned,' he said, 'in connection with allegations that you used your position as a police officer to procure, through intimidation, the sexual services of one or more female sex workers.'

Henshall looked shaken. 'This is bullshit!' he said.

'In which case,' Ince told him, 'we should be able to clear it up in no time.' He held up the warrant. 'I have here a warrant to search these premises, and any vehicles belonging to, or used by, you. Also to seize any property or effects that I reasonably believe may be connected with these allegations. I suggest you get dressed.'

In the hall the search team had put on their Tyvek suits, gloves, and overboots. They had been briefed to begin with his car, since that was the only part of the property that was identified as a potential crime scene. Jo decided to accompany them to the garage. The large family saloon took up so much of the space that there was barely enough room to open the doors.

Jack Benson had arrived with a small team of crime scene investigators. He shook his head. 'Can't search the vehicle in here,' he said. 'I need you to wait in the drive, Ma'am.'

Jo watched impatiently as the car was driven out on to the driveway. Benson exited the car, and walked across to her.

'Good news, or bad news?' she said.

'Bad news,' Benson replied. 'I'm guessing he's cleaned it inside and out within the last twenty-four hours. Good news is it's not a professional valet, so there's a reasonable chance he'll have missed something.

We've arranged for it to be flat-loaded, and taken back to the garage so we can do a thorough forensic examination. We'll do a basic visual check first. Is there anything in particular we're looking for?'

'A rug or a small carpet – something like that,' she told him. 'Any floor covering that's not standard for this car. It could be in the vehicle, the garage, or elsewhere in the house.'

'Anything else?'

'Collections of human hair. Short or long, loose, twisted, or braided. And anything else that might suggest an obsession with women's hair in particular.'

'Such as?'

'Photographs, magazines, wigs. Honestly? I'm not sure. Just record and bag anything you think might fit such a preoccupation. Oh, and any diaries or journals. If you're in any doubt, give me a shout and I'll come and have a look.'

⌣

'Is this it?'

The female CSI stepped back from the open boot of the car. With her gloved right hand she held aloft a cream rug approximately three foot long by two feet wide. It was an exact match for the one independently described by all three of the girls. Jo didn't know whether to be elated or deeply saddened. She wondered if this was how Ince felt every time he snared a bent cop.

'Where was it?' she asked.

'Folded in two and laid over the spare tyre beneath the boot floor carpet.' She lifted a label on the underside, and proceeded to read out loud.

'*Heavyweight, Non-shedding, Dense Pile Carpet. Colour – Cream. Technique: Shag.*'

'Fit for purpose then,' observed the third CSI.

Just the kind of remark that Henshall would have made, Jo reflected. The female CSI pulled a face but carried on.

'*Machine Made in England. Professional Clean Only.* It's been cleaned recently by the looks of it.'

'Don't worry,' Ince told Jo. 'If there's anything deep in that pile – and there will be, trust me – we'll find it.'

Chapter 25

From the outside, were it not for the window display full of colourful stickers announcing this week's special offers, it could easily have been mistaken for just another two-storey clothes factory.

Max opened the door.

As he stepped inside, his presence was heralded by the first four bars of the *Radetzky March*.

Given the length and breadth of this supermarket, he could understand why the owners would want to know when people entered and left the establishment. Though why they'd chosen Strauss rather than a Hungarian composer was a mystery.

Despite the early hour there were already a handful of customers. At the far end of the shop a thick-set middle-aged man wearing a blue apron that strained against a generous belly was serving at the checkout. Max walked towards him past a chiller section full of salami, speck sausages, and chicken frankfurters. On the other side of the aisle, two of the shelves held tins of pork and pork liver. A young woman was busy stacking the remaining shelves with dozens of bottles of sour cherry squash.

He waited patiently for the man to finish serving an elderly woman for whom this was clearly more than a simple shopping expedition. He assumed they were conversing in Hungarian, but it didn't take a genius to know that chatting about the weather, her current state of health, and what the world was coming to was an essential part of the service.

The man smiled, and nodded for the final time, took a packet of sweets from the counter beside him, slipped it into her bag, and waved her goodbye.

He turned to Max and shrugged apologetically. '*Tejkaramella*,' he said. 'Creamy fudge. Sometimes I think they're the only reason she comes in here.'

'That and the conversation,' said Max.

The man smiled. 'That too.' He looked down at the empty counter and then back at Max.

Max held up his ID. 'Are you the owner?'

The man nodded warily.

'I need to talk with you,' Max said. 'About Clara.'

'Clara? I don't know any Clara.'

'I understand that she rented a room from you upstairs. Along with her friend Natalia.'

Comprehension dawned, followed swiftly by suspicion.

'Not Clara, Flora,' he said. 'You mean Flora.' He shook his head. 'I have not seen her this morning. Maybe she came back already. I can get my daughter to check if you like.'

'That won't be necessary,' Max told him. 'But I do need to speak with you about her. In private.'

The young woman who had been stacking the shelves took over at the checkout. The owner led Max to a small office at the rear, where he had no option but to sit low down in a battered and uncomfortable armchair. Behind the desk the owner slumped on to a swivel chair, which protested noisily.

'What are you, Immigration?' he asked. 'Because I can tell you she's Hungarian, like me. EEC. So she's entitled, no? Free movement?' He grimaced. 'For now at least.'

'Can we start with your name please, sir?' said Max.

'Matayas Boros,' he replied nervously. 'I'm her landlord. It's not a crime, is it?'

'No, Mr Boros. But that is not why I'm here. I'm afraid I have some bad news for you.'

Boros clenched his fists, and shook his head.

'*Istenem nem!*' he said in disbelief.

'The body of a young woman was found not far from here in the early hours of the morning. We were led to believe that she may have been your tenant.'

The blood drained from the landlord's face. Beads of sweat appeared on his forehead. He groped in the pocket of his apron, took out a crumpled handkerchief, and mopped his face with it. Max wondered if the man was going to faint. Instead he clasped his hands together, rocked back and forth, and muttered a torrent of words. It sounded like a cross between a lamentation and a protest. Had the girl been his daughter, he could not have appeared more distressed. Max waited patiently for him to recover.

'Mr Boros,' he said when the outpouring had become a trickle, 'we don't know for certain that it is Flora.'

'I warned her,' Boros replied. 'I told her if she didn't stop it would end like this. Foolish girl.'

'Perhaps if you were to describe her to me, sir.'

He mopped his face again, thrust the handkerchief back into the pocket, and gripped the edge of the desk with his hands.

'She was a beautiful girl,' Boros said. 'More beautiful before I think.'

'Before what, Mr Boros?'

The owner made eye contact. Wondering if he had been wrong to jump to conclusions. Maybe it wasn't her after all.

'Before she started doing what she does.'

He saw that the policeman understood. Dropped his eyes. Fell silent.

'Mr Boros,' Max prompted. 'What did Flora look like?'

Boros reached forward and took hold of a five-by-seven-inch brushed aluminium photo frame beside the computer. He stared at it for a moment and then turned it so Max could see for himself.

'An angel,' he said. 'She looked like an angel.'

Max saw instantly that the photograph was of the victim. Except that in this photo she was smiling, happy, and alive.

Chapter 26

It was a selfie taken on a carefree trip to the city centre.

Flora was in the centre, to her left the supermarket owner's daughter, and to her right another girl with short black hair, a few years her senior. Manchester Town Hall's clock tower formed the backdrop.

'The dead girl,' said Boros. 'It's Flora, isn't it?'

'I'm afraid so,' said Max. 'I'm sorry.'

Boros reached down to open the bottom right-hand drawer of his desk. He held on to the desk to prevent the chair from toppling over, and taking him with it. He removed a bottle of clear liquid and two shot glasses and placed them on the desk. The contents appeared slightly oily, leaving a distinct smear on the neck as the natural level was restored. Boros unscrewed the top, and filled one of the glasses.

'Not for me thank you,' said Max.

Boros nodded. Lifted the glass. Threw back his head, drained the glass, and poured a second, which he downed as swiftly. He began to pour again.

'Mr Boros,' said Max firmly, 'there will be plenty of time for you to finish that bottle when I'm gone. For now I need you to keep a clear head.'

He lifted the glass, held it suspended between desk and lips for what seemed an eternity, and then put it back down again. He nodded.

'Of course. What is it you want to know?'

'When you rented her the room. Everything and anything you know about her, and her friend.'

Boros turned the photo to face him, and stared at the image of Flora. 'They turned up one evening in February. They'd seen the advert in the window. A two-bedroom flat to rent. Upstairs. They offered cash. Enough for the deposit. At first I wasn't going to let them have it.'

'Why not?'

'Because they had no papers. No passport, no *személyi igazolvány*.'

'Excuse me?'

'*Személyi igazolvány*. Our national ID card. It's not compulsory, but most Hungarians carry one. Especially young kids like these, who don't have a driving licence. I could see they were desperate, but . . .' He shrugged. 'They had no papers. I didn't even know for sure how old they were.'

'What changed your mind?'

'My daughter, Lina. She has a good heart. She said they'd told her they had been robbed in the city centre just after they arrived. Their bags snatched. Everything taken except the money they had on them. No family here. No way they could go back. Lina pleaded. So I told them they could stay till I found a long-term tenant.'

'They must have told you their names.'

He nodded. 'Flora Novak, and Natalia Nemeth.'

'Are those their real names?'

Boros shrugged. 'Their given names. I think so, because that's what they called each other. But their family names? Who knows? Without papers it was impossible to tell.'

'Did they say where they came from in Hungary?'

'Budapest. But I think that was a lie. The details were too . . . how do you say . . . ?'

'Sketchy?'

Boros nodded. 'Sketchy.'

'Why would they not want you to know?'

'I asked myself that. Then my Lina found out why. She told me. They didn't want anyone contacting their family.'

'Because they didn't want their parents to find out how they were earning their living,' Max guessed.

Boros shook his head. 'Not that. Okay, was part of the reason, but it was more than that. They were afraid.'

'Of whom?' Max asked, although he had a pretty good idea. A familiar story was unfolding here.

'Two young friends in search of adventure,' he began. 'One seventeen, the other nineteen. Seeking their fortune in the promised land. England. Just like many of their friends were doing. Just like I did. There was an uncle who had friend, who gives them the promise of jobs. In London. Jobs too good to be true. They arrived in London. They were taken to a house. Had their passports and papers taken away. They were locked in separate rooms. Raped. And put to work.'

Boros's fingers encircled his shot glass. He took a deep breath, lifted the glass, and tipped back his head. This time Max made no attempt to stop him. He placed the glass down beside the bottle, bowed his head, and closed his eyes. When he opened them, they glistened with tears. He pulled the handkerchief out again, and dabbed them.

'How did they escape?' Max asked.

Boros crumpled the handkerchief in his hand, and leaned back in his chair. 'One morning early Natalia went to the bathroom. Someone had left a set of keys – the keys to their rooms – on the windowsill. She took them, hid them in her panties. When the coast was clear, she let herself out, and unlocked Flora's door. It was their one chance. They managed to slip out. They were terrified what these men would do if they caught them. They had to get as far away as possible.'

'Why Manchester?'

'Lina said they hitched a lift, and this was where the driver was going.'

Time and again Max had seen a victim's fate sealed by such a random event. Walking home instead of taking a taxi; turning left rather than right; having one last drink. Had the driver been going to Leeds or Hull – anywhere other than here – Flora Novak would still be alive.

'They were like daughters to me,' Boros was saying. 'Kind and thoughtful. They were the best friends my Lina ever had. When I found out what they were doing, how they were making their money, I offered them both a job in the store.' He shook his head. 'I couldn't match the money they were earning. Natalia said they needed enough to get new passports, papers. I told her to go to the embassy. Get them for free. But it would mean going down to London. They were too frightened to do that. When Natalia left, I even offered to lend Flora the money, but she wouldn't take it.'

He fingered the photograph.

'Foolish, foolish girl.'

Max stood up. 'Can I see her room please?'

<hr>

The room was neat and tidy. Two single beds in a double bedroom. The beds were made. A small wicker table held a shaving mirror and three pots containing perfume, make-up, brushes, and a comb. On one wall stood a single pine wardrobe with drawers beneath. Max took a pair of nitrile gloves from his pocket, put them on, and opened the wardrobe door.

Two pairs of jeans, a pair of trousers, three dresses, a fur-lined anorak, two pairs of shoes – one flat-heeled casual, the other red patent with three-inch heels. Everything looked reasonably new. Probably bought from some of the hundred or so fake fashion outlets in lock-ups between here and Cheetham Hill. Hardly surprising if they had fled their captors with only what they stood up in.

He pulled open the first of the drawers. The underwear was folded into two neat piles. One sexy and skimpy, the other plain white bras and pants. There was also a bag of tights. The second drawer held two skirts, sweaters, and jumpers. He closed the drawer and turned his attention to the bedside table between the two beds.

The drawer held a box of tissues, a half-used packet of painkillers, and two months' supply of oral contraceptives. In the cupboard below was a neat stack of handkerchiefs, two large unopened boxes of condoms, a tube of spermicide, and a battery charger for a mobile phone. He closed the cupboard, felt under the pillow, and pulled out a plain pink cotton pair of pyjamas with a single white heart in the centre of the top. He folded them up, put them back, and sat down on the bed.

No photos, no diary, no letters. Nothing to link her to a past or a future. Only the trappings of a soulless present. He stood up, lifted the mattress, and looked underneath. Nothing. He knelt down, lay on his side, and looked under the bed. There was a metal box easily within reach. He retrieved it, and placed it on the bedside table.

It was a black metal, A4, six-inch-deep security box. There was a small chrome lock that required a key but of which a screwdriver would make short shrift. He held it to his ear, and tilted it. There was a faint brushing sound as something light and soft slid across the floor of the box.

Max stepped to the window. It looked out over a large yard, and the depressing backs of neighbouring Victorian factories and warehouses. He tried to imagine her standing here recalling a very different view back home in Hungary. He shook his head. If only they had gone to the police.

He chose from the dressing table a brush that still had hairs attached, and went in search of the bathroom. Finding nothing significant there, he went back down to the office.

Boros was slumped in his chair. The bottle was half empty. He looked up as Max entered the room.

'Did you find anything?' he asked. His speech was slurred.

Max held up the box, and the brush, which was now in a transparent evidence bag.

'I would like your permission to take these,' he said. 'I can always come back with a warrant if you insist.'

'Take them.'

'I'll also need the photo,' said Max.

Boros pulled it towards him, and clutched it protectively. 'It's alright,' Max told him. 'I'll take a copy with my phone.'

When he had finished, he handed the photo back to Boros.

'Has Flora's friend Natalia been in touch with you or your daughter since she left?'

He shook his head.

'No.'

'Are you sure, about your daughter?'

He looked up. His eyes were bleary.

'I'd know. She tells me everything. She's a good girl.'

Max had heard that too many times from parents doomed to be disappointed. Usually from the fathers.

'Even so, I'd like a word with her before I go.'

Boros heaved himself unsteadily to his feet.

'I'll get her,' he said. 'Someone has to be on the checkout.'

He paused.

'Working in the shop all hours, my daughter doesn't have many friends her own age.' He fingered the photograph. Sniffed, and corrected himself. 'Now she's alone again.'

He stopped in the doorway, and turned. 'One thing, Officer. How did Flora die?'

'Quickly,' Max replied, hoping that it was the truth.

Chapter 27

'How do you intend to play this?' Jo asked.

They were standing in the corridor outside Interview Room 2.

'With a straight bat,' Ince replied. 'Henshall's a serving officer, accompanied by his legal insurance solicitor, and his Federation rep. They all know the ropes.' He straightened his tie. 'Did the women who made the allegations come through with those DNA swabs?'

'They took some persuading,' Jo said. 'They only agreed to go ahead when DCI Holmes gave them written assurances about what would happen to the samples after the investigation, and any subsequent trial.'

'That gets us over the first hurdle,' Ince said. 'Now we have to pray they don't get cold feet if this goes to court.'

'*When* it goes to court,' Jo said. 'That rug is a coincidence too far. If you find their DNA on that rug or anywhere in his car, his only defence is going to be consensual sex. That's gross misconduct even without an element of coercion. And if he's capable of that, who's the jury going to believe?'

Ince looked sceptical. 'CSI said it looked like the rug had been cleaned. Any trace evidence is unlikely to prove that sex took place. It'll still be his word against theirs. He'll claim he stopped to move them on. He sat them in the back of the car while he spoke to them.'

There was a moment's silence. He shuffled his feet. 'Where are you and DCI Holmes up to in relation to any connection between Henshall and Firethorn?'

'The search of the house, car, and his work locker provided no evidence of his involvement in any of the Firethorn murders. What's more, he was still in uniform when the first of the Firethorn murders was committed. His work rota shows he was on nights in the city centre. He and his partner processed a drunk and disorderly, and an assault occasioning actual bodily harm. He's not our unsub. I never thought he was.'

'There you go then,' said Ince. He handed Jo a double-sided sheet of A4. 'This is the interview strategy. Given you're the one those women came to first and you were there when I arrested him, the Crown Prosecution Service will need you to give evidence if it goes all the way, so you're welcome to sit in. On balance, it's probably best that you do.'

The message was clear: keep your mouth shut, and let me do the interview. Jo wasn't the least bit offended. This was his case after all. She also had the impression he'd finally discovered that she was not the red-blooded heterosexual he'd taken her for. She smiled. It saved her having to tell him herself.

'What's so funny?' he asked.

'The thought of seeing DC Henshall getting his just deserts,' she replied. 'Not so much funny, more satisfying.'

Flanked by his solicitor and Federation rep, Henshall appeared to have regained his composure. He looked positively smug.

'To expedite matters,' said the solicitor as soon as the preliminaries were over, 'I should like to read a statement on behalf of my client.'

'Go ahead,' said Ince.

'DC Henshall believes that he is the victim of a conspiracy. He maintains that these are malicious and false allegations made by three common prostitutes solely because he has exercised his professional duty by reminding them that under Section 16 of the Policing and Crime Act 2009 it is an offence to persistently loiter or solicit in a street or public place for the purpose of offering one's services as a prostitute.'

'I am well aware of the law,' said Ince sourly. 'But I am surprised that neither you nor DC Henshall appears to be aware that the term "common prostitute" no longer applies as a legal definition.'

Jo took vicarious pleasure in seeing the grin wiped from Henshall's face.

'Be that as it may,' his solicitor responded, 'this is a clear case of three sex workers fabricating a story against an officer who, unlike many of his colleagues, chose to enforce the law rather than turn a blind eye.'

Ince raised his eyebrows.

'By threatening them with arrest unless they availed him of those very services for which they were soliciting?'

'That's not—' the solicitor began.

Ince held up his hand.

'You've read out your client's statement,' he said. 'Now I would like to hear from your client himself. Specifically I would like DC Henshall to answer a few questions.'

The Federation rep leaned forward across the table.

'Before you do,' he said, 'I would like to know what an officer from the National Crime Agency is doing here.'

'I can tell you that,' said Henshall. 'She's working the Firethorn investigation. The murders of those other prostitutes? She's hoping to pin them on me. This is a fishing expedition. That's what it's all about.'

'That is not true,' said Ince. 'SI Stuart is here at my invitation firstly because the allegations against your client were originally made to her, and secondly in order that your client can be eliminated from Operation Firethorn. I can confirm that DC Henshall is not now a person of interest in relation to that investigation. Isn't that right, SI Stuart?'

'Yes,' Jo said. 'At this moment in time Mr Henshall is not a person of interest to us.'

Henshall slammed the table with the flat of his hand. '*At this moment in time?* What the hell does that mean?'

His tone was angry, his stare threatening. This was the flip side of the laughing policeman, Jo realised. It wasn't difficult to imagine how each of those girls must have felt when he came on to them. His solicitor placed a warning hand over his.

'That was what I was about to ask,' the solicitor said.

'It means what it says,' Jo replied. 'I have no reason to suspect that your client is involved in the murder of sex workers. However, should new information emerge that causes us to revise that view you'll be the first to know.'

'Now that we've clarified that,' said Ince, 'I suggest we get on with this interview.' He glanced down at his notes.

'DC Henshall, do you recognise any of these women?'

He placed three photographs side by side on the table. The solicitor and Federation rep leaned forward to look at them. Henshall gave them a cursory glance. He sat back and folded his arms.

'Are these the bitches that have cooked the story together?' he said.

'Take your time,' said Ince.

Henshall looked to his solicitor and then his rep for a lead. Jo read the unspoken question on the tip of his tongue: *Do I No Comment this?* When neither of them responded, he sighed, leaned forward, and pretended to take a proper look. He sat back again.

'Well?' said Ince.

Henshall shrugged. 'They look familiar. Can't say where from though.'

'How about the red-light district around Piccadilly station?' Ince prompted.

'It's possible,' Henshall replied. He smiled thinly. 'But then they all look the same, don't they?'

'The same?' said Jo, unable to contain herself.

Beneath the table Ince nudged her with his knee. Henshall's smile became a sneer.

'Knee-high boots, pelmet skirts, skimpy tops. Fixed smiles cracking their make-up. Desperate. Pathetic.'

His Federation rep whispered in his ear. It wasn't difficult to imagine what he was saying.

'But it is possible that you've spoken to these girls?' said Ince.

'I might have come across them,' said Henshall. 'When I was on the streets working Piccadilly station, and Beswick. I would have told them to move on. Doing my job.'

'What about more recently? Since you became a detective?'

'Maybe.'

'And while you were doing your job, might you have asked them to sit in your car?' Ince asked. 'Any of them?'

Henshall stared up at the ceiling as though trying to remember. Jo knew he was considering his options. The cars and vans he would have used during that time would have been used by dozens of officers by now. The interiors routinely cleaned. Valeted after every service. Okay, so he'd cleaned his own car. But if the slightest trace of any one of them was found in his car. If he denied it now and they found the slightest trace . . .

'You don't have to answer that,' said his solicitor.

Ince ramped up the pressure. 'I'm sure I do not need to remind you,' he said, 'that it may harm your defence if you do not mention when questioned something that you later rely on in court.'

'It's possible,' said Henshall.

The look his Federation rep gave him spoke volumes.

'That one or more of these women sat in your car? And why would you ask them to get in your car?'

'So I could speak to them. It's got to be better than standing in the cold and the rain, hasn't it?'

'So where did they sit?'

'Objection!' said the solicitor. 'That's a leading question. My client hasn't said they did.'

'This isn't a courtroom,' Ince reminded him. 'However, I'm happy to rephrase the question. So, DC Henshall, had they hypothetically been sitting in your car, where would they have sat? In the front passenger seat? In the back?'

'It's a hypothetical question. You do not need to answer that,' said the solicitor.

Ince turned to Jo. 'Either the front passenger seat or the rear near-side passenger seat.'

'Standard procedure for an officer on his own,' she agreed. 'Mind you, an unaccompanied male officer inviting a lone female sex worker into a car that is not equipped with internal camera footage?' She tutted. 'Sounds like a hell of a risk.'

'My client did not—' the solicitor began.

'Moving on,' said Ince, 'I wonder if you can tell us what this is, DC Henshall.'

He placed another photograph on the table.

Jo spotted the sudden dilation of Henshall's pupils. It never failed to amaze her that however prepared a person might be – and in this case he must have known they would find it – there was little or nothing they could do to suppress an autonomic response.

Henshall stared defiantly at DCI Ince. 'It looks like my rug,' he said.

'I think we can safely say that it is your rug,' Ince replied, 'given that it was hidden in the boot of your car.'

'It was not hidden,' Henshall replied. His knuckles were white, betraying the struggle he was having to hold back his anger. 'I always store it on top of the spare wheel.'

'What do you use it for?' Ince asked.

'To kneel on if I have to change a tyre. To put over the seats if I have to arrest someone who's covered in puke or blood.'

He folded his arms again, and leaned back in his chair.

'You know how it is. Then again, maybe you two have forgotten.'

Ince shuffled the photos together, and placed them in the file. He leaned across to the console, his finger on the switch. 'This interview terminated at 11.27am.' He eased his chair back. 'Thank you for your time, gentlemen,' he said. 'I am going to recommend that during the ongoing investigation of these allegations DC Henshall is reassigned to an administrative role entirely outside of the Force Major Incident Team.'

'Is that really necessary?' said the Federation rep. 'These are after all only allegations. What you're proposing will make it look as though you've already decided DC Henshall is guilty.'

'I agree,' said the solicitor. 'My client has not been charged. He has answered all of your questions. And as I understand it, you have no compelling evidence to support these fabrications.'

'My recommendation stands,' said Ince.

He stood up.

'Further to which, I have to warn DC Henshall not to make any attempt to approach any of these three women or any of their known associates in any way. Including through third parties. To do so will be regarded as an attempt to subvert this investigation.'

Henshall stared at Jo. A look so cold and malignant that just for a moment she wondered if they had got it wrong. That he might indeed be the man they were looking for.

Chapter 28

Jo stepped out of the lift. Max was striding towards her across the atrium.

'How did you get on?' he asked.

'Henshall denied everything. He'll be transferred to a desk job with CID pending the analysis of his work diary, car log, and phone locations against the relevant dates of the alleged assaults and the results of the forensics on his car and the rug we found in the boot.'

'The one the girls described?'

'The very same.'

'You say he's as good as admitted they sat in the car but claims nothing ever happened? His word against theirs.'

'Three against one.'

'Sex workers versus officer of the law,' Max said. 'It'll come down to the judge's summing-up, and the make-up of the jury. Assuming the CPS have the balls to pursue it.'

'I know,' she replied. 'It's a pity Public Standards Branch had their hand forced. A couple of weeks' surveillance may well have caught him in the act.'

'They didn't have a choice,' Max reminded her. 'Two murders in seven days, four in total. Henshall had to be eliminated as the unsub.'

'I know it sounds absurd,' Jo said, 'but I'm still not sure about him.' She shook her head to chase the doubt away. 'So, what did you find out about the latest victim?'

'It's an all too familiar tale,' Max said. 'Two friends lured over here with promises. End up in an anything-but-safe house near King's Cross. Passports and ID confiscated. Beaten, raped, and moved to a nearby brothel.'

'How did they end up here?'

'Lucky escape. Hitched a lift. Found sanctuary over a Hungarian supermarket. Owner treated them like his own daughters. Tried to get them off the game. Even offered them jobs.'

'Couldn't match what they were getting?'

'Exactly. He's taken it badly. Promised to identify the body when he sobers up. His daughter is coming with him.'

'What about the victim's friend?'

'Natalia? No hide nor hair of her since she left. Not even a phone call or a text.'

'What about social media? Facebook, Snapchat, WhatsApp, Instagram.'

'Neither of them had any accounts set up. Probably scared witless it would enable the men who enslaved them to track them down.'

'What if they did it?'

She shook her head.

'It wouldn't explain the MO. The same person who murdered the others killed Flora. Besides, there's no evidence any of the other Firethorn victims were connected to London or to sex trafficking.'

'I know,' he said. 'But we'll be expected to eliminate that possibility. More time-wasting.'

'Not if it means we get those bastards too. I've just spoken to Harry Stone and he's promised to see if he can get the Agency team running an operation on sex trafficking into North London to see if they can identify the gang that held those girls.'

'How was he, Harry?'

'A bit distracted I thought. He warned me to not get diverted by the Public Standards investigation. He wants me back on Firethorn ASAP.'

'Good advice,' said Max.

He glanced at his watch.

'I'm off to brief DCI Holmes. Are you back on the case?'

'Almost,' she said. 'I promised DCI Ince I'd speak to Henshall's ex-wife. Find out if she knew about his nefarious activities. If that was the reason she left him.'

He pressed the lift button.

'Speed the plough,' he said.

'I've never understood what that's supposed to mean.'

The doors opened. Max stepped inside, and turned to face her.

'Good luck, or lift the sod and start again,' he said. 'Take your pick.'

⌣

As Jo swung out of the car park, a dozen cameramen and reporters pressed forward. In front of one of the Fujitsu buildings, two TV cameramen stepped into the road. Those on the nearside pavement jostled dangerously, risking sending someone stumbling beneath her wheels. She took the crown of the road, cursing as a series of flashes imprinted jagged ghosts upon her retina. On the other side of the roundabout a smaller media scrum had assembled outside the Force headquarters building. She imagined the heated conversations up on the Fourth Floor, and thanked God that their ire would inevitably be directed in Gordon's direction. But it was only a matter of time before some of it washed her way.

She sighed with relief as she entered the underpass, and switched on the radio. Willie Nelson was singing *On the Road Again*. Jo identified with the sentiments behind the lyrics, except that in her case it was because sitting alone in the car was one of the only opportunities for quality thinking time. That and the feeling of being in control. Of heading somewhere even if the investigation was not.

Jo knew that one of the things her colleagues past and present admired about her was the impression she gave of being on top of things. Of being able to stay positive and focused no matter what. If only they knew.

Just because it didn't show, that didn't mean she was immune to feelings of self-doubt. That she wasn't angered by senseless cruelty and deeply affected by the suffering it inflicted on others. She felt impotent and frustrated. Hedged in by policies and procedures. Perhaps that was why she took the risks on the job that she did. Why she loved her sessions of Krav Maga. What was it Rule Three said? You will never ever win a defensive fight. But first they had to identify their enemy.

She turned up the volume, and eased her foot down on the accelerator.

Chapter 29

'You'd better come in.'

Denise Henshall had clearly got the better deal in the divorce. This was a five-bedroomed Edwardian semi-detached house in affluent Heaton Moor. Easily close to £700,000. Not quite Didsbury but getting there. Jo and Abbie had talked about this area as a possible next step. Five or so years down the line. That conversation seemed a lifetime ago now.

'You didn't ask to see my ID,' Jo said as she followed her into the open-plan kitchen-diner.

'No need,' she replied. 'I know who you are. I saw you on television last week. Appealing for information. The three murdered women. Is that why you're here?'

Jo had not anticipated this. It was almost as though Henshall's wife had been expecting her.

'What makes you say that?' she asked.

The former Mrs Henshall pulled two stools out from beneath a marble-topped island, placed one beside Jo, and sat down on the other one. 'No reason,' she said. 'I just wondered.'

Jo didn't believe her but she decided to let it ride. She sat down, and placed her tablet on the island.

'What do I call you?' Jo asked. 'Mrs Henshall?'

'Murray,' she replied. 'I've reverted to my maiden name. But please call me Denise. *Miss* sounds like a school teacher.'

'It's about your former husband, Denise.'

Denise Murray searched Jo's face for a clue. Her own remained deadpan.

'What's he done now?'

'What makes you think he's done something?'

'Why else would you be here?'

It was a fair question.

'Has something happened to him?' she continued.

It sounded to Jo as though Denise was simply curious rather than concerned.

'Nothing has happened to DC Henshall,' she replied. 'And I'm afraid I can't disclose the nature of this inquiry. I was just hoping I could ask you a few questions about your husband. About your life together.'

The former Mrs Henshall folded her legs, entwined her fingers, and leaned on the marble-top with her elbows.

'Where do you want me to start?' she asked.

'From when you first met.'

'He wasn't in the police at the time. He was a member of staff and a trainer in a health club I joined. He became my personal trainer. He was fit, attentive, kind. He had a great sense of humour. We liked the same music, the same films, the same TV shows. I fancied him that very first training session I had with him. We dated for just under a year, and then we got married.'

Denise's face clouded over. 'My mum liked him, but my dad said he was a wrong 'un.' She sighed. 'He's a good judge of character, my dad. I should've listened to him.'

'When did he join the police?'

The cloud darkened. 'A year after we got married. That was when it began to fall apart.'

'In what way?'

'I know it sounds ridiculous, like I was jealous or something, but suddenly I came second to the job. He loved the police. Everything about it. It made him feel important.' She thought about it. 'Powerful if you like. Then there was the social side. The camaraderie. The drinking culture. He really bought into that. I went to a couple of events with him early on, at the police club. An engagement party. A German beer and brass night featuring the Greater Manchester Police Band. He made himself the centre of attention. The joker of the party. Only I could see what his so-called mates were really thinking: *What a prat.* Only he couldn't see it. Not at first.' She paused. 'I think it slowly dawned on him.'

Jo recognised the pattern. There was something about the nature of the work that had that effect on people with certain personalities, most often the outwardly self-confident overcompensating for a serious lack of self-esteem. It wasn't just the police. It happened in the other services too. These were the people you didn't want handling guns on the front line.

'I wondered,' Jo said, 'if you could tell me why the two of you decided to get divorced.'

Denise shook her head. '*We* didn't, I did. It was my decision.'

'He didn't want you to leave?'

'He didn't have a choice. And before you go running to conclusions, there wasn't anybody else. There is now, but not then. I didn't meet my current partner until Morton and I had been eight months divorced.'

'Why didn't he have a choice?'

Denise hesitated, sat back, and folded her arms. 'Because I told him that if he didn't give me an uncontested divorce, I'd report him to his boss.'

'For what?'

Another pause. 'Domestic abuse.'

'Physical or emotional?'

'Both.'

'I'm sorry,' Jo said.

'Don't be. It wasn't your fault. Well, not directly anyway.'

'I don't understand.'

'When it did finally dawn on him that he was less the joker and more the joke, his mood changed. He began drinking at home. Solitary drinking. When he was drunk, he got angry. When he was angry, he'd lash out. Oh, he was always apologetic afterwards. Pleading, crying, saying it wasn't him, it was the booze. It was stress at work. He blamed everything and everyone but himself. I gave him three chances, then I handed him the ultimatum. I went to stay with my sister while he made up his mind.'

'How did he seem between then and when the divorce came through?'

Denise shrugged. 'I didn't see much of him other than at the solicitor's. He'd cut down on his drinking I think. He put a brave face on it, but I could see he was depressed. Ironically, after the divorce I heard he'd cheered up. Stopped drinking altogether. Made detective.' She frowned. 'Maybe it was my fault all along.'

'Never think that,' said Jo. 'It's what abusers always want you to believe.'

Denise Murray looked down at her hands. 'He wasn't always an abuser.'

She stood, and pushed her stool back under the lip of the island. 'Look, I'm sorry,' she said, 'but I need to get moving. I have to be at work in twenty minutes.'

'What is it you do?'

'I'm a staff nurse. At the Royal.'

Just as Abbie had been. It was a painful reminder.

'One last question,' Jo said. 'Did you ever suspect your husband might have been seeing other women?'

Denise Murray sighed, and placed one hand on the island. 'There we have it,' she said. 'The final question is always the most important.'

Jo waited.

'And the answer is?'

'There were things that made me wonder.'

'Such as?'

'About a year before we broke up he became impatient with the way we made love. And the frequency.'

'In what way impatient?'

'Let's say he wanted it to be more adventurous.'

'And you didn't?'

'No. I told him I wasn't comfortable with that. And if that was what he wanted, he should have married a porn star.' She smiled at the memory.

'How did he respond?' Jo asked.

'He sulked. Became morose. When we did have sex, he was rougher. I started fabricating headaches. He stopped asking. The well dried up.'

'You said signs. What were the other ones?'

Denise shrugged. 'Nothing concrete. I sneaked a look at his mobile phone from time to time. No suspicious texts or names in his contacts. The same on the computer. He tended to wipe his search history, but when he did forget I could see there were porn sites he frequented. I'm afraid I accepted that as the inevitable consequence of our not having sex. To be honest, I was relieved it wasn't another woman. I saw that as a greater betrayal.'

'Is that it?' Jo asked.

'The occasional whiff of cheap perfume on his clothes. A smear of lipstick on a shirt collar. But we were already sleeping in separate rooms by then.'

She stood up straight, and checked her watch.

'That's it,' she said. 'I really do have to go.'

'Thank you,' said Jo as she followed her into the hallway. 'You've been really helpful.'

Denise Murray opened the door, and stepped back to let Jo pass. 'If it is about those women,' she said, 'you can rule Morton out. He only hit me because he was angry with himself. And he never really hurt me. Not badly. He isn't a murderer. He isn't man enough.'

Jo thought she was probably right, but for all the wrong reasons. 'Thanks again,' she said.

Jo was at the gate when Denise Murray called after her.

'I'm sorry,' she said.

'What for?'

'I didn't offer you a drink. That was rude of me.'

'Don't worry,' Jo told her. 'It wasn't a social call.'

Chapter 30

Tuesday, 9th May

It was 8am and the Central Park Major Incident Room was a hive of activity. Jo looked around for somewhere to put her bag down.

'Is it my imagination,' she said, 'or have you squeezed more desks in here?'

'More bodies,' DS Carter replied. 'People are having to share workstations. It's not gone down well, but we needed the manpower.'

'None of them are women then?'

He grinned.

'You spent too long working with DCI Caton.'

'How is he getting on at the College of Policing?' she asked. 'Have you heard?'

'His secondment finishes at the end of the month. He can't wait to get back. He's missing Kate, and the baby.'

'I'm not surprised.'

'He's missing me too apparently.'

'In your dreams,' said Gordon entering the room with Max.

Helen Gates pushed past them both and stormed into the MRI. 'The press and social media know that a police officer was arrested and questioned in connection with the murders,' she said. 'DC Henshall's house is under siege. I've had to send uniformed officers out there to get them to back off. The Chief Constable wants to call a press conference to calm things down. I need chapter and verse on Henshall. Is he in the frame or not? And if so, what the hell is he in the frame for?'

'We've ruled him out of Operation Firethorn,' Gordon told her. 'He was at work on at least two of the occasions when murders were committed. And there's no evidence to link him with any of them. Not unless you consider a predilection for prostitutes as evidence.'

'What about the allegations?'

'He's still in the frame for those, Ma'am,' Jo told her. 'We'll know more when we have the results of the forensic analysis of his car, and items taken from the house.'

'And when will that be?'

'By tomorrow morning at a push.'

'Then you'd better push harder. And what am I supposed to tell the press in the meantime?'

'That an officer is assisting the police with enquiries on matters unrelated to Operation Firethorn. An internal investigation has begun, led by Professional Standards Branch, and it is far too early to comment. Any speculation on the part of the press or media would be both unhelpful, and ill-advised. Future enquiries should be directed to the Press Office.'

Helen Gates nodded approvingly. 'Don't get too comfortable down there on The Quays,' she said. 'We could do with you back here on a permanent basis.' She turned her attention to Gordon. 'The second the forensics are back on Henshall I want to know. I don't want to hear it from Professional Standards, do you understand?'

'Yes, Ma'am,' Gordon said.

'As for Firethorn, I've arranged for the Operation Sumac deputy senior investigating officer to come up here to give you the benefit of her experience. She'll be here a week from Thursday.'

Gordon frowned. 'Is that really necessary, Ma'am? Can't it wait for the next case review?'

'No, Detective Inspector, it can't wait. This is a linked series investigation. I'm just following the Association of Chief Police Officers guidance. Section 2.6.5 of the *Murder Investigation Manual*. I assumed that you were too.'

'Sumac,' he said, ignoring her barbed remark. 'That the Ipswich murders?'

'Correct. Since they bear a striking resemblance to ours, her input could be extremely valuable.'

'If I remember correctly, Ma'am,' he said, 'they had over three hundred dedicated officers work that investigation. I have seventy, plus twenty civilians. And we're liaising with twenty other forces. We are receiving over two hundred and fifty calls from the public every day, and that's only going to escalate. I need more bodies, Ma'am.'

Gates's eyes narrowed. 'Point taken,' she said. 'I'll see what I can do.'

She started to leave, then turned in the doorway. 'Don't push your luck, Gordon,' she said. 'It's running out.'

He waited for the door to close. 'Luck,' he said. 'Since when did we get any of that?'

Jo shared his anger and frustration. The upper echelons spent more time pandering to the bean counters and the ACPO guidance than providing the tools to finish the job. Every investigation needed a little luck. Those involving serial predators needed a great deal more. Gordon had been doing everything by the book, and he was right: they needed more resources to work the detail, to mine the mass of information building up. Somewhere in there lay a nugget of gold that would give them their first real lead. Experience told her that even with the right resources it could take days or months to find it. That was where the luck came in. And somewhere out there was another victim, for whom time was running out.

Chapter 31

SATURDAY, 13TH MAY

Max hung his jacket on the coat stand that Dorsey had magicked up, and came to join Jo and Ram by the coffee machine. He held aloft two brown paper bags.

'Breakfast's up!' he said. 'Come and get it.'

'Perfect timing,' said Jo, handing him a mug of coffee.

'Where's Andy?' he asked.

'His wife gave him a three-line whip. She takes Oliver to chess club on Saturdays, so Andy has to ferry Harriet to football.'

'That's the price you pay for married life,' said Ram. 'Your life's not your own. Unlike us lucky so-and-sos.'

Jo was no longer sure about that. Perhaps if she'd paid as much attention to her relationship with Abbie they'd still be together. And would it have been such a hardship having to take their children to sports clubs instead of working these insane hours?

'What have you brought us?' said Ram, seizing one of the bags.

'Two bacon baps, one bacon and egg for me obviously, and three pains au chocolat.'

'Do me a favour,' said Jo. 'Remind me to go to the gym this evening. If I hang around you two much longer, I'm going to end up looking like DCI Holmes.'

'Speaking of whom,' said Ram, 'we've set up a video conference with him. We were just waiting for you to arrive. Let's take this lot through to our MIR and get stuck in before he calls.'

'Glad to see you lot are enjoying yourselves,' Gordon grumbled. 'Don't mind me.'

Ram waved a half-eaten bacon bap. 'We won't.'

'Ignore him,' said Jo. 'His mother's just flown back home and he's bingeing on everything she forbade him from eating.'

'Next time get her to take him with her,' Gordon retorted.

'So where are we up to?' Jo asked.

'We've got the forensics results. Henshall's rug had been regularly steam-cleaned, which in itself is suspicious, and that eliminated any possibility of extracting DNA. However, there were fibre residues – black denim, and faux fur – deep in the pile that are consistent with the clothes described by two of his alleged victims. They've also retrieved two strands of hair from the rear footwell carpet that match one of his accusers.'

'He's already explained that away,' said Max, chewing fiercely. 'He let them sit in the back of his car to shelter from the rain while he told them why they had to move on.'

Gordon attacked his chin. 'I know. It's a shame they had to move in on him straight away. If it hadn't been for Firethorn, Professional Standards could have kept him under extended observation, and eventually had him bang to rights.'

'What about Firethorn?' Max asked. 'Have they found any connection?'

Gordon shook his head despondently. 'Sadly not. Save us a hell of a lot of trouble if they did. Forensic examination of his car, tablet, and desktop PC continues. Further analysis of his work diary eliminates him from two of the four Firethorn murders; he was on duty with a colleague when the first occurred, and on holiday in Spain when the second happened. We're having those verified as I speak.'

'So that just leaves the two most recent. Both in Manchester,' Ram observed. 'Where he's alleged to have committed these other offences?'

'That won't make any difference,' Jo pointed out. 'If we're saying the crime behaviour and the forensic evidence link all four to the same person, including the latest – where we know Henshall never left his house – then that eliminates him as our unsub.'

'Unless he has an accomplice,' said Max.

There was silence while they processed that.

'That's the kind of blue-sky thinking I can do without right now,' said Gordon at last.

'I wouldn't worry,' Jo told him. 'Andy more or less ruled that out.'

Gordon scowled.

'What was I saying about academics?'

'What have Professional Standards decided?' Jo asked.

'They've spoken to the CPS. He'll be suspended on full pay while they continue the investigation.'

'That sounds as though they intend to prosecute.'

'I agree,' said Gordon. 'Then it'll come down to whom the jury believes. Your alleged three victims or DC Henshall.

'In the meantime,' he continued, 'the mind-numbing sifting of witness statements, CCTV data, and responses from the public to the appeals for information continues. The only good news is that Helen Gates has been as good as her word. We're being given a further sixty officers to help with all that. There's no more room at Central Park, so they're giving us a satellite MIR in Longsight nick.'

He paused theatrically. Jo sensed some bad news on its way.

'Speaking of ACC Gates,' he said, 'she's called a press conference for this afternoon to try and get them off our backs. She wants us there, Jo. You and me both. Bring your flak jacket.'

Chapter 32

It was standing room only in the Major Incident Room. There were even people in the corridor beyond the fire doors straining to see. To Jo's dismay, Simon Levi, Deputy Director of the NCA Organised Crime Command, was here, deep in conversation with Helen Gates. He saw Jo, excused himself, and marched over.

'Stuart,' he said. 'This is becoming a regular occurrence. One to which I am not looking forward.'

So why you and not Harry Stone? she was tempted to ask.

'Have you any idea what the weekend train service is like from Euston to Manchester?' he continued. 'Diversions on the West Coast Main Line for track maintenance and repairs mean I'll be lucky if I'm home this side of midnight. And for what? To cover your back, and to try to keep the Agency out of the headlines.'

Levi hadn't been shy in coming forward at the end of each of the last two investigations, Jo remembered. He had bathed in her reflected limelight. Grinning like the Cheshire Cat in *Alice in Wonderland*.

'I'd be very happy to explain to the press the role that we in the BSU have been playing, sir,' she said. 'That is what the Assistant Chief Constable has asked me to do.'

Levi glared at her.

'You'll do no such thing!' he hissed. 'I've spoken to ACC Gates, and she agrees with me that a brief noncommittal statement from me will suffice. All you have to do, SI Stuart, is sit there trying to appear confident, and leave it all to me. Do you think you can manage that?'

Jo gave him the saccharine smile she reserved for arrogant and officious misogynists. She had learned a long time ago that it was a waste of time and energy making enemies of them. Besides, it was only a matter of time before he moved on and up, made a fatal error of judgement, and was quietly put out to pasture. Men like him always got their comeuppance in the end.

'I'm sure I can manage that, Deputy Director,' she replied.

The press officer called the meeting to order, and they took their seats. As soon as the usual ground rules had been laid, Helen Gates took the mic. 'With reference to Operation Firethorn,' she began, 'I can confirm that a person has been assisting us with our enquiries. That person has been interviewed and is no longer a person of interest. The investigation is ongoing and I would like to take this opportunity to urge members of the public, many of whom have already provided us with information, to continue to do so.'

A forest of hands went up. Jo was surprised at how much more orderly the newshounds seemed to be compared with the previous occasions. She wondered if it was because there was a disproportionate representation of local and regional reporters, given it was a Saturday.

The first question, from the BBC North West correspondent, came as no surprise. 'What about the police officer you arrested? Is he still a person of interest?'

'A serving officer has been questioned in relation to wholly unrelated matters. He has been released without any charges having been brought.'

Yet, Jo said to herself.

A red-top newshound was straight in. 'Is it true that this officer was a detective on the Firethorn investigation who was being questioned about his association with known prostitutes?'

Helen Gates managed to keep her composure, although the expressions on the faces of one or two of the others on the panel betrayed their disquiet. 'I repeat,' she said, 'this officer was questioned in relation to other matters. He is not a person of interest in relation to Operation Firethorn.'

Next she selected a journalist from the Manchester Evening News. 'Do you have any suspects at all?'

'We are following a number of leads,' Gates replied. 'It would not be prudent for me to be specific about them at this stage of the investigation.'

The atmosphere that fell over the room told Jo she was not alone in interpreting that as a no.

'Detective Chief Inspector Holmes is the senior investigating officer,' said the reporter from BBC Radio Manchester. 'Why isn't he here to answer our questions, Assistant Chief Constable?'

Helen Gates visibly relaxed at having been let off the hook. 'DCI Holmes is busy leading the investigation. It would not be an effective use of his time.'

'Isn't it time that someone of a much senior rank took over this investigation,' someone called out, 'given that it doesn't appear to be getting anywhere?'

Jo had been expecting something like this, just not quite so soon.

'I have complete confidence in DCI Holmes,' said Gates, sounding ominously like the owner of a Premiership football team about to replace her manager. 'He is supported by expertise from the National Crime Agency, and I have today drafted in a further sixty officers and ancillary staff to assist with the operation. I can also report that we have been liaising with Suffolk police, and a senior officer involved in the successful hunt for the killer of the five murdered Ipswich sex workers a decade ago will be coming to Manchester to give the benefit of her experience. I can assure you that we are leaving no stone unturned in our relentless pursuit of the person responsible for these murders.'

The Force press officer raised her handheld mic. 'One last question,' she said, pointing at a man two rows back.

Jo held her breath. It was Ginley again.

'Is it true,' he began, 'that all of the victims had human hair stuffed in their mouths?'

Heads turned to look at Ginley and then at the stony-faced Assistant Chief Constable, momentarily stuck for a response.

'I am unable to comment,' she managed at last. 'And any speculation around that could seriously jeopardise this investigation!'

There was a noisy buzz around the room as the reporters processed the implications. Jo could imagine the lurid headlines in tomorrow's papers. Sunday of all days. No self-respecting editor was going to heed Helen Gates's plea. Speculation would be beyond rife. It was going to be rampant.

'I want to take this opportunity,' she said, raising her voice above the hubbub, 'to thank those members of the public who have already contacted us with information, and to urge anyone with any information whatsoever, however small they may imagine it to be, to ring one of the numbers on the screen behind me.'

No one was listening. Some had already left. Jo was wishing she could do the same. She slipped out into the corridor that led to the anteroom where the debriefing would be held.

Gates stormed into the room. Jo had never seen her so angry.

'What a monumental cock-up!' Gates declared. She looked around for someone to blame. In Gordon's absence her eyes alighted on Jo.

'Who was that?' Gates fumed. 'And how in God's name did he know about the hair?'

'Anthony Ginley, Ma'am,' Jo replied. 'Independent Press Consultants, UK Ltd. You may recall that he was a thorn in our side during Operation Juniper.'

Gates rolled her eyes. 'I knew I'd seen him before. What's he doing? Stalking you?'

'No, Ma'am. As an investigative reporter I imagine he has an eye for a good story.'

'So how the hell did he find out about the hair? Please don't tell me we have another leak in FMIT. Or the Agency.'

'Those working the investigation are aware of the consequences of that leaking out,' Jo replied. 'Furthermore, DCI Holmes has reminded everyone of the need for total secrecy on a regular basis. There is an alternative explanation, Ma'am.'

'Which is?'

'The security guard who discovered the body of Mandy Madden, the third victim. Ginley will almost certainly have also spoken to him, as well as those people who discovered the other victims. Unless he's prepared to divulge his source, we'll probably never know for sure.'

Gates seemed relieved that her own officers were not responsible, but she was far from finished. 'And how do you suppose that other reporter became aware of the nature of the allegations against DC Henshall?'

'All of the girls working the Manchester red-light districts will have known about it,' Jo told her. 'The press have been all over them since Mandy Madden's body was found. And Ginley is usually several steps ahead of the pack.'

'So you're saying they're both down to bad luck?'

'Yes, Ma'am.'

Gates scowled. 'Well, it's about time our luck changed then.'

She turned her attention to Simon Levi, who had been doing his best to stay off her radar. 'What we need is all the support we can get,' she said. 'I have just managed to find another sixty officers for Firethorn, Mr Levi. How about the NCA providing more resources?'

'I'm sorry, Helen,' he began.

Big mistake, thought Jo. *She hates people using her first name in front of other members of her staff.* Levi ploughed on, oblivious to the change in the ACC's expression.

'As I've already explained, our remit is serious organised crime. We are effectively lending you the services of the Behavioural Sciences Unit in this instance because of the serial nature of these offences and their expertise in that field. Contrary to popular belief we do not have the resources to otherwise supplement murder investigations involving regional police forces.'

Double whammy, Jo reflected. *Overfamiliar* and *patronising*.

'Well, it seems to me,' the ACC retorted, 'that your BSU have been extremely lucky in relation to our two previous joint investigations. But two swallows do not a summer make! I suggest you give them a shake-up, just as I intend to do with my officers.'

She turned on her heel and left, followed by the rest of the panel and her coterie of press officers. Jo found herself alone with the Deputy Director. *Here we go*, she thought.

'There is a view, Stuart,' he said, 'that the Behavioural Sciences Unit is an expensive resource that has failed to prove its usefulness. That is a view with which I heartily concur. I can't speak for the Agency as a whole, but I can assure you that if Operation Firethorn is not resolved soon I shall do my damnedest to see that the northern unit is wound up. Do you understand?'

Jo did. What she didn't understand, though, was where the hell their boss, Harry Stone, was when they needed him.

Chapter 33

'Levi can't do that,' said Max when Jo arrived back at their base on The Quays. 'Harry won't let him.'

'Harry who?' said Ram. 'The Boss has gone AWOL.'

'I've sent him loads of emails and texts,' said Jo, 'and left several voice messages on his phone. I'm concerned that something serious has happened.'

'There's nothing more any of us can do,' said Max. 'I vote we just crack on.'

'Where you up to?' she asked.

'I've been collating the latest data Central Park have sent over, and Ram has been feeding it into the investigative analysis software, and the geographical analysis machine.'

'With any luck,' said Ram, 'it may help us predict where the next attack might come, and direct the resources to prevent it.'

'And has it?' she asked.

'Early days,' he replied. 'But if I had to stick my neck out I'd say that the indications are that if he is going to attack again it's going to be in South, or East, Manchester. That's where the geolocation data is veering. Having said which, I think any of us would have been thinking that simply on the basis that he started out to the west of the GMP area, and has been moving steadily eastwards.'

'Except that the most recent victim was just off the northern inner ring road,' she pointed out.

'Which is why,' Max said, 'everywhere inside the ring road has been flooded with uniformed and plain-clothes officers. The investigative analysis has taken that into account.'

Jo sighed. 'Let's hope that the software knows more about his risk aversion than we do.'

She slid off the desk and stretched. 'I'd better give Gordon a ring and let him know.'

'I'm glad I wasn't there,' Gordon said once she'd told him about the press conference. He sounded exhausted.

'Don't worry, Gordon,' Jo said. 'We are going to get him. It's only a matter of time before he slips up. They all do – you know that.'

'Well, I wish he'd get on with it. After today I reckon my time as SIO is running out.'

'You don't think Gates will take over Firethorn?'

'She's too wily for that. She'll parachute in a chief superintendent, and let him take the flak.'

He paused. She imagined him rubbing his chin again. 'You just caught me,' he said.

'Why? Where are you going?'

'You do realise that you and I have worked seven days without a break? Three of them with little or no sleep?'

'Tell me about it,' she replied. 'I'm using matchsticks to keep my eyes open.'

'There you are then. I'm heading home, and not coming back in until tomorrow night. There will be plenty of foot soldiers out there tonight, and with all the press attention I reckon the unsub would be mad to go anywhere near any of the city's red-light districts.'

'There's only one problem with that.'

'Go on.'

'He *is* mad.'

'So will I be if I don't get some sleep. Nick's going to take over today, and I've told him to take Sunday night and Monday off. Besides, if I don't it's either this or have Marilyn filing for divorce.'

'Again?' she joked.

'That's not funny, Jo. Too close to the truth.'

And too late for me, Jo realised. 'Sorry,' she said.

'Forget it. I suggest you go home too. Max as well. The last time I saw, you both looked like death warmed up.'

'Thanks for that.'

'You're welcome,' Gordon said. 'Now go home.'

She had no sooner come off the phone than Harry called. He sounded worse than Gordon.

'I'm sorry I haven't been in touch,' he said. 'I did tell you about my daughter, didn't I?'

Jo recalled how his daughter's mental health had led him to recuse himself from Operation Juniper. He had not mentioned it since, but they could all tell it still hung over him.

'Yes, Harry, you did.'

'She's had a relapse. I've had her admitted to a secure unit in the psychiatric ward. She still hasn't come to terms with losing her mother.' He paused. 'They think she stopped taking her medication. I blame myself. I wasn't there to check on her.'

'I'm so sorry, Harry.'

'It'll only be for a week, the doctors said. Once she is stabilised, she can come home.'

'Don't worry about us,' Jo told him. 'You concentrate on getting her well.'

'There is some good news,' Harry said. 'I've been given the opportunity to relocate north. I'll bring her with me. It'll be a fresh start for both of us. I'll be able to spend more time with her, plus I won't be worn down by the endless commuting, and I'll be able to get over to The Quays as often as needed.'

'I'll look forward to that,' said Jo. 'And to meeting your daughter.'

'You'll like her,' Harry said. 'And I know she'd love to meet you.'

'Look after yourself, Harry,' she said.

'And don't you worry,' he told her. 'I'll see to Simon Levi. He's all mouth and no trousers. By the time I've finished with him, he won't come within a hundred miles of The Quays.'

Chapter 34

It was two in the afternoon when Jo got back to the apartment. She kicked off her shoes, and lay on the bed.

When she woke up, it was ten to seven in the evening. She splashed her face and went to see what she had in the fridge. Not having done a shop for over a week, she discovered it was almost bare. She found the remains of a block of cheese, and paired it with a hunk of half-stale bread. Then she opened a bottle of wine.

Seated in front of the TV, she sipped her wine as she flicked through the TV channels hoping to find something distracting. *Line of Duty*, *NCIS*, *NCIS: Los Angeles*. Cop shows were the last thing she needed right now. She plumped instead for *Great Canal Journeys*, and began to eat.

It was hopeless. She was unable to shake off the thought of women walking the streets tonight, the unsub lurking in the shadows waiting for his next victim. Here she sat in her nice cosy apartment with a glass of red, watching a narrow boat chug along an idyllic stretch of British countryside. She drained her glass, put the bottle with the others waiting to go in the bin, grabbed her jacket and car keys, and fled the apartment.

If anything, there were even more bodies in and around the streets off Piccadilly station than in the immediate aftermath of the discovery of Mandy Madden's body. She counted less than a handful of sex workers, outnumbered ten to one by freelance photographers, reporters, and plain-clothes police. In fifteen minutes down here she hadn't seen a single punter foolish enough to expose himself – not in the literal sense – and had only been challenged herself on one occasion, by a pair of police community support officers looking to relieve their boredom. She decided to try Cheetham Hill.

The story was the same here. After five minutes of aimlessly criss-crossing the district, she gave up, and headed two miles south-west of the city centre.

She had just passed the junction of Alexandra Road with Yarburgh Street and Claremont Road, where Alexandra Park marked the boundary between Moss Side and Whalley Range, when she spotted Max standing talking to a specialist firearms officer armed with what looked like a Heckler & Koch semi-automatic carbine. They were on the pavement beside the railings of Alexandra Park. Max's car was parked behind an Xcalibre armed response car, and a blue-and-white Challenger van. Jo pulled in behind them.

The firearms officer spotted her first, and nodded in her direction. Max turned.

'Great minds,' he said.

'I couldn't just sit there twiddling my thumbs,' she said. 'I drove around Ardwick and Cheetham first, but it's like the circus is in town. I was hoping our unsub might try his luck down here, where it was likely to be quiet. I was obviously wrong.'

'This has nothing to do with Firethorn,' said Max. 'It's a joint Xcalibre and Challenger operation. Part training exercise, part show of force.'

'We have intel that the Moss Side Bloods and the Longsight Crips are planning to face off against each other,' the firearms officer told her. 'This is our way of letting them know we're not going to tolerate another turf war. No way are we going to let them take us back to 2007 or the 1990s.'

'Your presence has certainly deterred the punters,' said Max.

'Still a few toms around though,' the SFO observed. 'One of them was desperate enough to proposition me ten minutes ago.'

'They have to be desperate to do it at all,' said Jo. 'More so now with a killer roaming the streets.'

The firearms officer slapped the stock of his gun. 'Just let him try on my watch.'

'How long are you going to be here?' she asked.

'Your guess is as good as mine. Till the early hours of the morning here and hereabouts, so long as nothing kicks off in the meantime. There's a debrief and disarm at 6am, and the promise of bacon butties. Won't be missing that.'

'Sounds like our cue to leave, Jo,' said Max. 'God knows what we were thinking coming back out here tonight.'

'That's the trouble with living on your own,' she said as they made their way back to their respective cars. 'Anything's better than hours of aimless TV channel hopping.'

Max walked around the bonnet of his car, and paused, one hand on the roof, the other on the door handle.

'It's not just that,' he said. 'It's having nothing else to worry about. No one there to remind you that there's more to life than what we do. To point out that if some crazy bastard were to come running out of that park behind you, and blast us both to kingdom come, there'd be others stepping into our shoes before Flatman has started the post-mortems.'

He pulled the door open, and grinned apologetically.

'On that cheerful note I'll bid you adieu. Let's go get some sleep.'

Jo closed the door of her apartment, and stood with her back against it. She knew that what she had done tonight had been irrational. Compulsive obsessive, Abbie had called it. She had never understood how she could walk away from a critically ill patient every night knowing someone else equally competent was going to take over, and yet Jo couldn't do the same when the threat was so much less tangible, and the next victim as yet unknown.

We both save lives, she'd said. *So what's so different about your job?* Jo had never managed to find an answer to that. She still couldn't.

She walked into the lounge, picked up the bottle, and her glass, walked into the bedroom, and kicked the door closed behind her. Twenty minutes later the bottle was empty, and Jo was dead to the world.

Chapter 35

Sunday, 14th May

'This is a lovely surprise, Joanne,' said her mother. 'And on my birthday too! Leave your umbrella out there in the porch, and come in and give me your coat.' She shouted up the stairs, 'Dad! Get off that computer. Joanne is here.'

Jo handed her mum the bottle of wine, and the bunch of flowers she'd picked up from the Tesco Express on the corner, and shrugged off her coat.

'Ooh, Cotes Du Rhone!' her mum declared. 'Your dad's favourite. It'll go perfectly with the roast. However did you guess?'

Jo smiled.

'Because it's what you've cooked every Sunday lunch since I can remember.'

'Not on Christmas Day. Never on Christmas Day. You go through. I'll put these flowers in a vase.'

Before she'd had a chance to sit down, her dad appeared, filling the room with his presence. A big man with a big heart.

'How's my Jo-Jo?' he said, bending to give her a hug.

'Now, Jack,' said her mother from the doorway, 'you know how she hates being called Jo-Jo. She's a big girl now.'

Jo smiled. 'And how many times have I told you that I'm not keen on Joanne either, Mum? But you're never going to stop calling me that.' She sat on the sofa and waited for her dad to settle himself into his favourite high-backed armchair. 'We saw you on the TV,' he said. 'That's a wicked thing this man is doing. Those poor girls. It doesn't bear thinking about. But it's wonderful what you're doing, Jo-Jo. Stopping people like that. We're very proud of you, you know? Your mother and I.'

'I know, Dad.'

'You should be more careful though. You always seem to get into the most terrible scrapes.'

'She was like that as a child, Jack,' her mother reminded him. 'Do you remember? We were always at the doctor's or accident and emergency. Forever falling out of trees she was, and jumping off shed roofs. Do you remember that time she tried to do a wheelie on her bike around the children's playground and ended up falling backwards on to the kids' roundabout while it was whizzing round? An accident waiting to happen, Dr Gladstone called her.'

This is what I miss, Jo reflected. *The easy familiarity. The unconditional love.*

It continued throughout lunch. Her mum wittered on about people that Jo had either never met or only vaguely remembered. Dad tucked into his roast beef, roast potatoes, and two veg with a gusto undiminished by the years. Jo sipped her wine, and reflected on how lucky she had been.

Jack and May Stuart were not her real parents. It was something she had never told any of her work colleagues, not even Caton. Which was odd really, given he had lost his own parents at an early age, and had been brought up by an aunt. It wasn't that she was ashamed of the fact, rather that to have done so would have meant having to talk about what came before. *BS* was how she had always thought of that time. Before the Stuarts.

For years – right up to her eighteenth birthday – the story of how she came to be with May and Jack had been hazy and fragmented. She had built it together from what a succession of social workers had told her. Distant episodic memories, and stories she had constructed, to comfort herself. Only when she was given a copy of her case file did it all fall into place. Her parents hadn't been married when her mother, Jodie, became pregnant. She was fifteen and a half. Jodie's parents were staunch Christians. The kind that were bigger on mortal sin than on the Beatitudes. Proper Old Testament Christians for whom the Sermon on the Mount was meant for other people.

It didn't help that the father was ten years older than Jodie, feckless, and already married. Arrangements were swiftly made. As soon as the child began to show, Jodie was sent away to her grandmother's, in Hull. When the child was born, it would be put up for adoption. Jodie would return home. No more would be said about it.

Except that Jodie got off the train in Leeds and chanced upon a squat populated by would-be hippies who saw themselves as a reincarnation of the flower power revolution. They survived on begging, busking, and charitable handouts. While Jodie was in hospital giving birth, the squat was raided, and the occupants dispersed. It was a difficult birth for mother and baby. By the time Jodie was due to leave hospital, there was nowhere for her to go. She was sixteen years and two months old. Through the efforts of the hospital social worker, she was placed in a mother-and-baby home. At seventeen she was told she had to move out. Move on.

In less than a year poor Jodie's life had begun to unravel. How she ended up addicted to heroin was unclear. The outcome was not. She died of an overdose, in another squat in a disused warehouse in Oldham, as her daughter lay hungry and shivering in a cot bed just feet away. The coroner declared an open verdict. Jodie's parents were traced, and given the opportunity to raise their granddaughter Joanne. They declined.

Foster parents were found while the adoption was pursued. The first couple to come forward had reached the final stages when the husband admitted his heart was not in it. He had been going along with it, he said, for the sake of his wife. The adoption attempt failed, as presumably did their marriage. The second couple pulled out at the eleventh hour when the wife discovered she was pregnant after seven years of trying.

By this time little Joanne was three years old. Her then foster parents, Jack and May Stuart, decided she had been through enough, and applied to adopt her themselves. They were the only parents she had ever known. They would be forever Mum and Dad.

Jo could recall only two occasions when their perfect relationship as a family had been clouded. The first was when she had sat them down, and told them she was gay. It was only in hindsight that she had come to realise that their evident disappointment, despite their brave attempts to hide it, was nothing to do with generational homophobia. May had longed for a traditional wedding, and to become a doting grandparent. Jack had been looking forward to walking her down the aisle, and proudly delivering the father-of-the-bride speech. And taking his grandson to watch Stockport County. But their love for Jo quickly swamped their feelings of regret at what might have been taken. They even took Abbie into their hearts. And so Jo had disappointed them a second time when she and Abbie split up, and renewed hopes of grandchildren had been dashed. Yet here they were, their affection for her undiminished. *I am*, she reflected, *truly fortunate*.

Two hours later and Jack and May stood on the doorstep, arms around each other's waist. Jo gave them a final wave, and set off. *I should do this more often*, she told herself. *Why the hell don't I? Is it because the novelty would soon wear off?*

But then, supposedly absence made the heart grow fonder. The thought of Abbie marching out of their apartment shortly before Christmas flashed across her mind.

'Not always,' she decided. 'Not this time.'

Chapter 36

Yesterday he had been consumed, as he was every time he was reminded of his mother, with anger, regret, revulsion, and an overwhelming sense of loss. There was, he knew, only one thing that would release this pressure cooker of conflicting emotions. So here he was, and he could not believe his luck.

The target for his hunt this evening had been the Coldhurst red-light district, but the Metro News had headlined another Operation Derwent attempt to rid the Westwood streets of prostitutes for once and for all. And so he had headed here, three miles further north, to Richmond Street, hard by the Metrolink station.

The heavy police presence surprised him. On a single pass through the area he had counted three marked area cars, a video surveillance transit van, a dog patrol car, and at least a dozen uniformed and plain-clothes officers on foot. To have committed this number of officers eight miles away from the scene of his last two kills meant one of two things. Either they were taking no chances or they had guessed where he was going to strike next.

Guessed or worked out? If the latter, then he would have to move on. That would be a pity. But as far as tonight was concerned their strategy had played into his hands. The usual punters had been warned off, and so the girls were beginning to leave, hoping to find a client or two outside this tight police cordon. Away from their normal habitat they were more likely to work alone. To become easy prey.

He glimpsed her first as she crossed the Metrolink tramlines by the fire station, and began to stride past the Church of St John the Baptist. They made an incongruous pairing. The short busty redhead in knee-length boots, denim pelmet skirt, and short denim jacket over a thin cotton blouse beside the cathedral-like red-brick church, whose enormous dome seemed more in keeping with one of the burgeoning mosques around here. He waited to see which way she would go when she emerged from behind the tram stop, and reached the junction with Station Road. He smiled as she turned right, and, pulling his gloves tight, flexed his fingers, released them, and set off.

He felt exposed here, lit sporadically by the headlights of passing vehicles. He crossed over to the far side of the road to lessen the likelihood of her spotting him or of an onlooker believing that he was following the lone female forty yards ahead. After less than two hundred yards, she also crossed over, suddenly turned left into a side road, and disappeared from sight.

He paused to read the street name. Milkstone Road. It was a name he vaguely recognised but could not yet place. To his relief he caught sight of smudged glimpses of blue and red as she passed through shallow pools of light from street lamps. The last eye-catching flight of a firefly.

He smiled again, and nodded as he followed her across the stone bridge over the Rochdale Canal. It had not been a false memory. He had been here before. On she marched, picking up speed, her heels slapping the pavement. Now they were heading down Well I' Th' Lane. The streets were deserted and so, as he reached the Horse & Jockey public house, he hung back, allowing the distance between them to grow.

She was moving with purpose now, a familiar destination in mind. This was the kind of area where he envisaged her living. In the melting pot of the urban corridor that stretched across the western edge of Greater Manchester. He watched her bob of auburn hair sway in rhythm with her hips. Imagined his fingers stroking those locks. Twisting them into a curl. The blades slicing through them. Given the time and effort he had invested already tonight, he hoped she was not going to suddenly vanish down an alley, and enter a house unseen.

He realised too late that she was approaching the busy Queensway roundabout, where there would be multiple choices that she could make, and he speeded up as she disappeared around the corner.

There was no sign of her at the roundabout. He cursed. Worse still, she could have gone in any one of five directions. Taking a deep breath, he closed his eyes and waited for the hunter's instinct to kick in. In the time elapsed since he lost sight of her, he calculated that the most likely route was straight ahead. He jogged across the dual carriageway against the stoplights, and darted down a street replete with cheap booze emporiums, charity shops, and suntan salons. And there she was, close to a hundred yards ahead, moving with such purpose that he wondered if she had realised she was being followed. Determined not to lose her again, he speeded up, careful to stay in the shadows, confident in the knowledge that if he had to swiftly close the distance between them, he could.

Genna glanced right and left and withdrew her phone. It was 2.27am. She quickly shoved it back in her bag. It didn't do to advertise your mobile around here, or any device for that matter. The rats'd come out of a doorway, snatch it off you, and have it away on their toes before you realised what was happening. The little buggers on their mountain bikes were the worst. When they weren't keeping watch or delivering drugs for the dealers, they'd be perfecting the art of street robbery. She stopped outside the drop-in centre. There was a decision to be made.

The sudden invasion of coppers had ruined her night. Put her right off her stride. Janice had been goin' on and on, peckin' her head about trying down Coldhurst, but word was it was even worse down there. So she had decided to call it a night, come back home, and get a decent night's kip for the first time in weeks. But now that it came to it, she knew she'd be well down on what she needed to cover the rent this month. And even though she didn't like to pee on her own doorstep, there was always a chance of picking up a couple of punters among the truck drivers kipping on the business park on the other side of the motorway. Better a turn in a nice warm cab than in the back of a cramped family saloon full of litter and dog's hair or, worse still, up against a railway arch. Some of those truckers even had full-size beds behind the cabin. She smiled at the prospect. Why not? *After all*, she told herself, *if I have to come back I'm only five minutes from home. I have nothing to lose.*

He watched her cross *The Strand* and begin to walk away from the precinct, with its freshly painted steel-shuttered shops. Next door to *The Chippy* he noticed one with a bold blue sign over the top. Police Post. Definitely not manned 24/7. Not around here. And the bookmaker's on the next length were sure to give good odds against the bobby living over the shop, like they did in the old days.

He waited until she had reached the far side of the narrow footbridge over the motorway before he climbed the steps himself. She was now on a wide sandy track that ran between brooding moorland, and two large steel warehouses that stood like silver sentinels in the moonlight. Her intent was clear. She was going to turn right into the heart of the business park, where *there would be CCTV, night workers, even security. He hurried forward, calling out to attract her attention.*

~~~

Startled by the sound, Genna turned, her heart pounding in her chest. Her hand went instinctively to her bag. Phone in one hand as though ringing the police, the other curled around the pepper spray. There was no point in running. And she would only scream for help once she knew what she was dealing with.

He was less than ten yards away, and closing. She put the phone to her mouth, the bright blue screen flagging her intent. He raised his left hand. He was holding up something for her to see.

'Evening, love,' he said. 'Sorry I startled you.'

Genna lowered the phone.

'Bloody hell!' she exclaimed. 'It's you. What were you thinking? You nearly scared me to death.'

Chapter 37

Tuesday, 16th May

Jo switched on the bedside light, and picked up the phone. It was 4.30am. Before she even picked up, she had that sick feeling in the pit of her stomach.

'Sorry, Jo,' said Gordon. 'What I said about it getting worse? It just has.'

She threw back the duvet, and swung her legs over the side of the bed. 'Where?'

'Trows Lane, Castleton. Couple of miles south-west of Rochdale town centre. I'll text you the postcode.'

'I'll call Max and Andy,' she told him.

'The more the merrier,' Gordon said.

Max wasn't answering. Jo sent him a text and left him a voice message.

Andy's wife answered after just two rings. 'He's still asleep,' she whispered. 'Is it important?'

'I'm sorry, Rachel,' Jo replied, 'but I wouldn't dream of disturbing you if it wasn't.'

'It's not as though he's a police officer,' Rachel complained. 'He doesn't even get overtime. Have you any idea how many unpaid hours he's done this week? He's hardly seen the children.'

'Who's that, darling?' mumbled a sleepy voice in the background.

'Go back to sleep, love,' said Rachel. 'I'm dealing with it.'

'Mrs Swift, please tell your husband,' said Jo, 'that a young woman's body has been found. Just like the others. Mr Swift told me that he needed to visit these crime scenes at the same time as the rest of us. Why don't you let him decide? If he still wants to come, ask him to text me, and I'll send him the postcode. If not, that's fine by me. I'm sorry to have disturbed you.'

She ended the call. The golden hour was ticking down. This was no time to be faffing around.

It was a concrete-surfaced lane off the A664, just wide enough for two cars to pass one another. Deciduous trees crowded in on either side. A perfect place, she noted, from which to deal drugs from the back of a car. A quarter of a mile on, through a second police cordon, she was forced to stop by a small industrial unit, and park up behind a line of marked and unmarked vehicles.

'It's just around the corner, Ma'am,' the loggist told her. He pointed to a large plastic box beside him. 'Help yourself to coveralls and a pair of overshoes. But don't forget to bag them before you leave. And please keep to the marked area. That's the common approach path.'

Jo was tempted to ask him how many crime scenes he'd attended. She rooted around for a set that would fit, and put it on.

The young policeman grimaced. 'I'd brace yourself, Ma'am,' he said. 'It isn't pretty.'

When is it ever when someone's life has been ripped from them? Jo reflected as she slipped on a pair of nitrile gloves. She set off beside the six-foot-high red-brick boundary wall of the foundry.

After thirty yards she rounded a corner and stopped. The glass- and razor-wire-topped wall turned sharp right for five yards and then left for a further twelve, where it ended up against the side of a two-storey factory building. In the corner of this space, brightly lit by two LED Remote Area Lamps, six people stood with their backs to her. Gordon Holmes and Nick Carter, Dr Tompkins, Jack Benson, the crime scene manager, and a photographer. Three crime scene investigators were on their knees conducting an inch-by-inch search of the broken concrete floor.

She went forward, and touched Gordon lightly on his shoulder. He turned and nodded.

'Glad you could join us,' he joked. It was a half-hearted attempt to defuse the tension. Nick moved to Gordon's right to create a space for Jo. The scene that now confronted her was eerily familiar.

'Another skip, another town, another body,' Gordon muttered.

It sounded callous, but he had a point. This skip was the twin of the one in Cheetham Hill in which Flora Novak's body had been found. Except that it was red.

'Her name is Genna Crowden,' said Nick. 'Her bag was in the skip beside her. So was her mobile phone. We think she lives . . . lived on the council estate on the other side of the motorway. There was a betting slip from the local bookie's on The Strand, and she had an appointment at the medical centre on Friday that she won't be keeping.'

In the harsh white light the young woman's body had the appearance of a retail dummy or a waxwork. An impression heightened by the CSI photographer snapping away on the far side of the skip to the left of Dr Tompkins.

Genna Crowden lay on her back across a broken wooden palette, beneath which lay a muddle of assorted junk and metal shavings. Her right arm was twisted beneath her back; the left arm hung over the side of the skip. A trendily distressed blue denim jacket lay open. Despite the best efforts of gravity, her breasts strained against a white embroidered cotton vest that had ridden up, revealing a wide expanse of flesh between it and the waist of a matching denim pelmet-length skirt. She had a silver ring through her navel mounted with a diamond-cut stone, whose prism refracted a spectrum of vivid colours across her skin. She wore knee-length mahogany-coloured boots. Jo forced herself to look at the face.

It was puffy and discoloured, with patches of purple and red. Uncomprehending eyes, open and bulging, stared skywards. The jaw had dropped, forcing crimson cupid lips apart, revealing a tangled lock of peroxide blonde hair protruding from the mouth. Her own hair was auburn, cut into a bob that so closely resembled Jo's that she could almost have been staring into a mirror.

Dr Tompkins lifted her voice recorder and began to speak.

'The victim is prone. The face is distended and cyanosed. Both eyes are open, prominent, and display subconjunctival haemorrhages. The tongue lies within the oral cavity. It is swollen but has no other obvious injury. The oral cavity is partly obstructed by a foreign substance that has the appearance of human hair. There are two concentric circles of reddish-purple bruising, one on, and one immediately below, the laryngeal cartilage. The depth of the indentations appears to be consistent around the entire visible circumference of the neck. This is suggestive of the use of a ligature, although none is present. The mouth, ears, and nostrils are free of bodily fluids. Cyanosis is present in the earlobes, fingernail beds, and hands. There are no other visible signs of injury.'

This cool, detached professional account gave little clue to the final moments of this poor young woman's life. It protected them in some small way from the horror of it all.

Jo, however, had a duty to imagine exactly how it must have been. To mentally reconstruct every tiny detail. To try to interpret what that might tell her about the perpetrator. His motivation. His state of mind. The artefacts he brought with him to the scene, and those he took away.

And with that came a duty, on the one hand, not to let it become too personal, such that it might overwhelm her, and, on the other, not to become so jaded, and deadened to it all that she lost the anger that would strengthen her resolve, and drive her on. She had seen that happen to others. She resolved that it was never going to happen to her.

Chapter 38

'Sometime within the past three to six hours,' said Dr Tompkins in response to a question from Gordon Holmes. 'Nearer to four than to six.'

'Jo!'

She looked over her shoulder. Andy Swift was standing by the corner of the wall, uncertain as to whether he should join them unbidden. She waved him forward.

'I'm sorry I woke you,' she said while he took in the scene. 'You did say to tell you if we had another one.'

'No need to apologise,' he replied. 'Rachel's a bit stressed out. The school has an Ofsted inspection starting today. It's her first.'

He adjusted the hood of his protective suit, pushed his spectacles further up the bridge of his nose, and focused on the corpse. 'Same MO I take it?'

'It looks that way.'

He nodded thoughtfully. 'That makes five to date, and the second to have been dumped in a skip.'

'Do you think that's why he chose this place?' Gordon asked.

'That would assume he was aware that the skip was here. That he'd already scouted this area. Given that it's off the beaten track, then it begs the question, why would the victim choose to come here with him? Or did he drive her here?'

'Was the body moved post-mortem, Doctor?' Jo said to Tompkins.

Tompkins thought about it. 'Difficult to tell without a full examination. The Home Office pathologist will be able to tell you. But if you're pressing me . . .'

'We are,' said Gordon.

'Then I'd say that, given what little post-mortem lividity I have been able to see without moving her, she was almost certainly placed here within a few minutes of meeting her death.'

'There were light showers around midnight last night, followed by a heavy dew,' Nick observed. 'So far no fresh tyre tracks have been found.'

'Then it was luck,' said Andy. 'And his decision to dump her body, and the one in Cheetham Hill, in a nearby skip is an expression of his contempt for his victims. He chooses these sex workers not only because they are vulnerable, and accessible, but also because he considers them worthless and therefore disposable.'

'If that's the case,' said Jo, 'how can he derive pleasure from the trophies he takes if they come from women he regards with such contempt?'

'Because the killing itself is the ultimate expression of power and control. And almost certainly connected with something in his formative years that affected him deeply. That is his primary source of gratification and release. The taking of a trophy, and his use of it to recapture the moment, almost certainly as a sexual act, prolongs what would otherwise be a fleeting experience.'

'But not long enough to stop him needing to do it again,' Nick Carter observed.

'Because all pleasurable experiences, especially ones of a sexual nature, have two things in common: firstly, they are addictive; and secondly, the degree of excitement and pleasure experienced diminishes in inverse proportion to the rate of repetition. Put simply—'

'The novelty wears off!' Gordon growled.

Andy nodded. 'Exactly. I call it the serial killers' law of diminishing returns. It explains why the interval shortens between each successive murder.'

'There were three weeks between the first and second victims,' said Gordon. 'The same between the second and third. Then just a week between Mandy Madden and Flora Novak. So why has he waited another eight days before this one?'

'He has almost certainly been out there,' said Andy, 'looking for opportunities to strike again. By flooding the red-light districts with officers, you've made it more difficult for him. Not to mention all the media attention.'

'Which would explain why he's moved further east,' said Nick.

'He will strike again,' said Andy. 'Sooner rather than later.'

'If you're done here,' said Jack Benson, 'could you move back on to the road to let my CSI get on?'

'I'll get back and file my report,' said Carol Tompkins. 'Mr Flatman will be here in an hour or so.'

Tompkins looked up at the sky. Jo followed her gaze. Dawn was breaking, the first golden rays of the sun painting the underbelly of a light grey sheet of cloud moving towards them from the Pennines.

'There are showers on the way,' Tompkins observed. She turned to Benson. 'It would help if you could erect a tent to preserve the scene. Unless you're prepared to brave Mr Flatman's ire.'

The detectives left them to it, and headed for the concrete apron of a driveway opposite.

'What's this place?' Jo asked, pointing to the black-and-white property behind them, partly obscured by trees and bushes.

'It's a registered childminder's house,' Nick told her. 'This'll be a nasty shock for the mums and toddlers when they arrive.'

'There's a cattery about a hundred and thirty yards further down the lane,' said Gordon. 'A car body repairer beyond that, and then a big private house. After that, it's a dead end, unless you happen to be on foot or going to one of the lodges.'

'Lodges?' said Jo.

'There are six of them. They belong to a local angling society. It was an angler who found her. He's currently sat in a van where the cordon starts. He was in too much of a state to make any sense. Should have calmed down by now though. Why don't you go see what he can tell you while Nick and I sort out the wider search team, and brief the officers who are going to conduct the door-to-door enquiries?'

'What will you do, Andy?' she asked.

'Have a mooch around, see what else I can pick up that might be relevant, and then go back and mend a few bridges before Rachel sets off for school with the children. Then I'll head to The Quays and update my crime behaviour analysis.'

'I can save you some time with that,' said Gordon.

Andy raised his eyebrows.

'Go on.'

'Based on his behaviour to date, I think we can safely assume that our unsub is a nutter. A sad, sick, evil, miserable nutter!'

'Thank you, Detective Inspector,' said Andy. 'I'll bear that in mind.'

'That wasn't fair,' said Jo as they watched the psychologist walk off down the lane towards the cattery.

'Maybe not,' Gordon replied. 'But if your colleague doesn't pull his finger out, and come up with something we can use, this bastard is going to end up making Jack the Ripper look like Mickey Mouse.'

Chapter 39

'I nearly missed her.'

In his mid-sixties, Jo guessed. It was hard to tell because his face was white and drawn with the shock of it all. The angler took a deep breath.

'It was the arm hanging over the side that caught my attention. But for that, I'd never have seen her.'

There had been the prospect, Jo realised, that a young child jostled around in the back of a 4x4 on the way to the childminder's house would have been the first to do so instead. In the Transporter's wing mirror she spotted Max walking towards them.

'Excuse me for a moment,' Jo said to the angler, winding down the window.

'Did you get my message, Max?'

'Eventually,' he said, stooping to her level. 'Sorry I missed your call. My phone was on silent. So, what are we looking at?'

'See for yourself,' she told him. 'Up ahead. You can't miss it. I'll be here when you get back.'

Max nodded, and set off. There was something about the way he was moving – head down, shoulders slumped, hands in pockets – that bothered her. This wasn't the usual energetic Max, keen to get stuck in. She worried that she had no idea what was troubling him. She wound the window up, and turned back to the witness.

'Sorry about that, Mr Henderson. You were saying you nearly missed seeing the victim.'

'I wish I had. I don't think I'll ever get that image out of my head.'

'You will. Not immediately. But you will. Someone from Victim Care will be along shortly. They'll give you the name and contact details of a counsellor. Promise me that you'll follow it up.'

Henderson nodded. 'I will. Like I was saying, I was on my way to the John Player Lodge. It's stocked with tench, roach, rudd, and perch. Plus a few barbel and chub.'

It was like a foreign language to Jo. 'No trout then?'

'There's a separate lodge for trout. But I don't do fly fishing.'

Jo was out of her depth. 'What time did you start fishing?'

'Three o'clock this morning.'

At least an hour after the killer had struck if Dr Tompkins was right.

'And you walked from where?'

'From the main road. I left my car on the dirt track opposite the car dealer's. I didn't want to risk the water keeper recording my licence plate.'

'What time did you park up, and start walking to the lodge?'

'About quarter to three?'

Still too late to have seen the killer leaving.

'Is it usual to fish during the night?'

'Late evening, and early morning,' he said. 'That's when they like to feed. Besides . . .' He tailed off nervously.

'Go on.'

He shifted in his seat.

'The fact is I've got an Environment Agency rod licence, but I'm not a member of the society that owns these lodges. There's less chance of being caught by a water keeper if you're away by five thirty. Nobody has to know, do they?'

'Not if you don't tell them. But you might want to keep your head down when you leave. The press will be waiting at the end of the lane. We would prefer that you didn't speak to them.'

'Thanks.' His relief was palpable.

'Did you see anyone at all from the time you left your car until the time you discovered the body?'

'No.'

'You're sure?'

'Positive. When you're worried someone might catch you fishing without permission, you're permanently on the lookout for other people.'

'Did you see anything at all suspicious?'

'Like what?'

'A vehicle parked near the entrance to this lane or on it.'

'No. I'd have noticed for the same reason as before.'

He saw the disappointment on her face.

'I'm sorry,' Mr Henderson said. 'Not been much use, have I?'

'On the contrary,' Jo replied, 'you chose to report what you found, and wait for us to arrive. Given the circumstances you could have decided to tell no one, and get the hell out of here.'

'I nearly did,' he admitted. 'Then I asked myself what the police would think if someone had noticed my car. Maybe even recorded the licence number.'

Henderson had a point.

Through the windscreen, Jo could see Max walking back towards them.

'Stay here,' she said. 'Someone will be along to take a formal statement. Make sure you ask for the details of that counselling service before you leave.'

She opened the door, and jumped on to the lane. Max joined her. They walked in silence side by side towards the cordon. She looked up at his rugged face. He looked half asleep. There were dark semicircles beneath his eyes, and a whiff of alcohol on his breath.

'Are you alright, Max?' Jo asked. 'You look dreadful.'

'Thanks for that,' he replied. 'I had a late night.'

'Should you be driving?'

'Should you?'

'As it happens, I had an early night. You, on the other hand . . .'

He shrugged. 'Who's to know?'

'They will if they breathalyse you.'

'They'll need due cause to stop me. I won't give them one.'

'How about driving without due attention?'

'That's never going to happen.'

She lowered her voice.

'Seriously, Max, I'm worried about you. You've been doing so well. You don't want to blow it now.'

He grimaced.

'Now you're beginning to sound like my ex. And seriously, Jo, how many of this lot do you think are still over the limit from a Sunday-night session? You know how it is. None of us count on being dragged out in the early hours like this. It's an occupational hazard.'

He was right of course. When the call came in the early hours, your first thought wasn't to wonder if you should call a taxi.

'Gordon is expecting the Home Office pathologist any time now,' he said. 'He wondered if you and I might visit the victim's house. It's on the estate.'

'What did you tell him?'

'That we would.'

'Why don't we go in mine?' she said. 'It's only a spit away. I'll drop you back here when we're done. With any luck you'll be sober by then.'

'I am sober.'

'And pigs'll fly.'

'You'd better not let any of this lot hear you,' he said, nodding towards the uniformed officers manning the cordon. 'You'll get us both arrested.'

Chapter 40

'What is this place?' Max asked.

Jo had just turned off a dual carriageway a mile or so from the crime scene, and was taking them into the heart of the estate.

'It was built by German prisoners of war in 1945,' she told him, 'on a wave of optimism for the future. About nine thousand souls lived here to start with. Now it's nearer six and a half thousand, mainly older tenants living on state pensions. The young ones without kids tend to live in the flats. Then there are vulnerable young parents on benefit. Unemployment is double the national average.'

'Sounds familiar,' he said. 'The rich are getting richer, and the poor end up in places like this.'

'There's a scheme to turn it around,' she said. 'But they need to get a grip on drugs and crime first.'

'Looks like some decent public facilities wouldn't go amiss,' he observed.

'Do you remember *Waterloo Road*?' she asked. 'The one about a comprehensive school turning into a virtual war zone? The first seven series were filmed here. Then the council decided to close and demolish the school. Where do you think they moved the filming to?'

'Eton?'

'May as well have done. They moved into a former academy school in Greenock, in Scotland, and miraculously turned Waterloo Road into a fee-paying independent school.'

'A case of art not imitating life.'

'Except there was a silver lining here. The kids from the high school moved to a new one on the other side of Queensway that's giving them a much better chance in life.'

'*You have reached your destination,*' the satnav intoned.

'Really?' said Max, staring out of the window.

They had arrived at a large grassy roundabout with a tree in the centre. To the left was a crescent-shaped precinct of shops with metal shutters. To the right was a triple-width three-storey block of flats.

'My money's on the flats,' said Jo, circumnavigating the roundabout. She pulled into a bus stop lay-by in front of the flats.

'No glass on the bus shelter,' Max observed as he unbuckled his seat belt. 'And there are as many CCTV cameras on poles as there are lamp posts. That tells you something. Make sure you lock your car.'

Jo tried the left-hand entrance first. Max headed for the other one.

'Flats 1 to 9,' she called across to him. 'Hers is Number 14. It must be one of yours.'

'It is.' He rang the buzzer on the box set into the panel beside the glazed door.

'Who is it?' asked a heavily congested female voice. She sounded a great deal older than the victim.

'This is the police,' said Max.

He turned to Jo, and lowered his voice to a whisper. 'I'm not going to say National Crime Agency, am I? It'd probably give her a heart attack.'

'What do you want?'

'It's about Genna,' he said.

The woman cursed and then cleared her throat. 'Don't tell me. She's gone and got herself arrested.'

'Actually, no she hasn't. Who is it I'm speaking to?'

'I'm her mother. And if she hasn't been arrested, why are you here?'

'If you let us in, Mrs Crowden,' said Jo, 'we'll tell you.'

'Bloody hell! Sent you mob-handed, have they? Well, I can't come down, so you'll have to come up. We're on the third floor.'

There was a long buzzing sound. The door opened inwards.

Jo and Max climbed two flights of stairs and found themselves outside a solid door inset with a spyhole and letterbox. Jo rang the doorbell. Nobody came.

'I think I can hear someone shouting,' Jo said.

Max knelt, and put his ear to the letterbox. 'She says she can't come to the door but there's a key behind the letterbox.'

'Watch out for DIY anti-burglary measures,' said Jo, recalling a colleague who'd sliced a finger to the bone on an artfully placed razor blade behind a drug dealer's door in Benchill.

Max gingerly inserted two fingers, felt around, and withdrew a length of string, on the end of which was a Yale key. He stood up. 'Not so much prevention as invitation.'

He inserted the key, and opened the door. Jo followed him down a narrow hallway that led to an open-plan lounge, kitchen, and diner.

Mrs Crowden lay on a large double sofa bed that had been placed in a corner facing an outsize wall-mounted television screen. Beside the bed was a mobile electric hoist, the reason for which was self-evident. At somewhere around five feet five inches tall, and pushing two hundred and ninety pounds, the victim's mother was morbidly obese.

On the wall to her left was an intercom for the front door of the flats. In her right hand she held a television remote control. From a cord around her neck hung a Careline fob. A bedside table held a water jug, and a tray piled high with empty plates and food wrappers.

'Go on then,' she said. 'What's she gone an' done this time?'

'Is there anyone else in the flat, Mrs Crowden?' Jo asked.

'Does it look like it?'

'We wouldn't know without searching the other rooms,' said Max. 'So please just answer the question.'

She gave him a withering look.

'No, there bloody well isn't. It's just me and Genna. She's my carer. And for your information I'm starving and I'm desperate for a wee. So the sooner you tell me what the hell's going on, and get her back here, the better.'

Max and Jo exchanged looks.

'Is there a neighbour who could come over and sit with you?' said Jo.

'Not one I'd trust not to run off with the housekeeping.' Even as she spoke, the import of what she had just been asked began to dawn on her.

'Now you're scaring me,' Mrs Crowden said. She let go of the remote control, placed both hands on the bed, tried to lever herself up, failed, and fell back against the pile of pillows.

Jo took a chair from the dining table, brushed it clean with her sleeve, and set it beside the bed. Max took another, and sat it beside her.

'I'm sorry, Mrs Crowden,' she said. 'There's no easy way to say this. I'm afraid that the body of a young woman has been found in the vicinity of Trows Lane. We have reason to believe it may be your daughter, Genna.'

Mrs Crowden's brow furrowed. Her mouth fell open, multiplying the rings of flesh beneath her jaw. She stared at the ceiling.

Jo and Max waited for the reality of what they had told her to sink in. For her to burst into tears. To wail, to scream, to do something.

Jo glanced at Max. He shrugged. When she finally did respond, it took them both by surprise.

'What am I supposed to do now?' Mrs Crowden moaned. 'Who's gonna look after me?' Her fingers plucked at the covers. 'The stupid cow. I warned her over and over again.'

She turned her head and stared at Jo. 'Trows Lane?' she said. 'What the hell was she doing down there?'

'That's what we were hoping you might be able to tell us, Mrs Crowden,' said Jo.

But Mrs Crowden wasn't listening. Instead she fumbled for the Careline fob that had got lost among the folds of her bosom, and pressed it between forefinger and thumb. There was a loud insistent beeping noise. 'And who's gonna pay for the funeral? I certainly can't.'

'Don't worry, Mrs Crowden,' said Max. 'I doubt the coroner will be releasing your daughter's body any time soon. You'll have plenty of time to save up.'

Jo jabbed him with her elbow.

'What's the matter?' he asked.

'That was cruel,' she whispered. 'Can't you see she's in shock?'

She need not have bothered. Genna's mother was listening to a disembodied voice emanating from a speaker somewhere in the hallway.

'Mrs Crowden? Is that you?'

'Of course it's me.'

'Good morning, Mrs Crowden. My name is Margaret. Would you prefer me to call you Gladys?'

'*Mrs* is fine!'

'And how can I help you today, Mrs Crowden?'

'My stupid daughter's gone and got herself killed, and I need someone to come and look after me. For a start I need a wee, and something to eat.'

There was a stunned silence at the end of the line.

'I bet that's not on their checklist,' said Max quietly so that only Jo could hear.

'Is there someone there with you now, Mrs Crowden?' The voice from the speaker was clutching at straws.

Mrs Crowden looked across at Jo and Max. 'There's a couple of dozy police officers,' she said. 'Some use they'll be.'

'Police officers? So you won't need us to call the emergency services.'

Jo had had enough of this. 'Margaret,' she said, 'my name is Joanne Stuart, with the National Crime Agency. I think that what Mrs Crowden needs is someone from social services who knows her situation and can arrange an urgent package of support for her. Can you assist with that?'

'Absolutely.' She sounded mightily relieved. 'I have the emergency contact details on Mrs Crowden's file, and I'll do that immediately.'

Gladys Crowden turned her head to look at Jo. 'Not so dozy after all,' she said.

———⌣———

The social worker lived on the estate and arrived within minutes. She brought a care worker with her. Jo was greatly impressed. She and Max were in the hallway preparing to leave. It had become clear that the victim's mother was unable to shed any light on her death or why she might have been on Trows Lane. The care worker was attending to Gladys Crowden's immediate needs.

'A family liaison officer should be here within the hour,' Jo told her. 'Can you stay till then?'

'Of course, although I will have a problem if it's any longer.'

'Don't worry,' Jo told her. 'We'll make sure they get a move on. Incidentally, did Genna have a partner?'

'Yes, a lorry driver. One of those big articulated trucks. He's somewhere in southern Spain at the moment picking up a load of fruit and vegetables from Murcia.'

'Do you think he knew she was a sex worker?'

The social worker shook her head. 'I got the impression he had no idea.'

'So what did he think she was doing?'

'Genna told me once that she worked in a call centre from midnight to 4am. Her mother tells the same story. Course, we all know the truth. There are few secrets on this estate.'

'And he fell for that?' said Max.

The social worker shrugged. 'It helped that before she became a prostitute she was working in a call centre, except it was a telephone sex line that folded under competition from the Internet chatlines. That was when she decided to go on the game.'

Max opened the front door. 'It's not a game though, is it?' he said. 'Not when you end up dead in a skip.'

Chapter 41

'Good to know she'll be sorely missed,' said Max.

'That's not fair,' Jo responded. 'The mother's probably in shock. When it finally hits her, I think she'll feel differently. Then there's the partner. He's bound to miss her.'

'You're too soft for this job, Jo. You do know that?'

She signalled right, and drove carefully through the media scrum by the entrance to the GMP headquarters' car park.

'The day I stop trying to see the good in people,' she said, 'is the day I'll pack it in.'

Max laughed. 'That's any time now then.'

She parked up, took her bag from the back seat, and got out.

'By the way,' she said as they walked towards the reception entrance, 'next time you call me soft I'll expect you to join me for a Krav Maga session.'

'Stupid I may be,' he replied, 'suicidal I am not.'

Gordon was crossing the atrium ahead of them. They rode the lift together up to the MIR.

'How did you get on at the house?' he asked.

Jo told him.

'At least with all the others there was someone who cared,' he reflected.

'How about you, Gordon?' she asked. 'Have you anything at all to go on?'

'Not a lot.'

The doors opened and they stepped out into the corridor.

'The Neighbourhood Team tracked down some of her fellow sex workers. We know she started off up by the railway station around midnight. The heavy police presence put the punters off, so most of them either went home or tried their luck elsewhere.'

Andy had warned them, Jo reflected, that doing so could have the effect of pushing the girls away from the red-light areas and making them more vulnerable. It was hardly the moment to remind Gordon.

'Presumably Genna did too?' said Max. 'Which would explain why she ended up not far from home.'

'We'll get a better idea when we've seen the CCTV,' said Gordon.

He held his security tag against the panel, and pushed open the door to the MIR.

'It's bristling with cameras around the town centre, and the Metrolink station in particular. Duggie's going through the footage right now with a forensic digital media analyst. Why don't you go and see how they're getting on while I update the policy book?'

'Duggie?' said Max as Jo led him to a carrel in the far corner of the suite, where a tall man in his forties was leaning over a younger man seated in front of a monitor.

'Duggie Wallace. He's the syndicate collator and senior intelligence analyst. We've worked together for years.'

'Indeed we have,' said Duggie, turning to greet them. 'Good to see you, Jo. DCI Caton will be chuffed when he finds out you're working with us.'

'Caton's back?'

She was surprised at how much that meant to her.

'Next week.' Duggie lowered his voice. 'Not a moment too soon. DCI Holmes is doing a good job, but we need all the experience we can get right now.'

'He asked us to check on how you're getting on,' said Max.

'We've identified seven kerb-crawlers, most of whom left the area without picking up any of the girls. Probably scared off by our guys. However, there were two rather persistent characters that hung around a bit longer.'

Duggie clicked on a Google Earth folder on the desktop menu bar. A 3D map appeared in the top-right-hand corner of the screen.

'This is the relevant target area,' he said, tracing the route with his trackpad arrow. 'The vehicle we are most interested in repeatedly cruised the two blocks to the east of the station bounded by Richard Street, High Level Street, Oldham Road, and the A640. We're pretty sure he also wove in and out of the backstreets inside that perimeter, where there's nothing but small workshops, warehouses, and industrial units. We won't know for sure till the rest of the CCTV is brought in. I've linked together the footage from six cameras on the main roads so far. This is the result.'

He opened a video file on the desktop, and started the playback. They watched as a car came into a view. While the footage ran, the forensic analyst followed its progress on the Google Earth map.

'The other reason we've chosen this one,' Duggie told them, 'is this same vehicle is among those picked up in the Fallowfield red-light district the night that Mandy Madden died.'

'Someone with an interest in prostitutes and railways stations,' Max observed dryly.

'It's a red Mazda 3 1.6 Venture,' Duggie informed them. 'The registered keeper and insurance holder is Jenson Hartley, forty-two years of age, from Tameside. He's a sales representative for a paint manufacturer.'

'One thing's for certain,' said Jo. 'Whatever else he's doing in that area, he isn't working.'

'He was there for over an hour,' said Duggie. 'Driving round and round. I'm amazed nobody stopped him and asked what he was doing. He left the area shortly after the victim, and in the same direction.'

'You've actually identified her on CCTV?' asked Jo.

'Based on the description DS Carter sent us, plus a photo from the crime scene.'

'This is her now,' said Jack, starting a second video.

They watched as Genna emerged from a side road on to Rochdale Road, crossed over, and disappeared down a ginnel. The time on the screen said 1.55am. It was surreal and uncomfortable knowing that in less than an hour she would be dead.

Fifty seconds later she appeared again, turned right, and walked down beside the Metrolink tramlines before crossing over by an impressive church, and disappearing behind the raised platform of the station. Thirty seconds later she appeared again, walked to the end of the street, and turned left on to the A664.

'That's all we've got so far,' said Duggie. 'When the rest comes in, we should be able to track her most of the way down to wherever she turned off on her way back to the estate.'

'Assuming that's where she was going,' said Max.

'It's the only thing that makes sense,' said Jo. 'And if she did, then she's bound to have shown up on some of those cameras you pointed out around the precinct.'

'I'll get on to that straight away,' said Duggie.

'How did you manage to get this footage so quickly?' Max asked.

'Rochdale Council has sixty-four cameras operated from one central point on their behalf. Plus there are half a dozen on the Metrolink stop. It was just a matter of two phone calls quoting RIPA.'

The Regulation of Investigatory Powers Act; a curiously apt acronym, Jo reflected, given their unsub.

'You mentioned a second vehicle,' she said.

'Yes indeed,' said Duggie. 'This guy. Only it's not a car or any other motorised vehicle. He's on a mountain bike.'

The final video showed a cyclist dressed in a black biker hoodie, black trousers, and a black ribbed helmet riding a mountain bike at a leisurely pace around the same district as the Mazda. There were hi-vis patches on his sleeves and the front and rear of his jacket.

'Are you sure that's not a GMP bike patrol officer?' said Max, leaning closer to the screen.

'Definitely not,' said Duggie. 'We did check to see if any had been deployed there last night. And when you zoom in . . .'

The forensic digital media analyst obliged.

'. . . you can see this guy has no police markings on his helmet. It is also black, when ours are white. And that's not a standard police marked hi-vis jacket. He has a tinted visor obscuring his face.'

'Be an easy mistake to make though,' Jo observed thoughtfully.

'That was our thinking too,' said Duggie. 'He does two circuits, each an hour apart, which is what made us suspicious.'

'Is there any possibility that he may have followed the victim when she left the area?'

'We'll only know that when we've got the footage from the cameras on the A664,' Duggie told her.

'The sooner the better then,' she said. 'In the meantime, let's see what Mr Hartley has to say for himself.'

Chapter 42

It took Gordon Holmes a little over an hour and twenty minutes to rush through a search warrant for Jenson Hartley's car, company office, and home. Ten minutes later his Mazda was spotted by an ANPR camera heading north on the M60.

'A Traffic car pulled him over, and is waiting for instructions,' he told them. 'How about you and Nick go and pick him up, Jo?'

'What about his car?' Jo said. 'For all we know, he may have used it to pick her up.'

'I'll send a vehicle recovery low-lifter to bring it back for forensic examination,' Gordon said.

'What about me?' said Max.

'It would help if you were to accompany the house search team,' said Gordon. 'You can find out what his wife thought he was doing in the early hours of this morning.'

⌣

'He doesn't look very happy,' Nick said as he pulled over on to the hard shoulder of the motorway, and stopped in front of the Traffic car.

Jo unbuckled her seat belt. 'That's not a good sign,' she said.

Nick frowned. 'How so?'

'If Hartley's just a pathetic sex-starved kerb-crawler, I'd expect him to be nervous. A psychopath would be sitting there confident he's got all the angles covered and in the belief he can talk himself out of anything.'

'What's that? *The Gospel According To Dr Andrew Swift*?'

'I am capable of doing my own research,' she said, getting out of the car.

'What, and he's never wrong?' he called after her as he carefully checked the traffic before exiting the driver's side.

'No one is infallible,' she replied, and then added sotto voce, 'Not even me.'

'Sorry, Ma'am? I didn't catch that,' said the Traffic officer through his open window.

'Just talking to myself,' Jo said, holding up her ID.

'Occupational hazard,' the officer replied. 'I do it all the time.'

'How did you know who I was?'

He raised his eyebrows. 'Apart from being told to expect you? And this?' He pointed to the screen in the centre of his console. It featured the number plate of Nick Carter's car in bold letters, below it a live display of the rear of the vehicle, and a text confirmation that it belonged to GMP.

'Very good,' she said. 'You might want to think about applying for CID.'

He chuckled. 'Become a detective? And lose all that overtime? The wife would kill me.'

'How's he been?' said Jo, nodding towards the car behind them.

'Nervy. He assumed I'd pulled him over for a traffic offence. When he found out I hadn't but I couldn't tell him why and he'd have to wait till you got here, I thought he was going to have a panic attack. He's not going anywhere though. I've got his car keys.'

'Good,' Jo replied. 'That's how we like them.'

'What is it he's wanted for, Ma'am?'

Nick Carter answered for her. 'When you've swapped your candy bar for a detective badge, we'll let you know.'

'Sorry about him,' said Jo. 'He's been up half the night.'

They approached the suspect's car.

'You've been spending too much time with Gordon,' she said. 'One of these days you may need that guy to come to your rescue.'

'Not me,' Nick replied, 'I'm with the Automobile Association.'

Hartley spotted them coming in his wing mirror, and began to get out of the car. Jo placed her hand against the door panel.

'Stay in the car please, sir,' she said. 'And wind down your window.'

'What the hell's going on?' Hartley asked. 'I haven't done anything wrong.'

'That's for us to establish,' she told him.

Nick Carter walked around the bonnet, and stood by the passenger door.

'Can you confirm your name for me please?' Jo said to Hartley.

'Jenson Hartley.'

'And your address?'

He told her.

'And can you confirm that this is your car?'

'Yes, but what—?'

'In which case I would like you to climb over to the passenger side, and get out of the car.'

'But—'

'Just do it!'

She watched as Hartley struggled to clamber over the gear stick with his long legs and plate-sized shoes. It did seem ridiculous, but there was no way she was going to risk him running straight out into vehicles speeding past in the inside lane. Nick opened the door and stood back to let him out. Jo walked around the rear of the car to join them. At well over six foot three, and thin as a rake, he struck her as far too conspicuous to be their unsub, whom Andy Swift had previously asserted would need to blend in to commit his crimes without being caught. Nor did he fit the profile of any description provided by sex workers they had interviewed.

'We would like you to accompany us to GMP North Division headquarters, Mr Hartley,' she said. 'To help us with our inquiries.'

'I can't,' he said. 'I told the other policeman I've got an important meeting in Leeds in forty minutes. I'm already going to be late.'

'Our meeting trumps yours, sir,' said Nick Carter. 'No pun intended.'

'Jenson Hartley,' said Jo, 'I am arresting you under Section 51A of the Sexual Offences Act 2003 on suspicion that you did solicit, in a street or public place, for the purpose of obtaining a sexual service from another person as a prostitute.'

'You can't,' he said. 'Kerb-crawling is not an arrestable offence.'

'It may not have been when you started out,' said Nick, 'but it is now. You need to keep up. Where have you been for the past sixteen years? Timbuktu?'

'You do not have to say anything,' she continued, 'but it may harm your defence if you do not mention, when questioned, something that you later rely on in court. Anything you do say may be given in evidence. Do you understand?'

'Yes, but—'

'Good.'

Jo unbuttoned her jacket, took a pair of handcuffs from her belt holster, clamped one around her own wrist and the other around his.

'That's not necessary,' he said.

'Just a precaution, sir,' she said, leading him towards Nick's car. 'We wouldn't want you to end up as road kill, now would we?'

Chapter 43

'Please,' Jenson Hartley said. 'Can we just get on with it?'

Hartley stared back at them across the interview table. His initial panic, worsened by the taking of a mugshot, fingerprints, and a DNA sample, had been replaced by a determination to get this over with as quickly and quietly as possible. It was a common reaction Jo had found among kerb-crawlers. It wasn't so much about the conviction or the fine but rather the desperation to avoid public shaming. She and Nick had agreed to tread carefully. They had no evidence that Hartley had solicited any of the women. Only that he appeared to have been behaving suspiciously. If he came up with a plausible reason for cruising both of the red-light districts, they were going to have to let him go until they found one or more of the girls, who might be willing to confirm that he had at some time approached them for sex. And that was not something any of them would be keen to do. Outing your punters was a sure-fire way to lose custom. Even to invite revenge.

'Very well,' Jo said, 'my colleague has some questions for you.'

'Let's start with last night,' said Nick. 'Where were you between midnight and 2am?'

Jo could see Hartley trying to decide the best course of action. Should he lie? Fabricate a story with elements of the truth? Or confess?

It all depended on how much he thought they already knew. He stared at the two of them, clearly hoping for some clues.

'Come on, Mr Hartley,' said Nick. 'We're talking less than twelve hours ago. Surely you can remember.'

Hartley clearly decided to hedge his bets, and went for the middle option. 'I was driving around.'

'In the middle of the night? Do you do that often?'

'As a matter of fact I do.' He switched his attention to Jo, as though seeking an ally. 'I suffer from insomnia. I find it helps if I have a drive before I get my head down.'

'And this insomnia,' said Nick. 'Would your GP happen to know about it?'

There was a flicker of panic in his eyes.

'She started me on a benzodiazepine a few years ago,' he said. 'But you don't need to check with her. I can show you my prescriptions.'

'Or we could ask your wife,' said Jo.

The panic deepened. 'No! You don't need to bother her.'

'No bother,' she said. 'We can get the officers who are searching your house to ask her.'

He jerked upright as though struck by lightning. 'Searching my house? What the hell for? Kerb-crawling you said, not robbery. Please don't tell my wife,' he said. 'Please!'

'That shouldn't be a problem,' said Nick. 'If you were just driving around.'

'I was.'

'There you go then. So, where exactly were you driving around between midnight and 2am?'

Hartley looked down at the table and tried to order his thoughts.

'I left home about midnight,' he said. 'And then I drove up to Rochdale.'

'That's, what, twelve miles from your house?'

'Eleven.'

'Do you have many friends in Rochdale, Mr Hartley?'

'No, not really.'

'Is that a few or none at all?'

'None at all.'

'Acquaintances then?'

Hartley shook his head forlornly.

'For the record please, Mr Hartley.'

'No.'

'Not even among the street walkers?' said Jo.

If looks could kill, Hartley's would have done. 'No!'

'So why did you spend an hour driving around those particular streets?'

Hartley shrugged unconvincingly. 'No reason.'

'How about Monday the 8th of May?' said Nick.

'Sorry?'

Nick raised his eyebrows. 'What for?'

Hartley looked doubly confused. 'What?' he said.

'What are you apologising for, Mr Hartley?'

'Nothing. I'm not apologising for anything.' He looked from Nick to Jo and back again. 'I don't understand what you're asking. I wasn't anywhere near Rochdale last week.'

'We know that, Mr Hartley. What I'm asking is what you were doing driving around the Manchester Fairfield Street red-light district in the early hours of Monday the 8th of May.'

Whatever tenuous conviction he had harboured that he might bluff his way out of this evaporated before their eyes.

Nick smiled. 'I see the penny has finally dropped,' he said. 'Five young women have been brutally murdered. Two of them within the past eight days. And you just happened to have been driving around the areas where those two young women were last seen. So if you're still maintaining that you were not kerb-crawling on those occasions, then we'll have no option but to rearrest you on suspicion of murder.'

Jo resisted the temptation to look at Nick. It wasn't exactly what they had agreed. Neither the timing, this soon into the interview, nor the form of words. Not that it mattered. It appeared to have had the desired effect. Hartley grasped the edge of the table and tried to push himself away, as though attempting to distance himself from what he was hearing. He stared wide-eyed at Nick and then at Jo.

'No! No!' he pleaded. 'You can't believe that I'd actually kill someone.'

'Why not?' said Nick. 'We don't believe in coincidence. You were in the right place at the right time on both occasions. You clearly have unmet needs. In our experience that can drive a man to do crazy things.'

Hartley's eyes sought out Jo's. *Help me*, they said. She placed a hand on Nick's sleeve, and leaned forward.

'Jenson,' she began, 'this is your last opportunity to convince us that you are not the man who has been killing young women in red-light districts.'

They watched as his shoulders slumped and his resistance crumpled.

'Alright,' Hartley said. 'I'll tell you the truth.'

Chapter 44

'I was looking for one girl in particular,' he said. 'I was one of her regulars whenever I went to Rochdale.'

'Which was how often?' said Nick.

'When Manchester was being targeted by the police. Once a month or so.'

'What is her name?'

'I only knew her as Frankie.'

'How many years have you been availing yourself of the services of street sex workers?' asked Jo.

'Since my wife and I stopped making love.'

Making love. The phrase sounded incongruous in the circumstances. He certainly wasn't making love with Frankie and the other girls, Jo reflected. Maybe he had never gone beyond releasing an animal impulse. Perhaps that was why his wife had shut him out.

'That doesn't help us, Mr Hartley,' said Nick.

'Oh, er . . . about twelve years ago.'

He would have been thirty at the time. It hadn't taken long for that side of the marriage to stall.

'You've been cruising red-light districts for twelve years or so?'

Hartley nodded sheepishly.

'For the tape please.'

'Yes.'

'You were driving around in the vicinity of Piccadilly station in Manchester, intent on soliciting sex, in the early hours of Monday, 8th May this year.'

'Yes.'

'And again in the early hours of this morning in the vicinity of Rochdale Metrolink station.'

'Yes.'

'You must have been aware that the police were hunting a serial killer believed to be active in the region's red-light districts.'

'No.'

'No? It was all over the papers, the television, social media. How could you not have known?'

'No. What I meant is that I didn't know about those other women. The first I knew about it was Tuesday before last, after that woman's body was found near Piccadilly.'

'Her name was Mandy,' said Jo. 'Mandy Madden.'

He nodded.

'Yes. Mandy Madden.'

'Had you ever had sex with her, Mr Hartley?' There was no longer any point in using his given name. The familiarity had served its purpose.

He bowed his head. His voice was unsteady. 'I think so,' he said. 'A few years ago. But she wasn't one of my regulars.'

'Why was that?'

Hartley looked up and shrugged.

'She just wasn't. That one time she was just a . . .' He saw the disgust on Jo's face, and tailed off.

'A what?' said Nick. 'Stopgap?'

'I'm sorry,' he said.

'It's not us you need to apologise to,' said Jo. She glanced at her notes. 'Even if we accept that when you were in Manchester last week you did not know about the previous attacks, you most certainly did when you set out for Rochdale on Sunday night. Isn't that so?'

He nodded tentatively.

'Yes.'

'And when you arrived there, you must have noticed a large police presence.'

'Not at first. It built up during the night.'

'Yet you continued to drive around and around looking for your "regular". What was her name again?'

'Frankie.'

'Your need must have been great to risk being stopped, and arrested,' Nick observed.

'I was only there for an hour or so,' Hartley said. 'And I was careful.'

'Not careful enough, evidently.'

'Would you like to help us catch this killer, Mr Hartley?' said Jo.

Hartley's eyes lit up. He seized this apparent lifeline. 'Of course. I'll do anything. Anything.'

'Then perhaps you could cast your mind back to last night, when you were driving around Richard Street, High Level Street, Oldham Road, the A640, and the side streets that come off them.'

'Of course.'

'Good. Now, do you recall seeing anyone or any vehicle behaving in a suspicious manner?'

Hartley's brow furrowed. But he was staring straight back at her. Either he was preparing to lie or he wasn't trying to remember.

'No.'

'Mr Hartley,' she said, 'this is really important. For you and for us. Please think again. Take as long as you need.'

This time his eyes went up to his left. Then down to the left and back up again. This was better. He was accessing his visual memory, and having an internal dialogue.

'I do keep looking in my rear-view mirror,' he said. 'In case I'm being followed. So I see quite a lot.'

'And?' said Nick.

'Well, there were a few other cars obviously doing what I was doing. Not as many as usual, but a few. But none of them did anything out of the ordinary. I saw a couple of them pick up girls.'

'Can you describe the vehicles?'

'One looked like a dark Mondeo. The other one I'm not sure. A Honda saloon maybe?'

'Were either of those girls wearing a blue denim jacket, a matching short skirt, and dark brown knee-length boots?'

'No.'

'You seem very sure.'

'I am. I'd passed them several times looking for Frankie. I took careful note in case—'

'You needed a fallback?' said Nick.

He nodded mournfully.

'Anything else?' asked Jo. 'Anything at all out of the ordinary?'

'I was coming to that,' he said. 'There was someone. Someone I saw in Manchester last week as well as last night.'

The two detectives glanced at each other. Now he had their attention.

'Go on,' said Jo.

'There was this guy on a mountain bike,' Hartley said. 'At first I thought he was one of you.'

'A policeman?'

'Yes. He was dressed in black, on a mountain bike, wearing a cycle helmet, and one of those luminous jackets.'

'So what made you decide that he wasn't a police officer?'

'The helmet was wrong.'

'In what way?'

'Normally they're white-ribbed. This one was black. And it didn't say POLICE in capital letters on the jacket.'

'He could have been undercover,' said Nick.

'I suppose. But he didn't really behave like one.'

'How did he behave?' said Jo.

'Well, when I saw him in Manchester he was talking to one of the girls on Fallowfield Street.'

'Can you describe her?' said Jo.

Hartley shook his head. 'I'm sorry. It was under the railway arches. She was in shadow. He was between her and my car as I went past. Then I saw him a bit later as I was leaving, standing at the side of that old pub on Fairfield Street.'

'The Star & Garter?' asked Nick.

'That's the one.'

'And what was he doing when you saw him that morning?' Jo asked.

'The first time I saw him was shortly after I got there. He was cycling slowly down Richard Street. Then about ten minutes later I saw him again walking his bike down Wood Street. The last time I saw him was about an hour later as I was leaving to go home. He was just sitting on his bike to the right of the railway station entrance. I wouldn't have noticed but for my dipped headlights catching his fluorescent vest.'

'And what time was this?'

'About twenty to two.'

'And what did you do then?'

'I went straight home.'

The two detectives looked at each other. Hartley's account fitted with what they'd seen on the CCTV. He seemed to be telling the truth. It wouldn't take long to track his exact route home. Nick leaned across, and whispered in Jo's ear. She nodded, and they had a brief conversation. Nick sat up straight.

'Mr Hartley,' he said, 'we are going to release you on police bail, pending the results of the search of your house and effects, and the examination of your car. The Crown Prosecution Service will then be asked to decide whether you will be charged, and if so with what offence. In the meantime you must stay away from any places where street prostitution is habitually carried on. And I urge you, Mr Hartley, for your own sake, not to talk to anyone, other than a solicitor whom you choose to represent you, about the reasons why you have been detained and questioned. Do you understand?'

Relief flooded Hartley's face. 'Yes. Is my car here?'

'I'm afraid not. It has been impounded, and is being forensically examined.'

'How will I get home?'

'Don't worry about that. We'll arrange for someone to drive you home.'

'A police car?'

His relief was short-lived.

'Is that a problem?'

'Yes. I don't want my wife to know.'

'Don't you think she might be curious about why your house is being searched?'

'I'll think of something to tell her.'

'If I were you, Mr Hartley,' said Jo, 'I would tell her the truth. One way or another it's going to come out. It always does.'

Chapter 45

'I'll drive him,' Jo said.

'Why would you want to do that?' said Nick. 'Leave it to Uniform.'

'Because I want to make sure he gets the message about keeping his mouth shut. And I want to find out how the search of his home is coming on. They should be nearly finished by now.'

'In which case I'll tell Gordon where we're up to,' he said. 'And I suggest we get CIS down to the Star & Garter. In case that cyclist left anything behind. A cigarette butt. Some chewing gum. A food wrapper. Anything.'

'It's been a week, Nick,' she said. 'There'll be all sorts of stuff accumulated in that time.'

'I know. But it's worth a try.' He grinned. 'Besides, it's not you or me who is going to have to sift through it all.'

'Can you check what Duggie turns up in relation to Hartley from the CCTV footage from cameras south-west of the station?' she said.

'Sure. And if there is any evidence that he actually followed Genna Crowden, we'll have him back in faster than a presidential tweet!'

'I only meant for elimination purposes. You do know he's not our man?'

'Of course I do.' He stared at her quizzically. 'Is that the real reason why you're babysitting him? Please tell me that you don't feel sorry for him.'

Her expression hardened. 'If you believe that, Nick, then you don't know me at all. If it weren't for men like Jenson Hartley, there wouldn't be vulnerable women and young girls on the streets, and in brothels. And those five girls would still be alive.'

Hartley had been keen to talk, but Jo had blanked him. She was annoyed with herself, not least because Nick had been right. Part of her felt sorry for Hartley. Another part was thinking about her birth mother. And how men like Hartley had used and abused her.

By the time they reached the house, she had calmed down.

'Oh God!' said Hartley, staring disconsolately through the windscreen.

Jo followed his gaze. A short, shapely, raven-haired woman similar in age to her husband was standing beside the front door remonstrating with one of the search team. She turned as the two of them exited the car, and hurried down the path towards them.

'What the hell have you done?' the woman demanded.

Hartley cowered beside Jo despite his height and weight advantage.

'Sam,' he pleaded. 'Can we do this inside?'

'Want some privacy, do you?' she shouted. 'It's a bit late for that, don't you think?'

She pointed at the houses on the opposite side of the road, and those flanking their own side. There were at least a dozen people watching from their windows and doorsteps.

'Mrs Hartley,' said Jo, 'it really would be best if the two of you discussed this inside.'

'Best for who?' she demanded, switching her wrath to this interloper. 'Hang on a minute,' she said. 'I know your face. You're that policewoman on the television.'

Jo saw the wife's expression freeze and her hand move towards her mouth.

She swore beneath her breath, and hurried towards the house. Nick Carter had been right. She had been mistaken coming here. If Mrs Hartley had recognised her, and put two and two together, then so would some of the gawking neighbours. It was only a matter of time before one of them sent a tweet, or uploaded a video to a social media account and the whole world would know. Within the hour this place would be a media circus.

Jenson Hartley brushed past her. 'Thanks for nothing!' he said. 'I'd have been better off locked up.'

He disappeared into the rear of the property.

Duggie Wallace came down the stairs. 'Was that him?' he asked. 'The husband?'

'Jenson Hartley,' Jo told him.

'Where's he gone then? We need the screen passwords for his PC and tablet.'

'He went that way,' she told him. 'Before you go, where are you up to?'

'Just the garage, those passwords, and we're out of here.'

She stepped back against the wall as Samantha Hartley brushed past in pursuit of her husband. Jo lowered her voice.

'Anything sus?'

He shook his head.

'Nothing obvious. The computer's our best bet.'

Fifteen minutes later the vans were packed and they were sitting in the front of Jo's Audi.

'Did you get a look at the computer and the tablet?' she asked.

'Just a quickie,' said Duggie. 'Although I should really have just bagged it and waited for my forensic techies first.'

'I won't tell anyone,' she said. 'So? Are you going to keep me in suspense?'

'I concentrated on his search history, and his downloads. There's nothing so far that would suggest he'd been planning any of those attacks.'

'Such as?'

'Map searches. Using search engines to scope the area. Photos of likely attack or dump sites, that sort of thing. And there was one tenuous connection.'

'Go on.'

'He's a regular on adult sex sites, and he's downloaded a tidy amount of porn.'

'Hard or soft?'

'Mainly soft.'

'No snuff movies?'

'Nothing like that.'

'Anything that suggests an obsession with hair? Women's hair in particular?'

Duggie shook his head. 'Mind you,' he said, 'he may have tried to permanently delete loads of stuff, so we won't know till his caches have been restored.'

Both car windows were down. Despite the fact the front door was closed, they could still hear Mrs Hartley yelling at her husband.

'Sounds a bit one-sided,' Duggie observed.

'What did you expect? They'd kiss and make up?'

'It would have been a damn sight less embarrassing for both of them if she'd given him a chance to explain. Then they could've told the neighbours it was a case of mistaken identity.'

'That option went south the minute I stepped out of this car,' Jo said. 'And it's certainly too late now.'

She pointed to the rear-view mirror.

A motorcycle with two large panniers, its rider clad in black leathers and a matching helmet, had just turned into the avenue. Behind it was a mobile radio news van.

'We'd better get out of here,' she said. 'I'll catch up with you at the MIR when you're done.'

She waited for him to exit the car and then executed a U-turn. Twenty-five yards before the end of the avenue two school children turned the corner, a boy and girl in their early teens. They looked like brother and sister. The boy was larking around, attempting to push his sister into a garden hedge. She wriggled free, stopped, and pointed past Jo's car in the direction of the Hartley house. As she spoke, her brother followed her gaze. Their expressions morphed from confusion to concern. The two of them began to sprint, their bags bouncing awkwardly on their backs.

Jo shook her head. That was the trouble with investigations like this one. The backwash kept sucking innocent people in.

Chapter 46

'Listen up!'

It was 7.30pm. The syndicate had gathered for the briefing. Every desk and chair was spoken for. Gordon, Nick, Max, and Jo stood by the progress board, facing the throng.

'I'm going to ask named persons to give us an update,' said Gordon. 'I don't want a peep from any of you while they're doing so. Save your questions for the end. Is that clear?'

'Yes, Boss!'

'Roger that, Boss!'

'Good. I imagine you all want to know where we're up to with the person who was brought in for questioning.'

He turned to Jo and handed her a remote for the whiteboard.

'SI Stuart.'

Jo began by clicking the remote to reveal a head-and-shoulders mugshot. 'Jenson Hartley,' she said. 'His name stays within these four walls until it becomes public knowledge.'

'Which won't be long,' muttered a wag at the back.

'DC Hulme!' Gordon bellowed. 'What did I tell you about no comments?'

'Sorry, Boss.'

'Do that again and you will be. Carry on, SI Stuart.'

'Jenson Hartley has subsequently admitted to having been kerb-crawling around the Fairfield Street and Rochdale Metrolink station on the nights, and around the times, when Mandy Madden and Genna Crowden met their deaths. He also admitted having had sex with Mandy Madden on a previous occasion. We are still waiting for the results of forensic tests on his car, and items removed from his home and workplace. We're also waiting for analysis of CCTV footage covering the last known sightings of Genna Crowden. We do know that he left both of the red-light districts before either Mandy Madden or Genna Crowden. That does not rule out the possibility that he may have doubled back. Initial indications suggest he is unlikely to be our unsub.'

She waited for the groans to subside. Her own disappointment far outmatched theirs.

'I must stress, however, that he has not been eliminated from this investigation, although he has been released on police bail pending the results of those tests and further CCTV analysis.'

She handed the remote back to Gordon.

'Thank you,' said Gordon. 'Mr Benson.'

The CSI team leader stepped up. 'The latest information I have for you is that hairs and fibres retrieved from Mr Hartley's car are being tested for matches with the clothing and DNA of all of the Operation Firethorn victims. Likewise, traces of semen found on the upholstery and front and rear carpets of his vehicle. His computer devices are undergoing forensic digital analysis. Nothing so far has been discovered that might link him directly or indirectly with any of the murders here in Manchester or in the Wigan division. The lack of significant trace evidence from any of the five crime scenes, including the most recent, suggests a perpetrator who is forensically aware.'

Another reason, Jo reflected, why Hartley was a most unlikely suspect. Andy had agreed. His observation of Hartley during the interview led him to conclude he was too weak, and pathetic to be capable of such organised planning, and such cold-blooded murders.

'Next we'll hear from SI Nailor,' said Gordon.

Max still looked the worse for wear, Jo thought, and tired too, but his physique and rich baritone voice were sufficient to make his presence felt. 'SI Stuart and I interviewed Genna Crowden's mother. She was more concerned about herself than her daughter, however. The little she did tell us, together with door-to-door interviews with neighbours, rules out the likelihood that her killer was related to Genna Crowden or from the immediate neighbourhood. Nor was there any awareness that Genna suspected someone may have been watching or following her in the vicinity of her home in the days prior to her murder. Her partner, who is a long-distance lorry driver, was in Spain at the time of the attack. He has been informed of her death, and is on his way home.'

'Before you get too despondent,' said Gordon, 'Mr Wallace has some better news for us.' He handed the remote to Duggie Wallace.

The intelligence analyst clicked the remote and filled the whiteboard with a series of images. They showed a cyclist dressed in black, and sporting a hi-vis jacket with a mountain bike. The top-right-hand corner of the board showed an inset image of a map.

'Thanks to the work of my colleague from the forensic digital media unit,' he began, 'we have been able to track this person following Genna Crowden last night from Rochdale to the estate on which she lived.'

A buzz of excitement fizzed around the room. People at the back craned forward to get a better look. Duggie traced the route that Genna and this unknown man had taken by highlighting each image in turn and using a moving red blob on the map to indicate its exact location.

'We lost sight of him at this point,' he said, 'shortly before the two of them entered the estate on which Genna Crowden lived. However, we picked him up again here, on the estate itself, by the shopping precinct. If you look closely, you can just see Genna at the top of the screen. She is entering Ruskin Street, which leads to the A627M motorway footbridge. Here you can see the cyclist walking with his bike in the same direction. None of the cameras recorded either of them returning. It is reasonable to assume that he followed her over the footbridge and on to Cripplegate Lane, less than a quarter of a mile from where her body was discovered.'

Duggie handed back the remote to Gordon.

'This man is now our primary suspect,' said Gordon. 'We need to find out who he is and if there have been any sightings of him in the vicinity of any of the other murders. Several of these images, together with descriptions, have been circulated to every front-line officer and detective in GMP. Are there any questions or observations?'

A hand went up. It was DC Hulme pushing his luck again.

'For someone who is forensically aware, he doesn't appear to be camera shy. Okay, so he's got a tinted visor, but I thought that the infrared cameras can see through that.'

'They can indeed,' said Holmes. 'Show them, Duggie.'

He selected an image, and zoomed in. There were muted gasps. Several people swore. Underneath the visor the man was wearing a balaclava.

'There is one thing we could do to help identify him against other images or live suspects,' said Jo.

She felt everyone's eyes on her.

'Go on,' said Gordon.

'These are still images,' she said. 'But they've been taken from video capture. In some of these images he is walking with his bike rather than riding it. We could commission a gait analysis.'

'I wish I'd thought of that,' said Gordon. 'I can see a few blank faces out there, SI Stuart. You'd better explain.'

'Forensic gait analysis examines a person's stance, leg swing, step length, and stride length. Also time parameters, such as step time, stride time, cadence, and velocity. Add in the patterns of movement of the torso, head, and arms, and you have an extremely detailed analysis of how a person moves. Some experts claim that an individual's gait is as unique as his or her fingerprints.'

'Is this form of analysis accepted by the courts?' someone asked.

'Has been for over ten years,' said Max. 'I was involved in a number of convictions in the Met where gait analysis helped to convince the jury when we had no eyewitness identification.'

'And we've used it extensively in FMIT for a number of years,' said Gordon. 'So those of you for whom this comes as a surprise had better wake up and smell the coffee!'

He looked at the clock on the back wall. 'It's an early start in the morning. I have no doubt that in addition to the backlog of information from members of the public, there'll be a string of blokes in black Lycra on mountain bikes waiting to be eliminated. So I want everyone, apart from those like me who know they are working late, to go home now. No excuses. Just stop whatever you're doing, and go.'

As the exodus began, he turned to Jo and Max.

'That includes you two,' he said. 'Neither of you have had much sleep in over a week, and you, Max, look absolutely—'

Max held up his hand. 'You don't need to tell me. Jo already has.'

'What about you, Gordon?' Jo said. 'You've had even less than us.'

'I'm too old to need beauty sleep,' he replied. 'Besides, I won't be able to rest until we've caught this bastard.'

'That's how I feel,' she said. 'And I don't have a wife and children waiting for me.'

He nodded. 'I know, Jo. But this is my case, and as far as Genna Crowden's concerned, it's less than twenty-four hours since she was killed. Tomorrow morning I'll be the one that looks like Max and I'll need the two of you, and Nick Carter, as fresh as daisies. So please go home. Both of you.'

'You go, Jo,' said Max. 'I've a couple of calls to make, then I'll be on my way too.'

Jo was walking across the foyer towards the exit when she heard some-one call her name. She turned. One of the receptionists stood with a phone in his hand.

'It's Detective Chief Inspector Holmes,' he said. 'He'd like a word with you.'

Chapter 47

Gordon held a printout in his right hand. Jo could tell from the grave expression on his face, and that of Max, that this was not good news.

'Someone just texted this to one of our SMS-enabled public appeal lines,' Gordon said. 'It's addressed to you.'

'Me?'

He handed it to her.

'See for yourself.'

Jo took the printout. Her pulse quickened as she began to read:

> *For the attention of Senior Investigator*
> *Joanne Stuart.*
>
> *She is the fairies' midwife, and she comes*
> *In shape no bigger than an agate-stone*
> *That plaits the manes of horses in the night,*
> *And bakes the elflocks in foul sluttish hairs,*
> *Which once untangled, much misfortune bodes.*
>
> *PS I love your new look, DI Stuart. I cannot*
> *wait to run my fingers through it!*

'I know this,' said Jo. 'It's from *Romeo and Juliet*. Mercutio's speech.' She read the question on Gordon's face.

'I played Juliet at high school. And they took us to see it in Stratford-upon-Avon.'

'What the hell does it mean?'

'If I remember rightly, elflocks refers to a European folklore tale, where during the night imps, or fairies, knot or tangle the hair of sleeping humans and horses. This can only have come from someone with intimate knowledge of the killings.'

'I agree,' said Max. 'And that stuff about foul sluttish hairs speaks volumes for how he regards his victims.'

'He's taunting us,' said Jo. 'Taunting me. How the hell does he know I've just changed my hairstyle? I wasn't on Operation Firethorn when I had it done.'

'He only had to google you,' Max pointed out. 'There must be loads of images of you out there from Operation Hound. And Operation Juniper.'

Max was right, of course. Not that it made her feel any better. All she could think about was the way in which, seven years ago, she had been stalked by her abductor. How just last year a serial rapist had sent flowers to her apartment. Now it was happening again. This time it was a serial killer.

'Have you been able to trace the source?' she asked.

'Ram's working on it,' said Max. 'But I wouldn't hold out too much hope. Not given how careful the unsub's been this far.'

'At least he didn't send it to the press,' said Gordon. 'We should be grateful for that.'

'Grateful?' said Jo. 'I've become an object of desire for a madman who goes around strangling women, and I'm supposed to be grateful he hasn't put it on social media? What if it was you or your wife? Would you be telling her she should be grateful?'

She thrust the printout against his chest, turned her back on them, and stormed from the room.

Chapter 48

Jo had tried everything.

Comfort food in the shape of a ready-meal chicken korma, and the best part of a bottle of red wine. Another four catch-up episodes of *Coronation Street*, a long hot shower, and a mug of camomile tea. Her mobile phone and her tablet were both switched off and on charge in the lounge. There was nothing to stop her from going to sleep. Apart from the enemy within.

There was a fine line, she learned during the counselling she received following the Bluebell Hollow incident, between uninvited voices, and your own. It was better to embrace internal dialogue than to allow more malevolent voices to emerge. Forty per cent of people heard voices at some time in their lives, she had been told. When her PTSD had been at its most extreme, her internal voice had belonged to her captor. Not simply in the form of flashbacks, but as though from the grave. These days it was her own voice that kept her awake.

Tonight the voice was telling her to take a long hard look at herself. To acknowledge how lonely her life had become since Abbie left. To recognise that it consisted of nothing but work, and sleep. And precious little of the latter. That it was devoid of any form of social activity or entertainment. That she had become friendless, sad, unloved, and unlovable.

'I know!' she found herself shouting. 'Don't you think I bloody well know?'

And then she began to cry.

When the tears finally dried up, Jo made herself two promises. When this investigation was over, she would take two weeks' leave and have a proper holiday in the sun somewhere. Secondly, she was going to make a real effort to shift her mindset and at least admit the possibility of another romantic relationship. With that she turned over, and closed her eyes. Within minutes she was fast asleep.

⌣

Max placed the letter on the bedside table, kicked off his shoes, and lay back on the pillow. He had always known there was no going back. His wife would never forgive him for having exposed her brother Ben's corruption and that of his tight-knit band of fellow police officers. Never mind that Max had risked his own career by warning Ben, and giving him the opportunity to put a stop to it. When it all came crashing down, Ben and the other four had lost their jobs and pensions and were handed a seven-year jail term apiece. Never mind their stupidity and greed; it was Max his wife had blamed. Blood had proved thicker than water and infinitely more important than the vows Penny had taken. The message was unequivocal. Family before justice, and duty. Ben was family; he was not. He would never be able to forgive her for that. Nor she him.

It only added insult to injury that she had been able to move on. Word was that she was seeing someone. Her brother's defence counsel of all people, despite the lawyer's ineptitude in advising Benny to plead not guilty having added at least three years to his sentence. The only upside was that once the private detective he had hired, a former colleague from the Metropolitan Police, had furnished the evidence of her adultery, it would mean a quicker and hassle-free divorce. At least there weren't any children to worry about.

He, on the other hand, had not been able to move on. Moping around, drinking more heavily than usual, and putting on weight weren't the worst of it. His work was suffering. This new job was supposed to be his salvation. A renaissance. He was supposed to rise like a phoenix from the ashes of his career. It wasn't working out like that. He was finding it difficult to concentrate, making silly mistakes, and prone to childish outbursts of anger at the least provocation. The irony was that he had an MA in conflict resolution.

Harry had made it clear that time was running out. Max was on a final warning. This case was make or break. It didn't help that he had got off to such a bad start with the Lancashire SIO leading Operation Gannet. Worse still that they'd now pulled the plug on NCA involvement. Now he had come to terms with playing second fiddle to Joanne Stuart. It didn't seem to help that he really liked her. And she'd proved herself with both of her previous investigations, even if she had ridden roughshod over standard protocols. He smiled. It wasn't as though he was averse to cutting corners himself.

He swung his legs off the bed, went over to the minibar, and took out the remaining bottle of beer. Then he lay back down on the bed, and picked up the remote. Maybe there were a couple of films on the pay-per-view that would blot this all out. For tonight at least.

Chapter 49

WEDNESDAY, 17TH MAY

'The Boss has gone home,' said Nick. 'You just missed him.'

'He's been up all night?' said Jo. 'That's crazy.'

'I know. I managed to persuade him to let us get an area car to take him home. He wasn't fit to drive.'

'What about you?' she asked.

'I'm okay,' he replied. 'I was away not long after you. I've only been back in half an hour. Listen, the Boss wants us to manage this between us while he's not here. Is that alright with you?'

'Of course it is. You're the deputy SIO though, so there's no way I'm going to step on your shoes.'

He grinned. 'But I bow to your experience and seniority.'

She poked him with her finger.

'Give over, Nick. It was a toss-up which of us passed our Inspector's Board first.'

'I know that,' he replied. 'I've got my own Board in a fortnight's time. Don't tell anyone though. I don't want anything jinxing me.'

'You'll be fine,' she said.

He shook his head.

'Not if we don't catch this bastard soon.'

'We will,' she replied. 'We have to.' She pointed to the Policy File he was holding. 'Where are we up to?'

'The post-mortem results are in. No surprises. She died in exactly the same manner as the others. Strangled with a ligature made of human hair. A section of her own hair had been cut, and removed. This time, however, there were a few defensive injuries.'

'Where?'

'Light bruises on her arms that had not been evident at the crime scene, but no fingerprints or DNA, which suggests he was wearing gloves. They will give us some indication of the size of the perpetrator's finger pads. Only trouble is, we can't be sure that they are the perpetrator's rather than one of her clients'.'

'They will if the report says they are perimortem,' Jo pointed out.

'Also CIS found mountain bike tyre tracks at the scene. They've been photographed, and lifted.'

'We're inching closer,' Jo said.

The remark didn't seem to cheer him. 'But how many girls need to die,' he said, 'before we actually get there?'

'What about the tests on Hartley's car?' she asked.

'They've come back negative for any of the victims. There were traces of cocaine, which we assume came from prostitutes, since there were none in Hartley's house and he tested negative for drugs when he was arrested.'

'Has anyone spoken to the CPS?'

'The Boss did. They've decided that despite the fact that he didn't actually solicit anyone on the night in question, he should still be charged because he has admitted that was why he was there and that he had done so regularly in the past.'

'Do you mind if I tell him?' she said.

'Rather you than me,' he said. 'Be my guest.'

Jo swore.

It looked as though the entire press corps was camped outside the suburban semi-detached. There were two vans with satellite discs on the roof, and a fleet of cars. She counted at least three motorcycles. There were more photographers snapping the property than you see at a Premiership football match. A reporter was in the process of talking to camera.

Jo parked well back from the nearest car, and walked purposefully up the path of a house next door but one to the Hartley home. Head down, facing away from the assembled mob, she rang the doorbell. A little old lady opened the door on a chain, and peered nervously through the gap.

'Yes?'

'I'm sorry to bother you,' said Jo, shielding her warrant card with her body. 'I'm with the police. Could I come in for a second?'

There was a moment's hesitation, and then the chain was slipped and the door opened. Jo stepped nonchalantly inside.

'My name is Joanne Stuart,' she said. 'And you are?'

'Mrs McGonagle. Maggie McGonagle.'

She led the way into the lounge, then turned to face Jo, and lowered her voice as though someone might be listening in.

'Is this to do with Number 35?' she asked. Before Jo could reply she added, 'Who'd have thought it? Poor Samantha. And those poor wee children.'

'Mrs McGonagle,' said Jo, 'I know this may sound strange, but would you mind showing me your back garden?'

'My garden?'

'Please.'

'Well I never,' Mrs McGonagle muttered, shaking her head as she went back into the hall, and straight to the kitchen.

Jo leaned over the kitchen sink and looked out of the window. It was exactly as she had envisaged, given that this was a relatively new estate. The gardens were lawned and divided by low wooden fences. She stood up, and smiled.

'I need your help, Mrs McGonagle,' she said. 'I am going to go outside and climb over your fence and that of your neighbours so that I can reach the back of Number 35 without having to battle my way past the press. Would that be okay with you?'

Mrs McGonagle's eyes twinkled behind her spectacles.

'How exciting,' she said. 'Of course you can. Will you be coming back the same way?'

'I will,' said Jo.

'In that case I'll have a cup of tea and a slice of Madeira cake waiting for you. How long do you think you'll be?'

'That's very kind of you,' said Jo, 'but it really isn't necessary. I'll only be a moment.'

'Nonsense. It's no trouble.'

Before Jo could object, she pulled the bolt on the back door, turned the key in the lock, and opened the door.

'Off you go then.'

Jo turned in the doorway.

'Your neighbours. They don't have dogs by any chance, do they?'

Mrs McGonagle's eyes twinkled again. 'No, dear. But you might want to watch out for the tortoise.'

Jo negotiated the first fence without any difficulty. As she crossed in front of the patio windows of Number 33, a woman crossing through the lounge stopped in her tracks and stared at her open-mouthed. Jo held up her warrant card, smiled, put a finger to her lips, and carried on.

She raised her left leg over the fence. As it landed on the far side, she felt a tug, and heard a ripping sound. She swore for a second time that morning, and did what she should have done to start with. Look over the fence.

A young pyracantha, replete with red berries, was being trained along and up the side of the fence. Her trousers had caught on several needle-sharp thorns. She gingerly swung her right leg clear of the offending bush, and bent to free her trousers. There was a two-inch rent at the top of her calf, but at least her skin had not been penetrated.

She walked to the back door of Number 35, and knocked twice.

There was no response. She knocked again, harder this time. She heard a key turning in the lock. The door opened. An astonished Samantha Hartley stood there. Her face was free of make-up, her eyes red-rimmed.

'What the hell?' she said.

'I'm sorry, Mrs Hartley,' said Jo. 'I didn't want the press to see me, and I assumed that you would prefer they didn't see the police calling on you again.'

'It's a bit late for that,' she said, pointedly blocking the entrance with her body. 'What do you want?'

'I need to talk to your husband, Mrs Hartley.'

'Why?'

'I'd rather discuss that with him.'

'Well, you can't. He no longer lives here.'

'Where will I find him, Mrs Hartley?'

'He's staying at his brother's.'

She gave Jo the address.

'When you see him,' she said, 'you can tell him he can collect the rest of his stuff on Saturday morning. I'll be out, and so will the kids. My father will be here to make sure he doesn't try to change the locks.'

'Very well,' said Jo. 'And I want to say how sorry I am about the way in which this has impinged on your family.'

'Impinged!' she shouted. 'Impinged? It's bloody well destroyed it. No, correction. *He's* destroyed it.' She took a breath to steady herself. 'I'd like you to leave now.'

Jo turned to go and then stopped.

'Your husband is no longer a suspect in the Firethorn investigation,' she said. 'And he has done his best to help us. I thought you should know.'

Mrs Hartley stared back at her. Her face was expressionless. She closed the door, locked it, and slammed home the bolts.

Jo looked down at her flapping trouser leg and back at the pyracantha. *Sod it!* she told herself. *I've had enough of tiptoeing through the bloody tulips.* She pulled open the side gate, and stormed out to the front of the house and down the garden path.

She shouldered her way through the throng of reporters and cameramen, enjoying the contact her elbows made with the odd rib or two. Head up, shoulders straight, she stared down the camera lenses as she marched to her car. They could make of that whatever they liked. She didn't give a stuff.

Chapter 50

Hartley's brother lived twenty-five minutes away in leafy Reddish Vale. Having made the fatal decision to use the M60 ring road, it took Jo closer to forty. A tanker spillage had closed two lanes, and the hard shoulder was out of use because of the smart motorway improvement work. She had sat fuming for fifteen minutes with her air vents closed while scores of diesels in front of her, their drivers too ignorant to turn off the engine, spewed carbon monoxide into the atmosphere.

When she finally arrived at the brother's house, it was Hartley's sister-in-law who answered.

'He's in the garden room,' she said. 'I think it's best if I left you to it. Would you like a drink? I can offer you tea or coffee.'

'No, thank you,' said Jo. 'I don't expect that it's going to take long.'

The sister-in-law paused in the hallway. 'Go easy on him,' she said. 'He's in a bad way.'

'How bad?'

'Somewhere between fragile, and totally devastated.'

The sister-in-law led the way through an open-plan lounge to a pair of patio windows, beyond which a large conservatory with brick walls looked over the golf course. Jenson Hartley was slumped on a long wicker sofa, his face turned away from them, half-hidden by cushions.

'Jen,' said Hartley's sister-in-law, 'it's the police for you.'

He burrowed deeper into the cushions.

His sister-in-law gave an apologetic shrug.

'I'll be in the kitchen when you've finished,' she said.

Jo dragged a matching wicker chair closer to the sofa, and sat down.

'Mr Hartley,' she said, 'it's SI Stuart. I need a word with you.'

There was no response. 'Jenson,' she said, 'please look at me.'

Reluctantly he pushed himself into an upright position, and turned to face her.

The transformation shocked her. In less than twenty-four hours he had become a shadow of his former self. His hair was in disarray. His eyes, red-rimmed like his wife's, had dark half circles beneath them. His cheeks glistened with tears of self-pity. Mucous clogged his nostrils, and he was unshaven. The overall impression was of a haunted man who had surrendered to despair.

Jo was torn between sympathy and anger. Hartley had brought this upon himself and upon his wife and children too. He had been happy to exploit those vulnerable women, at least one of whom was now dead. And his overwhelming response was self-pity. A score of men had been caught kerb-crawling in the round-up over the ten days since Mandy Madden's body had been found. She wondered how many of them would have been reduced to this state.

'I have some news for you, Mr Hartley,' she said. 'You are no longer a person of interest in relation to the death of Genna Crowden or any of the other young women.'

There was a flicker of hope in Hartley's eyes.

'However, you do need, within the next twenty-four hours, to come back to the station where you were interviewed, where you will be formally charged under Section 51A of the Sexual Offences Act 2003 with soliciting another, in a street or public place, for the purpose of obtaining a sexual service from that person as a prostitute.'

Hartley sat there slack-jawed.

'When you have been charged,' Jo continued, 'you will then be bailed to appear at the magistrates' court, along with a number of other men charged with the same offence. You are likely to receive a fine up to a maximum of a thousand pounds, and you should know that since you were using a car at the time of the alleged offences the magistrates' court would have the discretion to disqualify you from driving.'

That jolted him into action. To Jo's surprise, Hartley fell forward on to his knees, and grasped the arms of her chair with his hands. His eyes were wild, his voice full of desperation. She tried to scoot the chair across the floor away from him.

'No!' Hartley pleaded. 'You can't do that!' he shouted. 'If I can't drive, I'll lose my job.'

Jo managed to wrestle herself free, and stood up. Hartley sank back on to his heels, and stared up at her.

'Please,' Hartley said, 'I've already lost my marriage. My children hate me. Now I'm going to lose my job and my reputation. Without those she'll never take me back.'

Hartley's sister-in-law appeared in the doorway.

'I warned you to go easy on him,' she said, hurrying to his side, and crouching down beside him.

'I'm sorry to have been the bearer of bad news,' said Jo, 'but it's not something I can avoid. It comes with the job.'

'Then I'm glad I'm not you,' replied the sister-in-law.

'I'm afraid that your brother-in-law has to report to the North Division Headquarters police station at Central Park by the end of the day,' Jo told her. 'Otherwise he'll be arrested again. I'll let myself out.'

She stepped into the lounge, remembered something, and turned back.

'Oh and by the way, Mr Hartley. Your wife asked me to tell you that you can collect the rest of your things on Saturday. She will not be there, but her father will.'

As Jo turned to leave, the sister-in-law's parting words rang in her ears.

'Put the knife in why don't you?'

Chapter 51

Thursday, 18th May

2.18am

Jacinta shivered. It wasn't the cold. It was one of the telltale signs that she was in withdrawal. Her runny nose was another. She wiped it with a tissue and threw the tissue into the gutter. Another couple of hours and the sweats would start. Come dawn there would be muscle spasms, and nausea, her heart beating like a subwoofer on speed.

She hadn't wanted to go out again. Not with that monster roaming the streets. Killing at will. Kenny said she had no choice. A score for a score. That was the deal.

Kenny Kebab. His mates had started calling him that as a joke on account of his favourite hangover cure. He'd quickly taken to the nickname when he found out that an infamous New York gangster had been known as Johnny Sausage.

Kenny Kebab. A big fish in a small pool. Her pimp, landlord, and dealer rolled into one. If she didn't have enough money by morning to both pay him and score, she didn't know what she was going to do. Her body still ached from the last time. He was clever was Kenny. He always made sure the bruises never showed where it mattered.

Jacinta was bright too. Bright enough to know she was trapped between three hells: the punter, the pimp, and the smack. Dumb enough to see no way out. The only way was forward, one of the other girls had told her. Place one foot in front of the other, and keep going till you either find an exit, or fall over the edge of a cliff. The way things were going, all she could see ahead was the cliff. Some nights, like this one, she'd have welcomed it. A sudden drop and then oblivion. But that was what the skag was for. Except with heroin you woke and had to start all over again.

It was Kenny that insisted they drive out here. There were now too many coppers round the red-light district, he said. She couldn't disagree with that.

'There's a big one going down tonight,' he'd said. 'One that'll set me up for a couple of months. I'll come back for you in the morning. If you need me before then, text me.'

Then he'd driven off, and left her standing there. At least it was an area she knew, having grown up just a mile or so away. She was past caring someone might recognise her. More worried that there was nobody to watch her back. But her overriding concern was, would there be any punters? She had to make a minimum of fifty quid to keep Kenny sweet and the same again for the skag. At twenty quid to give head, forty for full sex, and fifty for both, that meant a minimum of four punters, and more likely six or seven to make it worth her while.

To her surprise there had been three in quick succession. Two, like her, had shunned the red-light district and were driving round on the off-chance of finding a tom. One had been an opportunist, who had spotted her as he was walking home from the pub, and fancied a quickie down by the side of the railway embankment. Nothing since then. She'd been here for over three hours now, and was still thirty quid light. The trouble was the best of the night was over. Only the sad, the desperate, and the sickos trawled streets like these after 2am. Still, one good punter and she'd be sorted. Then she'd text Kenny to come and get her.

That was all it would take.

Just one good punter.

⌣

Tonight he felt good. The last one had not gone entirely to plan. He had been forced to expose himself in ways he had not anticipated. No matter. They would assume he was a creature of habit. In which case they would be following both the form and pattern he had given them so far. They would be looking for the man in the CCTV images. The man on the mountain bike with a hi-vis vest. What they would not be expecting was that, like the chameleon his father had bought him for his tenth birthday, he had changed his appearance, and modified his modus operandi.

He whispered it softly. Let it roll off his tongue.

'Modus operandi.'

The initials were bland, and understated. Like BO for body odour, or KO for knockout. Modus operandi had a grandeur that reflected the seriousness, the professionalism, the preparation, the thought, and the effort that went into the hunt. And the skill that lay behind every kill.

He had another reason to feel pleased. The rest of the press had adopted the name that the reporter Anthony Ginley had given him: the Backstreet Barber.

Every serial killer had a special name. One that struck fear into those of a nervous disposition. It spoke of power. It showed respect. Like some of those he most admired: the Grim Sleeper; the Yorkshire Ripper; the Night Stalker; the Suffolk Strangler. And now he had his own. The Backstreet Barber.

He smiled to himself. There was a special irony about their choice of name. They were oh so close and yet nowhere near close enough.

From his hiding place on the tarmac path beside the bushes opposite the pedestrian entrance to the brewery, he spotted her coming towards him down Joshua Lane. His pulse began to race. He felt for the locket around his neck. This was how his mother must have been, returning home in the early hours. Happy. Confident. Unquestionably less sober. Blissfully unaware of her son's sweat-soaked sleepless nights. Desperate for the sound of the key in the lock. The footsteps on the stair. He let go of the locket, patted his pocket, and tightened the straps of his backpack. The gap narrowed.

'*Turn left,*' *he whispered.* '*Turn left.*'

Jacinta paused at the junction with Green Lane. Decision time. Go straight on, which meant sticking to the main road, or turn left, and repeat the circuit where she'd picked up her first, and most profitable, punter. If she had a coin, she'd toss it. Fate decided for her. Beyond the traffic lights she caught a flash of blue and yellow as a police patrol car approached. She turned left down Green Lane, and prayed she had not been seen.

Chapter 52

'We need to stop meeting like this.'

'That's not funny, Max,' said Jo.

He shrugged, and slammed the boot of his car shut.

'I never said it was.'

Jo picked up her shoes, placed them in the boot of the Audi, and closed it. The two of them walked side by side towards the tape marking the start of the common approach path.

'You realise this is number six?' she said.

'Looks like he was going for the record,' Max replied.

'Meaning?'

'The Ipswich serial killer? Also known as the Suffolk Strangler. Five prostitutes in just over a month. Our guy's killed six in just three months, four of them in the past seventeen days.'

'You think he's a copycat?'

'There are three points of similarity,' he said. 'They were all prostitutes, there is no evidence that any of the victims had been sexually assaulted, and death was by asphyxiation. Not identical I grant you, but similar.'

'If I remember rightly,' said Jo, 'the Suffolk victims were all found naked, and some of them were displayed with their arms out in cruciform pattern – I don't remember anything about him having taken trophies. And then there's the hair fetish. There was certainly none of that in Ipswich.'

They halted at the end of the row of red-brick terraced houses to show the crime scene loggist their IDs. They then began to follow the blue-and-white tape down the metalled path that ran between the side of the end house and farm field. Two CSIs were already searching a line of blue, brown, green, and black recycling wheelie bins beside the field fence.

'It's only two days since Genna Crowden was found,' Max observed. 'There was just over a week between her and Flora Novak, and before that seven days between Novak and Mandy Madden. I've heard of escalation, but this is ridiculous.'

'It's not ridiculous,' Jo said. 'It's horrific, and it's frightening.'

All the more so, she reflected, on a day like this. The early-morning sun shone brightly in a cloudless sky, drying the dew, leaving behind an earthy fragrance. Swifts swooped and darted low across the fields, oblivious to the tragedy unfolding beneath them.

The path ended after less than thirty yards. Now they were following a narrow grassy track that led on to undulating open land consisting of rough grass and heather. The tape took them left, where it ran beside an even narrower grassy track, uphill at first, and then down for a hundred yards between two small hillocks to a sandy track that led to a six-foot-long bridge made of stone slabs laid over a narrow gully over the dried bed of a stream. A tent had already been erected ten yards down the gully on the far side. Gordon emerged from the tent, and waved them over.

'Better late than never,' Gordon said grimly as he pushed the hood of his Tyvek coverall clear of his forehead.

'Is it him?' asked Jo.

He rubbed his chin with the back of a gloved hand.

'If it isn't, it's a bloody good copycat.'

The two NCA investigators exchanged a glance.

'Who's the pathologist?' asked Max.

'Professor Flatman's on his way. Apparently he's staying in Manchester for a conference at the university. Said to expect him about an hour from now. We'll have to wait on him for approximate time of death. But the paramedic reckoned she'd been dead at least four hours.'

'Who found the body?' asked Jo.

'Couple of thirteen-year-old lads on their off-road dirt bikes. Hoping for a practice before school. Got the shock of their lives.'

'What time was this?'

'Half seven. Paramedic arrived fifteen minutes later. I wasn't called out till eight thirty. Her bag wasn't near the body, unlike the other victims, so we don't yet have a name. I've told the search team finding it is a priority.'

Gordon stared at the tent.

'You'd better come and have a look before Flatman gets here,' he said. 'When he does, there won't be room to swing a cat.'

He lifted the flap, ducked his head, and entered first. Jo followed him; Max brought up the rear.

She lay on her right side with her back towards them. Her right arm and leg lay on the upper bank. Her left leg, drawn up at right angles, and her outstretched left arm clung perilously to the side of the gully. She was fully clothed, but her blue denim skirt had ridden up and exposed the strap of a scarlet thong. Her hair, dyed a dramatic emerald green, was cropped short, exposing telltale purple bruising around the neck.

'What is this?' asked Jo, breaking the brooding silence. 'A hundred and fifty yards from the road? A quarter of a mile from Middleton Junction? If the paramedic is right, she must have been killed sometime between 2 and 4am. Why would she come here with a punter in the dark? That's assuming this was where she was killed.'

'Evidence suggests it was,' said Gordon. 'You see where those markers are? There are two pairs of footprints in the sandy soil. The smallest in front of the other pair. Those smaller prints are badly scuffed, suggesting she was struggling, her feet scrabbling to get a purchase, whereas his are firmly rooted, presumably as he braced himself.' He pointed to the side of the top of the bank, close to where they stood. 'And here, from the flattened grass, you can see where she was lowered to the ground and then dragged away from the path before being left as you see her now.'

'So my question stands,' said Jo. 'Why would she agree to come down here?'

'Because this isn't her usual patch, and he says he knows the perfect spot to do the business?' Max suggested.

'I don't buy it,' said Jo. 'We passed plenty of safer spots than this between the bridge and here.'

He shrugged.

'What if he was prepared to pay enough to make it worth her while?'

'Or he used force,' said Gordon.

He bent close to the woman's head, and pointed with his index finger. 'There's dried blood behind her left ear. Looks like it must have come from this nick. The kind of thing the point of a knife might make.'

'Or a pair of scissors?' said Jo.

Gordon nodded. 'Or a pair of scissors.'

Jo bent closer. The injury was barely three millimetres wide and a couple of millimetres deep. She visualised the unsub with his right arm wrapped around her chest, his left hand holding a pair of scissors against her neck. The poor girl, knowing this was unlikely to end well, dragging her feet to try to slow him down. Pleading with him not to hurt her. Stumbling on the rough ground, causing the point to pierce her skin. First the pain and then the trickle of blood warm on her neck.

Lower down were the familiar concentric circles where the garrotte had been applied. The bruising was thicker and the indentation deeper slightly left of centre of the nape of the neck. She pointed to it.

'This looks as though it was the point where the two hands met as the garrotte was tightened,' Jo said. 'That suggests someone who is right-handed. But if that was the case, I'd expect the scissors or knife or whatever the weapon was he used to have been held to the right side of her neck.'

There was silence while the three of them pondered the anomaly.

'There's no sign of the garrotte,' said Gordon. 'We won't know till Flatman's performed the PM, but it looks identical to all the others. Who'd have thought that human hair could be used like that?'

'It's not as strong as steel,' said Max, 'but it's not far off. Did you know that a head of hair like yours, Jo, would support the weight of two elephants?'

'It's not something I've ever contemplated. How come you know this?'

'Circus performers do it all the time,' he said. 'Besides, we had a case in the Met about ten years ago where a woman was found hanging by her hair from the banisters in her own house. One of the neighbours alerted us when she heard the screams. It was one of her husband's little ways of letting her know who was boss.'

Jo shook her head.

'Bloody men!' she said. 'Present company excepted.'

'We'd better move away and let CSI get on with their work before Professor Flatman tramples all over it,' said Gordon.

He lifted the flap of the tent, and led the way.

Chapter 53

They reassembled by the bridge. Gordon pushed his hood back, and rubbed his chin with the back of his hand.

'This is worse than a recurring nightmare,' he said. 'Gates is threatening to ask the Association of Chief Police Officers to find someone from another force to take over the investigation. Though God knows what they're going to do any different. I've already got three syndicates working on it.'

'No surprise she doesn't want to do it herself,' Max observed.

'When's the Sumac deputy SIO coming up to Manchester?' asked Jo.

'God, I'd forgotten about her,' said Gordon, looking at his watch. 'She'll be arriving at Piccadilly station in half an hour. I'll get Nick to pick her up and babysit her till we're ready for her. He can fill her in on where we're up to – at least that'll save time.'

'There's no point in Max and me hanging around waiting for Mr Flatman,' said Jo. 'Why don't we scout the area and see if we can work out how she got here? That way we'll know which CCTV to harvest. Then we'll head back to the MIR, and meet you there.'

'Fair enough. There'll be a full briefing at eleven thirty. I'd appreciate it if all your team could be there.'

'Of course.'

'By the way,' he said, 'an area car reckons they might have seen her round about 2am turning off Joshua Lane into Green Lane. They assumed she was a tom but didn't see any point in having a word. After all, she wasn't actually breaking the law.'

'That time of night they were probably heading for a coffee break or a power nap,' said Max.

'Either way I bet they're regretting it now,' said Jo.

As they emerged from behind the row of terraced houses, Jo and Max were confronted by a mass of reporters and photographers. Their cars were parked on both sides of the road for as far as the eye could see. Three uniformed officers were gamely trying to hold them back.

'Don't say anything,' said Jo. 'Not even a "No Comment".'

'Don't worry,' he told her, 'I wasn't going to. What I am tempted to say would get me sacked.'

They had to suffer the indignity of being photographed taking off their coveralls, bagging them, and dropping them into the receptacle provided. Then, heads down, they shouldered their way through the crowd, jostled at every turn, ignoring the camera flashes, the microphones shoved in their faces, and the insistent questioning. When they were finally clear and walking towards their cars, a voice called out. One that Jo recognised. She turned.

Agata Kowalski was following them. Jo touched Max's arm.

'You go on,' she said. 'I'll join you in a minute. I need to see what she wants.'

The reporter advanced, grim-faced. 'I'm sorry,' she said to Jo. 'This was the last thing you needed.'

'That any of us needed,' said Jo. 'Except that lot behind you. It seems to have made their day.'

'Look,' said Agata, 'I'm not after any information. I want to offer you some help.'

In Jo's experience, when a reporter offered to help you there was always a catch. 'In return for what?'

'Nothing.'

'Nothing? Not even a promise to give you an exclusive?'

Agata smiled. 'That would be nice. But no, I'm not asking for anything.'

Jo sighed. 'I'm grateful for the way you persuaded those girls to talk to us about DS Henshall,' she said. 'I'm just not sure how else you can help. But I am open to offers.'

'The only reason he's able to keep murdering these girls, Jo, is because, despite everything, they are still out there on the streets. Putting themselves in harm's way.'

'That's because their need is greater than their fear. Not having food to put in their children's mouths, not being able to pay the loan sharks, being slashed or beaten by their pimps, or going cold turkey because they can't afford a fix – those are real and present dangers. Certainties if you like. By comparison, the odds of falling victim to this killer must seem remote.'

'Tell that to your latest victim,' said Agata.

Jo couldn't argue with that. 'What do you propose?'

'There is one person who could prove far more persuasive in getting these girls off the streets of Greater Manchester, albeit for a short while, than all these leaflets your officers have been giving out. At least it would give you and your colleagues a breathing space while you hunt him down.'

'And this person is?'

'Her name is Selma Strangelove. She's the Convener of the North West Association of Prostitutes. And there's another reason you might want to have her on your side.'

'Go on.'

'She's on the warpath. She believes the only reason these girls are so vulnerable is because successive governments and local politicians are not prepared to face the reality that this is the oldest profession in the world and it's not going to go away. She's about to lobby the media with her view, and those of the national body, that there are simple solutions out there and it's the failure to implement them which is allowing this man to murder at will.'

Jo could see it now. It was bad enough having to defend their failure to catch the unsub without having also to deal with the fallout from a national campaign to liberalise prostitution focusing all the attention on Firethorn. It would up the ante for everyone. Helen Gates, the Chief Constable, the Mayor of Greater Manchester, and the Leader of the City Council. Even her own bosses at the NCA would rapidly lose patience with them if they hadn't already after this morning's discovery.

'Can you arrange a meeting with her?' Jo said.

'Today.'

'Very well,' Jo said. 'Do it.'

Chapter 54

'Do you want me to tag along?' said Max.

'I'm not sure that's a good idea,' she replied. 'Are you?'

He looked relieved.

'No, you're probably right.'

'Why don't we leave the cars here and walk up to the junction?' she suggested. 'That way we'll be able to talk as we go, and get a better feel for it.'

'Why do you think she offered to do this, Jo,' he said, 'if there's nothing in it for her?'

'I don't know. Doing her civic duty I suppose. Or in the hope that we'll credit her for it. That would certainly help her to sell her story. Isn't that what all investigative journalists get out of helping the police?'

'Or could it be that she happens to fancy you?'

Jo laughed it off, but secretly she had been wondering the very same thing. If it wasn't for all the unfinished business with Abbie, she might even have been hoping that it was so.

She pushed the thought to the back of her mind when an elderly man, in his late eighties or early nineties even, with a Jack Russell straining at its lead stopped in the centre of the pavement, leaving them no choice but to do the same.

'You're police, right?' the man said.

'What makes you think that?' Max replied.

Silly question, Jo thought. *No cameras, no mic. Observant faces*, and *an air of authority. Who else would we be?*

'That's right,' she said to the elderly man. 'Do you have some information for us?'

He grinned. 'Funny you should ask.'

The dog lunged forward to nibble the toe of Jo's right shoe. 'Rufus! Get back!' the man shouted, tugging the dog's lead, and reeling it in.

'We haven't got all day,' said Max. 'Do you have some information, or don't you?'

Jo was surprised. It wasn't Max's usual approach. She hoped he wasn't reverting to his time with the Flying Squad.

'Don't mind my friend,' she said. 'Mr . . . ?'

'Roberts, Alf Roberts.'

'Well, Mr Roberts, we'd be grateful for whatever information you can give us, however small.'

'That's more like it,' he said. 'A bit of local knowledge never goes amiss, does it?'

'You live around here?' she asked, determined to keep him on side.

'That's right. I got a little cottage on Springs Road.' Mr Roberts pointed behind him towards the junction. 'Hundred and fifty yards that way. Lived there all my life, man and boy.'

'Local indeed,' she said. 'And this information, Mr Roberts?'

'That woman's body they found this morning,' he said. 'In the gully, was it?'

'How do you know about that?' said Max.

The old man gave him a withering look. 'Not much of a detective, are you? Everyone round here knows. Stands to reason those lads were going to go straight home and tell their mums, doesn't it? And their mums are not going to keep something like that quiet, are they?' He chuckled. 'Checked your Twitter feed lately?'

'Please, Mr Roberts,' said Jo. 'What was it you wanted to tell us?'

'That whole area where she was found used to be known as Drummer Hill. It's rough farmland, right? And up till a quarter of a century ago so was that estate up on the hill behind it. But afore that in the 1920s it was the Laurel and Baytree Mills, and afore that a coal mine.'

'What's that got to do—?' Max began to say.

Jo cut him short. 'Go on, Mr Roberts.'

'Well, when I was a lad we were told to stay away from Drummer Hill because it was haunted.'

Max sighed impatiently.

'By whom?' Jo asked.

'Story is there was a coal-pit mining disaster, and among the dead were pit ponies, who were buried alive, and never recovered. Sometimes if you woke up in the night you could hear the beating of their hooves.' He looked up at Max. 'You may scoff. But I heard them myself.'

'That's very interesting, Mr Roberts,' said Jo. 'What makes you think it has any relevance to the body those boys found this morning?'

'Ah well,' he said, 'the point is, apart from the farmer, kids on their bikes, and a few people who walk their dogs, not many people go up there. An' I certainly never heard of anyone going there at night. Superstition is a powerful thing once the sun's gone down.'

'Your point being?' said Max.

The old man ignored him, and spoke directly to Jo. 'That place is hidden from the road by all those trees along here. I don't reckon you'd know it existed unless you were a local. An' if you were a local you might think it an ideal place to do a murder. Somewhere you weren't likely to be disturbed.'

Jo thanked Roberts, and let him go on his way. They watched him struggling to walk, holding on to the fence with one hand, and the dog lead with the other.

'That dog's going to kill him one of these days,' said Max. 'He'll either trip over the lead, or get dragged under a car.'

'What do you think?' Jo asked as they continued towards Middleton Junction. 'About what he said?'

Max shook his head.

'If this was the only murder, I'd give it some credence, but what he said about local knowledge could equally be said about all of the other murders too. Especially the first two in Wigan and Leigh. The unsub can't have been local to all those places.'

'There's another difference this time,' Jo said. 'All of the other crime scenes have been within spitting distance of a well-known red-light district. But this one wasn't. It's unlikely she was followed here. There's no evidence of a car having been used. And it's unlikely the unsub just happened to be hanging around here on the off-chance.'

Max didn't seem convinced. 'I can think of several flaws with that. Not least of which is if this isn't a red-light district, what was she doing here?'

'Assuming she is a prostitute.'

'Come on,' he said. 'You saw her hair, and the short skirt. And the boots.'

'Don't judge a book by its cover.'

'Why not? It's always worked for me. This place, for example.' He nodded towards the public house just ahead of them. 'Look at the pub sign. The Railway & Linnet. What does that tell you?'

'Search me. It's near a railway and it served the navvies that built the railway and the passengers that travelled on it?'

'What about the Linnet?'

'I don't know. Maybe the original landlord kept a bird in a cage on the bar.'

'Nice try,' Max said. 'Actually linnets love the kind of habitat you find along railway embankments. For feeding, and nesting. So that's what you have here. A railway, and linnets. Exactly what's on the cover.'

'I never took you for a twitcher.'

'I used to be as a kid.' He grinned. 'I grew out of it when a different species of birds caught my fancy. But you know how it is with childhood obsessions. You never really forget them.'

Jo did. She wondered if that was how it had been with the killer. Was his fetish connected in some way with his mother or a sister perhaps? With a dramatic or traumatic childhood experience? She sighed. They would have to catch him to find out for sure.

Chapter 55

'This is Detective Superintendent Hazel Truckett. Suffolk Constabulary.'

While Gordon introduced each of them in turn, Jo studied the woman standing to his left. She was a head taller than him and dressed in a trouser suit and white blouse. The entire ensemble looked custom-tailored. She had the bright eyes and natural air of authority that accompanied unstoppable ambition.

They took their places at the table.

'Superintendent Truckett is in the middle of a serious investigation,' said Gordon. 'She has to catch the 4.50pm train from Piccadilly. We have agreed that the best use of her time and expertise is for her to listen to where we're up to, and comment as appropriate. Nick has already briefed her, and she's had a look at both the murder book and the policy book, so we're going to crack on with this morning's developments.'

He turned to address her. 'Is there anything you'd like to say first, Superintendent?'

She smiled warmly. 'Only to remind you that when Operation Sumac began, I, like Gordon here, was a newly promoted detective chief inspector. The only difference is that I was the deputy senior investigating officer. My boss, the SIO, was a chief superintendent. He's retired now, which is why they sent me. When the bodies began to pile up, they also drafted in a commander from the London Met as an adviser. Frankly I'm surprised that you haven't done something like that here.'

'Yet,' muttered Gordon.

'I'd take it as a compliment if I were you,' she said. 'From what I've seen so far, I'm not sure we, or anyone else, would have done anything different in terms of the way in which you're currently running Operation Firethorn. Frankly you have a much more challenging situation than the one that faced us.'

'How so?' said Gordon.

'Well, whilst Sumac, like Firethorn, was an A+ linked-series homicide, ours was pretty much contained. Although the deposition sites were spread out, the victims were all working in or close to the same small red-light district when they were abducted and killed. We were pretty sure from the outset that our man was local and almost certainly someone who used the services of prostitutes. In the case of Firethorn the perpetrator is moving around to different red-light districts, and his modus operandi is far more resonant of a stranger serial predator. But I don't want to get into that until I've heard about today's discovery.'

An imperious rap on the door interrupted Gordon's response. The door opened. Assistant Chief Constable Helen Gates walked in.

'Apologies,' she said. 'The Mayor of Greater Manchester demanded an update on Firethorn.'

She pulled out a chair next to Gordon, and sat down.

Gordon introduced her to Hazel Truckett.

'We learned a lot from the review of your Sumac operation,' Gates told her. 'Aside from catching the killer, our overarching strategy is focused on preventing further murders of street sex workers within Greater Manchester, providing appropriate and sufficient resources to support the investigation, and maintaining the confidence and trust of our partners and the wider community. The day-to-day investigation is, as I'm sure you've been told, down to DCI Holmes.'

'Yes, Ma'am,' said the Suffolk superintendent, whom Jo could see had already made a swift assessment of the new arrival.

'Good,' said Gates. 'So where are you up to, DCI Holmes?'

'All three syndicates are working flat out, Ma'am,' he told her. 'Deskbound and front-line officers and staff are on a three-shift pattern so we have 24/7 coverage. We're handling over three hundred calls a day from the public, and averaging one hundred and ninety face-to-face follow-up interviews. Over one thousand five hundred vehicles caught on CCTV in and around the various crime scenes have been traced and eliminated. Likewise thirteen male cyclists broadly matching the description of the man recorded following victim number five, Genna Crowden. Two hundred voluntary DNA samples have been taken. There are seventeen males due at the magistrates' court later this week on charges under 51A of the Sexual Offences Act 2003. The forensics tests are ongoing.'

'That's impressive,' said DS Truckett.

Helen Gates looked far from impressed. 'Unfortunately,' she said, 'since we don't have a single suspect, it counts for nothing. Tell me about victim number six.'

Gordon nodded to Nick, who swiped his tablet and brought up an image on the whiteboard at the end of the table. It was a colour photo of the latest victim in situ, taken before the tent had been erected. The emerald hair struck a discordant note and gave the impression of a discarded clothes shop mannequin. Despite the fact that Jo had stood right beside the body, this image still brought a lump to her throat. Gordon gave them time to digest what they were seeing.

'Victim number six,' he said. 'We have a name. Jacinta Quinn. Her handbag was found close to the path, halfway to the road.'

Another image appeared. Jo wondered how she, Max, and everyone else who had trod that path could have missed it.

'She was twenty-nine years old. Older than the other victims. She is believed to be of MI ethnicity – mixed white and Afro-Caribbean.

According to the Neighbourhood Policing Team, she lived in a six-bed house of multiple occupancy on Rochdale Road. The landlord, Kenneth Albert, aka Kenny Kebab' – he looked up – 'don't ask . . . is alleged to be her pimp, and is a known drug dealer with two previous. He's nowhere to be found, but we're proactively looking for him.'

He nodded again, and a third image appeared. It showed a BMW 3 Series black saloon with tinted windows.

'This is his car, and this is her getting out of it. As you can see, the time is 11.48pm yesterday evening.'

The image began to move. The car door opened. Jacinta Quinn alighted from the front passenger side, and closed the door. They watched in silence as the car performed a tight U-turn and sped off towards Middleton. She looked around for a moment, as though getting her bearings, and then set off in the opposite direction.

'How did you get this so quickly?' Gates asked.

'As soon as I heard the body had been found, I got my digital media officers to start harvesting the data from the static council-managed cameras, focusing on the main roads around Middleton Junction.'

'If we'd had access to as many cameras eleven years ago as there are now, we could have saved some of those women,' commented DS Truckett.

'Doesn't appear to be working for us,' said Gates. 'Where was this taken?'

'On Lees Street, close to the brewery. We know she entered the Brookside Business Park. There are lots of modern units: industrial equipment supplies, a print works, a fire and safety firm, and refrigeration business, for example. There's a security barrier manned in daylight hours, and operated remotely thereafter. The park is bristling with private CCTV cameras. I have officers collecting footage as we speak. We are still tracking her progress, but we do have some evidence that she then tried a triangular route comprising of Lees Street, Green Lane and Grimshaw Lane.' He nodded again. 'Nick?'

Nick brought up another piece of video footage. It showed Jacinta Quinn walking into shot as a dark 4x4 appeared on the same side of the road and came to a halt just ahead of her. They watched as she bent to speak to someone through the front passenger window. After a brief exchange she opened the door and got in. The car set off slowly, then after thirty yards turned left, and out of sight.

'This is timed at ten past midnight,' said Gordon. 'We have the licence plate, and the name of the registered owner and keeper. It hasn't been reported stolen, so we should have him in here for questioning any time now.' He rubbed his chin nervously. 'But don't get excited.'

Without being asked, Nick replaced the image with another video.

'This is him dropping her off in the same place he picked her up. Timed at just gone half past twelve. I think we can all guess how they filled the intervening twenty minutes.'

Helen Gates scowled. Nobody else responded.

Couldn't resist it, could you, Gordon? Jo thought.

He looked around the room.

'That's all we've got for now, but more and more footage will have come in while we've been sitting here.'

'Let's hope for all our sakes you get lucky this time,' said Helen Gates.

How about for the sake of the next potential victim, and *the one after that?* Jo reflected.

'What did the pathologist have to say?' the ACC continued.

'Professor Flatman is of the opinion that this victim was killed in an identical manner to all of the others. He tentatively puts the time of death at between 2am and 3.30am this morning. He's reasonably confident about that because there had been a relatively small change in ambient temperature overnight and up till the time the body was discovered.'

'It is definitely the same killer then.'

' "Definite" isn't a word I'd use lightly, Ma'am,' said Gordon, just managing to avoid it sounding like a rebuke. 'But apart from the manner in which she was killed, there was a section of hair cut from her head, and a foreign clump of hair placed in her mouth. So the same modus operandi, if not the same killer.'

'Clump?'

'I used that term because it was impossible to tell without removing it if it was a knotted or tangled lock of hair, as in all of the previous cases. Come the post-mortem results, I will be better placed to describe it accurately.'

That did sound like a rebuke. He was saved by a knock on the door. Helen Gates tutted. Jo pushed back her chair and went to investigate. It was Duggie Wallace, the senior intelligence analyst. His eyes were wide, and shone with excitement.

Chapter 56

'Tell DCI Holmes that I've just uploaded to the whiteboard some footage from a camera on the side of the brewery at Middleton Junction,' Wallace whispered. 'I think he'll want to see it right now.'

'Thanks, Duggie,' said Jo.

She returned to her seat and told them what the analyst had said. An air of expectancy filled the room.

'Right, Nick, let's have it,' said Gordon.

It took a moment for Nick to locate the file. When he did, it showed a jogger emerging from a path between bushes on the opposite side of the road to the camera. He wore a dark hooded anorak, tight black leggings, black training shoes, and a small, dark runner's backpack.

Jo recognised the spot from their walk around the area.

'This is from the side of the brewery at the junction of Grimshaw Lane and Lees Road,' she informed them.

The man jogged to the junction, noticed he had a lace undone, bent to tie it, and then walked across the road before jogging off down Grimshaw Lane.

'Look at the time,' said Jo, pointing to the bottom of the screen. 'It's 2.17am.'

The import was not lost on them. Max leaned closer.

'If we get another gait analysis on this one and compare it with the one of the cyclist in the Genna Crowden murder, then we'll know if it's the same person,' said Jo. 'And a biometric analysis should give us his height and weight, and establish whether there is a match with the footprint recovered from the Middleton crime scene. We should also be checking with street sex workers, including going over existing statements, for any sightings of both cyclists and joggers.'

'Mr Swift,' said Helen Gates, 'I would like an opinion on what the killer's behaviour, assuming this is him, is now telling us.'

Jo was just as keen to hear what he had to say.

Andy looked up. 'The first thing that this is telling us,' he said, 'is that if there was any doubt – and there wasn't in my mind – that this multiple-series homicide is the work of a serial killer, then that doubt has been completely dispelled. Secondly, his compulsion to kill is escalating. Thirdly, whilst he is a meticulous planner he is also something of an opportunist.'

'What leads you to that conclusion?' asked Gates.

'The fact that the last two victims had moved out of the recognised red-light districts, and yet he was still comfortable in following the first to, and finding the second in, places outside the neighbourhood he had presumably reconnoitred.'

'Reconnoitred? You make it sound like a military exercise.'

'In his mind it is. We are the enemy. His victim is both the target, and collateral damage. A better metaphor would be a hunting expedition. He is the poacher, we are gamekeepers.'

Andy let them digest that and then continued with his original list. 'Fourthly, the fact that he is modifying and adapting his behaviour to avoid detection suggests he is both of above-average intelligence and intent upon continuing to kill. He will strike again, and soon. Ironically that is your best hope of catching him. However, if he isn't apprehended soon, he may go to ground. Adapt again. And re-emerge at a later date, and in another place.'

'Is that likely?' asked DS Truckett. 'It certainly wasn't the case with our perpetrator.'

'It is unusual but not unknown,' Andy told her. 'There have been cases, in the States for example, where an escalating serial killer has suddenly gone to ground and either re-emerged sometime later or never been heard of again. Which doesn't mean, incidentally, that he stopped killing. Only that he had become more cautious and sophisticated in doing so.'

'None of which takes us any further forward,' said Gates.

Andy was not the slightest bit offended. It probably helped that he was an academic. Plus the fact that Gates was not his boss.

'I am aware of that,' Andy replied. 'I do, however, have a few suggestions.'

'We're all ears,' Gates responded.

He smiled benignly. 'Firstly, I think that you should be concentrating on the fact that if, as we now suspect, he is moving around his hunting grounds either by bicycle or on foot, it implies that he must have good local knowledge, and spend some time scoping the immediate vicinity. But since the crime scenes are spread along two lines, one fourteen miles to the west of Manchester city centre, and the other nine miles north-east of the city, he must have another means of getting to each new kill zone. Find that means of transport, and you will be able to concentrate your search more effectively.'

'We've been tracing every car, van, and lorry that was caught on cameras at the relevant times within three miles of the crime scenes,' said Gordon Holmes with an air of exasperation. 'I don't see what more we can do.'

'And secondly,' Andy continued as though he hadn't been interrupted, 'as has been noted before, the lack of defence injuries on any of the victims implies someone who has gained their confidence. Someone charming, reassuring, whose presence neither surprised nor concerned them. There will be other street sex workers whom he has approached or who have seen him. SI Stuart is correct. It is vital that DCI Holmes's officers talk to as many of the girls as possible about joggers and cyclists and anyone who might fit the profile I drew up, however sketchy it may have been.'

'Agreed,' said Gates. 'And while we're about it, apart from the leaflets we discussed last time, what are we doing about reassuring the sex workers, and persuading them to stay off the streets?'

Jo seized the opportunity. 'I have just been offered a meeting with the Convener of the North West Association of Prostitutes, Ma'am. She is apparently our best hope of achieving that. At least until we have apprehended the unsub.'

'Sounds like a good move,' said DS Truckett. 'That was something we were slow to do.'

'Better get on with it then,' said Helen Gates.

'Unfortunately there is a quid pro quo,' said Jo.

The ACC's eyebrows arched. 'Go on.'

'She is not prepared to go ahead until a meeting has been arranged for her and a representative of the national association with the Chief Constable and the Mayor for Greater Manchester to consider the setting up of a safe zone like the one being trialled in Leeds.'

All eyes turned to Helen Gates.

The colour drained from her face. She clenched her hands. Jo imagined the long, perfectly manicured nails biting into flesh. She inhaled, and exhaled. Inhaled again. 'That kite has already been flown,' she said through gritted teeth. 'Several months ago, before all this started. The answer was no then, and I have no doubt it will be no now. Besides, it's only three weeks since the mayoral elections were held. I imagine that the last thing he'll want to get embroiled in is a political and moral hot potato like this one.'

The look on her face was enough to dissuade anyone from challenging her. To Jo's surprise, it was Andy who put his head above the parapet. 'With respect, Ma'am,' he said, 'that was then and this is now. And I have no doubt that the Mayor will already be taking a singular interest in the fact that a serial killer is wreaking havoc in his fiefdom. If the promise of a meeting is all that is required for this person to assist the investigation, what harm can it do? It is not as though you will be promising the outcome she seeks.'

Helen Gates's face remained impassive. After what felt like an eternity, she gathered up her papers, and pushed back her chair.

'Leave it with me,' she said.

'Excuse me, Ma'am,' said Jo. 'Just a thought, but the UAV we used on Operation Juniper. The SkyRanger drone that GMP were trialling. Is it still available?'

Gates frowned. 'Sadly not,' she said. 'I don't need to tell you that the trial was a complete success. The Chief Constable pencilled two into this year's budget. The previous Police and Crime Commissioner rubbed them out. He said we already had access to a helicopter, and a fixed-wing aircraft through the North West Air Operations Group. In the light of continuing cuts he couldn't justify the cost of the two staff needed for each of the drones. Not when they wouldn't be operational 24/7.'

'Merseyside Police have one,' Jo replied. 'Perhaps you could borrow it.'

'Had one,' said Gordon unhelpfully. 'I enquired. They lost it in the River Mersey a few years ago. Haven't replaced it yet.'

'I believe the Greater Manchester Fire Service possess two,' she persisted. 'Perhaps they might lend us one through the Blue Light Collaboration Programme.'

The Assistant Chief Constable stood up.

'Speaking of collaboration,' she said, 'from what I hear the National Crime Agency have drones coming out of their ears. Why don't you talk to your superiors, SI Stuart?'

Jo felt her cheeks burning as Gates stalked from the room.

'Damn,' she whispered to Max. 'I should have thought of that.'

'Don't worry,' he said. 'Just proves you're human.'

Chapter 57

It took three hours for Helen Gates to come through. Another two for Jo's meeting with Selma Strangelove to be set up.

They met under the blue awning of Odd Bar on Thomas Street, in the Northern Quarter – a stone's throw from Jo's apartment. It was seven thirty in the evening. All of the polished chrome pavement tables were taken.

'Let's go upstairs,' said Jo. 'It's quieter.'

They found seats on a sofa in a corner that looked out over the street, and placed their bags and jackets on the adjacent seats to ensure their privacy.

Strangelove was not at all what Jo had been expecting. In her early fifties, dressed in a smart twinset over a crisp white shirt, she could easily have been mistaken for a Conservative Member of Parliament.

'I don't know about you,' said Jo, 'but I haven't eaten since this morning. And there's fifty per cent off main courses on Thursdays.'

'That suits me,' said Strangelove.

They ordered their food, and the waitress brought Jo a Flying Dog Easy IPA, and Strangelove a cider.

'You do realise, Ms Strangelove, that I can't promise the politicians will go for a safe area,' said Jo. 'Only that they are prepared to hear you out.'

'I know. But it's more than they've agreed to before. It's Selma by the way.' She held up her bottle. Jo clinked it with her own. They both drank, and placed their bottles on the table.

'I can't believe how difficult it's been to persuade the working girls to stay off the streets till we've caught this man,' said Jo.

'You have no idea, do you?' said Strangelove. 'I know I said that for some of these girls sex work is a career choice, and a lifestyle choice. That is what we are fighting for. For those few it may well be possible for them to work out of a well-managed brothel as an independent, but only if they are really lucky. And if they can find one that isn't run by foreign gangs using young girls trafficked for the purpose. And besides, the law makes the keeping of a brothel illegal. So what alternative do they have?'

It sounded like a rhetorical question, but Jo responded anyway.

'Can't they join an escort agency, where the big money is?'

Strangelove shook her head.

'Competition is fierce for the best agencies. Once you have worked the streets, your chances of making that transition are minimal.'

'Because?'

'Because the agencies are looking for professional women, for students, for graduates. For girls and women who can make a man feel as though he is on a special date with someone who is on his wavelength, who can engage in intelligent, empathetic conversation, and who can make it feel like a girlfriend experience rather than a hurried and tawdry transaction. It requires girls who look the part. Who can walk into any hotel lobby, and head straight for the lifts without the concierge, the desk clerk, or security giving them a second glance. When you have worked the streets, it wears you down and it leaves its mark.'

Jo knew exactly what she meant. The physical and emotional scars that showed when you were close up with a working girl and their constant hypervigilance as they scanned the vicinity not just for punters but for police, pimps, and potential predators.

'There are other escort agencies of course,' Strangelove continued. 'Over fifty in Manchester alone. I personally would not work for most of them.'

'Why is that?'

'Because they are run by people trying to get around the law. They provide no security for their girls or health checks, and don't bother to vet the clients. Most of the girls you see out on the streets have tried one or more of these agencies and decided it is safer, and more lucrative, to work for themselves.'

'The only other alternative would be for them to work from home,' said Jo. 'An option they have already ruled out.'

'Precisely. What if they have children or a partner who is unaware of their secret life? If there are two or more of them in the house, they could end up being accused of managing a brothel. And if they live alone, do they really want to invite strangers into their home, which is legal, but where they may be at even greater risk than taking their chance out on the street?'

She drained her bottle, and put it down on the table. 'So, SI Stuart, you tell me. Having discounted those options, how much notice do you believe these girls are going to take of me when they are feeding a drug habit, struggling to pay off crippling debts, or to pay a pimp, or trying to support their children when their benefit has been removed? None of them woke up one morning thinking, *I'm going to become a prostitute*. They all – *we* all – have a story to tell.'

'I understand that,' said Jo.

She saw the scepticism in Strangelove's eyes.

'No, I really do. I worked Vice for several years, including one occasion when I worked undercover. I've seen the type of men who cruise these streets. Heard every demand imaginable. I've listened to the girls. Heard their stories.'

'But you never had to do what they do.'

'No. Thank God.'

'Even with your experience I doubt you can really understand how it is to live such a life. Constantly fearful, without backup or protection. Face it, SI Stuart. You are a tourist in their world.'

Jo knew she was right. For a fleeting second she realised this must have been how it was for her mother. She shuddered at the thought.

Strangelove misread Jo's body language. 'If you want to stop girls being trafficked for sex,' she said, 'enslaved, and brutalised, and men living off the proceeds of prostitution, there is only one solution: make prostitution legal, and subject to regulation. The only way to stop this trafficking in, and profiting from, the use of women's bodies is for prostitution to be legalised. Legalisation will open it up to regulation, and regulation means safety. That's what the Home Affairs Select Committee recommended and the Government Review is looking at right now.'

Strangelove and Jo saw that the people on the nearest neighbouring tables had stopped talking, and were staring at them.

Strangelove lowered her voice. 'As long as prostitution remains criminalised, then any woman whose sexuality is overt, whether or not she openly sells it, will be regarded as immoral and therefore "asking for it". That more than anything else explains the attacks on sex workers in the Western world and in those cultures where the notions of shame and dishonour are used to excuse the gang rape of women and girls.'

'I accept all that,' said Jo, 'but what I'm faced with right here, right now, is that the working girls in Greater Manchester are at even greater risk than ever of losing their lives. We can't sit around waiting for the politicians to change the law.'

'They don't have to. All you need is for the local authority to designate an area of the city – preferably the safest of the existing red-light districts – as a prostitution zone, a managed area where street workers can ply their trade between the hours of 7pm and 7am unhindered. They don't need to change the law for that. They can vote it in tomorrow.'

'Managed in what sense?'

'Overseen by a Safer Manchester partnership involving the police, and sex worker charities. The police are still around but less visible, and they are not out to criminalise anyone. There is a police liaison officer who has won the trust of sex workers, and as a result there is a massive increase in the willingness of the girls to report attacks and rapes, with a number of men having been apprehended, and jailed.'

Jo nodded thoughtfully. 'In an ideal world I could see them going for that,' she said. 'Especially in the light of these murders. But they are also being told that, since the Ipswich murders, a zero-tolerance approach to kerb-crawlers has completely eradicated street prostitution there.'

Strangelove shook her head. 'In which case it's probably swelled the numbers in those badly managed brothels and escort services.'

Jo sighed.

'I'm sure I can get you that meeting, but I can't promise that they will go down that road.'

'That's all I'm asking. You persuade them to let me bring some people from the Leeds managed approach to talk with them, and I'll do what I can to help you. But you can warn them that if there isn't some movement on this we'll go big nationally. We'll organise press releases, protest marches, television interviews.'

She picked up her empty bottle, and paused with it halfway to her lips.

'Promises were made after the Ipswich murders. There was going to be a major review of the laws on prostitution. Apart from one minor change, nothing was done. And now this. Well, they won't get away with it a second time, Jo. You tell them that!'

Before Jo could respond, a waitress appeared with their food. While they were eating, Strangelove made a number of phone calls to contacts among the working girls. Her final conversation was with the journalist Agata Kowalski.

When she had finished, she smiled at Jo. 'Keep your phone on,' she said. 'You should expect a call.'

Chapter 58

It was 10pm when Jo and Selma parted company.

Jo walked slowly back to her apartment through the jumbled network of streets that was the epicentre of Manchester's bohemian nightlife. Past New York fire escapes snaking down the sides of red-brick former textile factories, now upmarket apartment blocks. Past brightly lit shopfronts of bookshops, florists, artisan bakeries, and independent cafes. Music pulsed from dozens of bars, thronged with live-in-the-moment millennials, and young-at-heart members of Generation X.

She paused beside the iconic twenty-foot-high David Bowie tribute mural in Stevenson Square by graffiti artist Akse. One of a score of portraits created for the festival, Cities of Hope. Bowie had his finger to his lips. Jo knew what he was saying: *Keep our secret.* There was one secret in this city that she was desperate to discover, and to reveal.

Cities of Hope.

She carried on walking. Ahead of her two couples tumbled out of a bar on to the pavement. Their laughter echoed along the narrow street. Jo had not felt this alone in years. Not since before Abbie. Maybe not even then.

Jo's phone rang. It was Agata. The reporter sounded breathless. As though she had been running.

'Are you okay?' said Jo.

'Jo,' she said, 'Selma came good. A cyclist matching the description you've circulated has approached some of the girls. I have one of them with me. She's prepared to speak with you, but only if you come right now.'

'Where are you?'

'The Marble Arch. It's a pub on—'

'The corner of Gould Street and Rochdale Road,' said Jo. 'Get me a can of Wild Beer Bibble. I'll be with you in ten.'

Floodlit brickwork on the upper storey, marble stone and pillars below, Number 73 Rochdale Road – a Victorian pleasure palace for work slaves of the Industrial Revolution – stood proud like the bows of an ocean liner.

Jo shouldered her way through the crowd at the bar. Agata spotted her first, and waved her over. She followed the line of mosaic floor tiles to a table tucked into a corner at the far end of the pub.

'This is Sylvie. Sylvie, this is Senior Investigator Stuart.'

Twentyish, going on forty, Sylvie tried to make eye contact. Heavily mascaraed eyes lingered warily for a second and then slid past Jo to the far end of the room.

'Thank you for agreeing to speak with me, Sylvie,' said Jo.

'S'okay. You're paying.'

Jo looked at Agata.

The reporter shrugged apologetically. 'I've already sorted it,' she said. 'Don't worry, it's on me.'

'So, Sylvie,' said Jo, 'you saw a man matching the description we've been circulating.'

'Yeah, I saw him a few times.'

'Where was this?'

'Piccadilly the first time. Ancoats the second.'

'Where exactly?'

Agata pushed a hand-size reporter's pad in front of Jo. 'I made a note.'

The page was covered with longhand notes, as were the next five pages.

'You've already interviewed her?' There was no escaping the accusation in Jo's tone.

'No. I just asked a few questions to make sure it wouldn't be a waste of your time.'

'If you two are going to spend all night arguing,' said Sylvie, still staring into the middle distance, 'I'm out of here. Time is money. Besides, I've got my reputation to think about. Less time I spend here with you, less chance there is someone'll get the wrong idea. Wonder if maybe I'm a grass.'

She had a point, Jo realised.

'Have you been interviewed before about this investigation, Sylvie?' she asked.

'Yeah,' Sylvie replied.

She took a drink from the glass in her hand. When she put the glass down, an oily slick of clear liquid marked the original level. Neat gin, Jo decided.

'Twice,' she continued. 'Once by a dick, once by a couple of plastic plods.'

Agata Kowalski frowned.

'A detective and a pair of police community support officers,' Jo explained. 'Why didn't you say anything to the officer who interviewed you?'

'Because the guy on the bike was one of yours.'

'One of ours? A police officer?'

'That's right.'

'How do you know?'

'Because he said so. He showed me his warrant card.'

'What did he say to you?'

'That he was part of the team investigating the murders. He was a detective working undercover. He offered me an official GMP card with advice on.'

Could this really be a coincidence, Jo wondered? First DC Henshall, now this mysterious stranger, potentially the unsub. Had the killer observed Henshall coercing the street girls? Or could they possibly have been working together? That was a nightmare scenario she didn't wish to contemplate.

'How do you know the card was official?' she asked Sylvie.

'Because I'd already been given one the same.' Sylvie rooted in her bag, and produced the card.

'What else did he say?'

'For a start he said he was working for you.'

Jo's heart lurched.

'Me?'

'Yeah. SI Stuart.' She looked at Agata. 'That's what you said her name was, didn't you?'

'Yes,' said Agata.

'There you go then. That's what he said. "I'm working for SI Joanne Stuart. She's in charge of the hunt for the Backstreet Barber. You may have seen her on the television." '

Agata lightly touched Jo's arm with her hand. It felt like an instinctive, protective gesture.

'What else did he say?' asked Jo.

'He asked if I'd seen anyone behaving suspiciously.' She laughed. 'I said, what, like every punter who comes down here?'

'How did he respond to that?'

'He laughed. Told me to take care. And then rode off towards the Green Quarter.'

'Can you describe him?'

'It's difficult. It was dark and he was wearing a cycle helmet.'

'What else was he wearing?'

She turned her body towards them, and looked up at the ceiling for inspiration.

'A black top, black trousers. Dark trainers. He had a rucksack on his back. Black.'

'Any reflective patches like the ones our bike patrol officers wear?'

'No.'

'And you didn't think that was suspicious?'

'No. Like I said, he was undercover.' Her eyes widened. 'Hang on, are you saying he's the killer? I was face-to-face with the killer?'

'We don't know that. I just need to eliminate him from our investigation. So, can you describe him? How tall was he, for example?'

She was now a lot more focused. 'A couple of inches taller than me with my heels on.'

'So about five six?'

'Something like that.'

'Was he white, black, Asian, mixed race?'

'White.'

'How old would you say he was?'

'Older than me, younger than you.'

'What would that make him? Late twenties, early thirties?'

'Something like that.'

'Did he have an accent?'

'He sounded local. Definitely local.'

'A Manchester accent?'

'Yeah.'

'You're sure about that?'

'I'm sure. Not rough though. A bit formal . . . like a policeman.'

'Authoritative?'

Sylvie's lips moved, as though she was committing the word to memory. She nodded.

'Was there anything else you remember about him? Anything distinctive?'

'Like what?'

'Like his mannerisms?'

'What's them?'

'How he used his hands when he spoke, for example.'

'He didn't. He just held on to the handlebars, apart from when he showed me his warrant card, and offered me that advice card.'

'You mentioned that he laughed. How did that sound?'

Sylvie shrugged. 'Like a laugh.'

'How did he make you feel?'

'Feel?'

'Feel. Did he make you feel uneasy in any way? Suspicious or wary, for example?'

'No. He seemed alright. He wasn't as bossy and judgemental as most. I quite warmed to him.'

Jo remembered Andy's sketchy profile of the unsub.

'Would you say he made you feel comfortable?' she asked.

She nodded.

'That's it, comfortable – that's the word.'

Jo searched for one final meaningful question.

'How do you know it was a warrant card?' she said.

Her face became a sneer.

'I've seen enough of them, haven't I?'

'Thank you,' said Jo, closing her notebook. 'You've been really help-ful. If you see him again—'

'Don't worry,' she said. 'I'll run like hell.'

'And dial 999 straight away,' said Jo. 'No messing.'

Jo and Agata watched her leave.

So did a dozen pairs of greedy male eyes. Lust and disgust jostling for attention. To Jo she looked like another lost soul, rudderless on an unforgiving ocean. They drank their beers in silence.

'For what it's worth, the other girl on Cheetham Hill told me an identical story,' said Agata at last. 'Except for the part about working for you. Why would he risk exposing himself like that?'

'Perhaps he was trying to establish himself as innocuous so that when he did strike it would take his victims by surprise. But I can guess what our psychologist will say.'

'What?'

'That it is all part of the game he is playing with them, and with us.' She paused. 'And with me. He's feeding off the excitement that risk-taking brings. Taunting us.'

Agata thought about it. 'Okay,' she said. 'So where did he get the GMP advice cards he was handing out?'

'From his last two victims? I think we can assume they would have been given them like everyone else. And we didn't find one in either of their handbags.'

'Maybe he works for the printers.'

Jo shook her head.

'Too much of a coincidence.'

They stared at each other, neither of them wanting to be the one to say it. The reporter gave in first.

'Unless he works for the police.'

Jo was already ahead of her. Working through the arguments. It would explain a lot. How he was able to move freely around the red-light districts. How he would know which areas were being targeted for close surveillance, and which were not. The fact that most of his attacks had taken place at weekends, when the majority of detectives, and civilian staff would be off-duty. It was too awful to contemplate. But then so was most of what she did.

She drained her beer, crumpled the can and stood up.

'I owe you,' she said.

The reporter smiled. 'Don't worry, Jo,' she said. 'I'll remind you.'

For the first time Jo noticed that each of Agata's eyes was a slightly different shade of blue and there were tiny dimples in her cheeks.

Chapter 59

FRIDAY, 19TH MAY

Another fitful night.

On the edge of wakefulness, Jo sensed for the first time in months the flashbacks she had experienced after her abduction by the Bluebell Hollow killer pushing against the steel door of the mental vault into which she had consigned them. Just as the counsellor had taught her, she steadied her breathing, closed her eyes, and called up the memory palace she had created.

Step by step she climbed the imaginary stairs to the attic, reached beneath the bed, and pulled out the ribbon-wrapped box of treasured photographs that transported her to happier places, and happier times.

She woke at six, put on her kit, and tracksuit, and headed out. This was only her second time at the gym since the killings had begun. In those thirteen days another four girls had died. She vented on the grappling dummies her pent-up anger and frustration with a ferocity that left her physically exhausted yet mentally and emotionally invigorated.

It was seven forty-five when she arrived at The Quays. To her surprise Harry was already there.

'I came up to Warrington yesterday,' he said. 'Stayed over at the pentahotel. Four-star luxury for sixty-five quid a night, including breakfast.'

He sounded cheerful. He didn't look it.

'I'm making myself a coffee,' she told him. 'But I'm guessing you won't need one.'

'You're only on secondment,' he replied. 'I can always send you back.'

They sat with their drinks on one of the sofas in the breakout area. Unsurprisingly Harry looked tired and drawn. It was bad enough that his daughter suffered from schizophrenia. Worse still that she had been sectioned.

'How is your daughter, Boss?' she asked.

He blew distractedly across the surface of the mug.

'She's back home, and stable.'

'Have you told her you're planning to move up here?'

'I had to before I put the house on the market.'

'How did she take it?'

'She seemed pleased. I think she knows that it's a chance to make a clean break. So long as we're living in the house where Marge and I raised her and where her mother died, it's going to be a constant reminder. Her psychotherapist agrees. And to be honest I think it's what I need too.'

'How long do you think it'll be before you move?'

'A couple of months at the outside, according to the estate agents. The buy-to-let sharks are already circling.'

He smiled for the first time.

'Looking on the bright side,' he said, 'I'm planning to downsize. With the difference in property values I'll be set up for the rest of my life. I'll be able to retire whenever I want.'

'And we'll get to see a lot more of you.'

He smiled again.

'Be careful what you wish for. Speaking of which, I've managed to secure that drone team you asked for. They'll be arriving in Manchester late this afternoon.'

'Boss, that's brilliant,' she said.

'They'll be exclusive to Operation Firethorn until at least the end of next week. Try to catch this bastard before then, Jo. Simon Levi is giving me a hard time.'

He frowned.

'You do know that he's got the BSU in his firing line?'

'He's made a point of telling me twice since the operation began. He can't really close us down, can he?'

'Not by himself. But he's got the bean counters on his side, so I wouldn't discount it.'

'I'm going to set up a video link to the incident room at Central Park,' she told him. 'DCI Holmes needs to know about the drone. He'll have some ideas about where best to deploy it. Do you want to join me?'

***

'Now you're talking!' said Gordon. 'And I've got some good news for you.'

'Go on,' said Jo.

'Given how high-profile Firethorn is, I managed to persuade ACC Gates to get the guy who did the original gait analysis to come in last night and work on those images from Middleton Junction. It's a match! He claims it's as unique as a fingerprint, and impossible to disguise. Having said which, convincing a jury of that will be another matter.'

'It's another piece in the jigsaw,' Harry said. 'A bloody important one.'

'All I need,' said Gordon, 'is a suspect to compare it with. The same with the profile from the biometric analysis of him from a still shot taken from that camera. He's five foot seven inches tall, well built, and an ectomorphic mesomorph, whatever that is.'

'Muscular with a tendency to leanness,' she told him. 'What you'd call an athletic build.'

'Right,' he said. 'With size seven shoes. Which also fits with the footprint from the Middleton kill site.'

'At least we know this is almost certainly our man,' said Jo. 'And if he's using a bike or jogging, it would explain why we haven't been able to spot him on the CCTV. He'll have been able to avoid places where the cameras are, stay in the shadows, escape down ginnels, and along tracks. Just like the drug couriers do. Now we have the drone, we can track him. All we need is one sighting.'

'Easier said than done when he's moving around like he is,' said Gordon. 'What's the range of that thing?'

'If it's the same as the one we used on Operation Juniper, just under two miles.'

He folded his arms and sat back.

'That's only enough to cover one red-light district at a time.'

'We need to get word out there to all of the street workers that if they see a jogger or a cyclist matching his description they should not approach him or take him on if he approaches them, but instead they should ring or text us straight away.'

'We've already pulled in a load of cyclists,' Gordon pointed out. 'Our unsub is probably aware of that.' He sat bolt upright. 'Odds-on that's why he's now masquerading as a jogger.'

Jo was sure Andy had already suggested that at their previous meeting at Central Park. Had Gordon been listening?

'Then you still ask them for sightings of either, but prioritise the joggers,' Harry suggested.

'Max and I can help with that,' said Jo. 'And I can ask Selma Strangelove to spread the word.'

Harry stared at her.

'You haven't read my latest update on the shared drive, have you, Boss?' she said.

'It's illegal to read and drive at the same time,' he said. 'I thought you knew that, SI Stuart.'

'Fair enough, Boss,' she said.

Then she told him her plan.

Chapter 60

'What the hell are we doing here?' asked Max.

It was a rhetorical question.

They were sitting in his car, parked halfway down Moston Lane. Three miles north-east of the city centre. Two miles south of the latest crime scene. Five miles south of the Trows Lane deposition site. If the unsub was moving back towards the city, this was the next most likely target area. It was either here or Failsworth. They were close enough for the SkyRanger team to move between them at one-hour intervals.

'Are you going to finish that?' she asked. 'Because it's making me feel sick.'

Max laughed. 'That'll be the kimchi,' he said, shovelling a ball of glutinous rice into his mouth.

'What the hell is that?'

'Fermented vegetables. It's brilliant. You should try some.'

Condensation from the two boxes of takeaway had all but obscured their view through the windscreen. Jo leaned forward and rubbed it with her glove. Sodium street lights fought the resultant smear.

'I'd switch the engine on,' Max said. 'Give the aircon a blast. Only I don't want to draw attention to us.'

'Don't worry,' Jo told him. 'The smell's already done that.'

He laughed again, dropped the fork into the box, and closed the lid. She took it from him, grabbed the other box from the dashboard, and opened her door.

'Where are you going?' Max asked.

'To dump these in a wastepaper bin. It's either that or you'll have the sweet smell of vomit to deal with.'

Five yards in front of her, bolted into the pavement outside a takeaway was a metal bin. She turned up her collar as she walked towards it. High pressure had settled over the country, giving the impression summer had come early. The night air felt chilly after the heat of the day.

Every third shopfront was an off-licence or takeaway. Here and there a charity shop or a betting shop broke the monotony. Hanging baskets and lamp-post banners provided by the council hinted that better times were coming. *For Sale* signs, and a crowded estate agent's window suggested otherwise.

She was surprised by the number of people about. Presumably either without the inclination or the disposable income to spend their Saturday night in the city centre. The takeaways were busy. Here and there groups of youths had congregated, cans and bottles in hand, oblivious to the street alcohol ban. This place had a long way to go before it became the Didsbury of North Manchester.

When she climbed back in, the blowers were working flat out.

'What kept you?' Max asked.

An area car sped past towards Victoria Avenue, lights and siren assaulting the senses.

'He's not going to come here,' she said. 'I told Gordon that. It's far too busy. There are cameras all along the main drag. And besides, there's always a police presence.'

'Why is that?' Max said. 'Manchester's not exactly Detroit or St Louis.'

'Maybe not. But in January alone there were forty-five recorded incidents of violence and sexual offences within a few hundred yards of this street. And that was a good month.'

'Sounds like he'll blend in then.'

'I don't think that's how he'll see it.'

Max turned to look at her. 'Do you really think he's going to go online and check out the latest crime stats before he decides where to strike next?'

'People do that when they choose where they're going to live. Why not where they're going to commit a crime?'

'Are you serious?'

She shrugged. 'Just passing the time.'

'It's a thought, though,' he said. 'The GMP website uses cookies. There'll be a log of everyone who uses it. We could ask them to draw up a list of users around the time of each of the murders. If the same computer crops up on more than one of those lists, it might be worth following up.'

Their radio crackled into life.

'Sierra Romeo 1. We have a contact. Do you copy?'

'We copy,' said Jo, securing her seat belt. 'Where?'

'On grassland about a mile and a quarter to the east of you. Suspect is running due south towards Oldham Road. His coordinates are . . .'

Jo punched them into the satnav as he read them out.

'Fifty-three degrees, thirty minutes, thirty-seven seconds north, two degrees, ten minutes, twenty-one seconds west.'

'Roger that, Sierra Romeo 1,' she said. 'We're on our way.'

Max was already pulling away from the kerb. Heads turned to watch as their blue lights strobed the shopfronts.

'Straight on,' she told him, toggling the screen to map view. 'It's on the other side of the railway. We'll have to cross over and come back on ourselves. Closest we can get is down here, just off Oldham Road.'

'How far?'

'Two point one miles.'

'Should we call for backup?'

The tyres protested as he swerved right at the junction with Nuthurst Road, and put his foot down again. Jo clung for dear life to the grab handle.

'Let's make sure it is him first,' she said. 'So long as Sierra Romeo has eyes on him, there's no need to panic.'

Chapter 61

Ninety miles an hour down Broadway.

'You need to do a U-turn at the bottom,' she told him.

The lights were on red. The sign said no U-turns. Max ignored both. His brake turn would have done justice to a skid pan. He was about to accelerate away again when she yelled.

'Stop! Pull in here.'

A four-metre stretch of pavement had been dropped to permit access to a tarmacked lane with barrier gates across.

'We'll have to go on foot from here,' she said. 'He can't be far away.'

Max unclipped his safety belt. 'Depends on how fast he's been running.'

'Sierra Romeo 1. Sitrep, please,' said Jo, speaking into the radio.

'Suspect is approaching a large property due south of him. A big house with what looks like tennis courts, and playing fields.'

'Copy that,' said Jo. 'We are leaving the car now. Expect to see us approaching the house from the south.'

She plugged her earphones in, and climbed out of the car.

'Do you know where we are?' said Max as they squeezed around the post holding the barrier.

'The Lancaster Club,' she told him. 'Home of Avro Football Club. Sports and social club for BAE Systems. The people who built the

Lancaster bomber, the Avro Vulcan.' They were jogging now, and she was pulling away from him. 'There's always been a Northern power-house,' she told him. 'It's only you Southern Jessies that weren't aware of the fact.'

The lane became a broad drive that led to a three-storey Georgian mansion. Jo waited by the steps for him to catch up.

'I told you to join a gym,' she said.

'I have,' he panted. 'Don't have the time to go.'

'Make time. Before it's too late.'

She clicked her radio, and whispered into the speaker. 'Sierra Romeo. Sitrep please.'

'Sierra Romeo. We have eyes on you,' came the reply. 'Suspect is at the back of the house, jogging west along the treeline that borders the playing fields.'

'Roger that,' she said.

They jogged to the edge of the playing fields. They were huge. Big enough for at least four full-size football pitches.

It was the first night of a full moon, less than one per cent of which was visible.

'I don't see him,' whispered Max.

'Neither do I,' said Jo. 'If he's wearing black and his hood's up, he won't show against those trees. But if Sierra Romeo says he's still there, then he is.'

'Assuming he's following the treeline, we can cut him off if we head straight across these fields,' said Max. 'But what if he's got a weapon beside those scissors?'

'It's a bit late for a risk assessment,' she said as she began to run.

It was just over two hundred yards to the far side. On damp grass, and in the dark, Jo covered it in just over thirty seconds. Max was some way behind her. She was concerned that the sound of his breathing would alert the suspect.

'Sierra Romeo 1, sitrep,' she whispered.

'Suspect is closing in on you. If you can't see him, you should at least be able to hear him.'

They listened.

Above the hum of traffic on Broadway there was another sound. A rhythmic scrunching sound. Coming closer.

They unclipped their Maglites and waited.

A dark, moving shape began to form.

'Now!' said Max.

Twin beams of light pierced the night. The runner put a hand to his face, stumbled, and fell heavily.

'Police!' Jo and Max shouted in unison.

'Stay where you are!'

'Show me your hands!'

'Put them behind your head!'

'Do it! Now!'

They made him sit up.

'You've done my fucking ankle!' the runner complained. A youthful whining voice. A local accent.

Max pulled off the suspect's hood, revealing a callow youth in his late teens. He had a rucksack on his back.

Jo held up her warrant card and shifted the beam of her torch so that he could see it.

'My name is SI Stuart. My colleague is SI Nailor. Tell us your name please.'

'Am I under arrest?' the youth asked. A sure sign he was not a stranger to the law.

'No,' she told him. 'But you will be if you refuse to identify yourself. My guess is you're on the system. In which case we'll find out who you are sooner or later. Save us both time. Just answer the question.'

He rubbed his right ankle while he thought about it. 'Desmond Neeley.'

'Where do you live, Mr Neeley?'

He gave her an address. It sounded familiar.

'Is that off Oldham Road?' she asked.

'Yeah. Behind the Lamb.'

The Lamb Inn. A small estate of back-to-back terraced houses Jo had been called to less than a year into the job. A particularly nasty domestic. The kind you didn't forget.

'Is that where you were headed?'

'Yeah, till you busted my ankle.'

'For the record,' said Max, 'nobody touched you. And if it was broken you wouldn't be this lippy.'

'Where were you coming from, Mr Neeley?' said Jo.

If he could have shrugged, he would have done.

'Nowhere. Just out for a run.'

'What's in the rucksack?'

His expression was a total giveaway. Anxiety overlaid with a veneer of innocence.

'Nothin'.'

Max lifted the rucksack by one of its straps.

'Surprisingly heavy then,' he said.

'You can't search me,' he whined. 'I'm just out for a run. You got no grounds.'

'Ooh, I think we have,' she said. 'Out for a run in the dark dressed in black, wearing a hood, carrying an empty rucksack that weighs a ton. Doesn't know where he's coming from. Sounds to me like reasonable grounds to suspect burglary or street robbery. What do you think, SI Nailor?'

'Absolutely,' said Max. 'Don't worry, you're entitled to a copy of the search record.' He unzipped the backpack, lifted the flap, and shone his torch inside.

'Laptop, tablet, two mobile phones,' he said. 'And that's just for starters.'

He dropped the flap and zipped it up again.

'Desmond Neeley,' said Jo, 'I am arresting you under the Theft Act 1968 on suspicion of possessing stolen goods. You do not have to say anything, but it may harm your defence if you do not mention, when questioned, something that you later rely on in court. Anything you do say may be given in evidence. Do you understand?'

He spat on the ground beside her feet.

'What do you think? Pig!'

Chapter 62

His mind was on SI Stuart. Joanne Stuart.

He wondered what effect his message had had on her.

Had she been puzzled? Intrigued? Or frightened?

She didn't look the type to easily frighten.

But she had never had to deal with anyone like him before.

He could tell she thought she was his nemesis.

But she was wrong. He would be hers.

One day soon they would meet. And when they did . . .

He touched the locket around his neck.

A woman turned on to the lane, and began to walk towards him.

She looked perfect.

He smiled. If only she knew how lucky she was.

Tonight was about reconnaissance.

He had not come prepared.

He moved to the side of the lane, close to the bushes.

Best not to spook her.

Allochka saw him veer to the side, and slow his pace. A male. Medium height. Black hooded top and running pants. Just like she'd been told. An icy hand gripped her heart. There wasn't time to go back. And he would know why if she did.

Long blonde hair.
   Face moon-shaped.
   A pale orb against the night sky.
   He felt the heat in his groin.
   The pulse throbbing in his neck.
   Not tonight.
   Not prepared.

She felt for the zip on her shoulder bag, and began to unfasten it. Slid her hand inside. The houses to her right were in darkness. To scream or not to scream? *Wait*, said the voice in her head. *What if he's just a jogger?*

The gap between them closed.
   Her eyes were deep in shadow.
   He smiled reassuringly.
   Her body shrank away from him.
   Her face was tight with fear.
   He saw her hand move within her bag.

Knew that she was going to call for help.
To ruin everything . . .

She saw the smile freeze on his face, and his left shoulder drop as he began to move. She scrabbled for the rape alarm. Realised she would need both hands to pull the pin. She opened her mouth to scream.

Chapter 63

SATURDAY, 20TH MAY

It was 4am by the time they had delivered Neeley to the custody officer, persuaded a night detective to accept the handover, and completed the stop and search record, and their arrest reports.

It helped that Neeley had plenty of form. Over thirty previous offences as a juvenile. In the past five years he had graduated from a Secure Children's Home to a Secure Training Centre via a Young Offender Institution. The last of which he had left less than a month ago.

'We've already had two break-ins reported in New Moston,' the night detective told them. 'My guess is they're down to Neeley. Stuff missing. I'll get the day shift to pay a little call on his mum first thing, armed with a search warrant. Odds-on they'll find items from priors he hasn't been able to shift yet.'

He grinned.

'Best night's work I haven't had to do, thanks to you two. Any chance we can borrow your drone for a week or two?'

'Is that actually possible?' said Jo as they walked to the car park.

'What?'

'Where you told him to stick his truncheon?'

He chuckled. She'd never heard him chuckle before.

'Judging from the look on his face, probably not.'

'I checked with Sierra Romeo 1,' she told him. 'Not only have there been no sightings, but apparently as far as working girls are concerned it's eerily quiet out there. Not just Moston and Fallowfield either. I spoke to the control room, and they confirmed that all of the red-light districts are quiet as the grave.'

She stopped walking.

'Did I just say that?'

He stopped too.

'What?'

'Quiet as the grave. Hardly appropriate.'

'Sorry,' he said. 'I was trying to remember what sleep felt like. I don't know about you but I've just done another eighteen hours without a wink.'

They started walking again. Jo did a quick calculation. It was hard when you were this tired.

'Wimp,' she said. 'I've done twenty, and counting. The good news is I've stood the UAV team down, and told them to check in with Gordon tomorrow evening about another night shift. He can decide where he'd like to deploy them.'

Their cars were parked side by side.

'What are you planning for tomorrow night?' said Max, his hand on his door handle.

'I'm not. I thought I'd see what time I wake up, have something to eat, and then check in.'

He gave her a mock salute.

'Sounds like a plan,' he said.

Chapter 64

SUNDAY, 21ST MAY

It was 1.45pm when Jo left the apartment. On her way to the car, she picked up a copy of each of the top four-selling Sunday newspapers. Before she set off, she laid them on the passenger seat and checked them one by one.

Double-page spreads were devoted to Firethorn in three, and there were three pages and an editorial lead in the fourth. All of them paraded so-called experts in criminology, the criminal mind, and the conduct of investigations into multiple homicide. As far as Jo could tell, none of them had offered to assist the investigation, and judging by their comments nothing they had to say would have made a blind bit of difference.

Two of the papers were taking the opportunity to strengthen their ongoing campaign for tougher action by police and the Crown Prosecution Service, and for more draconian sentencing.

One focused on arguments in favour of the legalisation of prostitution, and the decriminalisation of the possession and misuse of drugs, quoting examples from around the world. An even-handed milksop article designed not to upset any of their dwindling readership.

The remaining paper was the only one to run pen portraits of the victims. And the only one to wonder what value, if any, the National Crime Agency was adding to the investigation, under a banner that read:

Britain's FBI? We don't think so!

Below the text was a photograph taken with a long lens showing Jo and Max walking towards their cars.

She cursed, started the engine, and headed for the exit of the multistorey car park.

She drove to The Quays; she needed to clear her in-tray, emails, and her mind without the distractions of the Major Incident Room at Central Park.

The office felt like the *Mary Celeste*. Harry was in Warrington. Andy was at home with his family, and Ram was having a much-needed rest day. She put her bag down on the desk, and walked over to the windows looking out over the Huron Basin.

It was a beautiful spring day. The Quays were crowded with people strolling in the afternoon sunshine. Couples hand in hand. Whole families, their children running excitedly ahead. Cyclists weaving perilously in and out of the throng. Canoeists on the water. She raised her eyes to where Beetham Tower, shining gold and silver, marked the bottom of Deansgate, and the start of the city centre. It was hard to believe that out there was a man with a trail of bodies behind him and only one thing on his mind.

It felt as though the whole world was on her shoulders. She sat down at her desk and brought her computer to life.

An hour and a half later she had emptied her in-tray, dealt with her emails, and made sure her log on the shared drive was up to date. She decided she had earned a coffee. She stood up and began to walk towards the machine.

Her mobile phone rang.

She turned and picked it up off the desk. It was Gordon.

'Where are you?' he asked.

'At The Quays. Why?'

Jo didn't need him to respond. The pause was answer enough.

'He's killed again?' she said.

'Possibly,' Gordon replied. 'Won't know for sure till we've seen for ourselves. Maybe not even then.'

Jo sensed that an explanation of exactly what he meant would have to wait.

'And Jo,' he said, 'there's something else. Not to do with this one. To do with victim number six.'

'Jacinta Quinn? What about her?'

'Best I tell you face-to-face,' he said.

There was something about the way he said it that set her nerves on edge.

'Where?' she said.

'Mitchell Street, Newton Heath. Off Briscoe Lane. Between the canal and the Medlock Valley Way.'

She picked up her bag.

'I'm on my way,' she said.

Chapter 65

Jo counted a dozen uniformed officers keeping people back behind the crime scene tape. It looked as though the entire estate had turned out to gawp. At least there was no sign of the press. Not yet.

Gordon was already there, leaning on his car as he struggled into his Tyvek all-in-one. Jo collected a new coverall from the loggist, and went to join to him.

'It's like the Rawtenstall Annual Fair!' Gordon grumbled. 'And where did all these kids come from? I thought they'd gone back to school.'

'If you ask, they'll say homeschooling. Avoids their parents being fined for truancy.'

Gordon pulled the zip up to his neck. 'I wish I'd known,' he said. 'Would have saved Marilyn and me a hell of a lot of grief and embarrassment.'

'What did you mean by us not knowing if it was the unsub till we'd seen it for ourselves?'

'None of what the first responder described matched up with the other crime scenes. Other than the fact that she's a known sex worker.'

They walked across the roughly tarmacked lane to the officer standing beside the start of the common approach path. Raised aluminium stepping plates snaked up a grass- and weed-covered bank and into bushes.

'You'll have to wait a moment I'm afraid,' said the officer. 'The crime scene manager is still recoding and retrieving evidence close to the focal point of the scene. As soon as he's finished, they'll lay the final plates and he'll give us the okay.'

Focal point. A CSI technical term. A neat way of avoiding mention of the body.

Jo drew Gordon to one side.

'Jacinta Quinn,' she said. 'What was it you couldn't tell me over the phone?'

He shuffled his feet, and rubbed his chin nervously.

'Come on, Gordon,' she said. 'Spit it out.'

'The forensics report on the hair he stuffed in her mouth,' he said. 'The results have come through. We got a match.'

'One of the other victims?'

He shook his head and looked away up the lane.

'No, not the victims.'

A sense of dread spread upwards from the pit of her stomach. A cold hand reaching for her heart.

'Tell me,' she said.

He turned back, his eyes nervously finding hers.

'It's you, Jo,' he said. 'You're the match.'

She shook her head. 'That can't be,' she said. 'I never touched her. I never went near it, not even after it was bagged and labelled.'

'You don't understand,' he said. 'Your DNA wasn't *on* it. It was the hair itself. It was *your* hair, Jo.'

'It's a mistake,' she said. 'It must be. The DNA and fingerprints they took when I joined up – they must have mixed them up with someone else. Where else could he have got it from? My locker at the gym? A comb, a brush?'

But that would mean he's been in my apartment.

Gordon read in her expression the shift from confusion to panic.

'It was only a couple of strands,' Gordon said. 'Yours was just one of seven different sets of DNA. There's nothing to suggest he targeted you, Jo.'

And nothing to suggest he didn't, Jo reflected. But right now the most important thing was to concentrate on this latest crime scene. To find something that would lead them closer to the killer. She turned to the officer standing beside the tape.

'Who found the body?' she asked.

'Woman in her eighties,' the officer replied. 'Lives in one of these bungalows behind us. Let her dog out to do its business. It usually nips over to that grassy bank. Performs. Comes back for a reward. Today it didn't. It disappeared into the undergrowth. She goes in after it. Stumbles on the body. Manages to grab Poppy.'

'Poppy?' said Gordon.

'The dog. Gets as far as her front gate, where she has a panic attack. Neighbour sees her and thinks she is having a heart attack. Sends for an ambulance. It's only when the ambulance crew get here and calm her down that she's able to tell them about the body. They have a quick look. Then they call us.'

'Where is she now? The pensioner?'

'Manchester Royal. They took her in for observation. Before they got around to assessing her, she actually had a heart attack. A massive one. They had to resuscitate. She's critical, so you could end up with a second victim.'

The bushes parted five yards in front of them.

'Right,' said Jack Benson. 'We're ready for you now. Try not to snag anything on the branches as you go.'

He gave a running commentary as he led them deeper into the undergrowth.

'Under these plates we found evidence that he'd dragged the body from the bank at the side of the road through the bushes, and between these trees. As you can see, they're all small shrubby trees. Mainly elder, dogwood, birch, blackthorn. Close together, with weeds and smaller bushes underneath. He left a trail of crushed grass, and snapped branches. We've already retrieved traces of fabric snagged on thorns and smaller branches. That's why I asked you to be careful.'

'He clearly wasn't,' said Gordon. 'That's one difference for a start.'

'How did an elderly woman manage to make her way through here?' Jo wondered.

'She won't have,' Benson told her. 'There's a cleared path off to the right. She'll have gone that way and then come in from the side, attracted by the dog barking. I brought you this way so you could follow in his footsteps as it were. We're only a few yards away from the path, but the perpetrator won't have known that in the dark.'

'Not unless he was a local,' said Jo.

Suddenly there were two rows of stepping plates leading into a small clearing, one curving to the left, the other to the right. There was barely enough room for the four of them – Jack, Gordon, Jo, and a CSI photographer, who was busy capturing images. In the centre of the clearing lay the body.

A young woman. Petite, and slender, arms by her sides, long blonde locks that trailed away from her head as though the killer had been dragging her by her hair, and had suddenly let go. In death she looked very young, and very fragile. Jo guessed her age as somewhere between sixteen and twenty. She wore a tan faux-leather blouson over a white tee shirt. Black fitted jeans tucked into tan side-zipped ankle boots.

There was fresh bruising on her right cheek. Both eyes were open, staring skywards. Blood-red blotches covered the sclera. The mouth gaped open in the classic rictus of a horrific death. There were bruises on both sides of her swollen neck. Even without leaning closer, Jo could make out the shape of several fingers and at least one thumb.

She didn't need the pathologist to tell them what had happened here.

'Manual strangulation,' she observed. 'No sign of a ligature.'

'And nothing inserted in the mouth that I can see,' said Gordon. 'Nor is there any sense that the body has been put on display.'

'We won't know if any hair has been removed until the doc has examined her,' said Jo. 'But it doesn't look like it.'

'So what do we think?' said Gordon. 'Is it him?'

'If it is, something must have happened,' she said, 'for him to change his MO like this.'

'I agree,' said a voice from behind them.

'Andy,' she said. 'How long have you been standing there?'

'Not long,' he said. 'But long enough.'

Gordon shuffled to his right so the psychologist could stand beside Jo. 'Is Nailor with you?' Gordon asked.

'No,' Andy replied. 'Too many cooks, he said. He decided to go over to Central Park and help DS Carter.'

'Good call,' said Gordon. 'So, what makes you agree with Jo?'

'Firstly, he's a methodical predator. Carefully choosing his targets, and locations. He comes prepared to carry out a sophisticated attack, the details of which – the use of a garrotte composed of human hair, the removal of a lock of the victim's hair, the placing of human hair in the victim's mouth – have special meaning for him.'

Andy pointed to the body. 'This is careless. Messy. It has more in common with rage than passion. An impulsive, reactive act of violence. Look at the bruise on her cheek. Whoever did this struck her. My guess is to subdue her. That has never featured before. Jo was right. If it is him, then something went wrong. He was rushed or spooked or both. Either that or he did not go out intending to kill. In which case, what happened to lead him to do this? One thing is certain: if he did do this, then it will have had a significant impact on him.'

'In what way?' asked Jo.

'He will be furious, and frustrated. With himself, and with whatever or whoever triggered this. He will have been knocked off course emotionally. From our point of view that's a double-edged sword.'

'How?' asked Gordon.

'It will mean he is more likely to make mistakes. To be less careful. On the other hand, it will also make him unpredictable.'

'Do we know yet who she is?' Jo asked.

'Her name is Allochka,' said Gordon. 'Allochka Burgos. She's nineteen years of age, from Ukraine. Came here three years ago to work in the hotel and catering industry. Met a man friend, who introduced her to drugs. She lost her job as a result, and went on the game to feed her habit.'

'How do we know all this?' said Jo.

'Because her mate reported her missing last night.'

'Last night?'

'They were supposed to be meeting up at a quarter to midnight before deciding where to peddle their wares. Allochka never turned up. Her mate tracked back to the house where she's living. She wasn't there. Texted some of her other contacts. Given what's been going on, she was scared enough to ring the numbers on the advice card we gave out. Area cars were sent to have a look around. Nothing. When she still hadn't turned up this morning, PCSOs and beat officers were asked to look out for her. The mate had provided a description, so when she was found we knew straight away it was her.'

'Is there room for a little one?'

Dr Carol Tompkins stood at the edge of the clearing, holding her black case.

'I'll get out of your hair,' said Jo. She turned to the crime scene manager. 'I'd like to have a look around, Jack. Is there any evidence the killer went further on to the heath?'

Benson shook his head. 'We'll probably never know, but since there's no obvious evidence he did I'm not going to stop you. Just don't disturb anything. I'll have Tactical Aid crawling over this place when the body's been moved to the mortuary.' He grimaced. 'They're going to love me. Mind, that's going to be the least of my worries when Gates turns up.'

'Come on, Andy,' Jo said. 'You're with me.'

Chapter 66

'Where is this exactly?'

They were standing on a hillock composed of loose grey shale. In the direction from which they had come, there were occasional glimpses of white-clad crime scene investigators moving to and fro between the trees and bushes. High above them, in a clear blue sky, a kestrel hovered expectantly.

'Newton Heath,' Jo said to Andy. 'At least what's left of it. We're three miles west of the city centre, a mile from the Etihad Stadium, and over there to the north are the GMP headquarters buildings in Central Park.'

'How far is that? A half a mile away?'

'As the crow flies. The whole area was once a vast expanse of heath-land that stretched all the way from Ancoats to Fallowfield. It was bounded by four waterways: Moston Brook, Newton Brook, Shooters Brook, and the River Irwell. Most of it was swallowed up during the Industrial Revolution. What we're standing on now is basically a slag heap from the coal mines that were around here. The only large expanse that's left is Clayton Vale and the Medlock Valley Way just over there, to the south-east.'

'Water again,' he observed. 'All of the murders have been within a stone's throw of a body of water.'

'You're going to tell me there's symbolism involved.'

He shrugged.

'If there is, it's in his head, which is precious little use to us.'

'I've got another symbolic connection,' Jo said. '*Slag* as in slag heap. Like the one we're standing on. *Slag* as in a lewd or promiscuous female.'

Andy nodded thoughtfully. 'That would fit with his dumping two of the bodies in waste skips as well as this slag heap.'

'Four years ago I worked on a case with DCI Caton,' she said. 'The one where I went undercover?'

She watched his face to see if he made the connection. He did. His expression softened, and there was a suggestion of empathy in his smile.

'The killer buried his victims on a slag heap much like this,' she said. 'Except that Cutacre was once the largest spoil tip in Europe. We wondered then if there was a connection, but none of the victims could have been described as promiscuous.' She forced a smile of her own. 'Least of all me.'

'That's the problem,' he responded. 'It's as likely to be a matter of convenience as a cryptic clue. You never know till you've caught the bastard. Sometimes not even then. Having said which . . .'

He removed his glasses and squinted slightly as he began to turn through 360 degrees. When he finished, he replaced his spectacles.

'He's doubling back on himself. Heading towards the city again. Except he's now staying away from the red-light districts, where he knows we'll be waiting. That begs the question, has he suddenly become risk averse, or was it part of his plan all along? Is he trying to taunt us by killing this close to the building where the hunt for him is being coordinated?'

'Or was this just an accident? You said yourself you didn't believe it was the unsub adapting his methods. That it looked more like panic than planning.' He sighed. 'And I stand by that. If so, and if it was him, what was he doing here?'

'Perhaps he's staying near here,' she said. 'But then why did he start killing in Wigan? That's miles from here.'

'Unidentified subjects,' said Andy. 'More questions than answers. That's the nature of the beast.'

He sounded the most pessimistic he had been since Operation Firethorn had started. Jo's attention was grabbed by the sound of a small biplane approaching from the west.

'I hope Jack gets the tent erected PDQ,' she said. 'The vultures are gathering.'

They met up with Gordon on the path between the Rochdale Canal and the River Irwell. He looked depressed and beleaguered. Not a good combination.

'Dr Tompkins's initial examination didn't add a lot. She's been dead over sixteen hours, which fits with the time she supposedly left home, and her not meeting up with her friend. So given the time it would have taken her to make that rendezvous, she must have been killed between 11.15pm and 12am.'

'A lot earlier than most of the other victims,' Jo observed.

'Correct. She's confirmed that death was almost certainly by manual strangulation and that there is no lock of hair in the oral cavity. Nor could she find any sign that her hair had been cut to provide a trophy.' He rubbed his chin vigorously. 'Basically we're none the wiser.'

'I can't explain why,' said Jo, 'but I still think this is our unsub.'

'I'm inclined to agree,' said Andy Swift. 'And if we're right, this is his first big mistake. Apart from what that will have done to him emotionally, and how that will affect what he does next, am I right in thinking he must have left a lot more trace evidence here than at any of the other crime scenes?'

'Absolutely,' said Jo. 'There'll be footprints, fibre transfer on the trees and bushes as he dragged her body through the scrub. And if he really hadn't come prepared, perhaps he wasn't wearing gloves. In which case Jack's team may be able to recover fingerprints and DNA.'

'None of which is going to help us catch him,' said Gordon. 'Not if he isn't already in the system. In the meantime, Gates wants to know what to tell the Chief, the Mayor, and the press. Does this one come under Operation Firethorn, or is it a separate parallel investigation? Either way I'm buggered. If it is him, they won't just be baying for my blood; they'll want their pound of flesh. And if it isn't him we've got another madman out there. Possibly a poor man's copycat. So much for protecting the public.'

Gordon's radio squawked. He stepped a few paces away, turned his back, and had a conversation. When he rejoined them, his cheeks were burning.

'Got to get back to Central Park,' he said. 'God knows what I'm going to tell them.'

Chapter 67

They watched him walk to his car. For such a big man Gordon looked diminished by the whole affair. As though the weight of responsibility was pushing down on his shoulders, bending him, shrinking him.

Jo's heart went out to him. He had resisted promotion for years, finally giving in to his wife's relentless pressure to ensure he left with the best possible pension. And on the day he heard that he had received the promotion board's endorsement he learned that his boss, DCI Caton, was off on secondment. Without Tom Caton beside him he was always going to struggle. And now this.

'It's at times like this that I'm glad I do what I do,' said Andy. 'That I'm not a senior investigating officer. I don't know how you do it.'

'Sometimes I wonder,' she said. 'But in truth, if I didn't do this I don't know what else I would do.'

Overhead, helicopter call sign India 99 was circling slowly, ensuring no other aircraft could get close enough to get photographic or video images of the crime scene. They had already observed it chasing away a light aircraft, and two drones. Like every other technological advance, for every benefit there was a downside. Jo had no doubt drones were set to become the greatest menace to the isolation of crime scenes.

'We're missing something, Andy,' she said. 'I just can't put my finger on it.'

He stared at her for a moment.

'Are you okay, Jo?' he asked. 'You're not yourself today. You haven't been for a while.'

A light breeze danced playfully around her new bob cut, and set the leaves on the birch trees fluttering. Her hand went instinctively to smooth it down.

'There's something I haven't told you,' she said. 'About the hair he leaves in their mouths.'

———

'I agree with Gordon,' said Andy when she'd finished telling him about Jacinta Quinn, and her own DNA. 'It sounds like a random event. A coincidence.'

Jo was not convinced. It seemed like everyone was just trying to reassure her.

'DCI Caton taught me there is no such thing as a coincidence,' she said. 'Not till you've proved it so. Besides, I've been targeted before. This is exactly what it feels like.'

'The question we should be asking ourselves,' Andy said, 'is if it is a coincidence, how could he have inadvertently got hold of a sample of your hair?'

Jo grabbed his arm. 'What was it you said about hairdressers being disproportionately represented among trichophiliacs?'

'You think he may be a hairdresser?'

'Or someone engaged in that industry. A wig maker. A make-up artist? I don't know. But it's worth exploring.'

The psychologist frowned.

'If Gordon had some DNA to work with, he could start by trying to DNA-swab every male who works in the industry within a ten-mile radius of the loci. I wouldn't want to be the press officer who has to justify that though.'

Jo unzipped her bag and reached in for her mobile phone.

'There's something I'd like to try first,' she said. 'Would you like to come with me?'

'Why not?' he replied. 'It sounds intriguing.'

———

'Joanna!' Rico exclaimed. 'What a delight to see you.'

'You too, Rico,' she said. 'But this isn't a social call.'

'Well, it's also too soon for a trim,' he said. 'I'm intrigued.'

Andy nodded.

'That's what I said.'

'Come, sit down and tell me,' said Rico, pointing to the couches in the salon waiting area.

'Somewhere private?' said Jo.

He led them through the salon to one of the rooms at the rear. There was a couch, a single hairdressing chair, and a mirror surrounded by gold LED lights.

'This is where I work my magic on those clients who value their privacy,' he said. 'The TV stars, the models, the WAGs.'

'Wags?' said Andy.

Rico raised his eyebrows for studied effect.

'Wives and girlfriends of Premiership footballer players. I thought everyone knew that.'

'Mr Swift moves on higher planes,' Jo explained. 'I deal with the mundane. For example, what happens to the hair you are left with at the end of the day, Rico? All of the tresses you cut, and the locks and split ends that I see Trenton sweeping up.'

Rico gestured dramatically with his hands like the conductor of an orchestra.

'I am disappointed! This is what you came to find out? Recycling? Really?'

'Really, Rico. It's important.'

He shrugged. 'Very well. In which case I can tell you that's all very simple. My apprentices collect the longer lengths of hair and place them in one receptacle. The sweepings from the floor they place in another. Three times a week a specialist waste disposal firm comes to collect them, and to replace the containers. I can show you if you would like.'

'I would like,' said Jo.

The four-foot-high rectangular containers were made of recycled cardboard. Jo recognised them as identical to those which the young man had dropped when they collided in the doorway as she was leaving three weeks ago.

'The small stuff they incinerate I think,' said Rico. 'The long hair is quite valuable. Some of it comes back to us in the form of wigs, and hair extensions. Foil, and plastic containers go in separate boxes. Why do you need to know all this, Joanna?'

Jo ignored the question. 'Could I have the name and address of the waste disposal firm?' she asked.

Chapter 68

Barnaby's Salon Waste Disposal Management sat in the middle of an industrial estate in Patricroft, just off the A57 Liverpool Road. The owner, Jason Barnaby, exuding self-made man, was eager to help.

'National Crime Agency,' Barnaby said. 'Never met any of you lot before. Not surprised though. It's the scrap metal guys in waste disposal you need to take a good look at.'

'Actually it's your specialism we're most interested in,' Jo told him. 'Salon waste collection and recycling. Do you cover many salons in the area?'

'Most!' he said. 'Not many, most. Two hundred and sixty in Manchester and Salford alone. I found a niche, made it my own, and fashioned an empire. We're a cut above the rest. You could say we're the crowning glory of salon recycling.'

Jo smiled politely at the onslaught of clichés.

'Is it a family firm?'

'If you count just me and the wife.'

'Can you tell us how it works exactly?'

Barnaby smiled broadly. 'D'you want the two-hour tour or the two-second tweet?'

'Is there something in between? A two-minute summary, for example?'

'That's the foot-in-the-door sales blurb. Goes like this. Confused by EEC recycling regulations? Worn down by snap council inspections? Desperate to avoid hefty fines? Then look no further! Barnaby's Salon Waste Disposal Management is the only company dedicated solely to your needs. We provide a bespoke collection and disposal service, fully compliant with current legislation, offering competitive rates, with discounts given for quality waste. We provide attractive waste boxes, regular collections determined by you, the client, a seven-day-a-week service, and a fortnight's free trial period. When would you like us to start?'

'Very impressive, Mr Barnaby,' said Jo. 'What exactly is quality waste?'

'Ah, that's waste for which there is a ready and lucrative market. Even after giving discounts, we earn as much, if not more, from selling on quality waste products as we do from charging for collection and disposal of the rest.'

'Can you give us some examples please?'

Barnaby was clearly enjoying his captive audience. 'The non-human stuff, like the silver foil, and the plastic product containers are boxed separately. Those are sorted, graded, and sent on to the council recycling centres. Most of the hair swept from the floors is incinerated. Although depending on the level of demand it may be sent off for use as organic fertilizer or to make into mats used to help mop up oil spills at sea.'

'The affinity of human hair to oil is amazing,' explained Andy. 'It just sucks oil up like a magnet does iron filings.'

'Exactly,' said Barnaby approvingly. 'The long tresses and locks are collected separately by the salons, and we sell them on to companies that manufacture hair extensions, wigs, moustaches, eyelashes, and beards for theatrical and fashion make-up.'

Jo and Andy glanced at each other. Jo's heart sank. That had just added another layer of potential sources for the unsub.

'I would be very grateful if you could let me have a list of those companies, Mr Barnaby,' she said.

He nodded enthusiastically. 'Of course.'

'How many employees do you have?'

'Nine. Three clerical staff in the office. Five here on the shop floor. And three lads who do the collections and deliveries. My wife does the admin. Strictly speaking, she's a fellow director, not an employee.'

'You've been immensely helpful, Mr Barnaby,' said Jo. 'I wonder if I could trouble you for just one more thing.'

'Anything.'

'A list of the names and addresses of your employees.'

Barnaby's face clouded over. 'Hang on,' he said. 'You never mentioned anything about any of my staff being part of whatever it is you're investigating.'

'That's because we don't have any reason to suspect they are,' she said. 'But it would be so helpful if we could have those details, and have a word with each of them. Just so we can eliminate them from our enquiries.'

His eyes narrowed.

'What is it you're investigating exactly?' he said.

'It's a murder investigation, Mr Barnaby,' she said. 'A multiple-murder investigation.'

For a moment she feared he was going to force her to seek a warrant for those details. Then he sighed, and she knew he had relented.

'Bloody hell!' he said. 'You'd best come up to the office.'

They followed him up the metal staircase on to the mezzanine. Jo paused at the top to look down at the scene below. Two men were unloading boxes holding salon waste from the back of a transit van. A second van swung into the hangar-like space with a squeal of tyres before coming to a halt. Barnaby stopped and cursed under his breath.

'I've lost count of how many times I've told him about that,' he said.

The driver's door opened and the driver climbed out.

'Beck!' Barnaby shouted. 'Get up here! Now!'

The young man looked up.

A cold hand wrapped itself around Jo's heart. She placed a hand on Andy's arm.

'Mid-twenties. Five foot seven tall. Athletic build,' she whispered. 'Curly black hair.' She had a nagging feeling she had seen him somewhere before. It was the hair.

The young man appeared to do a double take. Then he turned on his heel, and disappeared around the front of the van.

'Stay here, Andy,' Jo shouted over her shoulder. 'Get his name and address, and text it to me. Then let Gordon know what's going on. Ask him to divert India 99 in case we need them.'

The other employees stopped to watch as she sprinted across the factory floor, and out on to the forecourt.

The driver was sixty yards away, out of the saddle of a mountain bike, pedalling like an Olympic champion.

'Beck!' she yelled. 'Stop! Police!'

By the time the echoes had faded on the wind, he had disappeared around the corner of a building, and was gone.

Chapter 69

'His name is Beck, Bryan Beck,' said Barnaby, handing Jo a human resources file. 'Lives with his father. Calls himself Bomber Beck. God knows why. He's worked here for three years. Never given me any reason to sack him, although he can be a pain at times.'

'In what way?'

'He stands right up close. In your face. Flies off the handle at the slightest provocation, then before you've had a chance to have a go at him he's all nice as pie again and apologetic. His co-workers reckon he thinks he's a cut above them. He's always bragging, telling tall tales. He likes to do things his way rather than how he's supposed to do them. And his record-keeping is erratic.'

'In what way?'

'The salons sign off the number of boxes collected and delivered. Only sometimes the number on the sheet hasn't tallied with the number he checked in when he got back here.'

'What did he say when you tackled him about it?'

'That the salon owner got it wrong. He was sorry – he should have checked.'

'Does that happen with any of your other delivery staff?'

'Now and then. What is it they say? To err is human? But I'm talking once or twice a year. Not like Beck. I was wondering at one point if he was ripping us off. Selling quality waste direct to some of our customers.'

'How do you know he wasn't?'

'I checked. There's only a few local ones, and he doesn't have a car. They all assured me they hadn't been approached, and I believed them.'

'He doesn't have a car?'

'He said he didn't own one, and I've never seen him in one. Always comes on that bloody bike.'

'Why bloody?' said Andy Swift.

'Because in his lunch breaks he does tricks in the yard. Showing off.'

'Tricks?'

'Bunny hops, wheelies, nollies, spin turns. Jumping over crates and stacks of pallets. Thinks he's bloody Evel Knievel.'

Jo held up her tablet. 'I'd like your permission to take a photo of the front page of his file so we have his photo and address.'

When she finished, she handed him her card. 'If he comes back, Mr Barnaby, don't tell him why we were here. Make up a story about break-ins at neighbouring premises if you have to. Then ring me or text me straight away.'

'I'm sorry about the helicopter,' said Andy as they made their way back down the stairway. 'As soon as the scene was secure, the North West National Police Air Service control centre diverted it to look for a vulnerable missing person in Derbyshire.'

'Can't be helped,' she said. 'It's him though, isn't it?'

'I know what you're thinking,' he said. 'Barnaby's description could have been straight out of the manual. Invading personal space, emotionally erratic, haughty and braggadocious, inclined to risk-taking. That's five out of the top-ten signs of a psychopathic personality. Even so, do you know how many people there are out there who are like that?'

'A lot,' she replied. 'But only one who collects human hair from salons, and does a runner when he sees police officers. I'd like you to head to Central Park and tell DCI Holmes what we've learned from Barnaby.'

'What are you going to do, Jo?'

'Go to his home address. I need Gordon to apply for a warrant and send a search team to me there. If Beck is there, I'll arrest him and do a Section 18 search without a warrant. If he's not, I'll try to persuade his father to let us search. Either way we can't give Beck the chance to destroy evidence.'

'Be careful, Jo,' said Andy. 'You might want to do a risk assessment before you step foot inside that house.'

She stopped walking and stared at him.

'I already have. Does he pose a threat? Yes. To vulnerable women in the dark at night. Does he carry weapons? Yes. A pair of scissors and a garrotte composed of human hair. Does he scare me? No.'

Andy raised his eyebrows.

'I was thinking of his nickname.'

'Nickname?'

'Bomber,' he said. 'You might want to call the bomb squad.'

Chapter 70

Beck's address was a 1980s townhouse off Fog Lane, where Burnage morphed into upmarket Didsbury. A stone's throw from Sifters Records emporium, immortalised by Oasis's Noel Gallagher in *Shakermaker*. Jo parked up in a neighbouring street of terraced back-to-backs.

The doorbell was answered on the third ring. A man in his mid-fifties, Jo guessed, going on seventy. A frayed cardigan over a grubby washed-out white shirt. Baggy grey trousers. Worn slippers of indeterminate colour. His nose broken, and not reset. Several days' growth of beard. The cloudy eyes and stale breath of an alcoholic.

'Mr Beck?' she said.

His eyes narrowed. 'Who's asking?'

She held up her ID.

'Police.'

'He doesn't live here any more,' he muttered.

'Who?'

'Bryan. My son.'

The way he said the word *son* made it sound like a piece of excrement on the sole of his shoes.

'What made you think it was Bryan I was enquiring about?'

'Because it usually is. Or should I say, used to be.'

'Do you mind if I come in, Mr Beck?' she said.

He opened the door, and backed off down the hall. 'Close it after you.' He disappeared through a door on the right.

She followed him into a cluttered through-lounge cum diner with patio doors that looked out on to a small overgrown garden. The television was on. She recognised the programme as *Escape to the Country*. His son wasn't the only one living in fantasy land.

'Did he often get himself into a lot of trouble, Mr Beck?' she asked.

'His mother spoiled him rotten. If he didn't get what he wanted, he'd just take it.'

'Stealing?'

'Thieving more like.'

Jo wasn't sure of the distinction.

'Such as?'

'Sweets when he was little. Then records and such. And books.' He paused and rubbed his hand through the stubble on his cheek. 'Stuff from other people's washing lines when he was in his teens.'

'Women's clothing?'

'Bras and panties. Dirty little bugger.'

'When did you last see him?'

'Like I said, he doesn't live here.'

'Why did he leave?'

He sniffed, and wiped his nose with the sleeve of his cardigan.

'We don't get on. Especially since his mother died.'

'Why is that?'

'Because she was the only reason he stayed.'

'How did your wife die, Mr Beck?'

'Cancer. What's that got to do with anything?'

'I'm sorry,' she said.

He shrugged. 'Not your fault, nor mine. Though that's not what Bryan reckoned.'

'What do you mean by that, Mr Beck?'

'He reckoned the way I was with her helped bring it on.' He spat the words out. 'Stupid bastard!'

'The way you were with her?'

Mr Beck glared at Jo.

'I know what you're thinking,' Mr Beck said. 'But I never touched her. Not once.' He scowled. 'Not that I didn't have cause.'

'For example?'

His face darkened. 'What difference does it make? She's been dead three years.'

'I'm not sure,' Jo said, 'but please bear with me. I'd appreciate anything you can tell me about Bryan's upbringing.'

'What are you saying? That whatever it is he's done is down to me?'

'No. Not at all.'

'Good. Because I had bugger all to do with it. Whenever I put my foot down, she'd take his side. Whatever I said, she contradicted. That's why we parted ways. That's what he meant about the way I was with her.'

It felt to Jo as though he was speaking in riddles, but she had a feeling it would be worth persevering a little longer.

'Parted ways?' she said. 'She left home?'

'May as well have done. After he was born, she went through a bad patch. She bonded with him alright but went right off me. I spent more time in the gym, down the pub, and with the snooker team. She wanted the good life. I couldn't give her that on what I was making, so she started going out late at night with them who could.'

'Other men?' she guessed.

Mr Beck kicked a leg of the coffee table. 'What do you think?'

From the drop in his voice and the way his shoulders slouched, she had a sense of what that must have done to him. The big man in the gym cuckolded by his wife. To all intents and purposes neutered.

'Why did you stay with her?' she asked.

Mr Beck shrugged. 'You just do, don't you?'

She had no reply to that. In the silence that followed she realised how cold the room was, how empty the house felt.

'When did you last see Bryan?' she asked.

'Last Thursday. He calls every other week or so to see if there's any mail for him. It's usually the odd parcel or two. I reckon he only calls when he knows he's expecting one. Never stays. Doesn't even cross the threshold. Just grabs whatever it is, and beggars off.'

'Do you have any mail for him?'

'No.'

'Have you any idea where he might be staying?'

'No. He never tells me anything.'

'Does your son keep any of his things here?'

He shook his head. 'When he left, he took everything with him. There were boxes of books. Weird stuff.'

'In what way weird?'

'You name it, he collected it. He had shelves full of Shakespeare, and that true crime rubbish. I blame his mother. They were always reading to each other when he should have been out there kicking a ball around with his mates.' He shook his head despairingly. 'What was left was rubbish. I threw it all in the bin.'

'Would you mind if I had a quick look around?'

'Be my guest.' He smirked. 'If you find anything valuable, let me know.'

It took her less than five minutes to establish that the son was not hiding in the house. Nor was there any sign he had ever lived there. She had found a shiny steel rod propped up on the landing that enabled her to pull down a loft ladder and look inside the roof space. It was empty but for a thick carpet of recently laid floor insulation.

'Satisfied?' Mr Beck said as she descended the stairs.

'Your son is using the soubriquet Bomber,' she said, ignoring the sarcasm. 'Do you happen to know why?'

He scowled.

'Cheeky bugger. That was my moniker when I was an amateur boxer. I wanted him to learn to box too. So he'd be able to stand up for himself. Little wimp couldn't handle it. Now he's pretending he's a hard man. That's typical of him. He's a fantasist. A total loser.'

Unlike you then, she said to herself.

'I wouldn't be surprised,' he continued, 'if he wasn't gay. When she died, he started wearing those wigs she had after her chemo. How weird is that? When I took them out the back and burned them, he went spare. That's when he walked out. Left home for good.'

'And you're sure you don't know where he may be staying?'

'No. Mind you, about six months ago one of the blokes down at the Sun in September—'

'The pub on Burnage Lane?'

'That's the one. This bloke mentioned he'd seen Bryan drinking in The Ship Inn, on Rochdale Road. You might want to ask up there.'

'One last thing,' she said. 'Do you have a photograph of Bryan?'

Chapter 71

The search team arrived as Jo was leaving. She apologised to the inspector leading them and told him he could stand them down.

'Don't worry though,' she told him. 'I've a hunch we're going to need you again very shortly.'

'You know what they said about the little boy who cried wolf,' he replied.

'I do. But he was a boy. Big difference.'

She called Gordon, and told him where she was up to. When she reached The Ship Inn, she called him again.

'I'm standing on the towpath by the Slattocks locks,' she told him. 'The suspect was seen drinking in the pub behind me. It's only a mile from the Trows Lane crime scene, Gordon. This is it. This is what we've been missing.'

'Slow down,' he said. 'What are you talking about?'

'The canal. He's following the route of the Rochdale Canal. Look at the map on the wall in the incident room. West to east, then south to north and back again. Every one of those murders was within easy reach of a canal. The latest victim was found less than two hundred yards from the canal. He's using the canal towpath to get to and from the red-light districts. That's why the cameras never picked up a car, and why we've only had glimpses of him on foot or on his bike. I'm guessing he may even be living on the canal and using a boat to move along it. That's why he uses his father's house for his mail deliveries.'

'What do you propose to do now?'

'I'm going to show his photograph in The Ship and the other pubs that stand by the side of the canal. Could you ask Max and some of your team to start at your end and work out towards me?'

'Ask him yourself,' said Gordon. 'He's standing right next to me.'

'At last,' said Max when she told him. 'Proper detective work.'

It took less than ten minutes to confirm that Bryan Beck had indeed been seen drinking in The Ship. On several different occasions over the past twelve months. Most recently less than a week ago. Shortly before the murder of Genna Crowden on Trows Lane.

'Didn't have a lot to say for himself,' the landlord told her. 'That's one of the reasons I remember him. Standoffish. Mean too. Never said thank you. Never left a tip. That's another reason. People like that don't get served till I'm good and ready.'

'Did you happen to ask him where he was staying?'

'If I did, he never told me.'

'Did you get the impression he might be on one of the boats?'

The landlord shrugged.

'No way of knowing. But I can ask around. See if any of the other canal folk that come in here have seen him on a boat. You'll have to let me have a copy of that photo though.'

'How about you take a copy of it with your mobile phone?' she suggested.

'Hang on a mo.'

He disappeared, and returned holding his phone.

'What did we do before we had technology?' he said.

Jo didn't care; she was too busy counting her blessings.

By eight o'clock Jo had visited The Ship Inn, in Middleton, the Anglers Arms in Failsworth, and the Boat and Horses, and the Rose of Lancaster, both in Chadderton. Beck had been seen in the latter on two occasions within the past week. Again he had been a solitary drinker, and nobody could throw any light on who he was or where he lived. Jo was in the car park when Max called her.

'I'm in the New Crown Inn, Newton Heath, Bridge No. 82,' he said. 'He's been in here, and the barmaid is pretty sure he's living on a boat.'

'How come?'

'Because the last time he came in he ordered a pint and then had to apologise. Said he'd left his wallet behind. He'd have to pop back to the boat.'

'He actually said *the boat*?'

'Barmaid is certain. It isn't often someone forgets their wallet. She said Beck was back within five minutes.'

'When was this?'

'Last Thursday. The eighteenth.'

'Two days before Allochka Burgos was strangled. And the New Crown is, what, a couple of hundred yards from where she was found?'

'Nearer three hundred. And there's something else, Jo.'

He paused dramatically.

'For God's sake tell me,' Jo said.

'Another reason the barmaid remembers him is he complimented her on her hair. "Lovely texture," he told her. "*Silky.*" '

'It *is* him, Max,' she said. 'It has to be.'

'I agree. All we have to do is find him.'

'Stay there,' she said. 'I'll be with you in ten minutes.'

Chapter 72

They sat in Jo's car behind the pub, overlooking the canal and the lock gates. The dying rays of the sun cast a blood-red hue over the water. The excitement in Gordon's voice seemed magnified by the speakerphone.

'Now that we know who he is, it's just a matter of time.'

'I've checked on the Internet,' Jo told him. 'All boats on the two thousand miles of canals and rivers in England and Wales have to be registered with the Canal & River Trust. Can you get Ram or Duggie to check if there's a boat registered in Beck's name?'

'Leave it with me,' he said. 'What are you proposing to do in the meantime?'

'If he is on a boat, there's a limit to how far he can have got since he fled Barnaby's. All of the canal-side pubs east of the city centre as far as Slattocks have had a visit from members of our team. But there's one place we haven't checked where there's a good chance they'll be able to match him to the boat.'

'Where's that?'

'Islington Moorings. The marina. If he's been there, they may well have a record of it. Max and I can be there in ten minutes.'

Jo parked the car, and cut the engine.

'You know where we are?' she said.

Max shook his head. 'I haven't the foggiest.'

'This is the site of the former Cardroom Estate. Where Mandy Madden and Tricia Garbett grew up. Pin Mill Brow, where Mandy's body was found? It's a quarter of a mile away, across the canal.'

'So we've come full circle,' he said. 'This is where it started, our involvement.'

'Exactly.'

Her radio squawked. It was Ram.

'It's bad news I'm afraid,' he said. 'I've been on to the Canal & River Trust. There are two thousand miles of rivers and canals under their jurisdiction, and thirty-two thousand registered owners. They did a quick check, and there is no vessel registered or licensed to a Bryan Beck.'

'What about other Becks?'

'Negative.'

'So he's using a false name and he's borrowed or stolen a boat.'

'Or we're barking up the wrong tree,' said Max. 'And he isn't using a boat at all.'

'Please don't say that,' she said. 'This is our best lead yet.'

'Our *only* lead.'

'But he told that barmaid he was popping back to the boat.'

'It could just as easily have been a deliberate red herring as a slip of the tongue.'

'If you're going to continue to pour salt on the wound,' she said, 'I'd rather you did it with someone else.'

'Come on,' he replied. 'You can't break up Mulder and Scully.'

'The way you're going I was thinking Cagney and Lacey,' she replied.

'When you two have quite finished,' said Ram, 'is there anything else I can do for you?'

'Sorry,' said Jo. 'Can you let Harry know where we're up to, and ask DCI Holmes to contact the Police National Air Service? If we do come up with anything, the North West Air Operations Group is going to be our best chance of finding this boat.'

'Assuming there is one,' said Max.

She gave Max a withering look. 'Thanks, Ram,' she said into the radio. 'Tell Harry we'll be in touch.'

There were close to forty narrowboats moored within the marina. Some had lights on in the cabins.

'Where do they all come from?' Max said as they walked down on to the promenade.

'My guess is most of them are baby boomers spending their kids' inheritance.'

'You and me,' he said. 'We'll never get the chance to S-K-I.'

Not now that I've broken up with Abbie, Jo reflected.

'This is a needle in a haystack,' she said out loud. 'Where do we start?'

Max pointed. 'With him?'

Twenty metres away a man was locking a metal gate that surrounded a park-like area beside the towpath. Jo called out.

'Excuse me!'

The man waited for them to come to him. In his forties, well built, he regarded them with amused curiosity. Jo held up her warrant card.

'You're too late,' he said. 'I sorted it.'

'Sorted it?' said Jo.

'Storm in a teacup. A couple of lads on mountain bikes thought they could use it like a race track. I gave them a flea in the ear, and sent them on their way. It wasn't me that called you. Must have been the same person who rang me.'

'Nobody rang us,' said Max. 'We're here on a different matter. And you are?'

'Selwyn, warden and park keeper. I only work days, but if there's a problem I come down here if I can. We used to get a lot of this in the early days, but it's settled down now that the old estate's gone and new residents have moved in.'

Jo found herself drawn to the balcony high on the impressive Islington Wharf development, where Tom Caton and his wife, Kate, had their apartment. Five vertical blades of glass and steel lit up like a beacon. Perfectly mirrored in the still waters of the basin.

'We need to know if you've seen this man before,' said Max, holding up his tablet. 'We believe he may be staying on a boat.'

The warden moved closer, and took his time. 'I'm not sure,' he said. 'Have you got any more photos of him?'

Max flipped to the next one. The photo his father had provided.

The warden's eyes gleamed in the light reflected from the screen.

'Him I know,' he said. 'That's Barry Jones. He's house-sitting *Tit Willow*.'

'*Tit Willow*?' said Max.

'A lovely sixty-two-foot narrowboat. Registered in Middlewich. He's been house-sitting it for a couple of years. The owners are in Spain seven months of the year. They pay for their mooring in advance.'

'When did you last see him?' said Jo.

'Earlier this afternoon. Must have been about a quarter to one. He left his moorings, heading east. On to the Ashton Canal link.'

'Ashton Canal?' said Max. 'I thought this was the Rochdale Canal?'

'The two meet right here in the Islington Basin,' Jo told him. 'They both cross the Pennines. The Rochdale Canal heads north from here, the Ashton Canal heads east.'

She turned to the warden. 'How far might he have got?'

He puckered his lips. 'That depends on whether he sticks to the four-miles-an-hour limit, and how much traffic he meets in the locks. And if he decides to travel at night, which is strongly discouraged.'

'If you were us, where would you start looking?' said Max.

The warden thought about it. 'Three hours' cruising, plus around five hours' passing through the locks. That'd take him anywhere between Stalybridge and Mossley. I'd probably start at Stalybridge and work out from there.'

Chapter 73

It was so peaceful out here. Even the sounds were calming. The rhythmic putter of the engine. The soft slap of the wake against the banks. An occasional hoot from an owl. A momentary break in the clouds allowed a sliver of silver across the shimmering surface of the water, before the darkness closed in again.

He knew he ought to use the lights on the bows and stern, but he was confident enough to manage without, except in the locks, where not to do so was little short of suicidal. The only boats he was likely to encounter would be moored up. So long as he stuck to the centre of the canal it would be fine. The bridges were the worst. Then he had to keep his wits about him. If he failed to duck in time, it would be curtains. Even at four miles an hour a wallop from a slab of millstone grit was going to fracture his skull and propel him backwards into the water. There would be no coming back from that.

Not that he was worried about them finding him. After all, nobody knew about the boat. Not even his father. Least of all him. They would be looking for a cyclist. Or a jogger. Well, good luck with that.

He cursed his bad luck. If that bitch hadn't taken fright, that Stuart woman would still be chasing shadows. As it was, he'd have to start again. Get as far as Huddersfield – that was the plan. Then he'd have a choice *of waterways. The Aire and Calder Navigation, the Aire and Hebble Navigation. At some point – and he'd know when it was time – he'd ditch the boat, pack his rucksack, find a cycle way, and see where it took him. The world was his oyster. Full of pearls to pluck.*

'Don't mix your metaphors, darling.' That's what his mother would have said.

He smiled, and his hand moved to stroke the locket on the chain around his neck.

Jo and Max had parked their cars side by side, kitted themselves with their stab vests, belts holding holsters for their Taser, handcuffs, and loops for Maglite torches and an expandable baton. They had slipped on their black NCA cagoules, and were now sitting in Jo's car.

'I'm waiting for the Fourth Floor to tell me who's going to assume Gold Command,' Gordon told them. 'They can't decide if this is a spontaneous incident, or a planned operation. They're also in two minds about whether to tell the media we've started a manhunt, or keep quiet for now so the press doesn't get in the way.'

'Hopefully the latter,' said Jo. 'The last thing we want to do is let him know we're on to him.'

'I agree,' said Gordon. 'While they're making their minds up, I'm assuming Silver Command, and you're Bronze Command. I've put out an all-ports warning for Bryan Beck, and the alias he's using. With any luck we'll have it wrapped up before they get their heads out from between their backsides.'

'Luck doesn't come into it,' she said. 'How did you get on with North West Air Operations Group?'

'Good. There's an Explorer helicopter on its way. Our old pal call sign India 99. We're patching them into your channel. I also have two support cars, and a Tactical Aid Unit on standby. You let me know where and when you need them. They can be with you in under ten minutes.'

'Best we go operational speak then,' she said. 'You never know who's going to be listening.'

'Roger that, Bronze Command,' Gordon said. 'Where are you now?'

'In my car. Half a mile east of Ashton town centre on the A635. SI Nailor is riding shotgun. There's a wharf down beside a bridge that runs over both the River Thame and the Huddersfield Narrow Canal. We're aiming to park up there and await feedback from India 99.'

'Speaking of shotguns, Bronze Command, do I need to arrange for an Armed Response Vehicle and a strategic arms commander?'

'Negative to that, Silver Command. There is no evidence the suspect is armed. Besides, I have a Taser on board, and both SI Nailor and I are authorised users.'

'The suspect may be armed with a knife. He has been known to carry scissors on his person. You do both have stab vests?'

'Yes,' she told him. 'When the Tactical Aid Unit get here, we won't even need them.'

'Be careful, Jo,' he said.

'Roger that, Silver Command,' she said tersely, reminding him that all of this was now being recorded. It was enough that her reputation went ahead of her without him rubbing it in.

The Airwave radio crackled. 'Bronze Command, this is India 99. Are you receiving?'

'Loud and clear, India 99. Where are you?' said Jo.

'Six miles north of Stalybridge. Where do you need us to be, Bronze Command?'

'India 99, we are heading for the Huddersfield Canal Wharf on Mottram Road. Coordinates . . .'

She waited as Max read them out from the Google Map he had up on his tablet.

'Our ETA is three minutes . . . Can you rendezvous here please?'

'We'll be there before you, Bronze Command,' came the reply.

They became aware of the *whup-whup* of the helicopter as they drove over the first of the two bridges. By the time Jo drove down on to the wharf, her way was lit by the Nightsun searchlight slung beneath the undercarriage.

Max had already logged into the live downstream video link from the India 99 cameras. On the screen in front of them they could see Jo's car in the centre of a broad pool of intense light. The shimmering surface of the canal boiled beneath the vicious downdraught from the whirring blades.

'Bronze Command, please advise. What exactly are we looking for?'

'A sixty-two-foot narrowboat. Described as cream with black gunwales. The name *Tit Willow* is blazoned along both sides. It may be moored up, but we are assuming, or rather hoping, it's on the move.'

'Roger that, Bronze Command,' said the air observer. 'And where do you suggest we begin the search?'

'Just to be on the safe side, I'd like you to begin at Islington Marina, at the start of this canal, and work towards us.'

The pilot officer did a quick calculation.

'That's nine miles to the start, and nine miles back give or take,' he said. 'Should take us about thirty minutes if we're checking those boats that are moored up, as well as those on the move.'

'Roger that,' she said. 'We'll wait.'

He saw the beam of light swing away. Heard the sound of the helicopter recede. Breathed a sigh of relief. False alarm.

He used the pole to push the stern away from the canal bank, switched on the engine, reversed to ensure the propeller would not foul on the reeds, selected forward gear, and eased smoothly into the central channel.

The helicopter had unnerved him. Already he was revising his plan. That was what had kept him one step ahead, the willingness to adapt. Huddersfield was where he'd leave the boat.

Seventeen miles or so to go.

If he pressed on, he could be there by daybreak.

Chapter 74

'What if he's already left?' said Max. 'He could be miles away by now on that mountain bike. Then it could be weeks before we catch him. Years if he's smart.'

'He *is* smart,' she reminded him. 'So you'd better pray he's still on the boat. On the upside, he's also arrogant. My guess is he'll underestimate us. He'll assume it'll take us a few days to find out that he's been living on *Tit Willow*, by which time he'll have found a new rathole to slink into.'

They heard the helicopter working its way back towards them. Jo checked her watch.

'That was quick. I hope they haven't cut corners.'

'They're not here yet,' said Max.

'You're right,' she said. 'They're in the Ashton-under-Lyne basin.'

On the screen they could see the searchlight moving meticulously from one narrowboat to the next moored along the side of the canal against a backdrop of brooding railway arches. Jo turned her attention back to her tablet.

It was another ten minutes before India 99 was overhead. They had to shield their eyes from the dazzling light.

'India 99, can you switch that bloody searchlight off?' Max demanded.

They heard the pilot officer chuckle as he complied.

'Sorry, Bronze Command,' said the air observer. 'We've checked every vessel between New Islington Marina and here. No target sightings. Do you have a new search area?'

'Yes please, India 99,' said Jo. 'Please continue to follow the canal east and then north from here as far as the Stannige Tunnel at Diggle.'

'That's the *Standedge* Tunnel?' queried the air observer. 'Three miles long right through the middle of the Pennines?'

'Roger that,' Jo replied. 'Only it's pronounced *Stannige*. Blame the locals.'

There was a muffled exchange between the observer and the pilot. Jo imagined them placing their hands over their mics and having a joke at her expense.

'According to the Canal & River Trust website, the tunnel is closed at night, India 99,' she told them. 'There's a lock on the Diggle end, so there's no way he can have gone further than that.'

'Unless he's got some bolt cutters,' said Max.

'Roger that,' said the air observer.

They heard the helicopter swing away, and saw the searchlight come back on as it threaded its way westwards.

Jo turned to Max. 'If he is on this stretch, and decides to leg it when he sees the helicopter, it's going to be difficult to get to him in the dark. The terrain is increasingly rugged from here on, and there is a lot of woodland.'

'I agree,' said Max. 'And a dog would come in handy too.'

Jo pressed the Transmit button. 'Silver Command,' said Jo, 'I think you'd better send those two cars you have on standby just in case. And is there any chance you could arrange a Dog Unit?'

'Understood,' said Gordon. 'What about the Tactical Aid Unit?'

'Them too,' Jo said. 'Tell them to rendezvous with us here, on the wharf.'

'Roger that, Bronze Command,' Gordon replied.

Max motioned for her to put her hand over her mic. 'Do you get the impression Gordon's a little tense?' he said.

'I'm not surprised,' said Jo. 'He's got the world and his wife breathing down his neck.'

Their earpieces burst into life. 'Bronze Command, this is ACC Gates. If the suspect is spotted, I do not want anyone taking unnecessary risks,' she said. 'Is that understood?'

Me, Jo mouthed. *She means me.*

Max nodded in agreement.

She's not wrong, he mouthed back.

'Understood, Ma'am,' said Jo. 'Or should that be Gold Command?'

'There is no Gold Command at present,' Gates replied coldly. 'Should it become clear that interoperability is required with other services or police forces, then I shall assume that command. Until then, DCI Holmes is in charge as Silver Command.'

Jo smiled. 'Understood, Ma'am.'

Max elbowed Jo, and pointed at the live video stream from the camera slung beneath India 99. The camera was zooming in on a lone narrowboat moored by the right bank on a long straight stretch of canal. 'Light-coloured narrowboat, black gunwales,' he said.

'Stand by, Silver Command,' said Jo. 'Possible contact.'

She held her breath as the pilot manoeuvred for a sidelong view. Her eyes registered the name *Tit Willow* a split second before the air observer confirmed it.

'Target contact!' he said. 'I repeat, we have target contact. Do you copy, Bronze Command?'

Chapter 75

The second he heard the helicopter, and saw the beam of light moving closer, he knew it was him they were looking for. He judged the tunnel too far to reach before they were upon him. Besides, a vessel moving at night would attract more attention. He decided to pull over to the bank, and cut the engine. There was nowhere for them to land. As soon as they peeled away, he would make a break for it. Along the towpath, through the tunnel, and into the woods. For now there was nothing to do but wait.

'This is Bronze Command,' said Jo. 'What is your location, India 99?'

'Five hundred metres south of the Scout Tunnel,' the observer replied. 'Two thousand three hundred metres north-east of your current location. Switching to thermal imaging now.'

They watched with bated breath as the helicopter's Nightsun searchlight was extinguished. In the centre of the inky darkness, *Tit Willow* appeared as a long grey shape, one end of which emitted a red glow, shading to purple at the extremities. And there, a third of the way along the cabin, was the unmistakable shape of a seated human being, the torso an intricate mix of red and purple hues, the arms and legs bright yellow, the head a splash of magnesium white.

'His brain is working overtime,' said Max. 'And he's sweating like a pig.'

Jo handed Max her tablet with the Google Earth map still open, started the engine, and began to back out of the wharf.

'India 99 remain on station,' she said. 'We are on our way. Silver Command, please ask all support vehicles to rendezvous at . . .'

Max stabbed his finger at the tablet. 'The nearest access point to the towpath is on a bend of the A635 Manchester Road at New Scout Mill.'

He selected Street View, and zoomed in on the front of the building. 'It's a furniture factory. Plenty of parking space. A bridge opposite leads on to paths through woodland to either end of the tunnel, where the towpath can be picked up.'

'Did you get that, Gordon?' Jo asked.

'Roger that, Bronze Command,' Gordon replied. 'Scout Mill, A635. You are advised to contain the target in situ and wait for backup to arrive.'

'That'll be Gates,' she muttered.

'I heard that, Bronze Command,' said the ACC over the radio.

'Might be too late anyway,' said Max, pointing at the video feed. The figure was on its feet and moving towards the front of the boat.

From the integrated speakers came a deafening command.

'Police! Stay where you are. Do not attempt to move this boat. Do not attempt to leave this boat.'

The Audi's brakes and tyres squealed in protest as Jo performed a perfect rally turn on to Cocker Hill and sped towards the junction with the A365. Max clung on to his grab strap and began a running commentary.

'Target has emerged on deck. India 99 has reverted to laser-guided searchlight. Target is shielding his eyes, and crouching low to avoid being blown into the water. Target has leaped on to the bank. Target is now on the towpath running north-west towards the tunnel. India 99 in pursuit.'

On the screen she could see the unmoored boat slowly drifting away from the bank, turning broadside across the canal.

'Why is he running for the tunnel?' Jo asked, flooring the accelerator. 'What do we know about it?'

Max was already ahead of her. 'Scout Tunnel,' he said. 'Six hundred and fifteen feet long. That's one hundred and eighty-eight metres. Brick lined with some unlined sections of exposed rock and stone. It has a towpath running through it.'

'What does he hope to achieve?' Jo wondered out loud. 'He may lose the searchlight and the thermal imager inside the tunnel, but they'll pick him up the second he emerges.'

'It's animal instinct to try and hide,' said Max. 'Unless he knows something we don't.'

'Such as?'

'Secret doorways? Tunnels leading off? A 1960s underground bunker in case of nuclear attack?'

'Bronze Command, support vehicles approaching your rendezvous,' said Gordon. 'ETA four minutes.'

'Must be driving even faster than you,' said Max. 'If that was possible.'

'Not fast enough,' said Jo, rounding a bend and screeching to a halt at the entrance to a row of single-storey buildings.

'He's in the tunnel!' said Max, bracing himself against the dashboard.

'Report your situation please, Bronze Command,' came Gordon's anxious request.

Jo unclipped her seat belt. 'At the rendezvous location, exiting our vehicle. Target is entering the tunnel. We are in pursuit of the target.'

We? Max mouthed.

Jo clipped on her Airwave radio, checked that her earpiece was secure, and opened the car door. Max had no option but to follow her.

'You are advised to await backup, Bronze Command,' said an increasingly anxious Gordon.

'Negative to that,' said Jo. 'I assess the situation on the ground as requiring that we locate and secure the target as soon as possible. Not least for his own well-being as much as to ensure he does not avoid capture. If he makes it through the tunnel and into the woods we can see in front of us, he may evade us, even with the support of India 99.'

'I doubt that very much, Bronze Command,' came ACC Gates's acerbic response.

'Not a risk I'm prepared to take, Ma'am,' said Jo. 'SI Nailor agrees with me, don't you, SI Nailor?'

Even in the semi-darkness Jo could see his glare, and sense the gritted teeth through which he replied.

'Absolutely, SI Stuart,' he said.

'It's your call, Bronze Command,' said Gordon. 'Please be careful.'

Jo was already crossing the road towards a wooden bridge in a gap in a drystone wall. Max hurried to catch her up.

'What's the plan, Jo?' he said.

'According to the map, once over the river there are paths in both directions leading to either end of the tunnel. You go right, I'll go left. He'll be trapped between us.'

'Providing he doesn't emerge before we get there.'

'Better get a move on then,' she said, switching on her torch, and breaking into a jog.

Their feet drummed on the wooden planks. Beneath them the River Thame frothed in spate. On the far side the path was hard sand underfoot, narrow and winding. The branches of the trees plucked at Jo's hair and clothing. She ran as fast as she dared.

At a junction where the track merged with the northern towpath, Jo turned right down an even narrower trail that led to the opposite bank. Overhead, unable to penetrate the thick stone roof of the tunnel, India 99 hovered impotently. Jo had to crouch to keep her balance in the downdraught. Sensing this, the pilot climbed away. Jo paused and directed the beam of her torch down the towpath ahead of her. There was no sign of Beck.

'Bronze Command,' said the air observer. 'Target is still inside the tunnel. I repeat. The target is still inside the tunnel.'

Jo clambered down the bank and on to the towpath.

Now Gordon's voice was in her ear.

'This is a siege situation, Bronze Command. We strongly advise that you await backup. Backup is less than one minute from your agreed rendezvous.'

Jo ducked into the tunnel, slipped her baton from her belt, and held the torch in front of her.

'Sorry, Silver Command, you're breaking up,' she replied. 'Can you repeat . . . ?'

Chapter 76

He could still hear the helicopter. Muted now but with a slight echo thrumming insistently inside the tunnel. This had been a bad idea. The second he emerged, that damned searchlight would latch on to him and follow wherever he went. It was going to take every scrap of ingenuity to shake it off.

His decision not to bring a torch for fear of giving away his position had also proved foolhardy. It was pitch-black in here, and holding on to the metal railings to feel his way had slowed him down.

Up ahead a shape began to emerge. A slate-grey semicircle that could only be the exit. He prepared to launch himself on to the towpath and straight into the nearest cover.

A sudden noise caused him to look back over his shoulder. A pinpoint of light at the far end of the tunnel found the ceiling, and expanded outwards as it moved towards him. He loosened his grip on the railings, and began to run.

The first thing that struck her was the smell of diesel, coke, and sulphurous damp. The second was the sound of running feet. A long way off a beam of light pierced the inky blackness. That had to be Max. This was nearby. Coming ever closer. Jo angled the baton across her chest, braced herself against the wall to her left, and raised her Maglite. She switched it on. Simultaneously she heard the sound of his head hitting the roof, and there, not more than twenty feet away, was Bryan Beck, arms flailing, as he toppled sideways over the railings and into the water.

'Jo!' Max yelled. 'Are you alright?'

'It's Beck!' she shouted. 'He's in the canal.'

She walked to the spot and quartered the surface of the water with the beam of her torch. At first she could not see him. Then she realised why. He lay on his front, his head obscured by a black balaclava. His arms floated listlessly by his sides.

'I'm going in after him,' she shouted as she laid her baton and lit torch on the damp stone floor.

'No, Jo!' Max shouted. 'It's too dangerous. Wait for backup. Standard procedure.'

She had already squeezed between the handrail, and the one beneath, and was lowering herself into the canal.

'He's not getting off that lightly,' she shouted. Then she let go.

The shock of the icy-cold water caused her to gasp. Keeping her head above the surface, she managed two breaststrokes before her hand felt his body. She found his shoulders, managed to roll him on to his back, grasped the hood of his cagoule, and began to tow him towards the railings. Now she was hyperventilating.

Max's footsteps were close, his breathing heavy. The beam of his torch quartered the canal until it rested on her face, blinding her.

'For God's sake,' she gasped.

The beam slid past her, and found Beck. His face was inches away from hers. Had his eyes been open they would have been staring straight at her. Max knelt down, placed his torch on the floor, and put both arms through the railings.

'Give me your hand,' he said.

'Him first.' She struggled to prevent Beck's body from spiralling out of her grasp. 'I'm conscious, he's not.'

Reluctantly Max grasped a sleeve, and began to haul Beck's dead weight over the lower bar. Jo did her best to support the rest of Beck's body, at the cost of a mouthful of oily water. She trod the water, coughing and spluttering.

'Hang on in there, Jo,' said Max, anchoring his feet against two iron struts to give him purchase.

There were new voices now, and more torches stabbing the darkness. Hands reached down to help Max pull Beck on to the towpath. Both of Jo's arms were seized, and she found herself being plucked from the water, over the top of the railings, and into Max's arms.

'Why did you do it?' said Max. 'You could have waited.'

Jo shivered uncontrollably despite the thermal blankets. Her heart was working overtime. She knew the symptoms. Early-stage hypothermia. Thirty yards away India 99 was attempting to land on a gently sloping field.

'Because he could have died. And I want to hear him admit it. I want to see him locked up for life. And I want to know what drove him to kill those women. How is he?'

Max turned to look at the figure lying on the ground just yards away.

'He's alive, and conscious. He has a head wound, but it looks superficial. He's showing signs of concussion, and cold water shock, and he's hypothermic.'

'A head wound? How the hell did that happen?'

'That section of the roof is unlined,' Max told her. 'The rocks and stones are held in a cage. In places the cage is bowed and the contents protrude. There are traces of blood on the cage above where he went in. My guess is he hit his head, lost his balance, and fell over the railings. It's a good job you're not four inches taller, or the same could have happened to you.'

343

Jo tried to stand up. Max gently eased her back into a sitting position.

'We need to get him to hospital as soon as possible,' Jo said.

'Why do you think India 99 has just landed?'

'What about the Helimed air ambulance at Barton?'

'Civil Aviation Authority regulations only allow it to fly in daylight. You should know that, Jo. Are you sure you're not concussed too?'

One of the Tactical Aid officers walked up to them. He pointed to the helicopter, standing in a pool of light, rotors gently turning.

'They're ready for them both now,' he said.

'Good. Let's go,' Max replied.

'Both?' said Jo.

'You're going too,' Max said. 'Look at you. You're shivering like mad, your teeth are chattering, and you've probably swallowed a lungful of crap.'

He bent, hooked his arms under her shoulders, and lifted her gently to her feet. Two officers were strapping Beck on to a stretcher.

Max shifted his grip, and swept Jo off her feet. 'Bloody hell!' he said. 'You're heavier than I thought.'

'Put me down then.'

'No,' he retorted. 'Put your arms around my neck, and shut up.'

Jo was too exhausted, cold, and weak to protest.

'Go on then,' she said. 'But if you drop me or a video of this turns up on YouTube, you're dead!'

The journey to Manchester Royal took less than ten minutes. Throughout the flight Beck lay beside her, handcuffed to a steel ring. Jo couldn't tell if he was conscious, and didn't care. She was desperate to sleep. Every time she began to nod off, the officer accompanying them gently shook her awake.

The speed with which she was whisked from the helicopter straight on to a hospital trolley, and the hurry to pile blankets over her, and check her pulse and blood pressure, did nothing to ease her anxiety.

Chapter 77

Monday, 22nd May

'You look like death warmed up.'

'It's how I feel. And you can wipe that grin from your face. It doesn't exude concern.'

Max fell into step beside Jo.

'Should I be concerned? They only kept you in overnight.'

'Have you any idea what I've been through?' Jo said. 'Not just cold water shock, and hypothermia, either of which could have killed me. They insisted on stomach-pumping me. Then this deceptively angelic nurse rammed a syringe full of anti-tetanus serum in my backside, even though I told her I'd had a booster. Not satisfied with that, they've put me on a course of antibiotics for Weil's disease.'

'I did tell you to wait,' said Max. 'What difference was thirty seconds going to make?'

'Hindsight is a wonderful thing,' she said. 'What about Beck?'

'They gave him the all-clear before you. He's already been processed.'

'We should be there.'

'Don't worry,' he told her. 'Nobody is going to interview him till we're there. Gordon says he thinks it's only fair the two of us should have first crack. I think it should be you and him.'

He held open a fire door for her.

'What about my car?' she said.

He reached into his pocket, withdrew a set of keys, and handed them to her.

'I had it taken back to The Quays. I wasn't sure if you'd be fit to drive. We can go to Central Park in mine.'

'Quick as you can,' Jo said.

———

'They should have built an alternative route to the car park,' Jo complained. 'This is a nightmare.'

It looked as though all the world's TV and radio stations were represented. She could see CNN and CBS vans alongside the usual suspects. 'All we need now is for Fox News to appear.'

'What makes you think they're not already here?' Max said. 'You do realise you've gone global?'

'What?'

'Female Agent Saves Serial Killer from Watery Grave!' he announced. 'SI Stuart Risks Life So Killer Faces Music!'

'Damned right,' she said, hunkering down in her seat.

'There's a cap in the glove box,' Max told her.

She reached inside and pulled out a standard-issue navy-blue baseball cap with black-and-white-chequered sides and the POLICE logo. She pulled it on, and angled the peak low over her eyes.

He laughed. 'There's some sunglasses in there too. But I think our undercover days are behind us, don't you?'

'What idiot said all publicity is good publicity?' she moaned as cameras pressed against the windows, and filled the car with blinding flashes.

'Oscar Wilde.'

'And look how he ended up.'

The route from the car park to the front doors was mercifully free from reporters, if not from zoom lenses. As they entered the incident room, everyone stopped what they were doing, and applauded.

Jo felt herself blushing. 'It's not a done deal,' she muttered. 'Not until they've thrown away the key.'

'DCI Holmes and DS Carter are waiting for you next door,' Ged, the office manager, informed them. 'And I'd like to add my congratulations, SI Stuart.'

'Jo,' she replied. 'And thanks.'

Gordon and Nick stood up as they entered the room. And Swift was also with them.

'Thank God you're alright,' said Gordon. 'That was spectacularly you, Jo. You don't do things by half, do you?'

'How are you, Jo?' said Andy.

'Fine,' she replied. 'And if it's alright with everyone I'd rather we skipped the post-mortem.'

'Fair enough,' said Gordon.

The five of them sat down.

'Where are you up to?' she asked.

'I formally arrested him on suspicion an hour ago. Reminded him that he's under caution, and asked the police surgeon to have a look at him. He's fit to be interviewed.'

'How did he react?' Max asked.

'Like a lamb. Said it was all a mistake and he couldn't wait to sort it out. The only hiccup was when he was searched. He refused to remove a chain around his neck holding a gold locket. "It's my mother's," he said.'

'*Is*,' Andy pointed out. 'Not *was*. This is how he keeps the memory of her alive. He is unable to let her go. That's something you can work on when you question him. When the custody sergeant opened the locket, there was a lock of hair inside. There will be a link from this to his motivation, if only we can get him to reveal it.'

'Have they searched the boat yet?' said Jo.

'Inside and out,' Nick replied. 'The Underwater Search and Marine Unit have been inspecting the hull.'

'Don't keep us in suspense. What have they found?'

Nick reeled them off from his list. 'A mountain bike. Resealable plastic bags containing samples of hair behind wooden panels cladding the cabin. Ash and charred remains in the stove on the boat.'

'CSI say it looks like human hair,' said Gordon.

'A black waterproof jogging top and jogging bottoms, and pair of running shoes,' Nick continued. 'And best of all, a waterproof bag hanging beneath the waterline containing a false GMP police ID.' He paused. 'And a pair of scissors.'

Nick looked like the cat that got the cream. Full-fat Jersey cream.

'That's brilliant,' said Jo. 'But it's all circumstantial unless we can match any of it to a victim or crime scene. We know the killer is forensically aware. That clothing, for example. Beck regularly used the laundry room in the Boater's Hut at the marina.'

'Obviously,' said Gordon. 'But with all this evidence, something is bound to turn up. No one is that lucky. The question is, when do we start to interview him? Straight away with what we have already? Or do we wait and see what Forensics turn up?'

'Why don't we prepare an interview strategy now?' said Jo. 'And tweak it if something does turn up.'

'*When* something turns up,' said Max.

She stared at him. 'Since when did you become an optimist?'

'When you went in that canal,' he said. 'Otherwise I'd have pulled you out first.'

They both began to laugh.

'Am I missing something?' said Andy.

'A sense of humour,' Max told him.

'Enough,' said Jo. 'Is he going to have a brief with him?'

'At first he refused legal representation,' said Gordon, 'but when we took that locket away he changed his mind. He's with a duty solicitor.'

'That's because he needs an audience,' said Andy. 'At the same time he needs to make it hard for you. To prove his superior intelligence, his cunning. You need to get under his skin. Make him angry. One of the first things you'll want to do is ask him why he ran. My hunch is he'll have an answer ready and waiting.'

'Such as?' said Nick.

'Because he'd been stealing samples of hair from his employers, and selling it on to clients. That's what I'd say.'

'It's a good job it's him we're interviewing then,' said Gordon, 'and not you.'

Chapter 78

'Why did you run when you saw me talking to your employer, Mr Beck?' said Jo.

'Because I assumed you found out I was keeping back some of the stuff I was collecting from the salons.'

'Some of the hair?'

'Yes.'

'Why would you do that?'

'To sell it. You'd be surprised how much specialist wig makers will pay. It was stupid I know. I told myself I was just doing a bit of *moonlighting*.' Beck smiled as he used the word.

Jo imagined Andy Swift congratulating himself on his prediction.

'So, who did you sell it to?' Gordon asked.

Beck shrugged.

'I chickened out. I disposed of it.'

'How?'

'I burned it.'

He smiled again, and stared at Jo. 'You have lovely hair, SI Stuart,' he said. 'It was the first thing I noticed about you. The shape, the texture, the colour of your hair. Like silk-smooth caramel. Have you ever smelled burnt hair? Of course you have. When you use your straighteners.' He leaned forward. 'You do use straighteners, don't you?' He leaned back again, and sniffed the air like a wolf. 'That smell. Sulphur. It's how Pompeii must have smelled when all that ash rained down. Burning flesh and burning hair. Charcoal and sulphur. Did you know that because the shells of tortoises contain keratin they smell like scorched hair when you burn them?'

'Burned a lot of tortoises have you?' said Gordon.

'*He's playing games with you,*' Andy counselled. '*Don't give him the satisfaction of joining in.*'

'You're clearly well read,' said Jo. 'And intelligent. Something you share with the man that we are seeking.'

'Is that a question?' asked Beck's solicitor.

'No, it's an observation. I wondered if your client would agree, purely on the basis of what he's read about these murders.'

'You do not have to answer that,' said his solicitor.

Beck regarded Jo with what appeared to be a mixture of amusement and curiosity. 'Based on what I've read,' he replied, 'I would say we have much in common.'

The solicitor placed his hand on Beck's arm. Beck pulled it free, and continued. 'The killer appears to be a man of great ingenuity. Resourceful, adaptable, a master of both strategy and tactics.'

'Is that how you see yourself, Bryan?' Jo asked.

Beck raised his eyebrows. '*Bryan.* Do you know that's the first time you've called me Bryan? May I call you Joanne?'

'No you may not!' Gordon barked. 'You'll address her as SI Stuart or not at all.'

Beck's eyes slid lizard-like in Gordon's direction and then back to Jo.

'SI Stuart it is then,' he said. '*Gordon.*'

'I'm glad you agree about the killer,' said Jo. 'Which is why it is so hard to believe he could have been that careless.'

Beck's eyes narrowed. 'Careless?'

'Have you ever availed yourself of the services of a sex worker, Bryan?' Jo asked.

For the first time he looked confused, and uncertain. Then affronted by the question. 'Certainly not. Have you, SI Stuart?'

She didn't need Andy to tell her to ignore the jibe.

'Why so surprised?' she said. 'Eleven per cent of males in Britain have made use of these services. Why not you?'

'Because I don't need to.'

Jo smiled. 'You have a girlfriend then?'

Beck looked distinctly uncomfortable. 'No.'

'In between girlfriends then?'

'I don't see—' his solicitor began.

'You will,' Jo replied, cutting him off. 'Bear with me.'

'I'd prefer you to address me by my surname,' Beck said.

Jo smiled again. 'Do you have an aversion to sex workers, Mr Beck?'

'No.'

'So you wouldn't have a problem speaking to a sex worker, for example.'

She saw Beck's solicitor about to make another objection, and stayed him with a raised hand.

'No,' Beck replied.

'Have you ever approached sex workers, Bryan?' she said. 'On the street, for example.'

His discomfort grew. He attempted to hide it by cradling his arms beneath his armpits.

'I may have.'

'That's a yes then,' said Gordon.

Beck shrugged.

'*He knows you'll have found his false ID by now*,' said Max's voice in her ear.

Jo nodded to Gordon. He opened a box file that lay on the table between them, selected two transparent evidence bags, and slid the first across the table.

'What is this?' demanded the solicitor. 'These were not part of the pre-interview disclosure.'

'We are disclosing them now,' said Gordon.

'For the record,' said Jo, 'DCI Holmes is showing Mr Beck Item of Evidence FT719/3. Namely a false Greater Manchester Police identification card in the name of Brendan Barnes, featuring a photograph which we believe to be of Mr Beck. And Item of Evidence FT719/4, a pair of scissors.'

Gordon pushed the second bag across the table, but not far enough for Beck to reach it.

'These items of evidence,' Jo continued, 'were discovered in a waterproof bag suspended beneath the hull of the boat on which Mr Beck was living at the time of his arrest.'

'Do you agree they both belong to you?' said Gordon. 'And before you accuse us of having planted them too, you should know that the Forensics Branch retrieved from the surfaces of both items thumb and forefinger prints matching yours.'

He shrugged. 'Yes, they're mine.'

'And what are the scissors for exactly?'

He held up his hands. 'My fingernails. I'm very particular about my manicure.'

'So why hide them?'

'Because they're precious to me, and there are a lot of bad people breaking into boats on the canal. You really should do something about that, Detective Inspector.'

'And why would you need a false police ID?' said Gordon.

Beck yawned. Jo couldn't decide if it was nervousness or feigned indifference. 'I've never used it for anything illegal,' he said.

'You used it to get close to street sex workers in Manchester,' said Jo. 'We have at least one witness that has positively identified you as having passed yourself off as a police officer using an ID identical to this.'

'That's a criminal offence in itself,' added Gordon.

Beck unfolded his arms, and leaned forward. He appeared to have regained his composure.

'But I only used it with the best of intentions.'

'To hand out cards warning them of the dangers of staying out on the streets with a serial killer at large?' said Jo.

He smiled, nodded, and sat back. 'Exactly.'

'Or to gain their confidence so that when they next saw you they would allow you to come close enough to surprise, overpower, and kill them?'

'That is pure conjecture!' said his solicitor. 'And wholly circumstantial. None of it places my client at any crime scenes.'

Beck smiled serenely.

'That is true,' said Jo. 'But taken together they do amount to an overwhelming weight of circumstantial evidence that in our opinion would only require some form of evidence that *did* place your client at the scene of one of the crimes to convince a jury of his guilt.'

'Have you approached any of these sex workers recently?' said Gordon.

Beck shrugged. 'Maybe.'

'How about the evening of Sunday the 21st of May? Did you approach any women between 11pm and 1am on the night before last?'

Beck didn't need to think about it. 'No.'

'You're certain of that?'

'Yes.'

'Do you know anyone by the name of Allochka Burgos?' Jo asked.

'No.'

'Where were you between 11pm and 1pm on Sunday last, Bryan?'

'On my boat.'

'Did you go out at all? For a run perhaps?'

She could see him trying to gauge how much they knew. Had he been seen leaving the boat or returning to it? She decided to push him.

'It's a perfectly simple question. Did you or did you not leave the boat?'

He folded his arms.

'No.'

Jo smiled. 'Interesting,' she said.

Gordon retrieved the two evidence bags, and replaced them with two more from the box file.

Jo watched for Beck's reaction.

'For the record,' she said, 'DCI Holmes is showing Mr Beck Item of Evidence FT718/5, a forensic report on a sample taken from the clothing of one Allochka Burgos, a woman whom we believe to have been murdered at some time between 11pm and 2am on Sunday, 21st of May 2017. This sample matches a sample of blood provided this morning by Mr Beck, and more importantly, his DNA.'

She thought she detected a flicker of surprise in Beck's eyes, though his expression remained impassive, which of itself was a giveaway.

'DCI Holmes is also showing Mr Beck Item of Evidence FT718/6. This is a forensic report on a sample of soil taken from the sole of a pair of running shoes found in his possession during the search of his narrowboat. This sample has been matched to a sample of soil taken from the floor of the cabin of his boat, Item of Evidence FT718/11, and to soil from the deposition site of the body of Allochka Burgos. Finally, my colleague is showing Mr Beck Item of Evidence FT718/5. This is a forensic analysis of the right shoe of the same pair of trainers. This analysis matches a footprint recovered from the scene of yet another murder. That of one Jacinta Quinn. This evidence places you, Mr Beck, at the scene of not one but two murders. How do you respond to that?'

Beck stared back at her with barely disguised anger. His solicitor, in his turn, stared at his client.

'I am advising my client not to say anything at this point.'

'I have no idea how any of this could possibly have turned up where you say it did,' said Beck. 'I can only assume you planted it. I wouldn't blame you, with all the world's eyes on you, all the pressure from your bosses and the politicians. You must have been desperate to charge someone, anyone.'

'Let me help you with this,' said Gordon. 'We found a bloodstained slash in a black jogging top discovered in a washing bag on your boat. When you were admitted to hospital last night, the preliminary examination revealed a matching day-old two-inch-long gash on your upper right arm. Our belief is you caught your arm on one of the bushes, probably a blackthorn, on Newton Heath as you dragged the lifeless body of Allochka Burgos to the spot where you left it. We have also requested forensic palynology examination of samples of pollen from clothing and surfaces on the narrowboat on which you have been staying to match against samples from all of the crime scenes that are part of this investigation.'

He slowly gathered up the evidence bags, and placed them in the box file.

'Why did you kill these women?' said Jo.

'Was it because your mother was a sex worker?' Gordon asked.

Beck's face suffused with rage and contempt. For the first time Jo saw the devil within.

'Don't tell me,' said Gordon. 'Let me guess. No Comment? Not that it matters.' He turned to Beck's solicitor. 'Mr Fredericks, you can have an hour with your client, after which we will formally charge him with the murders of Allochka Burgos, and Jacinta Quinn. You can expect further charges in connection with the murders of Jade Scott, Kelly Carver, Mandy Madden, Flora Novak, and Genna Crowden. This interview is terminated at 13.27 on the 23rd of May 2017.'

Gordon picked up the box, pushed back his chair, and stood up.

'Come on, Jo,' he said. 'Let's get out of here. The stench is killing me.'

'You go,' Jo told him. 'There are a couple of questions I would like to ask Mr Beck off the record.'

Chapter 79

'You do realise,' said Beck's solicitor when the door had closed behind Gordon, 'that nothing my client may say in answer to your questions will be admissible in court.'

'That's not strictly true,' Jo replied, 'since your client is still under caution, and is being questioned by a police officer. However, given that none of this is being recorded, it would only count as hearsay.'

'Then why bother?' asked Beck. He seemed to have recovered his composure. His eyes bored into hers. She could tell she had piqued his curiosity.

'Because there are several things I don't understand,' she said. 'Let's call it tying up loose ends.'

'Don't you mean split ends?' he said.

Jo ignored the taunt.

'The strands of hair we recovered from one of your victims,' she said. 'How did they come to include some of mine?'

His eyes widened, his forehead creased, and his jaw dropped just enough for his lips to part. It was a classic surprise response.

'How intriguing,' he said at last. 'Perhaps the killer has been stalking you. Perhaps he has been inside your . . .'

The pause was imperceptible, but enough to tell her that he had no idea where she lived.

'. . . bedroom.'

Jo had her answer. It had been a coincidence after all.

'Moving on,' she said. 'That quote you sent me from *Twelfth Night* . . .'

'From *Ro* . . .' he began, stopping when he saw the smile forming on her face.

'Forgive me,' she said. 'You're right. From *Romeo and Juliet*. Is that how you saw yourself? A mischievous spirit? The fairies' midwife? Except you brought not life but death?'

His face had become a mask of indifference.

'Or was it your mother's foul, sluttish hairs that you were—?'

The mask slipped. Beck gripped the table and pushed himself to his feet. His eyes blazed, and the veins in his neck pulsed violently.

'That's enough!' shouted his solicitor. 'I think you should go now, before I report you.'

Behind her, Jo heard the constable standing beside the door step forward to restrain Beck. She put her hand out to stay him.

'It's alright,' she said. 'I'm finished here.'

As she began to leave, Beck called her back.

'Wait!' he said. 'I want to know how you felt when you got that text. The one the killer sent. And those strands of your hair. How did it feel to know you were being hunted? That it was only a matter of time before you became the killer's victim? Admit it. You were terrified.'

Jo spun round to face him.

'You never got near me,' she said. 'Not physically or emotionally. It was obvious from the start you were a coward. Someone who made up for his own inadequacies by preying on the weak and vulnerable. I wonder how you'll survive in prison for the rest of your life.'

She turned away again and headed for the door. As the officer opened it for her, she stopped, and looked back at Beck.

'I tell a lie,' she said. 'You did get close to me, although you never knew it.'

His brow furrowed.

'You're wondering about those strands of my hair,' she said. 'Do you remember colliding with someone three weeks ago in the doorway of Salon Rico Romano?'

His eyes widened. Comprehension flooded his face.

'I can see you do,' she said. 'Well that was me. And those strands of hair are what led me back to Rico's and then to you. Ironic, don't you think?'

She watched his expression change. She took no pleasure in the way in which his anger and contempt for her seemed reluctantly to give way to self-reproach.

It had never been about him or her.

It was always about the victims.

Chapter 80

'How did you know his mother was a sex worker?' asked Jo.

Gordon grinned. 'I didn't. But you did say her husband told you she used to go out all night with other men. And that they showed her a good time.'

'Perhaps she was,' said Andy. 'You certainly touched a nerve. And it would explain his motivation. A love-hate relationship with his mother. But we may never know. Though I can't help wishing you'd given him a chance to respond.'

'Whatever the explanation, nothing can excuse what he did,' said Jo. 'It isn't a question of mad or bad – he's both.'

'My hunch is he isn't going to give us excuses or explanations,' said Andy. 'He'll be one of those serial killers who paints himself as an enigma. The likelihood is that ninety per cent of his brain is simply wired up wrong.'

'We won't be calling you as a prosecution witness then,' said Gordon.

'Why not?'

'Because going down that road gives him a defence that'll see him in a cushy psychiatric facility, where you and your pals will be able to add him to your research portfolio until either some quack decides he's cured and it's safe to rejoin the community or he escapes.'

'That's never going to happen,' Andy replied. 'Pleading insanity will mean admitting he wasn't in control. You've already seen how he intends to do this. He'll try to bluff it out. Maintain his innocence. Cast himself as a victim of police corruption. That way he'll never have to show remorse. He'll be found guilty, and sentenced to life without the possibility of parole.'

'ACC Gates wants a press conference,' said Gordon, 'as soon as we have word from the CPS that we can go ahead and charge him. She's invited your boss to front it with her, Jo. A perfect example of inter-agency cooperation, she said. She wants us both to be there.'

'Count me out,' said Jo. 'Tell her I've got delayed shock.'

'Tell her yourself!'

Helen Gates was standing in the doorway. Harry Stone was by her side.

'I'm sorry,' Jo said. 'But I'm exhausted. I'd prefer to not have to do this.'

'There are lots of things in this life we'd prefer not to have to do,' Gates replied. 'But with responsibility comes duty.'

'It would be good for the Agency if you were there, Jo,' said Harry. 'Don't worry. You won't be required to speak.'

It didn't sound as though she had a choice.

⌣

Jo was waiting to enter the conference room when someone touched her lightly on the arm. It was Agata Kowalski.

'I'm glad you're here,' said Jo. 'I wanted to thank you. But can it wait till afterwards? We're about to go on.'

'I'm sorry, Jo,' said Agata, 'but before you do there's something I think you should know.'

'What do you mean?'

'I've had a text from one of my sources. He says that GMP have just found a body.'

Jo's heart lurched. Her head was spinning. Did he have a partner? Was this a copycat?

Agata saw her confusion. 'It's not a girl,' she said. 'It's Jenson Hartley. He has been found hanging from a tree in Wythenshawe Park.' She pointed to the assembled reporters. 'I thought you should know before this lot start asking questions.'

A rush of conflicting emotions hit Jo like a punch in the solar plexus, sucking the air from her lungs. She gripped the doorjamb. Two hours ago she had been congratulating herself on the part she had played in catching the unsub and feeling relieved that no more young women would die. Now all she felt was an overwhelming sense of sadness for Hartley, his wife, and children.

Chapter 81

'This was a good choice,' said Agata. Her smile lit up her face. 'Great food, great atmosphere. How did you manage to book a banquette?'

'I'm a regular,' Jo told her. 'I told them I wanted somewhere a bit private. I know Firethorn is already yesterday's news, at least until the trial starts, but the notoriety was getting to me. There's only so much backslapping and handshaking you can take. That's when they're not avoiding me because of what happened to Henshall, and to Jenson Hartley.'

Agata put down her knife, and placed a hand on Jo's.

'DC Henshall chose to abuse his position. He chose to coerce those women into having sex with him. Effectively to rape them. He deserves whatever's coming. As for Jenson Hartley, it wasn't your decision to charge him. And no one could have foreseen he might kill himself. Not even his wife. None of it was your fault. You were simply doing your job.'

Simply doing your job. How many times had Jo told herself that? How many times had she heard those words from someone else? Each time the logic had been inescapable. Why, then, did they never make her feel any better?

Her phone told her she had been sent a text.

'Don't mind me,' said Agata. 'It might be important.'

Jo checked. Her heart flipped. Abbie wanted her to call her. It was urgent.

'I'm sorry,' she said. 'I do need to respond to this. I'll only be a moment.'

The loos were deserted. Jo walked over to the washbasins, and stared at her reflection in the mirrors. She hesitated. Firethorn had been all-consuming. She had pushed Abbie to the back of her mind. Now here she was again, bringing with her that familiar sense of dread.

She made the call.

'Jo,' said Abbie. 'Thank you for getting back to me so quickly. Especially with . . . you know.'

'The investigation? Operation Firethorn. You've been following it?'

'It's been hard to avoid.'

A trace of bitterness clung to the words like a whiff of slurry on an autumn wind.

'Every time we switched on the TV or checked the news.'

We. Was that James the sperm donor or Sally, his sister? Jo bit her lip. *You had your chance,* she told herself.

'Look, Jo,' Abbie said, her tone now businesslike, 'there's no other way to say this. I need to move on. So do you. I'd like us to get on with the dissolution of our civil partnership.'

It hit Jo like a tsunami. Rearing up as the sentence unfolded, then smashing down to envelop her. She clung to a basin, fighting back the panic.

'Jo? Are you still there?'

Just a hint of concern, nothing more.

Jo took a few deep breaths.

'What's the hurry, Abbie?' she asked.

Silence.

Now it was Abbie stalling for time.

'I'm pregnant.'

The phone slipped from Jo's grasp. She tried to catch it as it bounced on the side of the sink and on to the floor. She bent to retrieve it, and took another deep breath before she responded.

'I'm happy for you,' she said. 'It was what you wanted.'

'It wasn't *all* I wanted.'

'I know.'

'Being in a civil partnership when I give birth will complicate matters.'

'We wouldn't want that, would we?'

Jo reproached herself. It wasn't like her to be so hurtful. 'I'm sorry,' she said. 'That was unfair.'

'Forget it,' Abbie replied, but her voce was brittle. 'I understand this is hard for you. For both of us.'

The toilet door opened. Agata entered.

'Jo, are you okay?' she asked. 'I was worried about you.'

Jo placed her hand over the receiver.

'I'm fine. I'll be out in a moment.'

'*Sorry*,' Agata mouthed. She left.

'You have someone with you?' said Abbie.

Less a question, more an accusation. *Not that hard then, since you've already moved on.*

'She's a reporter,' Jo explained. 'We're discussing a case, that's all.'

She realised she sounded desperate to explain it away, and to convince herself as much as Abbie, but there was nothing she could do about it now.

'Right,' Abbie replied.

The silence swelled until it became intolerable. Abbie was the first to bridge the widening gulf between them.

'I think we should apply for a separation order. You know, to kickstart everything.'

Jo's head began to throb. She kneaded her temple with the knuckle of her free hand.

'What would be the point? We've already been apart for seven months. You can file a dissolution petition in another twenty weeks.'

'You've been counting then?'

'Now who's being unfair?' Jo replied. 'I can't take this right now. Just do whatever you want, Abbie. Send me the form and I'll sign it.'

'Right, I will then.'

'Right.'

Silence.

'Bye then,' said Abbie.

'Bye,' said Jo.

But Abbie had gone.

No 'laters' this time.

Jo splashed her face with cold water, dabbed it dry, and looked in the mirror. The face that stared back made her heart lurch with sadness. She forced herself to smile, rearranged her hair with her fingertips, and opened the door.

Across the room Agata sat staring out of the window. Backlit in profile by a street lamp, the reporter looked like an angel. She turned, saw Jo watching her, and smiled. Jo took a deep breath, walked over to the table, and slid into her seat.

'I'm back,' she said.

Author's Note

Those readers who have read any of my previous titles will be aware that for reasons of authenticity all of my novels are set in real time in and around the city of Manchester. *The Tangled Lock* originally began shortly before, and ended in, what would have been the aftermath of the horrific events of Monday, 22nd May 2017. You will appreciate why I immediately revised the timeline, such that it now ends on the afternoon immediately prior to that event and shortly before the equally appalling events of Saturday, 3rd June, in Borough Market, London, the city where I was born and raised.

Those events reminded me that life can be far stranger, and crueller, than fiction, and that a minority of people are capable of acts of inhumanity beyond our comprehension. However, the overwhelming and uplifting response to that tragic event from the residents of Manchester and the wider region also affirmed that the vast majority of people are kind, brave, and compassionate. That good will always triumph over evil. Having lived in Greater Manchester for over fifty years, and worked for the city for eighteen of those years, I was unsurprised by the response of my fellow citizens.

Manchester is a diverse community which over the centuries has opened its arms to those fleeing famine and poverty, war, and genocide.

It is renowned for its sense of community, its civic pride, its solidarity, spirit of independence, generosity, and self-deprecating humour. All of those qualities stood it in good stead in the face of the events of 22nd May this year. I could not be prouder of Manchester and am honoured to consider myself an adopted Mancunian.

Bill Rogers,
June 2017

Acknowledgments

My thanks to the usual suspects whose specialist knowledge, technical advice, and generous encouragement has been invaluable. They know who they are.

My special thanks go as always to everyone at Amazon Publishing UK and their Thomas & Mercer imprint team. To Emilie Marneur for believing in me; my Thomas and Mercer editors, Jane Snelgrove and Jack Butler, for leading me through the process with great wisdom and sensitivity; editor Russel McLean and copyeditor Marcus Trower for their ability to get inside my head, their meticulous attention to detail, and their brilliant advice. And finally, Victoire Chevalier, Editorial and Marketing Assistant, and Hatty Stiles and Nora Dunne, my Author Relations Managers, who complete the seamless package of support that made it such an agreeable and gratifying experience.

Bill Rogers
August 2017

About the Author

Bill Rogers wrote ten earlier crime fiction novels featuring DCI Tom Caton and his team, set in and around Manchester. The first of these, *The Cleansing*, was shortlisted for the Long Barn Books Debut Novel Award, and was awarded the e-Publishing Consortium Writers Award 2011. *The Pick, The Spade and The Crow* was the first in a spin-off series featuring Senior Investigator Joanne Stuart, on secondment to the Behavioural Sciences Unit at the National Crime Agency, located in Salford Quay, Manchester. Formerly a teacher and schools inspector, Bill has four generations of Metropolitan Police behind him. He is married with two adult children and four grandchildren, and lives near Manchester.